"May I have my knife back?"

Morgana asked as she fastened the belt buckle at her waist.

Hugh swung his eyes back to the woman. Her intense gaze was leveled at his waist, where her blade rested in the same sheath as his dirk.

"Until I know you better, Morgana of Kildare, I think the blade best rest where it is. I applaud your skill with it. One man of six dispatched to his Maker, three others wounded. You are a dangerous woman."

"A desperate woman, sir," she challenged him without compunction. "I would feel far safer if the blade rested in my own sheath."

Hugh leaned over her, deliberately sliding his hand under her skirt to find the sheath neatly buckled below her left knee. His eyes met hers. "You will be safe in my care without it."

The rhythm of Morgana's heart arrested. She knew exactly what he was telling her—he was the one in control....

Dear Reader,

Elizabeth Mayne's first book, *All That Matters*, was released during our annual March Madness promotion in 1995, and recently won a RITA Award nomination from the Romance Writers of America. This month's *Lord of the Isle* is a classic Elizabethan tale about an Irish nobleman who unwittingly falls in love with an Irish rebel from an outlawed family. We hope you enjoy it.

The Return of Chase Cordell is a Western from Linda Castle, who is fast becoming one of our most popular authors. It's a poignant love story about a war hero with amnesia who rediscovers a forgotten passion for his young bride. Gayle Wilson, who is also a RITA Award nominee, is back with *Raven's Vow*, a haunting Regency novel about a marriage of convenience between an American investor and an English heiress.

Our fourth title for the month is Ana Seymour's sequel to *Gabriel's Lady, Lucky Bride,* the delightful story of a ranch hand who joins forces with his beautiful boss to save her land from a dangerous con man.

Whatever your taste in reading, we hope you'll enjoy all of these terrific stories. Please keep a lookout for all four titles.

Sincerely,

Tracy Farrell
Senior Editor

Please address questions and book requests to:
Harlequin Reader Service
U.S.: 3010 Walden Ave., P.O. Box 1325, Buffalo, NY 14269
Canadian: P.O. Box 609, Fort Erie, Ont. L2A 5X3

Elizabeth Mayne

LORD of the ISLE

Harlequin Books

TORONTO • NEW YORK • LONDON
AMSTERDAM • PARIS • SYDNEY • HAMBURG
STOCKHOLM • ATHENS • TOKYO • MILAN
MADRID • WARSAW • BUDAPEST • AUCKLAND

ISBN 0-373-28947-2

LORD OF THE ISLE

This edition published by arrangement with Harlequin Books S.A.

® and TM are trademarks of the publisher. Trademarks indicated with
® are registered in the United States Patent and Trademark Office, the
Canadian Trade Marks Office and in other countries.

Printed in U.S.A.

ELIZABETH MAYNE

is a native San Antonian, who knew by the age of eleven how to spin a good yarn according to every teacher she ever faced. She's spent the past twenty years making up for all her transgressions on the opposite side of the teacher's desk, and the past five working exclusively with troubled children. She particularly loves an ethnic hero, and married one of her own twenty years ago. But it wasn't until their youngest, a daughter, was two years old that life calmed down enough for this writer to fulfill the dream she'd always had of becoming a novelist.

Emma Frances Merritt
1940 - 1995

The mentor every young writer should have.

Book 1

The Heir of Dungannon

"Old Days! The wild geese are flighting,
      Head to the storm as they faced it before!
For where there are Irish there's loving and fighting,
      And when we stop either, it's Ireland no more!"

                      "The Irish Guards"
                      Rudyard Kipling

Chapter One

_____

*Ireland
May 1575*

Finn mac Cool named the moodiest river in Ireland *Abhainn Mor,* the great dark water. The subtle nuance of meaning inherent in Gaelic was lost in the translation to its English equivalent—Blackwater. To Queen Elizabeth and all the lackey governors, generals and deputies she sent to rule Ireland, the name Blackwater meant *border.*

Beyond its treacherous currents lay the heart of Ulster. That fierce, clannish northern frontier of deep glens, forest-covered mountains and impregnable sea cliffs had withstood English subjugation since the Norman Conquest. Ulster's marly earth had spawned generations of heroic men; giants of yore, saints of mystic faith, warriors of lasting renown and women of great heart.

Legend linked the Abhainn Mor's ravines, currents and swift rapids to the humor of the *ri ruirech Ui Neill,* the king of kings of the clan O'Neill. As night fell on the fifth day of May in the year of our Lord 1575, the deluge of a cold spring downpour exposed the river at its most dangerous.

Rushing waters scourged the ravine at Benburg so ferociously, the Abhainn Mor broke free of its ancient bed, and threatened to score a new path across Ireland. The angry crash of the flood deafened all near it to the crack of thunder and the whiptail shriek of a banshee wind.

Were legend to be taken as truth, the black temper of the river matched the mood of the heir of Dungannon. Mounted on his favorite charger, Boru, a dun beast eighteen hands tall, Her Majesty's favorite earl, Hugh O'Neill, watched as seven English soldiers rode out of Benburg, hot on the trail of another victim.

Queen Elizabeth would have been sorely distressed by the earl of Tyrone's raiment. Lord Hugh wore not the elegant clothes of an English courtier. Instead, her man dressed as the elements decreed any Irishman should dress, in plaid and leathers that were oblivious of the rain pouring down upon him and his horse.

Hugh's young face reflected displeasure with the scene in the glen before him. By private agreement between him and Elizabeth, all of Ulster was his to administer, and included in his right of pit and gallows. Redcoats had no business entering or patroling the razed wilderness of the late martyr Shane O'Neill.

Clan O'Neill had laid barren every scrap of fertile earth within two leagues of the bridge and Shane's empty castle atop nearby Owen Maugh. Such was their tribute to Shane following his murder on the Benburg bridge seven years ago. Most O'Neill kinsmen swore that Shane's headless spirit haunted the bridge, seeking revenge. Hugh knew of no facts proving or disproving their opinion.

Hugh took out his telescope, twisting the brass tubes into focus on the winding road leading from the village to the bridge.

The soldiers' prey outdistanced them, on a swift and surefooted palfrey Hugh did not recognize. The rider's cloak billowed out, obscuring most of the lead horse's markings and flying tail. Hugh trained his glass on the soldiers instead, seeking to identify one particular man.

Night closed her hands over the flooding Abhainn Mor, concealing a dozen kerns of clan O'Neill. The clansmen blended into their lofty perches in the wych elms above the rushing water. Wrapped in green-and-brown plaids, they awaited a decision from young Hugh to proceed or retreat back to Dungannon.

From the oldest, whose age was counted by the score, down to the youngest, a boy just past his ninth winter, all kept their ears open, listening intently for the keening wail of the O'Neill's banshee, Maoveen. As every clan had its hereditary officials, marshall of forces, master of horse, keeper of treasure, poets, inaugurator and deposer, so too they had a banshee, a spirit whose dreadful scream portended death. Hence Maoveen's cry would warn each kinsman of the imminent approach of Shane O'Neill, were he to appear on the bridge seeking ghostly vengeance.

Their silence spoke more loudly in Hugh's ears than the rumbling thunder. His kerns—or more rightly, Matthew, the baron of Dungannon's kerns—waited to see if the heir to Dungannon could come up to scratch. Not a man among them trusted a kinsman raised and educated in England.

Hugh believed his position as leader of this patrol served as a test. Hugh's avowed interest in taking revenge upon the man who had murdered Shane O'Neill conveniently matched each kern's desire to spill English blood.

"It's Kelly," Hugh announced after some study.

"Aye. It's him." Loghran O'Toole sounded more like a wintering bear snoring than a man speaking. "I hear Maoveen whispering the traitor's name behind the wind."

Hugh cut his mentor a cold glance, saying, "Don't feed me that nonsense about banshees. Where's Rory? That's not his horse the soldiers are after. Do you stop squinting your eyes against the rain and listening for bloody hungry banshees, you will realize that."

Loghran took exception to that criticism, but said nothing to rebut it. Despite a score and ten years' span between their ages, his eyes were as sharp as young Hugh's.

Down at the crossroad, a musket exploded. A cloud of smoke rose briefly from behind Saint Patrick's high cross.

It dissipated quickly, driven to earth by the pouring rain. A lagging redcoat crashed to the ground, unseated by the accuracy of an O'Neill musketeer. Loghran had found Brian. With increasing satisfaction, he assumed Rory had reived the mount, leading the merry chase into Hugh's well-planned trap.

Rory was to lure the soldiers to Tyrone. Brian's task at the high cross was to pick off any stragglers, any who attempted to turn back to Benburg once the trap was sprung.

"Perfect shot!" Hugh praised Brian's skill. "I couldn't have done better myself."

The carefully crafted brass tubes snapped closed between Hugh's broad, blunt fingered hands. He put two to his mouth, emitting a sharp, short whistle, alerting the kerns in the wych elms to get ready.

The kerns knew what to do once the English crossed the river. Hugh had been over his plan time and again before they settled like kestrels high in the trees. Even Hugh's discerning eyes had trouble locating each man amid the camouflaging foliage. It remained to be seen if the kerns would do as Hugh had ordered and wait till the exact moment the redcoats rode underneath them before dropping onto the unsuspecting soldiers' heads.

Shortly, Hugh surmised with grim satisfaction, this simple altercation would be over. Then Hugh O'Neill would detain as his prisoner one Irish traitor, James Kelly, captain of Her Majesty's musketeers.

Hugh planned to take James Kelly to the stone of clan O'Neill and sit in judgment over his trial by ordeal. A coward's death was a fitting end for the man whom all said beheaded the last leader of the O'Neills, Shane the Proud.

Compounding his sins, the Judas named Kelly had sold Shane O'Neill's head to the crown's lord deputy for a paltry bag of silver coin. The degradation of Shane's tarred head, staked on a pole outside Dublin Castle's northwest gate for all to see, had sealed Kelly's fate.

When James Kelly's own head stood on a pike above the sacred stone of clan O'Neill, young Hugh, heir of Matthew, the baron of Dungannon, and hostage of Her Majesty Elizabeth Tudor of England for fifteen long and lost years, would finally be vindicated.

When he had avenged the murder of his uncle, Hugh's honor would be restored and all that was due to him by birth returned. Blood for blood, and an eye for an eye. Then, and only then, could Hugh claim his birthright and assume the righteous and honorable title the O'Neill.

His carefully planned ambush at Benburg bridge awaited one last event; the English soldiers must all cross the bridge. Hugh raised his right hand as the foremost rider charged out of the woods and into view on the flood-swept verge below the bridge. Two redcoats bore down hard on the lone rider, to prevent him reaching the bridge and escaping into wild Tyrone. It was going to be close.

Hugh urged the rider to more speed and followed with a curse on Kelly's wily ways. Well-mounted Englishmen knew how to ride. Kelly's red-coated soldiers were no exception to that rule.

"Damn my eyes," Hugh cursed out loud. "That's not Rory, O'Toole! I told you that wasn't his horse. What's going on here?"

Hugh knew horses as well as any man in Ireland. That fleet-legged mare in the lead was an Arabian palfrey. No other breed ran with such nimble grace and speed. When the rider's cloak caught on the wind again, Hugh spied something he didn't like seeing at this moment in his life at all.

A woman's petticoats fluttered over gartered knees.

The mounted soldiers bore down on the palfrey, shortening the gap. Neither man was Hugh's quarry, Kelly. Hugh delayed his last signal, his hand clenched, but raised and visible to his men. The English must cross the bridge. His gut tightened. His simple plan to capture Kelly was about to be compromised.

Rory was supposed to lead the English into the trap. But Rory wasn't on the Arabian galloping toward the bridge.

Hugh spied the man he wanted in the second pack of redcoats, fifty yards behind the leaders.

At the same instant he saw his quarry, the gap closed. One lout sprang from his saddle and took the woman to ground on the muddy verge below the river. The palfrey bolted onto the bridge, then reared, frightened by the turbulent, raging, muddy water flooding over the structure.

Hugh ground his teeth. A curse issued from his throat. His breath locked inside his chest. This was not what he'd planned. A woman's scream pierced the wet air, matched by a shriek from the terrified horse.

Without a rider guiding it, the palfrey toppled off the bridge, into the flood, and careened downstream. It fought mightily to regain its footing and swim across the Abhainn Mor.

Kelly reined in his mount, ten feet shy of the bridge. His evil laugh echoed across the water as he dismounted. Redcoats and brown horses surrounded the unlucky woman. Hugh didn't need to see inside the closing circle to know the woman's immediate fate. The sounds of imminent rape were testament enough.

The valuable Arabian struggled to gain footing on the west bank. Art Macmurrough darted out of hiding and plunged into the river, snaring the trailing reins and taking charge of the beast. Hugh growled a shout, enraged that the man had dared break his given orders. His shout died between grinding teeth as he told himself not to be surprised.

That impulsive act by a battle-tested Irish soldier spoke to all that was wrong with Ireland and to why Hugh's homeland remained in a perpetual state of domination by English overlords. Celtic soldiers, unlike their English counterparts, followed their commander's orders to the letter only when the whim suited them.

Incensed, Hugh reached for his sword. Something dark and dangerous pushed him perilously close to slicing his own man in half.

Damning his Irish for their fatal caprices, Hugh dug gold spurs into Boru's sides, galloping out from under the shelter of the wych elms on the bluff above the ravine. His purpose was obvious. He was going after Kelly alone.

Loghran O'Toole immediately rode forward, physically barring Hugh's path with his war-horse. "'Tis not our quarrel. Bide a while yet, my lord. Give Rory and Brian a chance to make up ground. All is not yet lost."

"Get out of my way, O'Toole," Hugh growled, his voice laden with malice. "Had my orders been followed to the letter, that woman wouldn't be there. I'll not stand idle while Kelly takes his sport before my very eyes."

"You will," Loghran said, challengingly. "It's my sacred duty, sworn on the deathbed of your grandfather, Conn O'Neill, to see that no English blade carelessly takes your life. Give our men time to recover. Brian and Rory won't let you down. Think of the woman as—" Loghran injected a twist of gallows humor into his voice "—a minor diversion."

Hugh was not amused. He unsheathed his sword.

"My lord, I didn't bring you safely through fifteen years of English hell so you could risk all for a skirt. Stay, else I'll call the men and order you returned to Dungannon. Trussed if necessary."

"Get out of my way." Hugh's sword cut through the rain. Another wretched scream pierced the tumultuous dusk. The point of Hugh's steel pressed into the boiled leather carapace molded to Loghran's chest. The younger man's voice softened to a dangerous snarl. "You know what Kelly's men will do to a woman. We've seen their handiwork before."

"Aye. More than that, I know what he will do to you, should he be lucky enough to get his hands on another O'Neill. Heed my words. Stay to this side of the Abhainn Mor."

"To the devil with your counsel. I'm in command here."
Hugh drew back on the reins. Boru reared, flashing mighty
hooves at the horse and warrior that blocked the worn path
to the bridge. "Listen to me, old friend—cross me and you
lose your head. Move! That's an order. Defy me at your
own peril."

"My lord." Loghran tried one more time, unwilling to let
Hugh face unnecessary danger. "The fate of one lone
woman cannot alter Ireland's destiny in the same way that
your fate does. She is not your quarrel. Think you of the
united Ireland of our dreams. You know as well as I that the
wench is likely naught more than an abbess who cut and ran
with a soldier's purse."

"She may be Mary Magdalene, herself. On Tyrone land,
we will bloody well protect *all women* from English abuse."

Hugh O'Neill touched his gold spurs to Boru's sides once
more. The stallion charged.

O'Toole yielded ground, wheeling his horse around full
circle. With deep regret, he unsheathed his sword and followed, hard on the young earl of Tyrone's heels, down the
cliffside, to the flooded bridge crossing the Abhainn Mor.

Chapter Two

Morgana Fitzgerald drove one strong knee into the groin of the soldier attacking her. By the time his womanish howl split the drenched air, she had her blade in hand. With well-practiced efficiency, she slashed the dagger across his throat. He fell to his knees, clutching his throat and his cods, his scream now a dying gurgle.

Morgana bounded to her feet, balanced and ready. She was winded from the fall from her horse, but not terrified, as Kelly wanted her to be. The cut man's death rattle proved that English soldiers were not made of the steel Lord Deputy Sidney, the governor of Ireland, and his cruel and bloodthirsty adjutant, James Kelly, would have all Ireland believe they were.

She regretted her one reflexive scream, which might have made these soldiers think she were frightened. She knew from experience to act as though she were the one in control. To do anything less would give away her only chance to keep the upper hand.

Unfortunately, she had screamed. Any woman would, when being rudely and deliberately tumbled her off her horse.

Morgana Fitzgerald didn't have the luxury of pretending she was any woman. If that were the case, Sidney's soldiers wouldn't be following her. The second soldier stalked her as she circled the fallen man, edging her way to the bridge.

When she tried to run for it, he darted in front of her, blocking her path. Her knife was no match for the sword in his hand. He feinted at her with it, driving her back as the rest of the English arrived. James Kelly laughed as he dismounted.

In two heartbeats, four men surrounded Morgana, boxing her in, the river at her back. Morgana made a quick search of their crude circle, reading their true purpose in their eyes. Cold-blooded and deadly Geraldine anger calmed and fueled her now. She'd not be raped by a pack of English whoresons without killing two or three of them first.

The one with the drawn sword danced slightly away from the bridge, opening a wider gap in the circle, as he sheathed his weapon. He eyed her nine inches of razor-sharp steel caustically. "Here, now, Lady Morgan, there's no call for that. We only wanted a little sport."

"You'll not take it with me, cur," Morgana fired back, maddened far beyond mere insult at their game of cat and mouse. These men all knew who she was and why Kelly was after her. They were lower than the scum beneath London sewer rats.

One of them was responsible for poisoning Morgana's six-year-old brother Maurice. For that, she would gladly kill all five of them. She had arrived in Benburg innocently unaware of the trap that waited there for her. Kelly and his men had been swilling whiskey at the only inn in Benburg all afternoon, idly waiting for Morgana to arrive. The men she'd hired to protect her on her journey north had been slaughtered in a matter of minutes.

She had been so caught up in her secret negotiations with Bishop Moye she hadn't noticed there was a traitor in her midst. She had also mistakenly thought that Saint Patrick's Cathedral in Armagh had been untouched by the English order to seize and close all of Ireland's churches. There was no sanctuary to be gained by fleeing to a church. She'd not make that mistake again, either. From here out, Morgana would trust no one, only herself.

The traitor in Morgana's escort no longer mattered. The carriage yard at the Kittie Waicke Inn was littered with the bodies of every man Morgana had hired to protect her on her dangerous mission north to Dunluce. Their throats were slit as wide as the dying soldier at John Kelly's feet.

Kelly bent to revive his man and drew back, appalled. "Sweet suffering Jesus," he groaned, shocked so deeply he crossed himself. "The bitch has killed Rayburn!"

"You expected less of me, Kelly?" Morgana snarled. "You know perfectly well that anything you do to a Fitzgerald will come back to haunt you. Shall I repeat for these fools the curse Eleanor Fitzgerald laid on your head?"

Captain James Kelly's mouth twisted cruelly as he straightened. "Save your witch's curses, and your breath, Lady Morgan. You'll come with us quietly now. No more of your games and escapades."

A cold laugh slipped from Morgana's throat as she brandished her blade. "Don't count on it."

"Ah, Morgan, Morgan, don't tempt me to teach you the lesson I've got in mind. Lord Grey cares little about what condition you arrive in when I return you to Dublin." Kelly wagged his exceedingly dark eyebrows, which stood out in stark contrast against his distinguished head of silver. "Fight me, Morgan O'Malley, and I'll allow my men to take their pleasure of you, after I've taught you a woman's proper submission to English authority. Now, give me that damned knife. Prove that you've had some upbringing, by bending your knee properly to me."

"I'd kiss the devil's arse first, you whoreson. We're in Ulster now. I have it on good authority that the only law here is that enforced by the man called the O'Neill. Begone, John Kelly."

"Nice try." He sneered. "But wrong, very, very wrong. There is no man called the O'Neill these days, my dear."

At Morgana's look of suspicion, he continued, relishing taunting her in return for her stinging insults. "I personally saw to the destruction of Shane O'Neill several years back.

Believe me, clan O'Neill rues the day James Kelly came home to Ireland for good.''

"No." Morgana shook her head, refusing to believe him.

"Why, my dear Morgan, who do you think it was that severed Shane O'Neill's head from his body? Or presented it to Lord Grey to display on a stake outside Dublin's castle walls?''

"Truly—" Morgana shuddered "—I have no interest in knowing the answer to that question."

"Ah . . ." Kelly sighed elaborately. "So you would profess no interest in politics beyond the Pale, hmm? But we both know differently, don't we? I'm the only man alive with the balls to confront an O'Neill. Just as I'm the one who will bring you to heel." His head twisted on bull-like shoulders, and his eyes beaded inside narrowed lids.

He spun around so quickly for such a big and heavy man that Morgana failed to see the blow coming. His fist struck her in the face, knocking her to the ground. Her head reeled with a vile explosion of pain. Blood filled her nose and mouth.

While she was down, Kelly stamped his left boot at her right arm, trying to kick her knife from her hand.

But she was faster than him, and trained well enough in hand-to-hand combat to wield a knife with either hand. He jumped clumsily back, not quick enough to avoid the cutting path of her blade. She cut his red coat to the hem and gouged a cut in his thigh before he stumbled out of her range. Morgana bounded back to her feet, dazed but in control of her knife.

One of his men came at her from behind. A pair of crushing, heavy arms swept around her waist, dragging her off her feet. That man, too, paid the price of getting too close.

The soldier screamed as he clutched at his face, his eye bloody and bulging from its socket. Kelly kicked at her again. Morgana caught his heel and jerked his foot with all the force she had, toppling him onto his backside in the mud.

"Bitch!" Kelly shouted, grabbing her skirts. "I'll teach you to raise your filthy Irish hands against an Englishman!"

"Bugger yourself. I'm more English than you'll ever be. My Norman ancestors conquered Ireland while yours were filthy, naked Celtic peasants rutting in peat bogs."

"Augh!" Kelly grunted as he got back on his clumsy feet. He charged her like a raging bull, then caught himself up short, dodging another vicious swipe from her dagger. Morgana swept the blade back and forth with both hands, daring any of them to come close again.

Kelly caught the hem of his coat, briefly examining the gash underneath it and the trickle of blood running down to his knee. "Oh, you're going to pay for that, bitch."

"Come, you murdering whoreson," Morgana taunted him. "Come, let my steel kiss you again."

He motioned to the other men to get closer to her, but none seemed inclined to be cut. The fool who had lost his eye shouted like a castrated bull and charged her. She slapped her wet cloak into his injured face and let him go rushing past. Wet wool shrouded and blinded him as he slipped and crashed to the muddy ground.

Morgana saw her chance to escape then, and bolted for the bridge. She hiked her skirts clear of her strong feet. She slashed the hand of a soldier trying to catch her, and leaped over the man struggling to unwind his head from her cloak.

Despite Morgana's deep-seated fear of water, she ran for the bridge, praying the water rushing over its sunken planks wasn't as deep and treacherous as it looked.

At the brink of the raging flood, she choked, unable to plunge into what her mind perceived as certain death—water, deep and bottomlessly malevolent water. Morgana's terror at being captured by Kelly paled against her fear of drowning.

A third blow drove Morgana to her knees. Kelly hammered the hilt of his drawn sword into her neck. He fell upon her, flattening her, wrenching her blade from her fist.

She fought to breathe, crushed by Kelly's weight. Cruel fingers dug into her hair, lifting her face from the mud, bending her neck against the agonizing pains still rippling across her shoulders. Astraddle her back, he stuck her own blade against her throat and rubbed the knuckle of his thumb against the soft flesh under her jaw.

His breath fanned her ear as he clucked his tongue. "Now then, my little fighting Amazon, I have you at my mercy."

A large knuckle raked across the path the blade would take slitting her throat. He thrust his wet tongue inside her ear and ground his hips suggestively across her bottom. His fingers tightened on her hair, pulling harder to make her bow up from the ground. He laughed cruelly as he licked the sensitive flesh behind her ear. Then he slowly brought the point of the blade against her throat and turned it down. The dagger slipped between her breasts, severing the lacing of the embroidered stomacher covering her gown.

Taut linen was no match for well-honed steel. Powerless, Morgana pressed her hands into the mud, arched way back by his painful pull on her hair. She grit her teeth as he cut her gown and kirtle down to where her belly made contact with the earth.

"Well, well, well, boys, look at this," Kelly called. "Who would think an Amazon would have such big and pretty titties? Look at them well now, my good men, because they're going to get all soiled and dirty. Are you listening, Lady Morgan? I'm going to take you first on your face. An animal like you will probably like that."

Morgana clawed desperate fingers in the mud, searching for a rock or a stone that could be wrenched free, anything to use as a weapon. The mud rendered nothing. She twisted, balancing precariously on one hand, using her fingernails to scratch at him. He jerked his face out of range, tipping her blade under her right breast.

"Ah, ah, ah, Morgana. Mind those claws of yours. Else my hand slips and severs this lovely mound clean away from your ribs. Think what a curiosity you'll be in your cage outside Dublin Castle then, hmm?

"Why, you'll be the governor's prize attraction, the Irish savage with one tit—another Celtic freak of nature, rivaling the cyclopes of ancient Greece."

Morgana stiffened, sickened by the touch of his filthy fingers. His two uninjured men dared to come close. Spittle was clotted on their panting lips.

Kelly jerked Morgana's face toward them, commanding, "Look, Morgan le Fay. They all want to shove their pricks in you. And they will, soon, my little Irish witch. Soon. Then I'll have the pleasure of watching you grunt and heave to satisfy their lust. Think you I won't have my revenge for the merry chase you've led me from Dublin?"

Morgana's fingers itched to snatch her grandfather's Celtic dagger from Kelly's hand and skewer him with it. Soured whiskey breath fanned her face. White rage at his effrontery in threatening her with her own blade flooded through her. She would show Kelly no mercy when the tables turned.

He twisted her head more, bringing his foul-smelling mouth closer to her lips. She jerked her head away. "No!"

"Good, Lady Morgan, fight me." His fingers tightened, painfully ripping hair from her head, forcing her head far enough back that she could see his gray eyes darken with cruel pleasure.

"There's nothing I like better than a woman who struggles as hard as she can against being taken."

Bent as she was, she couldn't see where he poked the point of her blade. But she felt it. And she felt the knife score her flesh as he drew it between her breasts. It came to rest pressed into the hollow of her throat.

"Come on, my sweet, fight me." He taunted her with cold-blooded malice. She wouldn't give him the satisfaction of crying out, so he ran his thumb back down the line he'd cut, smearing her blood. His eyes gleamed diabolically as he put his thumb in his mouth and sucked it. "Ah, but I do like the taste of a woman's blood."

"Whoreson!" Morgana grabbed a fistful of mud and threw it in his face.

Blinded, Kelly screamed, stabbed at her. She was ready, driving her fist backward, smashing his nose, using his momentum to topple him off her. He swore viciously, blinded by the mud in his eyes, losing control. "Grab her!"

Morgana wrested her blade from his slackened hand, rolling free as she stabbed at him with all her might.

"You bitch! Get her, damn you cowards!"

"You're the coward, Kelly!" Morgana sank her blade into his neck with all the force she could muster. His men fell on her then, wrestling to get control of the knife.

Kelly knelt in the mud, clutching his shoulder, chest heaving. He recovered enough to make a fist and strike her in the face.

"Hold her down, you damned whoresons! She'll think twice about fighting more when I get done with her."

This time, Morgana's struggles achieved nothing. Her knife was pried from her fingers and cast aside. Waves of nauseating pain in her temples met up with the horrible ache radiating from her neck into her shoulders and arms. None of that was going to abate very quickly.

She had to think, to calm, to hold back the panic rising inside her. The last and final rule of Grace O'Malley's thorough training in the rigorous art of self-defense swam in Morgana's desperate brain. According to Ireland's famed female pirate when rape was inevitable, one must submit. Accept the pain. Retreat. Think only to the future. Plan your revenge. Convince yourself to live, just to taste that revenge.

Morgana Fitzgerald had no choice but to live. Sudden death was not an option. Sean Fitzgerald's life depended upon her finishing her journey to Dunluce. She had to live through this. Sean depended upon her! She clung to that thought as James Kelly straddled her. She clung to Grace O'Malley's rules of survival, but she could not accept rape, not at any price.

She bucked and twisted, nearly freeing her muddy hands from the grips of the soldier who held them. Kelly drew back his fist. She jerked her head to the side, taking the blow intended for her face on her ear instead. That was a blessing.

Her ears rang so fiercely from the blow, she couldn't decipher the crudities spoken as Kelly yanked on her skirts, trying to free the cloth from under his own weight. She nearly gave vent to her outrage when his coarse hands groped at her knees.

"God damn it all, help me spread her legs," Kelly commanded. "Orson, keep her damned hands out of my way."

Rain beat a steady drum on the earth. The chill of it striking her face made Morgana lift her cheek from the mud. There was daylight enough that she could see the trees on the other side of the Abhainn Mor.

Severing all connection with her body, she looked for Ariel, willing her horse to come back for her. Her heart thudded hard, bringing her back to the gruesome present. Kelly's harsh hands pawed at her breasts. The one called Orson twisted her wrists, nearly breaking her arms.

She bit down hard on her lips, vowing not to scream. She wouldn't beg or cry. They were all talking fast, collective hands on her body, twisting and crushing her limbs, laughing at their rude jests. She shuddered when she heard the leather of Kelly's belt whip free of his buckle. Every man crowed over the size of Kelly's manhood, praising its hardness and envying him the right to be the first to abuse her.

Morgana shut out their voices by chanting an ancient prayer, invoking the spirit of Gerait Og Fitzgerald. She occluded Kelly's face from her sight by staring into the haunted wych elms engulfed by that fearful raging river.

Not a one of them saw what she did.

A warrior swathed in green and brown rode out from the wych elms on the opposite bank. Morgana blinked, clearing her vision. Surely the preternatural creature was no more real than the Little People. Oh, but she wanted him to be real!

Desperately she chanted the ancient prayer invoking the phantom. She inveigled him with the spirit of her grandfather, Gerait Og Fitzgerald, the greatest and most powerful wizard to ever draw breath in Ireland.

Amid the rocks, trees and rain, Morgana's savior galloped forth, imbued with her thirst for vengeance and her soul-deep hatred. A warrior at one with the spectacular panorama of wind-torn branches, storm-filled sky and spuming white water breaking free of the river bed.

Save me, Gerait Og, she prayed with all her heart and soul. *Stop Kelly!*

She could bear all that had happened thus far, but not rape. Her spirit would surely die if such a repulsive, evil man made his body one with hers.

Her warrior pressed through the flood riding a dun horse. A fiendish war cry reverberated from his throat, mingling with Erin's howling wind. The specter's tartan molded around his torso, detailing his size and exposing brawny, hard-hewn banded arms. Lightning flashed off his upraised sword. War plaits streamed from his temples, as if to flee from the fierce visage under his helm.

Morgana lifted her head from the mud and spat in James Kelly's face. She let free a high, wild laugh of triumph.

"You are dead, James Kelly!" she shouted, believing in the magic of the witchcraft handed down to her from generations of ancestors more powerful than she. "Look to the river, cur! See you the revenge of the Fitzgeralds!"

"God and Saint George," whispered a soldier.

"J-J-Jesus Mariah! It's Shane O'Neill! The ghost that haunts the bridge!" Orson bawled.

Her attackers released their grip at once.

Kelly scrambled off her on all fours, crawling and clawing at the ground for the sword belt that he'd cast beyond Morgana's reach to torment and break her. He shouted frantic curses and babbled frenetic orders. His cowardly soldiers bolted, howling as they ran for horses. "Jesus save us! It's the ghost of Shane O'Neill!"

Shane O'Neill, indeed! Delighted, Morgana pushed herself up from the mud, snatching Gerait Og's blade back into her hands. She brought it to her lips and kissed the amber jewel embedded in the hilt, then staggered painfully onto her feet.

A wild notion made her kick James Kelly viciously in his pimpled arse. He slipped and sprawled facedown in the mud, his belly covering his sword. That made her choke with glee. She tried to find the strength to kick him in his ugly dangling cods. Much as she wanted to deliver that last indignity before he died, she hadn't the strength to do it. Her weakened energy went into fueling her mad, ecstatic laughter.

Morgana sobered the instant her gaze returned to the warrior. Burning eyes were fixed on her, not Kelly. Her gown hung loose from her shoulders, rent from throat to hem.

Her brain locked on to a truth. Her grandfather's supernatural powers summoned only demons. Years of strict convent teachings had drummed that fact into Morgana's head. This bloodthirsty, berserk Irish war god running circles around her with lust in his terrible eyes wasn't coming for Kelly. He was coming for her.

The conundrum of those thoughts brought more mad laughter surging from her lips. All demons, spirits, powers and dominions demanded a high price for their aid. A supreme irony struck her. What could she possibly offer her war god for a sacrifice? Her virginity? Hardly. She was a widowed woman.

At that ludicrous thought, Morgana laughed. She was truly a witch, as all in Dublin called her—Morgan le Fay! Tears squeezed from her eyes as she threw her arms wide and spun in a slow dance, chanting, "Kill them, kill them! Slay them all for me and I am yours!"

A soldier screamed, "Shane O'Neill!" as the warrior's sword cleaved his head from his body. Morgana stopped dancing. Could her vision-god be the ghost of the murdered Shane O'Neill?

And why not? She laughed again. Shane O'Neill had died on the bridge at Benburg. How very Irish of him to haunt the very spot where he'd died!

Her humor left her then.

Another warrior—a giant of the ilk of the legendary Finn mac Cool—appeared. The giant's hair gleamed curiously white. Adorned with Pictish blue war paint, he bore no other trace of humanity.

Lightning bolts flashed from their gleaming swords. Mud churned up from the hooves of their charging war-horses.

The Abhainn Mor erupted. Warrior after warrior spewed forth from the bridge.

Each was more ferocious than the last. Heads sprouted helms and horns. Targes grew spikes. All bore swords and dangerous dirks on their belts, while brandishing halberds, pikes, lochaber axes, tridents or wicked spiked maces.

James Kelly staggered to his feet, hitching his breeches to his waist to cover himself. His sword hung limp in his hand. He turned tail, and spying Morgana, ran behind her to hide himself while he fastened his breeches.

Morgana dragged her ruined gown onto her shoulders and clutched its pieces closed over her breasts. Past that, she had lost all ability to move or breathe. Every muscle in her body was locked rigid. Rape at the hands of the English was the least of her worries now.

Her dabblings in her grandfather's witchcraft had come full circle. As the good nuns at Saint Mary de Hogges's Abbey had predicted, the devils had come for Morgana's wicked, unrepentant soul. She lacked the ability to dredge up the words of confession or the sense to list her many varied and too-often-repeated wicked sins.

"Sweet Saint Brigit, save me!" she whispered.

For the first time in Morgana's tumultuous life, the sights before her overwhelmed her mind. She fainted dead away at James Kelly's feet.

Chapter Three

No redcoat escaped Hugh O'Neill's retribution. In short order, five curs fell under the stroke of Hugh's sword. Only Kelly remained alive, his heart still beating, as Hugh dismounted from Boru and tossed the war-horse's reins to his young nephew, Owen Roe.

"What farce be this, O'Neill?" Kelly demanded. He hid his fear behind a mask of sarcasm—that of a bureaucrat accustomed to wielding threats against lesser men than he. "Think you this some London stage, and you a hero of some play, wherein you ravish the maiden yourself?"

Hugh's cold smile sent Kelly staggering backward. He came up short, pinned to the point of Kermit Blackbeard's sword.

"Your sarcasm ill suits you, Kelly," Hugh crooned. He handed Loghran his sword to clean the blood from it. James Kelly and Hugh O'Neill went way back, fifteen long years, to Hugh's first days at the court of Elizabeth Regina. Kelly had been the bully of the queen's court then, just as he was the bully of Ireland now.

The soldiers were dead, but not the traitor. Hugh stepped around the broken body of the woman, drew back his fist and let it fly into James Kelly's face, dropping him like a stone at the feet of Shamus Fitz and Donald the Fair.

"Truss him and tie a rope around his neck. If he doesn't wake up, I'll drag him by his throat to the stone of O'Neill."

Hugh turned his back to the traitorous Kelly as he stripped off his gauntlets. He flicked a cold glance to the kerns milling all over the vale, examining the soldiers Hugh had dispatched. Before a one of them had so much as lifted a finger, Hugh had lopped off three heads and gutted a fourth.

Stoic Loghran O'Toole's only participation in the mêlée had been to make certain Kelly remained Hugh's prisoner.

A deep silence settled over the kerns as young Hugh O'Neill turned to face them.

"Macmurrough!" Hugh shouted. "Present yourself!"

At one time, Art Macmurrough had been a general under Shane the Proud, in command of a division of five hundred foot soldiers. He commanded no one now. Bereft of the heart of their leadership, the army of O'Neills had not marched anywhere since Shane's death. The old soldier came forward reluctantly.

"So your admiration for fine horseflesh exceeds your attention to duty, does it, Art?" Hugh asked in a controlled voice, though the angry edge was there. Every living soul near Benburg bridge heard it.

"My lord," Macmurrough answered in a voice as aged by the years as Loghran's, "'twas a fine mare. I couldn't let it drown in the river. Not a horse like that."

"So you gave my position away, then, for a piece of horseflesh? Good thinking, man. What if this had been the justiciar, Lord Grey's, vanguard, bringing siege to Dungannon's abbey? Did you turn your back on Shane as you just turned your back on me? Did you leave Shane vulnerable? Here at this bridge? Send him alone to his slaughter the last time the English tried to bring Tyrone to its knees?"

"Nay, Lord Hugh. I didn't." Macmurrough's grizzled face broke out in sweat. "It was winter then. You were in England. I was at Tullaghoge. Shane ordered all of us to stand down for Epiphany."

Seeing that Lord Hugh did not believe him, Macmurrough fell to his knees, his empty hands up, beseeching

Hugh's forgiveness. "My lord, I swear to you on the souls of my five sons, we knew nothing of the attack before it happened. I loved Shane. He was my heart, my blood brother. I'd have given my life for his, if I could have done. I swear on my sainted mother's soul, I'll never fail you again, O'Neill. I'll carry out every command you give me, trusting you as Abraham trusted God. Hail, Hugh O'Neill!"

The kern's hands clasped Hugh's. He kissed Hugh's battered knuckles and the signet ring of his earldom. Donald the Fair strode forward and extended his sword to Hugh, hilt first, as he, also, dropped to his knee in salute.

"I, too, am your man, O'Neill. My soul and my sword lie in your hand, to command as you will."

Loghran O'Toole's eyes misted as he watched sword after sword being placed in Hugh's strong hand as each kern knelt before Hugh O'Neill, giving him a solemn oath of fealty. Loghran had gone to England, gillie to the baron of Dungannon's son, the only Irish influence in Hugh's long sojourn at the queen's court. It was abundantly clear to O'Toole that the queen of England's court had failed to breed the Irish out of Hugh O'Neill.

Loghran's heart swelled with pride, loving Hugh O'Neill as the son he would never have. Now, at five-and-twenty, his charge had all the qualities necessary to become the next O'Neill—leadership, intelligence, compassion, courage and fierce loyalty.

One by one, they all came, twelve men and one boy, pledging their lives and souls to Hugh's hand. Hugh was stunned and humbled. Before tonight, not a one of them had trusted a kinsman raised in England as far as he could throw him.

These twelve were not all O'Neills. Numerous and varied kinsman, cadres and families made up Tyrone. The trust and loyalty of all the others remained to be gained by Hugh at some future date. But these twelve were Hugh's men now, and Hugh belonged to them. It was a start.

Hugh turned to Macmurrough and bade him run down the soldiers' scattered horses and transport all seven, and the Arabian mare, to Dungannon. He ordered Kermit to gather the dead soldiers' weapons, and any wealth or valuables they carried on their persons. Bounty was forever the tribute of war. Whatever was gathered would be divided fairly, each to his own needs.

Donald the Fair and Shamus Fitz volunteered to bury the remains. Loghran O'Toole handed Hugh back his sword, cleaned. He took out his breviary, stole and rosary, saying he would recite the Te Deum over the bodies and consign their souls to God's eternal judgment.

Satisfied that all was done that should be done, Hugh O'Neill unfastened his plaid from his shoulder and went to the woman's body. As he opened the cloth to spread it over her and cover the gaps in her gown, it occurred to him that he might never know who she was.

That, he thought, would be a great pity. A woman with her courage should be remembered, immortalized in the bards' songs and revered in the ages to come. Hugh closed his eyes, remembering the sight of her kicking Kelly in his naked arse, sending him sprawling facedown in the mud. She might have been murdered, but her spirit hadn't been broken.

Bending his knee to the ground, Hugh gently pried her swollen, cold fingers from the handle of her knife. He tucked it inside the sheath holding his dirk for safe transport. Then Hugh gave her other hand and her neck a cursory examination for identifying jewels or ornaments. She wore none.

Rain had washed some dirt and blood from her damaged face. Matted curls clung to her cheek and clumped in the mud underneath her. He could not help looking at her full breasts. They were exquisitely shaped, heavy and firm, the kind of flesh that filled a man's hands with pleasure and joy in the touching. Her soft white belly gleamed like fine porcelain beneath the mud smeared across it.

Before he covered her with the plaid, he thought to close her gown and return some dignity to her.

Her flesh was still very warm to the touch, resilient and supple as his knuckles passed over it to draw the rent cloth closed. She'd been wearing a stomacher over a rather finely woven linen kirtle. The laces of that close-fitted outer garment had been cut, though the buckramed garment itself was whole and could be relaced. He loosened the lacing of his doublet and pulled it free, thinking to thread the stomacher at least partway closed.

He had no sooner begun that difficult task than he felt that soft, malleable, womanly flesh move against the backs of his knuckles. Hugh jerked his hand back, stunned by the sensation of feeling a nipple pucker.

Her kirtle slid back off that plump mound of flesh. It was full dark. There was no moon. His sight was good. She'd looked dead to his eye from the distance, even this close a moment ago. He laid his palm over that breast, certain that a woman's nipples should have no reaction to any touch after death occurred.

As he gently formed her pebbling nipple between his fingers, definitely feeling it react to his touch, he brought his right ear close to her open lips, cocked to catch any sound of actual breathing.

"My lord Hugh!" Owen Roe shouted. His bare feet made squishy sounds as he ran down from the river. "Shamus Fitz says we best cross the Abhainn Mor with all due haste. It will crest any moment now."

"Be quiet!" Hugh scolded him. "I think the woman may be alive. Stand still and let me listen."

He dropped his ear to her breastbone, listening for sound inside her throat. Positive that he heard something, Hugh slid his arm under the woman's shoulders and lifted her. Her head dropped back on his arm, moist lips flexed open and parted. Both breasts spilled out of the kirtle, full and luscious and splendidly beautiful, lifting quite high as her lungs inflated with air.

"Splendor of God!" Owen gasped. He dropped to his knees, his eyes as perfectly round as the gold sovereigns minted at the Tower of London. "Please God, make her alive."

Hugh shot the boy a quelling look and hastily spread his plaid where he should have some time ago. He felt the woman's ribs contract, completing the cycle of breathing. Hugh spread his fingers across her exposed throat, easily finding a steady and even pulse. "She is alive."

"What are we going to do with her?" Owen Roe wanted to know.

Hugh's mouth twitched over the boy's inclusive and decidedly possessive pronoun. "*We* are going to take her to Dungannon, do you fetch my horse to me."

"But, my lord Hugh," the boy said, confused, "do you dare to take her there? Doesn't she have to be cast out by all the clans, now that she's a whore for the English?"

Hugh blinked, so stunned by the nine-year-old's assessment of Irish custom that he didn't notice the woman had roused. His tone was severely reprimanding when he did speak. "She is the victim of a crime, nothing more. That doesn't make a woman a whore, Owen Roe."

"Shall I sing hallelujah that you've said that?" Morgana asked, her voice a rasp, as she took a firm hold upon the sodden cloth laid up to her throat.

Startled, Hugh jerked. The woman regained her strength all at once, twisting away from his supporting arm. "Milady," Hugh sputtered, reflexively tightening his arm across her back, "Be careful."

"Oh, I intend to be," Morgana said with assurance. She tried to scoot away from him, seeking safety in distance, but failed to gain that advantage. Her head turned slowly right, then left as she tried to gain her bearings. Her last conscious thought returned—of fainting from the fear that she'd called forth a phalanx of demon warriors from the beyond.

Her eyes returned to Hugh, and her hand came up to stroke his cheek. "Are you real?"

"Real?" Hugh asked, confused by that question. Trembling fingers traced his jaw and splayed across his cheek. "Aye, I am real."

"You're not a ghost?" Morgana whispered. She swallowed hard. "Not the spirit of Shane O'Neill?"

"Nay, lady. Shane is dead. I am Hugh of the O'Neills."

Morgana exhaled unsteadily. A touch of the mad irony that had gripped her before she fainted returned. Wryly she said, "Hugh of the O'Neills, then. Has anyone told you you look just like Shane?"

"Not that I can recall, they haven't. Who are you?"

Morgana wet her lips. She took time to count the crumpled bodies of the queen's soldiers and the number of Irish kerns milling around in the night shadows. She took a second deep breath, this one shuddering inside her lungs.

Shock was beginning to set in. Her mind wasn't anywhere near as clear as it should be. Her fingers on his shaved cheek proved he was a man of flesh and blood, not an apparition. She swallowed, then said, "My name is Morgan."

Hugh repeated her word. "Morgan?"

"Aye, Morgana," she repeated, stopping herself from saying anything more clarifying.

"Morgana, then." He grasped a trailing corner of his plaid and wiped at the mud on her face. "What great error on your part made you the prey of an English patrol this stormy night?"

He saw the whites of her eyes flash, but she made no move to stop his hand.

Morgana wasn't looking at her savior so much as she was looking to see where her attackers were before she answered that loaded question. She noted that there was no one standing to contradict her.

"Truly, sir, I have no idea what their intentions were. Savagery, I suppose." Her voice shook on her last words, and that much was no act on her part. "Are you certain we are not dead? Is this the afterlife?"

"No, I assure you it is not. You have not gone on to your reward." A pair of distrustful and confused eyes looked everywhere but at Hugh O'Neill. She drew back from the casual, servicing touch of his hand as he mopped up her face. "By your language, I assume you are not of Tyrone."

Morgana grimaced, recognizing her first mistake. "You're right. I don't speak Irish."

"Then you are from the Pale, from Dublin, possibly?"

"Kildare," Morgana corrected. She could not afford to say more.

"And what brings you to Ulster, Morgana of Kildare?"

"I am on pilgrimage to Dunluce." Again, Morgana looked to the river, seeking Ariel. She exhaled a deep and tired sigh. "Now that I've lost my horse, I shall have to go back to Dublin and start all over."

Hugh could see her distress. He stroked his fingers over her throat, soothing her as he would a frightened animal. "Nay, you haven't lost your horse. It is safe on the other side of the Abhainn Mor. One of my men took pity on the beast and rescued it from the flood."

"One did?" Morgana turned her face back to the man, her eyes wary. "Are you certain?"

"As certain as I am of my own name."

"God and Mary be praised," she whispered reverently. A great gush of relief over that news nearly caused Morgana to burst into tears. If Ariel had made it across the river, her saddle and bags intact, then all was not lost. Morgana could continue to Dunluce with nothing lost beyond the cost of her escort. Given any luck, she could hire more men. She could use some of her ready coins to have masses said for those she'd lost.

Hugh did not urge her to quiet. A woman's tears after an ordeal were a good thing. He embraced her gently, waiting for the calm that would come soon enough.

"Tell me," Hugh asked as he sat her up, mindful that she had injuries other than the ones he could see in the limited light. "Do you think you can stand or ride?"

"Possibly." Morgana used her left hand to touch the back of her neck. She encountered mud, matted hair and excruciating pain. This wasn't the time to start cataloging her injuries. She nodded in the direction of Kelly's trussed body, easily distinguished from the others because of his silvergray hair. "Is Kelly dead?"

"Not yet," Hugh murmured. "By your question, I take it you are acquainted with him."

"Enough to wish I wasn't," Morgana replied tartly. She busied her hands, making order of her clothing, and what she couldn't order she wrapped securely under the sodden tartan to cover the gaps.

The curious boy kneeling at Hugh O'Neill's side took off his own belt and offered it to her as a means to hold the plaid secure.

"That was kind of you, Owen. Now go and fetch my horse," Hugh said, dismissing the boy.

"At once!" Owen popped to his feet, bowing deeply. Hugh thought the show of respect attributable more to the English lady's breasts than to any sign of hero worship honoring Hugh.

"May I have my knife back?" Morgana asked as she fastened the belt buckle at her waist.

Hugh swung his eyes from the departing boy, back to the woman. Her intense gaze was leveled, pointed at his waist, where her blade rested in the same sheath as his dirk.

"Until I know you better, Morgana of Kildare, I think the blade had best rest where it is. I applaud your skill with it. One man of six dispatched to his Maker, three others wounded. My gut tells me that you are a dangerous woman."

"A desperate woman, sir." She challenged him without compunction, proving that she was no stranger to speaking her mind. "I would feel far safer if the blade rested in my own sheath."

Hugh leaned over her, deliberately sliding his hand under her skirt to find the deadly dagger's sheath, neatly buckled below her left knee. She was an Englishwoman from the Pale, and not to be trusted. His eyes met hers. "You will be safe in my care without it."

The rhythm of Morgana's heart arrested. Her breath caught in her throat. The flesh on the inside of her thighs quivered. The touch of his hand was intimate and warm. The implication of that sheath at her knee might have gone unsaid, but his proprietary attitude needed no more vouching for. She knew exactly what he was telling her—he was the one in control, not she.

Trying to take control of matters between them, Morgana grasped his wrist and removed his hand.

"I find, sir, my personal security never rests well in anyone's hands but my own. I repeat, give me back my knife."

"Not now, Morgana of Kildare. Not before we know who you are and what you are doing in Tyrone. Come, I will help you to stand."

As Hugh assisted the woman back onto her feet, Kermit Blackbeard turned the contents of a filled water skin out on James Kelly's head and chest. The moment the traitor roused from his stupor, Kermit kicked hard toes into Kelly's ribs.

Kelly awoke spitting and cursing, shouting against the bonds restraining him. "God damn you, I'll have your head for striking me!"

He sat up, blinking his eyes, and glared at the man assisting Morgana to her feet. "Untie me, O'Neill!"

"O'Neill!" Morgana gasped. She jerked against the young man whose kind arm gave her the support she needed to remain on her feet. "You're *the O'Neill?*"

"Aye, lady, so he is," Kermit Blackbeard assured her. He dug his fist into Kelly's collar and hauled him onto his feet.

"Those are their words, not mine, lady," Hugh crooned softly into the woman's ear, to calm her.

"On your feet, man!" Shamus Fitz dug his heels into his mount's ribs, putting hard tension on the rope tied between his saddle and Kelly's fat neck. Kelly struggled, choking, his wild eyes searching for Hugh.

"O'Neill! Tell your men to desist! O'Neill!"

Morgana of Kildare reacted. Her hand shot out to snatch her blade from the sheath at the O'Neill's waist. He stayed her hand, gripping her fingers firmly, adding a command to desist. "Nay, lady. This is my land, and he's my prisoner, now. Unless you want to join Kelly in the ranks of the unwelcome, obey me."

"Damn you, O'Neill, tell these bastards to untie me!" Kelly shouted hoarsely. "You can't hold me! I'm an officer in the queen's army!"

Owen Roe returned Boru and stood fast, holding the charger's bridle by the bit, awaiting Hugh's next order. Hugh nodded to Kermit and Shamus Fitz. "Take him to Fort Tullaghoge. He'll be tried one week hence. Guard him well, Shamus Fitz."

"On what charges?" Kelly raged, loud enough to wake the dead as far away as Tara. "Nothing I did to that woman matters. She's my prisoner. I've a warrant to take her back to Dublin."

Morgana instantly refuted that charge. "That's a lie!"

It was a good thing that Hugh's hands were put to use staying Morgana of Kildare's vengeful fingers, else this time he'd certainly have broken Kelly's jaw. "Take him out of my sight."

"Wait!" Kelly shouted again, struggling against the ropes that bound him. "I demand to know why you are doing this, O'Neill. I can bloody well have your head."

"On the contrary, Kelly. It is clan O'Neill that will have your head."

"I'm not under your benefice."

"Are you not James Kelly, born at Tullaghoge in county Tyrone, bastard of Margaret Mary Kelly, scullery maid at Fort Tullaghoge lo these many years?"

"Aye, and well you know my father is Lord Litton. You can't lay a hand on me, O'Neill. You haven't a charge against me that will hold in any court in England."

Hugh carefully lifted the woman onto Boru's saddle, then mounted the steed behind her. He nodded to Owen Roe, and the boy handed him the reins. "Get you to your father's horse, Owen, and return to Dungannon with him."

Hugh turned Boru to face James Kelly. His dark eyes pierced the bully's soul.

"This is Ulster, Kelly. You have forgotten that you are a son born to the land of Tyrone, subject of the late Conn the Lame, Shane the Proud after him, and now my uncle, Matthew, by whose authority I arrest you.

"As for my having to lay my hand upon you, I will not stoop so low as to touch you again. It is the judgment of Tir-Owen and Tir-Connail that you will face, at the next gathering. Witnesses will be called to testify against you, many who claim you murdered Shane O'Neill."

"That's a lie! I dare any Celtic bastard to face me and swear against me. I'll have their bloody head if they do! I'm the law in this land now, O'Neill. Not you."

"Oh?" Hugh O'Neill's voice was deadly cold. "Then we shall play this game your way, Captain Kelly. By my own authority as Her Majesty the queen of England's earl of Tyrone, I, too, am invested with the power of pit and gallows over all criminals who enter Ulster under false pretenses. In Her Majesty's name, I arrest you and bind you over for trial in the nearest docket."

Suddenly this argument between the two powerful men cut through Morgana's shock at finding herself face-to-face with *the O'Neill.* She stared at Kelly, tasting revenge on her tongue, and through him found the means to ensure that the O'Neill would aid and protect her.

"He can't have my head or intimidate me," Morgana said. "Under both brehon and English law, I can testify against him. He confessed to the murder of Shane O'Neill, boasting to me that it was none other than he who took Shane the Proud's head to Dublin and sold it. You've got your murderer, O'Neill."

"You lying bitch!" Kelly lunged forward, only to be drawn up taut against the ropes restraining him. "A cage outside Dublin Castle is too good for you. I'll transport you to England. You'll be hanged, drawn and quartered, the same as all the cursed Fitzgeralds! O'Neill, listen to me. That woman is Morgan Fitzgerald, protégé of Grace O'Malley, both wanted in London for piracy and high treason!"

As if he hadn't been interrupted by either of them, Hugh continued, finishing his words. "And did you not want to be charged for the murder of Shane O'Neill, Kelly, you should have remained in England and never return again to Ireland. Take him from my sight."

The last five words spoken by the O'Neill were the only ones Shamus Fitz was listening to hear. He dug his heels into his horse's ribs, and the rope to James Kelly's throat stretched as his mount galloped to the bridge.

"Run or be dragged, Kelly!" Kermit Blackbeard hastened the traitor on his march by whalloping Kelly's arse with the flat side of his sword.

Morgana sat stiffly on the charger, glaring after the departing men dragging their prisoner into the deep waters coursing over the flooded bridge. The rain beat down on her head, striking her face and stinging her eyes, making her squint to see into the dark night.

She wanted the satisfaction of watching Kelly drown, nearly as much as she wanted the satisfaction of killing him herself.

Hugh O'Neill waited in silence until Loghran and Donald the Fair joined him for the short ride to Castle O'Neill. He put no questions to the woman, though many came to mind. The hour was late and the woman exhausted. Her identity and status could be determined at another time.

Loghran and Donald rode at Hugh's sides, which proved to be a good thing on the crossing. The Abhainn Mor had not calmed. Violent water surged high up Boru's tall legs, lapping over the war-horse's withers in the deepest portion of the flood. Hugh had all he could do to keep a firm hold on Morgana, whom he'd foolishly seated sidesaddle.

Where she had been fearless and indomitable in facing a band of rapists, the flood turned her into a terrified, shrieking female.

The very moment rough water came near her boots, she panicked, trying to kneel and then stand on Boru's back. She'd have climbed Hugh's back and toppled them both into the flood, had Hugh allowed such foolish action. It literally took all his strength to contain the frantic woman.

He thanked God he had Loghran and Donald making certain all three horses crossed without mishap. Otherwise, Hugh was positive both he and the woman would have been swept to their deaths in the floodwaters.

On the Tyrone bank, death still seemed imminent, judging by the choke hold Morgana had on Hugh's neck. They were both soaked to the skin from the crossing. Hugh halted Boru on the high bank, to let his horse rest and to get the woman better seated for the journey home.

"It's all right, Morgana, you're not going to drown." Hugh tugged her arms apart, loosening their death grip around his neck. Her legs, too, wrapped shamelessly around his waist. Their clothing mingled in a tangle of bared knees and lower limbs. "You can let go now. We've crossed the river."

Loghran grunted a Gaelic comment pertaining to the indecency of the woman's position, then galloped up the cliff, leaving Hugh to deal with woman on his own. Donald the Fair politely offered to wait at the bridge for Macmurrough.

Morgana swallowed hard several times, gulping down her fear, before she was able to speak. The river was behind her. No point would be served by voicing her deep-seated fear of water now. She managed to loosen her grip on Hugh O'Neill. She could exert no control over her shaking.

Hugh rather missed the tight bindings, once she'd righted herself on the saddle and sat astride before him. Again, she fussed with cloth—pulling down wet skirts, tugging hanging sleeves and covering tartan into modest disorder.

"I'm sorry," she murmured. "I didn't hurt you, did I?"

Hugh cleared his throat, preferring not to remark upon the strength and power he'd sensed in her legs when they wrapped around his waist so intimately. He, too, gave his hands to the work of replacing her fallen clothing. For a moment or two, the river's wild current had threatened to strip her naked. "Remind me not to attempt riding tandem with you over another body of water."

Morgana ran a wet hand over her face. "This is most unseemly. Look you there. My horse is tied to that tree. You've been most kind. I can continue on my own from here."

"Continue?" Hugh murmured in her ear as he tucked the salvage of his plaid over her shoulders. She shook so violently, her body felt as though it were convulsing. "Nay, Morgana of Kildare. A man of mine is coming with the soldiers' horses. He and Donald will bring your animal to Dungannon's stable. You are in no condition to ride unassisted."

"I say that I am," Morgana insisted. Dungannon was a stronghold of clan O'Neill. She had no interest in winding up there. If the truth were to be spoken, she had hired a guide to make certain she traveled north without passing within a league of Dungannon. James Kelly was a minor nuisance compared to the troubles she could expect from those who resided at Dungannon.

Morgana began again, guarding words, as well as tone. She didn't want to alert any suspicion, but was doubly convinced that they must part ways. "I must be on my way to Dunluce...."

"Save your breath. I'm not listening. We ride to Dungannon as we are."

Hugh cut off what he sensed would be towering argument. He'd learned young not to expend his breath arguing with women. Instead, he turned Boru to the path leading up the cliff and into Tyrone. She struggled some, protesting the leaving of her horse behind.

"This is outrageous," Morgana declared. "First I am attacked at the inn at Benburg, then nearly killed at the bridge over the Blackwater. Now my rescuer abducts me against my will! Some knight in shining armor you pretend to be, Hugh O'Neill."

Instead of correcting her, Hugh turned as silent as Conn the Lame's marble effigy. Fifteen years under the rule of the most strident woman alive had taught him to keep his tongue behind his teeth and measure his words before voicing his opinions.

"You're cold and miserable." Hugh's arms slid around her waist, drawing her back against his chest. "Whist now. We'll be at Dungannon anon. My men will not rape you when we get there. You're safe, Morgana of Kildare."

"And that's supposed to reassure me?" she asked waspishly, keeping a secure hold on his powerful wrist, where his hand pressed so firmly against her bare belly through wet and torn cloth. "Who is to protect me from you?"

Hugh chuckled at her apprehensions. "You're safe from my attentions for the moment, lady. At least until I know if you wash up well."

Morgana hissed, sucking in her stomach. His arm at her waist tightened more. God help her, but she'd never in her life found herself in a more vulnerable or embarrassing situation. Here the man who had saved her from certain rape now hinted that he might take more liberties with her person than James Kelly had dared.

She regretted calling upon her grandfather's magic. She had summoned a devil! Hadn't she woken to find this very man leaning over her, touching her intimately, speaking to another about her, as though she weren't capable of hearing his words? His men all thought her a whore. Most likely he did, too.

She would disabuse him of that thought as soon as she could. It wasn't decent to be so immodestly clothed and ride tandem with a man whose bare shanks touched her own legs.

The jarring gallop of his horse intensified the aches in Morgana's head and neck. Damn Kelly! Her thoughts swam in confusing circles. She felt foolish and silly for having imagined ghosts and warrior-gods, now that she was certain this man was no apparition.

Hugh was solid and warm-blooded and hard male flesh against her back. His heat warmed her sodden clothes and soothed her shivering body. She was shamed anew each time she remembered having both her legs wound around his waist. She wanted him to disappear. The last thing on earth she wanted to do was to face him eye-to-eye in any better light.

"How much farther is this Dungannon?"

"Not far." Hugh urged Boru to the crest of a steep hill. Hidden in the valley behind it was Dungannon. The fortified village skirted the north shore of a lake, its walls now enlarged to enclose all of the Dominican abbey within the fortifications. On a crannog jutting into the lake sat the dark and ominous castle of the same name, Dungannon. The rain beat harder on the lee side of the hill.

To Morgana's eye, the castle and its walled town looked like a great black spider crouched in the center of a shimmering, intricate web.

Her brooding unease shot to full-blown alarm. The castle was completely surrounded by water! She bolted upright, banging the crown of her head on Hugh's chin. "Put me down!"

Hugh tasted blood, because she'd caused him to bite his own tongue.

"Put me down, I say! I'll wait here for your man to come with my horse. I refuse to go one step farther in your company. Put me down!"

It was becoming difficult to retain sympathy for her plight in Hugh's mind. Where was the woman's gratitude? He'd put an end to the cruelty Kelly and his men had dealt her. He'd saved her life. She should be kissing his hands, begging his grace and expressing her thanks, not haranguing him at every turn. "No. I will not put you down."

"Why not?" Morgana demanded imperiously.

"You should know better than to ask that. A woman alone isn't safe in these climes."

"I command you to put me down. This instant!"

"Lady, you do not command me to do anything," he responded. "Be silent!"

"No!"

"Now, you listen to me," he countered, goaded out of his usual reticence. "This is Ulster. More than that, this is my land, Tyrone! Here a woman does not speak again when a a man commands her not!"

Morgana twisted on his thigh, turning halfway round to glare at him. "I'll scream my bloody head off if you don't put me down at once! I don't know who you or where you are taking me or what purpose you have to your actions. You're frightening me, and I've had quite enough fright for one day and night."

"Morgana of Kildare, I gave you my name. It is Hugh O'Neill. That is my home, Dungannon Castle. I am taking you there for the purpose of cleaning you up, giving you shelter for the night, then sending you on your way at first light."

"Will you swear by that on your immortal soul?"

"Woman, you delude yourself, thinking you've had fright enough for one day and night," Hugh declared in an ominous, threatening voice. "Do you provoke my temper at this hour, you'll know what true terror is before morning comes. Now, keep your tongue behind your teeth.''

To the north, over Slieve Gallion, thunder rumbled and lightning stroked the sky. A responding cord smote Slieve Gullion, whence Morgana had come.

Morgana's banked temper nearly burst forth. She knew better than to believe a word he'd said about sending her peacefully on her way. Come morning, someone might remember that James Kelly had named her as a Fitzgerald. She'd never get clear of Dungannon Castle then.

''Very well,'' Morgana said, having the last word. She snapped her shoulders and, head upright, glared at the castle. She mustn't give in to her weariness or let down her guard. If it cost her a night's sleep to stay alert to the arrival of his man bringing the horses, so be it. The very moment she was reunited with Ariel, she'd leave for Dunluce.

Chapter Four

Only a light rain was falling by the time they reached the portcullis. It was raised to admit Hugh and Morgana, and closed behind them. She shuddered when the gate groaned as it was lowered. That was not a good sign.

The village streets were dark and narrow and fairly quiet. She silently searched each crossroad, looking for a postern gate at the end of the cobbled street that might give exit outside the town walls.

In the town's square, there was some celebration occurring. Hugh spoke to numerous men who hailed him from the doorway of a tavern, but he didn't tarry. Morgana clutched the dripping tartan to her shoulders, her eyes on the open avenue ahead, which ended at a stalwart portcullis barring entrance to the castle.

It looked more terrifying up close than Traitor's Gate at Dublin Castle. Morgana's heart rose to her throat. A Fitzgerald woman in Dungannon—that couldn't be borne. Now, when it behoved her to faint, she couldn't.

Hugh held Boru still, waiting for the portcullis to rise. As soon as it had, he guided the horse at a measured pace over the long bridge, crossing the lake into the fortress. Morgana's fingers exerted incredible force where they gripped his forearm, which brought questions to his mind. How had she come to acquire her unusual and unwomanly strength? Was she a protégée of Grace O'Malley, piratess *extraordinaire*?

More importantly, was she actually a Fitzgerald, as Kelly had claimed?

Torchbearers and grooms rushed to meet him. Hugh dismounted and surrendered Boru's reins, then reached up to help the woman down to the cobblestones, saying to the servants, "Wake Mrs. Carrick and tell her to come to me in the round tower. Fetch hot water and clean cloths. Both my guest and I are in need of hot baths."

"I can't possibly go inside tracking all this mud and filth," Morgana stammered, clutching at every imaginary straw she could think of to avoid stepping foot in the castle proper. Hugh dropped his hands from her waist, letting her stand on her own. The light from the torches showed how filthy and battered she was. Few hags had ever looked worse. He inclined his head in the direction of the open well in the bailey yard. "Would you prefer that I have servants douse you naked with water from that well?"

"Of course not," Morgana answered, without looking for any well. Her gaze was fixed past Hugh's right shoulder. "I can't go in there! I can't!"

The desperation Hugh heard in her voice caused him to swing around to look beyond the wide-open doors of the great hall. A measure of pride filled him, for the well-lit, stately chamber, filled with dancing courtiers and elegantly dressed and coiffed ladies, gave proof of how hospitable and elegant his home was. The happy strains of melodious harp and lute accompanying a tenor's sweet voice entertained a bevy of noble guests.

"You can't possibly think I want anyone to see me looking like this? Isn't there a side or a back door I can go through?" Morgana pleaded.

Hugh lifted a clump of muddy, matted hair from her brow. "What difference could your *dishabille* make to others who have never laid eyes upon you? To what would they compare your appearance? Can you not be thankful that you are alive?"

"That's unfair." She lifted her sodden skirts free of her soaked boots, trying to wring the water from her hems with her hands.

Hugh took hold of her hands, stopping her from continuing such a useless and futile effort. "Nothing can be done for these clothes you wear, Morgana of Kildare."

He caught her chin, lifting it, to make her look into his eyes. The torches glittered back at him from pale irises. "Where is that courage you had in abundance a little while ago? No one will disparage you for the accident of being drenched in a flood."

"Were it only a flood that caused me to be in such *dishabille,* I would rejoice." Morgana stared back at his dark eyes, her pride surfacing in the upward thrust of her chin. "Very well, O'Neill. Let's get this entrance over with. The sooner begun, the better done."

"That's the spirit." Hugh's eyes twinkled as he gave her his arm. He didn't doubt for a moment that his elder sisters would have a fit when they saw this woman enter the great hall on his arm. But neither Susana nor Rachel would dare to cross him in his own house.

Morgana held her chin high, laid her hand on his arm and marched up the steps at Hugh's side. They hadn't taken too many steps inside the vast hall before the music stopped, the dancing ended and all heads turned to stare.

Susana O'Neill rose to her feet from her comfortable seat on the dais, alarmed by two things: young Hugh's tardy arrival to hall and his attire in the rough garments of a kern. Their uncle, Matthew, rarely came to hall, so Susana was by all rights the lady of the manor, and most entertainments she organized suited her pleasures. Since Hugh had returned from England, she'd made many accommodations to please him, but he really didn't care what sort of events took place in the great hall each evening.

"Young Hugh? What has happened?" Susana left her seat at the high table, rushing forward to intercept her little brother. "Who is this woman? What happened to the both of you? I expected you to hall hours ago."

"Yes, do explain this." Morgana challenged him before the woman, obviously great with child, came within hearing range of her voice. "I dare you, young Hugh."

"Ah, you just proved something else to me, lady," Hugh said under his breath. "You are a troublemaker."

Morgana's hand left his arm, reaching out to snatch her dagger from the sheath on his hip. Again Hugh kept her fingers from their prize.

He offered a soft warning. "Mind what you do, Morgana of Kildare. Tempt me not to make you officially my prisoner. Kelly did accuse you of being a Fitzgerald. That is reason enough to lose one's head, isn't it?"

Morgana's hand clenched into a fist, which she dropped to her side. She turned her back to Hugh, waiting to meet the approaching woman. Several more trailed her, young beauties all, making Morgana feel even more disadvantaged. She heard water drip from her clothes onto the polished tiles at her feet, but she'd be damned from here to eternity before she bowed her head to look at the damage she was causing.

"Ah, good eve, my dear sister. Forgive me for interrupting your *soirée.*" Hugh smiled disarmingly and bent to kiss Susana's fair cheek. "I've brought a guest to the house. You will see that she has had a rather troubling time on her journey. Morgana of Kildare, may I present my sisters, Susana and Rachel. Susana, Morgana will need some cosseting. The Abhainn Mor is a most rapacious river. I fear Morgana lost all of her possessions to the flood."

"Sweet Mother of God, Hugh, you weren't out crossing the river in this weather, were you?" Susana exclaimed, her alarm deepening. "And why on earth are you dressed like a kern? Have you forgotten that I invited Inghinn Dubh to be here this eve?"

"No, I hadn't forgotten." Hugh turned to another woman, trailing his sisters. He bowed to Inghinn, also, but did not favor her cheek with a kiss, as he had done with his sisters. "Inghinn, you are looking splendid this eve, as always. Ladies, please, do not allow us to interrupt your evening. I'll see Morgana settled by Mrs. Carrick. She'll take her under her wing and see to everything, I'm sure."

Hugh turned Morgana to the open stairs rising up to the minstrels' gallery. Ignoring his sister's gasp of shock, he led Morgana out of the gallery, to the supreme isolation of the round tower. It adjoined the castle itself at his mother's solar, on the second floor.

Both the tower and the solar had been closed following his mother's death in 1570. Five weeks ago, when he and Loghran returned from England for good, Hugh had decided to take up residence in the tower's comfortable upper rooms.

He had decided that Morgana could be housed in the solar and the sleeping chamber adjoining it on the second floor of the tower. His gut told him to keep her nearby. She was English, therefore not to be trusted. Servants ran ahead of him, opening doors and lighting candles.

Morgana hadn't missed the surreptitious look of alarm that had passed from Hugh's sisters to the beautiful black-haired young woman named Inghinn Dubh. The women surely thought their young Hugh was bringing a doxy into their house. Had Morgana been standing in their shoes, viewing a ravaged and filthy woman in these tattered clothes, that would have been her assumption. So she couldn't hold theirs against them.

Her feet were literally dragging on the last steps up a winding bartizan staircase that opened onto a lady's solar in some distant quadrant of the massive house.

Mullioned windows lined the solar's outer wall to the east, two of them partially open, letting damp night air mingle with the ripe, earthy scent of a peat fire in the hearth. Numb with fatigue, Morgana surveyed the solar's elegant furnishings, cushioned chaises, tapestries, painted walls, coffered ceiling and beautiful ribbon-fold paneling.

The chamber didn't fit with her preconception of what the inside of the clan O'Neill's stronghold should be. O'Neills were barbarians, brutal killers, savages. How could such ignorant, uncivilized folk have produced any such beauty? Morgana's mind was incapable of dwelling on that conundrum. She wanted to drop where she stood, and couldn't, because a man named O'Neill remained with her in this impossible-to-comprehend chamber.

The peat fire in the solar's wide hearth beckoned her. Morgana stretched cold, trembling fingers out to it. Hugh's wet kilt slapped on his ankle as he put one knee to a marble hearth and wrestled a stout log onto the fire.

"You'll be comfortable here," he said casually, casting a sideways look over his shoulder at her. Morgana swallowed, mesmerized by the breadth of his left hand as he rocked the log back and forth, breaking apart the coals underneath it.

Smoke and flames stirred to life out of white ash and soot-blackened peat. Sparks shot up, snapping and crackling with the blue flames that licked the log, and tried to kiss his hand. A warm glow gilded his profile, highlighting his straight nose and angular jaw.

Morgana caught herself staring at his mouth. It looked out of place against his otherwise strongly masculine features. His mouth was too pretty and too gentle by half.

A wild impulse to run her fingers across that Cupid's bow lower lip, to touch the cleft indenting it, just to make certain it was real, unnerved her. She restrained the urge by pressing both her hands tightly against the wet cloth on her thighs.

"Mrs. Carrick will be here momentarily. You may sit down, Morgana of Kildare. The chairs won't melt if they get wet."

"Perhaps not, but no one will thank me for ruining them with the filth covering me," Morgana told him. She spread her skirts toward the fire, abhorring the dirt ground into the cloth. It was not the best gown she owned, but it hadn't begun this day as a shabby rag, either. Disheartened, she let the cloth drop. "I may as well burn this as try to clean it."

"With two sisters and their offspring to the house, I'll have no difficulty replacing that with something more suitable." Hugh rose to his feet, dusting soot off his hands.

Both his knees popped loudly, making him grin at the incongruity of his own clothing. Standing beside Morgana, he towered over her. She was uncomfortable, and he knew the reason why. His bare knees, her torn gown. No wonder Susana had regarded him with such shock in her face.

The earl of Tyrone had not worn a kilt in his castle since he'd returned home from England. A wild grin edged Hugh's mouth. He hadn't liked dressing in a kilt and tartan earlier that day just to prove a point to his men, but he rather liked the feel of the cloth now. It had certainly contributed to his enjoyment of the ride home with a half-naked woman seated on his lap.

He crossed to a silver service set on a sideboard, uncapped a crystal decanter and poured a generous glass of spirits. Hugh put the glass in Morgana's hand, saying, "This might restore you somewhat."

Morgana brought the glass to her nose, sniffing its contents. She was as wary as a wet cat. "What is it?"

"Whiskey." His fingers remained at the bottom of the finely cut crystal, tilting the contents toward her mouth. "Drink it by little sips, not too much at a time. It's well proved. At the least it will warm your bones, at the most loosen your reticent tongue."

"What do you mean by that?" Morgana sputtered over the first taste. In her part of Ireland, whiskey was a man's drink. She was more used to wine—and that only in modest amounts.

"What would you like me to mean by that?" Hugh's back, which faced the fire, enabled him to study her more critically. In the hall he'd guessed her hair was as dark as Inghinn Dubh's. Under the better light of his mother's Waterford chandelier, he could tell that the wet, mud-caked mop wasn't black at all. Under the river's grime, that hair was redder than autumn apples.

Even filthy and battered, she was an attractive woman. Younger than he'd first supposed.

Morgana tried to hand him back the glass. "I'm not going to drink till I fall down in a drunken stupor, if that's what you've got in mind."

"I didn't say you would." Hugh helped himself to a glass of Bushmill's finest distilled spirits. "In fact, I'll join you. A dousing in the Abhainn Mor saps one's body heat."

"So does the bloody rain." Morgana tasted another sip, grimacing over the burn at the back of her throat. "Does the sun never shine on this part of the island?"

"I seem to remember it doing so upon occasion, but I will admit it has rained repeatedly since I returned from England. Does Kelly actually have a warrant for you, Morgana of Kildare?"

"I doubt it." She met the intensity of his dark eyes without flinching. "Nothing is too low for his kind, especially if it means he can steal from defenseless children or women."

"Are you speaking from personal experience?"

"Aye, I suppose I am." Morgana affirmed that much, but she deliberately clamped her mouth closed afterward, minding her tongue. She took another sip from the glass, swallowing purposefully.

Hugh sighed silently. He wanted her to open up and give him some reason to put his trust in her. "Kelly rarely picks on anyone his own size, but then, most bullies are like that. You still haven't said what it is that put you on his list of enemies."

"I haven't the foggiest idea."

Morgana tilted the glass to her lips and finished it. She rather liked the whiskey's immediate ability to start an internal heat. The ache in her jaw numbed, the back of her neck and her hip throbbed a little less ferociously. Her fingers trembled as she put the glass on the marble mantel.

"You will forgive me if I call you a liar to your face, then, won't you, Morgana Fitzgerald?" She jerked when he said "Fitzgerald." "A few years back, I had the dubious honor of attending Parliament when the latest writ of proscription against the house of Geraldine was read into law.

"More recently, Her Majesty insisted I attend the execution of an Irishman named Warren Henry Fitzgerald, as a lesson in prudent stewardship prior to my return to Tyrone. It is an act of treason to use the name Fitzgerald nowadays, isn't it? Is that why you claim to be known as Morgana of Kildare?"

Morgana chose to say nothing. She turned to warm her back at the fire. A pair of burly servants toted a huge wooden tub into the solar. Hugh directed them to place it near the fire.

Both he and Morgana stepped back, allowing a stream of servants bearing steaming buckets to fill the tub. A short, heavyset woman supervised that work, and the laying out of towels, soaps and fresh clothing.

"We shall have to continue this conversation on the morrow, Morgana." Hugh motioned the woman forward. "Here is my housekeeper, Mrs. Carrick, come to help you out of these wet clothes. A hot bath will soothe and restore you, though I do suggest you make a strong effort to stay awake after your bath, Morgana."

"Why is that?" Morgana asked suspiciously.

Hugh brought his hands to her cheek and chin, touching the bruises on her face. With uncanny accuracy, he found a throbbing lump at her temple.

"People who sleep too soon after taking serious blows to the head sometimes have the ill fortune of never waking up. I shouldn't want that to happen to you," Hugh said firmly. "It would bode ill for the O'Neills to have another Fitzgerald woman die in this house."

"I don't know what you are talking about." Morgana lied with deliberate ease. "I've told you, my name is Morgana of Kildare."

Hugh stopped himself from saying, *And I'm Richard III.* No good would be served by engaging in a verbal fencing match with her at this moment. She needed a bath and the cosseting of other women. The morning would be soon enough for her to answer his many questions.

Answer all of them, she would.

He realized then that he wanted to take this battered woman to the trial of James Kelly. Not because she could testify to Kelly's boastful confession of killing Shane the Proud—the council of elders would consider that hearsay—but because under brehon law, rape was a capital crime, punishable by death.

Hugh's corroborating testimony as a witness to that crime was enough to condemn Kelly. His kerns had also witnessed that crime.

Whereas Hugh had no proof that Kelly had murdered Shane the Valiant. He doubted they could elicit a confession before the council. The elder judges would not condemn Kelly without irrefutable proof that he had committed the murder. Rumors and gossip were not testimony.

Hugh turned to Mrs. Carrick, giving her instructions, and left Morgana in her care. He didn't bother with explaining how the woman had gotten in the shape she was. Some things were not to be spoken of, to Hugh's mind. Better that the women dealt with such things in their own way.

Morgana sagged onto a high-backed chair after the O'Neill departed. Without his presence in the chamber, she had no reason to continue to play the brave heroine while the last buckets were poured. She let her head drop to her knees and let go of all the worries and fears that had assaulted her from the start of this day to the end.

A babble of women's voices crooning in Irish wafted over and around her, soothing her, taking her back to Maynooth, before it was razed to the ground and burned.

Her wet nurse and nanny had been Irish. Their language lay deep in Morgana's memories of childhood safety, security and love. All that was gone.

Morgana had only her wits to keep her alive. She must get to Dunluce. She had time enough still. All wasn't lost. Grace O'Malley had promised she would put into port at Dunluce on the tenth of May. No sooner and no later.

Morgana had every intention of being there when O'Malley's ship, the *Avenger,* docked.

Chapter Five

Mrs. Carrick bent over the softly weeping woman to gently shake her shoulder. "Here, now, my lady. The tub is ready. Come. Let us get you clean. You don't have to do a thing."

It was good that the housekeeper felt that way, because Morgana couldn't have done anything for herself. Now that she was out of the elements, aches too numerous to count had increased tenfold. She knew without having to look for confirmation that her body would be bruised from head to toe.

Mrs. Carrick coaxed Morgana onto her feet and moved her to the tub. Two maids helped her to gently strip away Morgana's ruined clothes.

Morgana clung to Hugh's tartan, refusing to let go of it. Wisely, Mrs. Carrick didn't fuss over such a simple need. She let the poor dear keep the cloth clutched to her bosom.

A girl she was, Mrs. Carrick concluded after supervising the whole procedure of her bath. In Mrs. Carrick's experience, no woman grown retained a coltish, leggy body for very long past maturity. Certainly she was old enough to be married—all girls were, once their menses had begun. But this lady was young. Mrs. Carrick was convinced the young woman was no older than ten-and-seven.

They had to change the water in the tub twice once they wet her hair. Black Abhainn Mor mud held the tangled coils close and flat against her head. Washed and rinsed until the water ran clear, that head of hair hung past the girl's knees.

Mrs. Carrick suspected that when it was dry, it would be the color of winter's Hogmanay fires. Her brows and lashes, and the soft down on her forearms, were as red as autumn apples. Morgana's skin wasn't prone to freckles. Unless in the past she had taken great care not to be exposed often to the sun.

A cup of tea and a scone settled the girl's stomach when leaving the heated tub had made her woozy and dizzy-headed. The judicious use of a leech drained most of the blood swelling the lady's blackened eye and went a fair ways toward removing the worst of the bruising on her face.

Mrs. Carrick did not ask any questions about any of the injuries she treated. Morgana of Kildare did not offer any explanations or make any observations of her own, either. She seemed to be a stoic sort, and very private.

As for the rest of the physical damage the young woman had suffered, Mrs. Carrick knew time would heal each injury. The razorlike cut from Morgana's breasts to her throat was most likely going to leave a scar. The origin of that wound caused a troubling frown on Mrs. Carrick's brow. True, only the young woman's husband would ever see it, but he would very likely have questions about its origin, too.

On that subject, Mrs. Carrick came away from the solar with numerous questions to put to Sir Hugh. Most importantly, where had the lady come from, and how was it that she had met young Hugh?

For a short while, Mrs. Carrick harbored the idea that Morgana might have met Hugh at court in England. On that subject, Morgana had made the vehement claim that she had never been to England. She'd said she'd never traveled north of the Pale until she'd begun her pilgrimage to Dunluce.

Of the few things Morgana had said, none sounded more outrageous than that she was making a pilgrimage to Dunluce.

No one in his right mind would do that. Mrs. Carrick knew that pilgrims prayed at Saint Patrick's shrine in his cathedral at Armagh, climbed to the top of Croag Patrick in county Mayo and gave penance by fasting on Skellig Michael off the coast of Kerry.

There were no saints to be honored at Dunluce. Devils, demons, ghosts and fairy folk, yes. Dunluce had evil aplenty.

It was most peculiar.

Mrs. Carrick found a way to appease her growing curiosity when she found out later in the evening that Hugh had retired for the night. She made a supper tray and personally took it to his study, high in the tower. She found him in his upside-down seat, gazing at the clearing night sky through his optic instruments.

Hugh's tower was something else that bothered Mrs. Carrick. He allowed no servants to enter the uppermost chambers. He claimed that some of them might do unwitting damage to his inventions and banned all but Mrs. Carrick and his gillie, Loghran O'Toole.

The young man was obsessed with grinding tools and glass furnaces and sheets of gleaming brass. He personally shaped and welded brass into odd tubes, making all manner of aids for sight. He also cleaned and swept the chamber himself, when he thought it absolutely necessary. That was the one source of contention between him and Mrs. Carrick.

Now—she had another—Morgana of Kildare.

"I've brought your supper, young Hugh," Mrs. Carrick said, alerting him to her presence. He twisted his head around, disengaging himself from a strangely carved ivory eyepiece that left an indentation around his right eye.

"Ah, supper. Wonderful. Thank you, Mrs. Carrick. Put it there on my worktable, but do mind the glass lenses scattered on the felt."

It took him a moment to untangle his long body from the upside-down chair. As he came upright, she saw that he'd changed back to his normal clothing, a dark tunic, fitted trews and hose. His wearing a *philabeg*, and the woman he'd brought home, were the talk of the house.

Hugh O'Neill never dressed like an Irishman. To Mrs. Carrick's knowledge, he hadn't so much as lifted an eyebrow in the direction of any Irishwoman in the few weeks that he'd been home from England. Of course, he was a widower, but he was no longer required to mourn the loss of an English wife. None of clan O'Neill counted that a true marriage, since the vows had been spoken in the Protestant church and were therefore not valid.

To the clan's eyes, Hugh and Loghran O'Toole lived like monks in this tower. O'Toole's behavior Mrs. Carrick understood. He really was an Augustinian monk, ordained as a priest at Holy Trinity Priory in Dublin before the English razed the monastery.

Conn the Lame had provided the Augustinians sanctuary at Dungannon when Henry VIII had evicted them from their properties in Dublin. In return, O'Toole had been entrusted with the education of Conn's grandson.

Hugh padded on bare feet to his table. He towered over Mrs. Carrick as she set his supper tray on the cluttered worktable. Looking up at him, Mrs. Carrick always had trouble linking this tall man to the apple-cheeked, curious boy he had been fifteen years ago. How they had all fretted and worried when Lord Sussex took Hugh from Ireland, and none more than his grandfather, old Conn. Losing Hugh had killed him.

"What did you bring me?" Hugh eagerly rubbed his palms together. "Summat sweet, perhaps?"

"A bit of the mutton from the day's roast, and some shepherd's pie. Bread and cheese, too. And there's plenty of vegetables, do you care to eat them. I don't think you eat near enough good cabbage, milord. To wash it all down, I brought you ale."

"Excellent!" Hugh toed a stool, nimbly dragging it to the worktable without having to use his hands. He tossed the napkin covering the tray aside and gave a glance at his clock. "Good Lord, it's gone past ten o'clock. I'm famished, and could eat a whole oxen. Did you make a tray for my guest? What's she look like without the mud?"

"Look like?" Mrs. Carrick asked, surprised by the question. "Why, she looks as a girl of ten-and-six should look, Sir Hugh. Save for that awful bruise on her face. The poor mite's battered from head to toe. Such bruises as I've never seen the like. Not from an unexpected dip in Abhainn Mor, I haven't. But if you say that's how the poor dear was hurt, then so she was."

"I didn't actually say that," Hugh pointed out.

"Well, then, I suppose those rapids could cut a lady's gown to ribbons. Or scratch her deep from her belly to her throat. Why, if she tumbled off that Benburg bridge, that would account for blackening her eye and putting bruises the size of a man's fist on her back and her hip. Are you sure it was just the river you rescued her from?"

Hugh bit down on a biscuit, eyeing Mrs. Carrick's placid face. He knew better than to try and fool her. "All right, then, you've found me out, Mrs. Carrick. Aye, a brute of a man was intending her grievous harm. But I don't care for that to be common knowledge, or for there to be gossip down in the kitchens about her. She's a lady, and rightly in need of my protection."

Just what exactly had convinced Hugh of that fact, he couldn't lay his finger on. Certainly nothing tangible. Then he remembered her horse and her concern for the animal, or for what the horse might have carried in its saddle packs. He'd have a look for himself when Macmurrough arrived.

Mrs. Carrick beamed at him, saying proudly, "So you dispatched him, did you? Good for you, O'Neill. You're a better man than your father, if that be the case."

"Humph," Hugh grunted over the compliment that praised him at the expense of his father. His jaw worked, chewing a crisp biscuit packed with sausage and ginger sauce.

"I didn't exactly dispatch him. I dispatched five English soldiers, and I've detained the bastard who beat Morgana. Provided that I can convince Matthew to summon the council for a trial, he'll be dispatched once and for all. The man's wanted for other crimes, but you know my odds of convincing Matthew better than I."

"I heard talk in the kitchens that it's James Kelly you've brought to justice." Like most O'Neill kinsmen, Mrs. Carrick believed in speaking her mind. Hugh didn't imagine the bright, bloodthirsty gleam in her eyes. She'd served three O'Neills, and as loyal and trustworthy as she was, Hugh hoped she'd live to serve three more. "Is that true, young Hugh?"

"You've found me out. So I have done," Hugh admitted.

"You're not one to brag over your accomplishments, are you? But if you've captured James Kelly, then I say it's time you sat on the stone of clan O'Neill and declared yourself the O'Neill. It's high time we had a strong leader, milord."

"Last time I heard how it was done, one didn't sit on the stone of O'Neill and declare oneself anything. The clan's inaugurator does the proclaiming, else there isn't any claiming to be done, period." Changing the subject, Hugh asked, "Don't you find Morgan a peculiar name for an Irishwoman?"

"Irish? She's no more Irish than Great Harry or his harlot daughter," Mrs. Carrick replied, exasperated.

"She could be 'old English.'" Hugh referred to the descendants of the Norman conquerors.

Periodically the landed descendants of the Norman Conquest went into open revolt, as the whims of politics struck them. Queen Elizabeth claimed the tenth generation Fitzgeralds, Butlers and Burkes were more Irish than the real Irish, and too proud to admit it. That observation had stung Hugh years ago. Now that he was older, it no longer had the power to shame him into thinking he was less a man for his Gaelic ancestors.

"I gave that some thought, asking her of customs in the Pale—French wines and priest holes. She is very tired, tho' and 'tis hard to guard one's tongue when one is exhausted. I think she is English and titled, milord."

"What makes you say that?" Hugh asked, actively seeking the woman's opinion.

"Och, she was content to be served, as though it were her due. Only nobility take the service of others as their due."

"She was boorish? Rude?"

"Nay, milord, nothing like that. She graciously accepted without question any service offered her. That's the way of noble English ladies."

"You have experience serving noble English ladies, Mrs. Carrick?"

"A few times, Lord Hugh. You may think me not old enough, but I served the Lady Catherine Fitzgerald when she came to Dungannon as bride to your grandfather, Conn."

"You did?" Hugh's eyes widened at that bit of news.

"'Twas a sad time, and I was a young girl, then, but I remember how gracious Lady Catherine was. Young Morgana is of the same ilk, a lady. I'd stake my soul on that."

"A noble, you say," Hugh mused, somewhat distractedly. "That complicates things, doesn't it?"

"Yes, it does. Lady Susana will be hounding you about her. Susana was hoping you'd take favor with Inghinn Dubh."

Hugh judiciously cleared his throat. "The queen would never approve *that* alliance. She'd likely have a fit if I dared marry outside of her approval. I know earls who've met the headsman's ax for less."

"Mayhap you shouldn't have let her make you an earl, then." Mrs. Carrick's innate practicality came to the fore. She spoke freely to Hugh, still thinking of him as a young boy needing a mother's good counsel and direction.

"As I wasn't given any choice, I couldn't refuse the honor," Hugh answered, just as forthrightly.

"Och, you could have if you'd been at Dungannon when your grandfather died. He cursed all the Irish who make terms with the English. That curse made Matthew the weakling he is, God save his tormented soul."

"I thought a fall from his horse broke my uncle's back," Hugh said, with no facetiousness intended. He tried to think back to his early childhood, to remember his uncle walking, or moving his legs unaided. No image of that came to mind, though he knew perfectly well that his uncle's accident had happened after Hugh went to live in England.

Mrs. Carrick gave evidence of how deeply her own superstitions ran, by crossing herself before speaking. "A deathbed curse bears more weight than others. There are those what say it's the weight of it on Matthew's shoulders that broke his back. In the olden days, it was always an eye for an eye, tribute for tribute and ache for ache. Then Conn the Lame made terms with Great Harry, and you know the rest."

"Fascinating," Hugh said as he bit deeply into a bun stuffed with slabs of mutton. "You believe those old tales, Mrs. Carrick? Of witchcraft, and curses that pass on from generation unto generation?"

"Believe them?" She laughed a little too brightly, then reached over Hugh's shoulder and took a pinch of salt from the cellar on his tray and tossed it over her left shoulder.

"I'm Irish, laddie. I believe in all of it, from leprechauns and pots of gold under rainbows on down to our Lord Jesus Christ and all his blessed saints. You'd be well served to believe in things you can't explain, too."

Now it was his turn to laugh, and Hugh did, chuckling deeply, but not scorning what the old woman said. "Ah, you'd have loved attending Queen Elizabeth's court, Mrs. Carrick. She's an astounding wizard in her employ, a Welshman by the name of John Dee. Some say his skills put the fabled Merlin to shame. I've seen him do fabulous tricks with my own eyes."

"Such as?" Mrs. Carrick demanded, distrusting anything that came of England's court out of hand.

"Why..." Hugh paused, thinking for a moment of Dee's most outlandish trick—sawing people in half, which was pure fakery and illusion, not magic. "I saw him levitate a yeoman guard in full armor in the bailey at the Tower of London."

"You don't say?" Mrs. Carrick inhaled deeply. "There must be many a sorry prisoner that wished for the same skill and craft to escape that hellhole."

Reminded of the true nature of the Tower, Hugh agreed. "I expect their grieving womenfolk were of the same mind, and would have gladly paid for any bit of magic that would have enabled their men to escape the queen's clutches."

"That reminds me, your Morgana of Kildare wants to be woken at first light on the morrow, so she can continue her pilgrimage to Dunluce." Mrs. Carrick fixed Hugh with her steady eyes.

"I'm not surprised." Hugh replied, easily enough.

"Do you ken why she would want to make a pilgrimage specifically to Dunluce?"

"I haven't the faintest idea, though she did mention that as her destination, once in passing."

"It doesn't seem right." Mrs. Carrick went on. "What with Drake harrying all of Antrim, bombarding the coast and laying siege to Glenarm by sea. I've advised her not to go, but I don't think she cares for my wisdom. Perhaps you should talk to her about that. Surely you'll not let her leave Dungannon to travel north without suitable escort."

Hugh knew very well what roving factions of soldiers could do to a woman traveling alone and unprotected. Today had been a prime example of that folly at its worst.

"Morgana of Kildare will not be leaving at dawn or noon or at any time alone," Hugh said firmly. "I'll see to that. Did she tell you why she wants to go Dunluce?"

"No, milord. I was hoping she'd told you."

"Humph." Hugh considered Mrs. Carrick's words carefully. "I'll tackle that tomorrow. She's exhausted by her...uh...ordeal. So we can assume she'll sleep long and deep. The best way round about detaining her is to just let her sleep in. Don't let anyone go to the solar to wake her."

"But you said she shouldn't sleep, and I left Brigit chattering to her to keep her awake."

"Ah, but Mrs. Carrick, you don't know a woman can be perverse? She'll sleep, just because I told her not to."

"And aren't you sure of yourself?" Mrs. Carrick teased. "Oh, and by the way, milord— Her hair's as red as holly berries."

"Is that so?" Hugh chuckled softly under his breath. "No wonder she fights with such passion. A redhead, then?"

Mrs. Carrick left him to his thoughts. On her way out the door, Hugh detained her with another question. "Did you send a tray to her yet?"

"No, but I will."

"I'll fetch it to the solar. Say, in a quarter hour."

Mrs. Carrick glanced at the standing clockwork next to the bank of oaken bookshelves that covered one interior wall. "A quarter hour it is, milord."

Chapter Six

Sleep was the last thing Morgana intended to do in Dungannon Castle. The bath restored her as nothing else could have. Once she had something substantial to eat, she was certain, she'd have the energy to get on her way.

The chattery maid Mrs. Carrick left to watch over Morgana was no citadel against Morgana's inborn ability to dominate and influence. First she requested that Brigit find her something more substantial than a night rail to wear. Brigit didn't hesitate for a moment to open two trunks and a wardrobe in the spacious chamber and let Morgana take her pick from the carefully stored-in-tissue gowns.

"Everything in these trunks belonged to Sir Hugh's mother," Brigit explained. "They've gone to waste these many years. No one ever uses these rooms, you see."

"Why's that?" Morgana gingerly eased one knee down onto the hard floor, examining a trunk's contents.

Brigit shrugged. It wasn't her place to tell the girl the solar was haunted. She'd know that soon enough, if she actually had to sleep here. "I expect that if His Lordship gave you these rooms to sleep in, he won't mind you making use of the clothes, too."

"Well, I'll just have to see if there's anything that I can use. Could you go and fetch me something to eat? I hate to be an outright bother, but I'm fair starved. It's been a very long and exhausting day."

"You won't go to sleep if I leave you, will you?" Brigit asked. "Lord Hugh said you were to stay awake. He'll have my head if I don't do my work right."

Morgana answered that question with the absolute truth. "I couldn't sleep here if you gave me ten sleeping potions."

"Are you certain? A little while ago, you looked as if you would drop right off in the tub."

"Oh . . ." Morgana stalled while she looked around the room for a suitable answer to that question. "Shall we say, I feel the presence of ghosts?"

"You do?" Brigit's eyes rounded. She gulped and crossed herself, hurrying out, saying, "Och, then, I'll get yer food."

Morgana held on to the urge to laugh. Claiming she felt ghosts lingering in Dungannon Castle wasn't stretching the truth all that much. Her greataunt Catherine Fitzgerald had died within a week of arriving at Dungannon Castle.

Morgana knew from reading all of Gerait Og Fitzgerald's journals that he'd done everything in his power to unite all of Ireland's powerful clans. The one mistake he'd never gotten over was the unexplained death of his favorite sister after she was forced to wed Conn O'Neill.

Prior to her death, Catherine had been mentioned often in her grandfather's journals. Very little had been written about her following his terse words regarding her death. He blamed himself for forcing a loveless marriage on a young and precious sister. After that, he never mentioned the O'Neills again, except to damn them and their portion of Ireland forever.

All the other political marriages Gerait arranged between his numerous siblings, nephews and nieces had worked to his benefit, uniting by blood nearly all of Ireland's most powerful families and separate counties.

Morgana removed a suitable gown from the trunk and stood up, holding the gown to her shoulders to judge its possible fit. She was tall for a woman. The skirts of the gray silk were long enough that without a farthingale or too many petticoats, it would sweep the floor at her feet.

One of the maids had taken charge of Morgana's boots, cleaning and drying them. She found silk stockings aplenty in the other trunk, and kirtles galore, though she did have to exert some care in choosing from the other trunk. Most of its wools had been ravaged by moths. Samites, linen and silks were apparently less palatable to marauding insects.

Morgana dressed with practiced efficiency, making do with an old-fashioned short-waisted stomacher to lace over the shapeless gown, giving it some form. It accomplished what she wanted it to accomplish, lifting her breasts enough to support them against the uncomfortable and sometimes painful jarring that a woman's unbound breasts suffered when she rode horseback. The only trouble with it came from the fact that it was designed to lace up the back. As her right hand was somewhat impaired, she couldn't pull the laces as tight as she was used to wearing them.

Her hair had dried sufficiently that she could braid it and turn the coils into neat order. She was seated at Lady Dungannon's vanity, doing that task, when the chamber door opened without a knock.

Hugh O'Neill arrived bearing an ample supper tray for his guest, and was greatly surprised to find the lady seated at his mother's vanity, vainly tucking an unruly plait into a curious coil over her right ear.

"You're not asleep?" he asked, rather foolishly. Not for his life would he have admitted that finding her awake had just contradicted every assumption he'd made about her. English women were perverse. That was a given. Why she'd chosen to confound him would be revealed soon enough.

Morgana came to her feet, and the coil unkinked and slid down her shoulder. She most certainly hadn't expected the O'Neill to walk through the chamber door. "No. I'm not."

Morgana kept her answer bland. She knew she couldn't have said as much for her face. Her surprise showed as much as his did. She blushed at the intensity of his inspection of her bosom. The silk gown was cut for a larger-breasted woman, revealing a great deal of décolletage. Morgana would have covered that with some kind of cloth insert once she finished with her hair.

Hugh grinned wolfishly as he set the heavy tray on a gateleg table beside his mother's fainting couch.

"Come, Morgana of Kildare. I've brought you sustenance for your belly and wine to soothe your soul. Sit you down and eat, while I feast my eyes on your loveliness. That gown suits you."

Morgana managed to keep both hands at her sides, resisting the urge to let them flutter to her throat to hide what was already obvious and exposed. She did wet her lips with her tongue and swallow twice before stepping forward to meet him at the small table.

He placed a candle branch on the table and brought a high-backed chair away from the fireplace. Setting the chair opposite the couch, he waited until she sat before taking his seat. His hands flew over the tray, removing steam covers from hot dishes and linen cozies from a woven basket full of bread. "There, a feast for your eyes, as well as your belly, is it not?"

Morgana's mouth watered instantly at the sight of wafer-thin slices of peppered salmon, lentils swimming in a rich, creamy sauce and an appetizing thick vegetable soup. She leaned over the table, inhaling deeply of the aromas rising on the steam, admitting, "I'm famished."

"I thought you would be." Her expression pleased him greatly, making him proud of Mrs. Carrick's efforts in the kitchens. "Don't be shy," he said, coaxing her to eat. "I was fed some time ago, so I'll join you in polishing off the wine. It's imported from Burgundy, a favorite of mine, and quite good."

Morgana gave him credit for knowing his own stomach as well as she knew hers. She took up the spoon and tucked into the soup, too hungry to argue about polite sharing. That gave Hugh another reason to smile as he uncorked the wine and filled two chased goblets to the rim. She was too consumed by hunger to notice his intense inspection.

Morgana of Kildare had washed up very, very well. Her hair appeared dark in the bedchamber's limiting shadows, but he'd have had to be blind not to see the red highlights shimmering in the candlelight. Unlike the beauties of Queen Elizabeth's court, she did not shave her eyebrows, and it didn't appear to him that she even went so far as to pluck them. They were thick enough to make him want to smooth his fingers over their naturally high arches.

Her skin was clear. Her nose as straight and neatly formed as an arrow. Her mouth, well, he could have wasted his time composing poetry to those lips that deftly opened to take in spoonful after spoonful of hearty soup. They were red and full, a touch swollen on one side, where Kelly had struck her hard. A small bruise marred a corner, but they were not mangled so badly that she couldn't be gently kissed.

He brought his goblet to his mouth, putting a mental brake on his wildly rampant, lusty thoughts. Hugh found himself unable to take his mind away from the idea of savoring the taste of her mouth with his own tongue.

"How's the soup?" he asked gruffly, taking hold of the basket of breads and extending that to her.

"Delicious." Morgana looked up from her soup to the basket his hand held so close to her. The five different breads all appealed to her. She choose the nearest, a plump rye loaf no bigger than her fist. Now that the edge was off her hunger, she remembered her manners, asking, "What made you bring the tray to me?"

"Isn't it obvious? I'm checking on you," Hugh replied easily. He set the basket down and raised his hand to her chin, turning her face toward the lighted candles.

"Even with a black eye, you are pretty to behold." Oblivious of her hunger, he held on to her chin as his right hand took the supreme pleasure of tracing and smoothing her eyebrow, where the worst bruising remained.

Unlike the grand ladies of the queen's court he'd bedded and never regretted leaving, Hugh knew he could never be immune to her eyes, were they ever to fix upon him with even the slightest trace of heat or desire.

He gently traced the boundary of the bruise across her cheekbone. "Does this hurt?"

Morgana frowned. "No, of course not. I have black eyes all the time. I'm used to them."

"Tsk." Hugh clicked his tongue, releasing her chin so that she could resume consuming her meal. "Such waspish sarcasm is not very becoming, Lady Morgana. I feel rather certain you've been trained to do better."

"When did I get the promotion? I was plain Morgana when you introduced me to your sisters." His scold didn't stop Morgana from taking another shot.

"No, you were never plain Morgana. I've had time to look up a few references lying about my study. You are Lady Morgana Fitzgerald, oldest daughter of the exiled earl of Kildare, James FitzMaurice Fitzgerald. By some curious twists of fate, I also know you entered the Arroasian novitiate at Saint Mary de Hogges's Abbey in March of 1569. Four months later, your father fled Ireland for France."

He was right, but Morgana wanted to know how he had learned those facts. "What makes you so certain of that?"

"I have copies of all the convent rosters, from Sussex's articles of dissolution, through 1574. In fact, I have rosters of all the monasteries and abbeys in Ireland, including the justicar's official valuation of the properties seized for the crown." Hugh took his time forming his next words. "I also know that you have two brothers that your father was also forced to leave behind. It's very dangerous to be a boy named Fitzgerald in this clime, isn't it, Morgana?"

She sat very straight, her marvelous blue eyes so cold with suspicion that Hugh feared he'd done more than upset her digestion. He was very glad he'd disarmed her, and doubly glad he'd insisted there be no knife of any kind put on the tray.

"What is the price of your silence?" she asked.

Lord of the Isle

"My silence?" Hugh frowned, distracted and not following her reasoning.

Her chest rose and fell deeply three times before he picked up his goblet and drank from it. Hugh withstood the temptation to look again at the lovely white mounds of her breasts swelling over the gray gown's neckline. It would be better if he kept firm control over his passions—at least for the moment. She'd been brutalized this very night, and he wasn't such a scoundrel that he'd take advantage of her now. His body responded otherwise, reacting like a randy goat's to her abundant physical attributes.

"I said, what's your point? Or should I say, what is your price for silence?"

"Ah, you think I would stoop that low, milady? Blackmail you? I am not an unconscionable bastard."

"Aren't you? You are the O'Neill, aren't you?"

"*The O'Neill?*" Hugh laughed.

"Your men claimed you are he."

Hugh laughed bluntly. "That is wishful thinking on their part. I am most certainly not *the O'Neill.* If I were, I'd have run my sword through James Kelly's belly and left him staked out for the carrion crows to pick the meat off his bones. I am no more than Hugh O'Neill, lately the good-conduct hostage of clan O'Neill at Her Majesty's court in London.

"Thanks to interference from the powers across the water, there will never be another revered as *the O'Neill.* As I, might add, there will never be another Fitzgerald earl of Kildare. A right pity it is, too."

Digging into the soup, Morgana asked, "How so?"

"It took the English five hundred years to establish a toehold on our island. But it has taken we Irish only two generations to destroy ourselves. Lift your goblet, Morgana of Kildare, and drink with me to a dying land. Erin's death throes surround us. Yet no one sees what is as plain as the noses on each other's faces."

Morgana swallowed and carefully laid the silver spoon down on the table. "I don't follow you."

"I think you do." Hugh picked up her full goblet and put it in her hand. "Tell me, Morgana, late of Kildare, when someone asks you what country you claim allegiance to, what do you say? 'I'm Irish'? Is that your answer?"

"No. Of course not," Morgana answered immediately. "I'm not Irish, I'm English."

"Yet you were born in Maynooth castle in county Kildare, Ireland. Your father was also born at Maynooth, and his father and his father going back twelve generations, to the year 1069. How much more Irish do you have to be?"

Morgana broke the small loaf of bread in her hands and bit into it, chewing on the tough bread as if it were dried meat. "You Irish don't accept us."

"And the English do?" Hugh lifted a skeptical brow. "You told my housekeeper that you've never been to England. Is that true?"

"And if it isn't, am I to be cast out into the night? Will you take the food from my mouth and the clothes from my back?"

Hugh brought his fist down on the table, making candles jump and goblets totter. "Woman, don't you dare sit there accusing me of cruelties to you! It was not by my hand that you were stripped of your dignity and raped this day. I have given you nothing less than fairness, generosity, and the hospitality of my home. When in truth I owe you nothing, for your kind are the usurpers of all that was and is good in Ireland.

"Well, by God's grace, *I'm* Irish. Since the dawning of all memory on this island—from the great battle between the Firbolgs and the Tuatha de Danann—an O'Neill king has ruled over the rocks of this lake and the hills that surround it. We've been overrun by Vikings, Scotchmen, Normans, Englishmen. We Irish *savages* have been converted by saints to Christianity, saved from eternal damnation by kings who proclaim they rule by divine right and lesser kings who rule only by the might of their own hand. But, by God, I'm Irish. I know exactly who and what I am. Can you say the same?''

Morgana picked up a slice of salmon with her fingers and laid it between the bread in her hand, folding it into a convenient bite-size morsel. ''Obviously, I can't speak with the same eloquence and passion to answer your question. But, yes, I do know exactly who I am and what I am.''

She shoved the whole bite into her mouth and chewed hard, as though his bread were made of gravel, not milled grain. Hugh sat back in his chair, drinking his wine, his eyes glittering as they assessed her.

''Then tell me, Morgana of Kildare. Who are you, really? What are you doing here in Ulster, where you are not welcome and not wanted? For what reason do you travel to my liege man in Dunluce?

''If you are an English spy hired by Walsingham, sent here deliberately to tempt and compromise me, I have the right to know the truth.''

Morgana almost choked. The bread stuck in her dry throat and wouldn't budge past her windpipe. She raised one hand to her throat and reached for the goblet with the other.

Hugh made no move to assist her. In fact, he didn't even blink as he stared at her, watching her gulp down swallows of wine as she tried to dislodge the wedged bread and salmon. Her color was quite high when she set the goblet aside and finally brought her pale eyes back to his.

''You think I'm an English spy?'' she whispered, her voice barely a croak. ''Sent here by Walsingham?''

''Circumspectly, I believe that what I witnessed today was just a little too patent to be real. I find it curious that in the heat of his passions James Kelly would confess his crimes to you. Forgive me if I tell you it doesn't ring true. I won't be set up to fall victim to Walsingham's treacheries.'' *Not this O'Neill.*

''Now, young woman...'' Hugh reached forward and took the hourglass on the table in hand and turned it over.

"You have exactly ten minutes to tell all and convince me that every word you utter is the Gospel according to Mark, or else you will find yourself locked away in the same pit in the earth that James Kelly occupies this very moment. Begin at the beginning."

Morgana sat back, staring at him blank-faced, appalled. Every word he'd uttered rang as a true and dangerous threat, to her ears. She closed her lips, which had parted with dismay, and folded her hands into her lap, saying nothing.

The fine sand trickled through the glass, making a minuscule white hill on the bottom. Morgana looked once at the hourglass, then back at the O'Neill's cold and heartless face. She wasn't going to engage in a test of wills with him. There was no purpose in doing that. She'd lose.

In fact, she realized belatedly, she'd already lost.

She would rather die than spend one minute in the same space as James Kelly. Morgana rose to her feet and crossed the room to the fireplace, picked up her boots and yanked out the crumpled tissue Brigit had stuffed inside them.

Hugh watched her jerk each boot onto her bare feet and deliberately tie the laces. He did not bother telling her she could not leave the room.

Loghran O'Toole guarded one door, Kermit Blackbeard the other. Did she try to run, she'd not live to regret it. Either would cut her throat before she had the chance to let out a single scream.

Bored with watching her fumble with the laces of her boots, Hugh looked at the hourglass, counting the time that remained. "Your ten minutes are rapidly running out, lady. Personally, I find your silence at this critical moment appalling."

"Go to hell, O'Neill!" Morgana muttered as she got to her feet again. She barely retained control of her rage.

"Do you play the game to suit me, my rewards to you will prove more generous than Walsingham's ever would be. I might be amenable to allowing you to remain at Dungannon as my mistress for a time. Do you serve me well, you'll be adequately pensioned after.''

Morgana paused at the mullioned windows to take a deep, calming breath. She glanced back over her shoulder as she twisted the lock on the window and pushed it open. A cold breeze caressed her cheek. Hugh O'Neill sat on his chaise as if it were a throne, watching her with the dispassionate eye of a Roman emperor.

Oh, his cold black eyes moved coveteously over her person, cataloging each movement that she made, but he was as blind to what she really was as the stones of his castle. Morgana swung her head and stared out the open window. The sky had cleared from the north to the east. A pale moon hung like a battered pewter cup in the dark, starless sky.

Beyond the window frame a soft, formless shape floated on the rising mist. Two hands stretched out opened palms of welcome to Morgana. The shade's soft, keening voice brushed across Morgana's eardrum, not registering any audible sound.

Don't trust him, cried Catherine Fitzgerald. *He is the O'Neill. All his people think it so. I have waited long years for a kinsman to come. You must help me, Morgana. Blood must stand for blood.*

Morgana's heart made a fierce racket under her ribs, banging against her breastbone. She swallowed and stared straight through the ghostly shape between the window frame and the distant hills. She refused to look down at the water in the lake. Water frightened her so. It always had and always would. If she was lucky, she'd hit the rocks and she wouldn't have to suffer the agonizing death of suffocating by drowning.

You must help me, sweetling, Catherine wailed, her lament sadder than the keen of little Maoveen when she had mourned the passing of Shane O'Neill. *I'm so lonely and lost.*

Agitated by the unaccountable rising of the wind, Hugh unclasped his hands, which had been deliberately laced to passive stillness over his flat belly.

He raised his voice to gain the woman's immediate attention. "Shall I point out to you now, woman, that your silence serves only as an admission of guilt to all the charges I've laid on you?"

He baits you. Don't listen to him! Catherine swirled in through the open window, circling her great niece as she spun on angry heels to confront the man. *Listen to me!*

"You are free to point out anything you like to a lowly creature such as I, O'Neill," Morgana said. "Count yourself right about one thing. There will never be a thirteenth Fitzgerald earl of Kildare. Without me, Sean's life is forfeit. I pray God you are right about one more thing. May there never be another O'Neill of Tyrone to strike terror into the hearts of the women and children of Ireland.

"Now I understand why Aunt Catherine chose to take her own life rather than live in this castle, married to an O'Neill!"

No! Catherine wailed. *I didn't! Stop! You foolish girl! Stop her, Hugh O'Neill!*

Morgana bounded onto the window ledge, crying out, "Goodbye, O'Neill! Till we meet each other in hell, sir, I bid you farewell!"

Hugh uncoiled from his chair. "What in God's name do you think you are doing?"

His shout reverberated off the coffered ceiling. Loghran and Kermit burst through opposite doors of the chamber instantly, dirks drawn and ready, expecting to find Hugh in a struggle for his life.

They ran past each other in the center and spun round, back-to-back, visually sweeping each dark corner.

"Jesus, Mary and Joseph!" O'Toole sprang to the open window and threw his long body across Hugh's kicking legs to anchor him inside the room.

"What?" Kermit bellowed. "Have you lost your mind, O'Neill?"

"Don't stand there jawing!" hollered O'Toole. "Help me pull him back in! The bloody woman jumped out the window!"

"Is she mad?" Kermit wasted words and breath, but no time, as he threw his own crushing weight over Hugh's hips, pinning them to the window ledge.

"Christ Almighty, are you trying to emasculate me?" Hugh thundered. "Get off my bloody cods and give me a hand out the bloody window, you fool. I've got her. I just can't pull her back."

Dumbfounded, Kermit pulled back enough to yank open the other window. He bent halfway out over the sill, stretching, trying to reach Hugh's hand. The woman spun by one arm, twisting back and forth, her wild feet kicking her skirts in the wind. Hugh's fingers were as white as Dover chalk where they clenched the bones of her wrist.

"Cut her loose," Loghran ordered, telling Kermit exactly how to wield the long knife he still clasped in one hand. "Chop off her hand. Save the O'Neill!"

"You do, and so help me God, I'll throw both of you down on top of what's left of her body," Hugh growled ferociously. A mighty shout followed as he jerked the woman up, catching hold of her clothing with his other hand. The laces on her vest held. "Morgana! Give me your left hand!"

Kermit groped down Hugh's sleeve, feeling for his wrist, stretching as far as he dared. His eyes bulged like the tendons in Hugh's forearm. Just beyond his fingertips, a clump of bunched cloth tore audibly.

The woman's fingernails scraped and clawed at Hugh's hand. The bloody-minded creature tried to pry his fingers from her wrist.

Kermit closed his eyes and clamped his fist on that talonlike hand of vicious, clawing fingers. The fingers crushed under his. He slapped his other hand over her wrist and grunted, hauling what resisted up to him. She felt like ten hundredweight of stone.

"I've got her." Hugh gasped. "Loghran, for the love of God, give me some help. I can't hold her much longer."

"Don't! Let me go!" Morgana snarled. She kicked her feet and spun around, only to twist violently back to where she'd begun.

Taller than either Hugh or Kermit, Loghran shifted his weight no more than necessary to keep Hugh from following the stupid woman to her death on the rocks. He unhooked his belt and positioned himself carefully, never taking most of his body weight from O'Neill's legs.

"All right," he said as he leaned over Hugh's straining body. "When I give the signal, the two of you hoist her as high as you can."

"Just do it! Now!" Hugh gave the signal. Both he and Kermit grunted deeply, jerking Morgana upward. Loghran snapped the leather around her body and caught the whipping tail, pulling both ends taut over her back.

"Got her!" He grunted. They pulled. She fought like a hooked marlin, cursing, raining blasphemies on the wet air and the castle walls.

Loghran got hold of her hair. Hugh found a leg. Kermit got an eye gouged by somebody's elbow. She shrieked more viciously than the banshee Maoveen when they hauled her over the ledge.

All four of them hit the floor—a heap of sweating, shaking tangle of arms and legs.

"God the Father Almighty, forgive us," Loghran croaked.

Panting as hard as a winded horse, Hugh clutched the woman to his chest and fought to catch his breath. Sweat ran freely down his cheeks and onto his neck. He swallowed twice, then put out his hand when Loghran moved to untwist his belt from its tight constriction beneath Morgana's ribs.

"Leave it," Hugh commanded raggedly. "I'm going to beat her to death, when and if I can ever move my arms again."

Kermit, who could not move his brawny arms at all, said, "When you finish, O'Neill, I want to murder what's left. She could have killed us, one and all."

Loghran raised his fingers over the woman's heaving back and made the sign of the cross. He found his voice and used it to beseech God to forgive all of them.

As the priest raised his hand in a sign of forgiveness and blessing, Catherine Fitzgerald put her hands to her face and faded into the tower's stone walls, weeping, as lost as she had been since the night of her death.

Morgana listened to the litany in Latin, numb with shock, unable to tell her tears from the sweat that coursed down Hugh's neck and throat onto her brow and cheek. His hand gripped her head, tightly holding her head flattened against his chest. His heart pumped erratically.

At some point, the cadence evened. Hugh's voice rumbled like distant thunder, repeating the same order twice. "Leave us."

Loghran got up and extended a hand to Kermit, hauling the soldier to his feet.

"Thank you." As Hugh gave vent to his gratitude, Loghran grunted and closed the windows, twisting the brass hasps so tightly the metal screeched.

The soft swish of their boots retreated across the wooden floor. Morgana tried to use her hands to wipe her face. The right one felt as if it were never going to work again. Hugh caught hold of her fingers and tucked them down between their bodies.

"It's all right to cry, Morgana." His lips nuzzled against her sweat-damp brow. "I thought I made it clear I won't let anyone hurt you. Not even yourself."

"I'm not a spy!" she managed to say, before Hugh's fingers pressed against her lips, silencing her.

"You don't have to explain anything else to me. I know who Catherine Fitzgerald was. Tomorrow I'll show you where her portrait hangs. You don't have to believe me, but she was deeply loved, and her death caused much grief and regret. Hush, now. Trust me, Morgana. I won't hurt you."

He lifted her chin, gently tilting her face, wiping away her tears with his thumbs. Then he kissed her mouth softly, hoping she would be able to tell that he meant what he said. He wanted her trust more than anything he'd ever wanted in his whole life.

Hugh shuddered then, unable to do anything more than to hold her close. He closed his eyes and shuddered again, shaken by the image of her poised on that window ledge, arms wide open to embrace death. The image moved as it had in reality, sluggish, ponderous, each weighted step he'd taken toward the window to stop her agonizingly slow.

Little by little, her flood of silent tears slowed. No words or sobs accompanied them. Hugh smoothed his hand across the back of her head continuously, massaging the tight muscles in her neck and shoulders. He tried to calm her, as a good father might soothe a frightened and terrified child. But he'd never felt less fatherly in his life as he sat on the floor beneath the closed windows, holding her in his lap.

"I never meant to drive you to do that," he said at last, finally able to face his own callous impatience and his inability to trust other people. Orphaned by war, and exiled by political expedience, Hugh had lived all his life alone, trusting only Loghran. Women were to be used. He was no better than Kelly. In some ways, he was worse.

"I'm sorry, Morgana. I only meant to frighten you, to make you believe my threats were real. The truth is, I could never raise a hand against you or any woman for that matter, not even were punishment deemed necessary by law or common sense. I am a man, and it comes easy to make such threats when fear holds me in its grips.

"I wanted you to tell me the real reasons why you feel you must go to Dunluce. It was wrong of me to use such underhanded methods. What I did was worse than anything Kelly did to you today. I'm sorry. I won't hurt you again.''

Hugh swallowed, then continued. "I give you my word of honor that you will be safe from all harm so long as you are here at Dungannon and in Ulster. If you will tell me when you must be at Dunluce, I will move heaven and earth to get you there on the very day you want to be there. No questions asked. We will just go. You and I. All right? Will you accept my word on that?''

Her head moved ever so softly under his hand.

"Is that aye?" Hugh asked, resting against the cold stone wall.

"Yes," Morgana whispered.

"All right." Hugh accepted that as answer enough. He wrapped both his arms around her and held her, asking for nothing more from her.

Some while later, the chill of the stone wall at Hugh's back roused him to the discomfort of stiffening, pressure-numb limbs. Morgana's breathing was as even and effortless as a sleeping kitten's.

"I'm not asleep," she told him.

"You were," Hugh said, challengingly.

"No. I've been thinking, that's all.''

"Thinking? Next you'll tell me I was snoring."

"You weren't. You've just been very quiet, waiting for me to say something."

"I told you. You don't have to tell me anything."

"I must be at Dunluce by high tide on May the tenth. Grace O'Malley is going to meet me at the Mac Donnell's stronghold."

"I see." Hugh took a deep breath, filling his lungs at the same time he told his numb legs to go back to sleep. She was a tall, full-bodied, flesh-and-blood woman, no sylph.

"Dunluce is twenty leagues north," Hugh continued. "I could ride that in a day, if pressed. We will leave Dungannon on the seventh, if that suits you. With you riding with me, I can afford to make a more leisurely progress. If it suits you, I'll have Susana's seamstress make you clothes for the journey—a new riding habit and gowns, to impress Sorely Mac Donnell. He's a right terror of a Scotsman, and deserving of his title of the laird of the Far Isles. He's been at war with England personally for fifty-eight years, and his rebellion has cost him two sons and three wives. He's a good example of how not to rule one's lands. I didn't know he was friends with Grace O'Malley."

"They aren't friends. O'Malley trades with him," Morgana explained. "I think I'd better get up now. My legs have gone to sleep."

"Oh, Morgana, what am I going to do with you?" Hugh said, more for himself than for her. He shook his head and let his arms drop. A moment passed before she moved off his lap. The rush of blood to his ankles was absolute agony. He didn't so much as breathe. She sat beside him, stretching her legs out, bending at the waist to reach down to her feet and rub them.

"I don't think I can stand up."

"That makes two of us," Hugh admitted, gnashing his teeth. "Just wait. It will pass."

Morgana sat very, very still, grimacing when the needle-and-pins sensation peaked. "Sweet Saint Brigit," she gasped.

"I second that."

Hugh rubbed his knees hard with his hands, but didn't dare press farther down, toward his deadened feet. He cast a longing glance across the room to the guttering candles on the gateleg table. A half-full bottle of wine enticed him to try getting onto his feet. There was whiskey in the solar, if he could drag his useless legs that far and snare the decanter off the sideboard.

"Would you like something really strong to drink? Something that will blot out everything else? I would."

"What would that be?" Morgana asked.

"Whiskey," Hugh said grimly. "It's in the solar. My legs are rubber. I can't get them to work." He could feel nothing from his knees down. Nothing.

"I'll get the bottle." Morgana managed to stagger to her feet. They felt very peculiar, hot and numb at the same time, but she could stand. Hugh's sort of collapsed, even though he was only picking one leg up, behind the knee. "Don't. I've heard of people breaking bones when they tried to walk on sleeping limbs. I'll bring the bottle to you."

Hugh didn't want her to step out of his sight. That was the trouble. How was he going to sleep, if he had to watch her day and night? What if she got it into her head to jump again? He wasn't certain his apology had reached her. He bit down on his tongue, holding all those doubts inside him.

She left the bedchamber, and was gone way too long to suit him. "Did you find it?"

"No." Morgana called back through the open door. "The lights have all died out. I can't see a thing. Where is the sideboard? On my left or on my right?"

How am I supposed to know that? Hugh wondered.

Chapter Seven

"Tell me—" Hugh caught hold of the door frame, needing its support "—do you think that I can actually see through walls, woman?"

Morgana yelped, so startled by the proximity of Hugh's voice in the dark that she dropped the decanter. The crystal crashed to the floor, shattering into pieces. Pungent liquor perfumed the heavy air.

"Oh, no!" Morgana gasped. "Look what you made me do! How could you sneak up on me like that? I've broken the crystal to pieces!"

"Lady," Hugh grumbled as he caught her waist, staying her from bending down to pick up the broken pieces, "you are the only person I've ever met who could accuse me of sneaking up on them. I haven't a quiet bone in this great, uselessly huge body of mine. Whew!"

Hugh turned his nose away from the spreading stench of potent whiskey, lifting Morgana clear of the path of glass. "Come with me. We can't stay here breathing these fumes. We'll both expire in it. I'll send a servant to mop up the mess."

"But I can't just leave it," Morgana protested. "I made the mess, and I'm certainly big enough to clean it up."

"Nonsense!" Hugh dismissed her concern. "I won't have cut fingers added to your catalog of injuries. Enough is enough, lady."

Hugh O'Neill, Morgana was rapidly learning, was one very determined and stubborn man. His grip around her waist was as sure and steely as it had been when she dangled from one hand over the rocks and the lake. He marched in the direction of the bartizan stairwell, carting her like a sack of grain slung across his hip. "Where are you taking me?"

"Upstairs," Hugh answered. He set her on her feet on the steep, winding steps. From the topmost floor, the resounding chimes of his clockwork marking the hour of midnight echoed down the cylindrical bartizan.

He paused at the landing to take a key from a pocket in his doublet, unlock a door and open it. Morgana peered around his shoulder into the cavernous dark chamber. Two dim and smoky oil lamps that were suspended from crossbeam rafters provided the smallest amount of light necessary to make out the chamber's details.

Hugh slipped his hand behind her back, gently nudging her over the threshold into the room.

"Why are you taking me here?" Morgana asked. The chamber was fitted out for only one use, sleeping. A monstrously huge bed dominated it.

"Do you hear the clock?"

"Yes," Morgana replied.

"It's midnight. It's time we both went to sleep."

"But there's a perfectly good bed already made up for me, downstairs."

"Aye, and you just spilled a whole bottle of whiskey in the anteroom. I'd have to wake the house to have the room cleaned and aired. To tell you the truth, Morgana of Kildare, I doubt if I could close my eyes the whole night long if I allowed you beyond the hearing distance of my ears. So, for my own peace of mind, I've decided you're going to sleep right here with me."

"Sleep with you?" Morgana sputtered. "I will not!"

"Aye, you will." Hugh stepped across the threshold and closed the door. He stuck his key in the lock and turned it.

Pocketing the key once more, he dusted off his hands as if to say, That settles that.

Morgana glared heatedly at him. "I am not going to sleep in this chamber."

"Oh, yes, you are." He put his fists to his hips, matching her scowl and towering temper.

Morgana sucked in her breath. "I don't believe this! You just said, not one quarter hour ago, that you wouldn't harm me in any way. Now listen to yourself!"

Hugh rubbed a weary hand across his face. His whiskers rasped on his callused palm, telling him he needed another shave. "Listen carefully to what I say, Morgana. I'm tired. I want to go to sleep. You need to sleep. I'm not going to touch you or harm you, but *you are sleeping here.* I've made up my mind about it."

Morgana had never heard such an audacious, irrational order in her whole life. In the span of several heartbeats, no rebuttal came to mind quick enough to prevent his stalking across to a jumbled Welsh dresser, muttering, "I'm going to have that drink, too. Speak up if you want one, as well."

He snatched a bottle off the highest shelf, uncorked it and tilted it over the rim of another glass. Amber liquid gurgled out the spout. "Well? Yes or no? Am I drinking alone?"

Morgana wanted to tell him yes, he was. She wanted to clobber him with something very large and preferably heavy, like an iron boat anchor. No such object appeared at hand in this austerely furnished room. There wasn't even a chair or a stool or a trunk to sit on.

Making up her mind to be more perverse than he, she stomped to the Welsh dresser and snatched a glass off the countertop and thrust it out to him. He tipped the bottle and filled her glass to the rim, saying, "If that doesn't put you to sleep, I know where there's another full bottle that will."

"Thank you very much!" Morgana snarled. He didn't offer to drink to her health, and she surely wasn't going to drink to his. As she brought the glass to her lips, she examined the room. She identified the chamber as a pie wedge, partitioned out of one floor of the tower.

Apparently no architectural effort had ever been made to make the room more comfortable. It boasted no fireplace and no windows. Two cross-and-orb slits in the stone work would allow a defender to fire arrows onto attackers below. Those apertures explained why he'd brought her here. With the door securely locked, she obviously wasn't going to jump out any windows or escape.

Morgana gulped a hefty swallow of the whiskey. This liquor burned the back of her throat. By the third swig, her whole mouth was numb. On the fourth, a cold sweat broke out across the back of her neck.

She stared rudely at him, watching his every move. He'd set his glass on the dressertop and begun disrobing. All sorts of thoughts, protests and demands clamored inside Morgana's brain, as though there were ten different people inside her, each shouting to be heard above the rest.

She blinked. He unfastened his belt, rolled it into a coil and tucked it on one of the dresser's cluttered shelves. Mesmerized, she watched his fingers deftly loosen the lacing of his doublet, tug the throat open enough to pull the garment off over his head. Her eyes widened as muscles across his back bulged and rippled their way out of the dark cloth, as if he were a snake shedding its skin. His head popped free, and he shook it negligently, making his thick, dark mane of hair fall back into place.

Morgana dipped her tongue inside the glass, lapping at the amber liquid the way a cat savors sweet cream, hardly even aware of what she was doing. She gulped a whole mouthful when he turned around, looking for her. His broad chest was completely exposed, and dark tufts of hair swirled across it, twisting into a needle-fine line that circled his navel, then slipped from her view, hidden by the concealment of his hose and trews.

He reached down, raising his foot to remove one soft-soled suede boot. The second he toed off and stepped out of.

"Come here, Morgana. I'll undo your laces. You can sleep in your kirtle."

"Oh, no." Morgana shook her head. Her eyes were huge with his magnificence. She wanted to scream and cry. Why was he doing this to her? Tormenting and tempting her like this?

Morgana knew what perfection was. The classical Greek standards had been drilled into her mind long before she entered the rigid, structured environment of Saint Mary de Hogges's Abbey. Knowledge of the arts, philosophy and humanities was part of the everyday life of a Fitzgerald son or daughter from the cradle onward. It had been thus for centuries.

So Morgana knew what the perfect man should look like beneath his clothes. And marriage, no matter how short its duration, had also schooled her in the pleasures to be had in a strong, virile man's bed. Somehow, she managed to drag her gaze away from the man who stood before her, wearing nothing more concealing than a pair of knit stockings, which clung to his body from hip to ankle. She stared at the amber liquid in the crystal glass in her hand, wishing it were a mazer, a golden bowl in which she could see the future.

Not that she wanted to know her future. That was already a given. Her fate was sealed, as her father's and her grandfather's—as every Fitzgerald's since 1534—had been sealed. All their lives were forfeit to England's crown on a trumped-up charge of high treason. It was only a matter of time before Morgana was caught and faced her own moment of eternal truth. So, right this moment, she wanted to know Hugh O'Neill's future.

Morgana tilted the glass once more, drinking deeply, her eyes never leaving Hugh O'Neill. Her head seemed to spin wildly. Her heart pounded heavily in her chest, slow and loud, its cadence rooted deep in preternatural elements of wind, rain, earth and fire, where time and logic held no meaning.

Catherine Fitzgerald raised her invisible hands before her grandniece's eyes, begging softly, *Nay, nay, look not beyond this moment.*

Stone walls faded. Hugh O'Neill stood before Morgana, alone atop a majestic rock fashioned into the throne of ancient kings. Around the hilltop, all the clans of Ireland circled, chanting, "Hail, Hugh, the O'Neill!"

Morgana gasped, pressing her hand against her heart, feeling its resounding beat echoed in chant ringing louder than thunder in her ears. "O'Neill, O'Neill, O'Neill."

Aye, Catherine whispered in her niece's ear. *Beware, my kinswoman. Wake not the dreamer. He is the one.*

Morgana put the glass to her lips and drank again. She shook her head hard to clear it. Stone walls solidified. The chant echoed to silence. Hugh O'Neill glared at her as though she'd done something unforgivable.

"What's the matter with you?" he demanded. "You look as though you've just seen a ghost."

Had she? Morgana wanted to know.

"No ghost." Morgana averted her eyes, taking a deep breath to calm herself. The future, perhaps, or the long-ago past. Or had she seen only what she wanted to see? As she had wanted to see a heroic warrior-savior in her moment of darkest need on the river. Did she want to invest Hugh O'Neill with all her dreams and her hopes, because she had no personal future at all?

Shaken, Morgana turned from him, seeking some place to hide.

The austere chamber offered no private retreat. So she must stand and face her own demons, and come to grips with the truth that her fantasies were just that—the vivid imaginings of a foolish and undisciplined mind.

Hugh finished his drink with a scowl at the woman. Heaven help him, but she was driving him to distraction. One minute he was consumed by the need to protect her, the next he wanted to wrap his fingers around her throat and throttle her. It was all the things she *didn't* say that were driving him out of his mind.

One minute her eyes blazed at him with adoration that could mean only one thing. The next she stared at him as if he was something strange and repelling.

Hugh couldn't decide whether he wanted to toss her onto his bed and bury himself inside her or unlock the door and throw her out. If this kept up, something terrible was going to happen. The odds were running high that come sunrise they'd both be dead, behind his locked door.

No. He shook his head, clearing it of that idiotic and fruitless train of thought. He was not going to harm her. He was merely making certain that nothing did happen to her. Her mind wasn't stable. Why else would any woman have thrown herself out a window?

Enough was enough, he told himself grimly. He set his glass on the dresser, empty. The bottle was empty. Her glass was empty. His bed was empty.

He crossed the room to her, took the glass from her slack fingers and set it next to the other, beside a jumbled stack of knit hose and leggings. Hugh caught her shoulder and turned her around, so that her back was to the better lamp.

His nimble fingers tugged on the bow knot at the bottom of her vest. It hadn't been tied all that tight to begin with, but the struggle to keep her from winding up carrion for the crows on the rocks below his tower had bound the knots.

She swayed with each of the determined tugs necessary to loosen the cords. Once the knots were freed, it took only moments more to loosen the crisscross lacing encasing her long back. He drew the slack garment off over her head, as he'd removed his own tunic.

Her poorly coiled braids fell free at the same time he tossed her vest onto a pile of his clothes. Hugh's mouth tugged in a wry smile at the way his possessions wound up in disorderly piles. He couldn't be bothered with such trivial things, when so many important things preyed upon his thoughts.

It hadn't ever mattered that he kept so few pieces of furniture in this room. He'd never used this chamber for any purpose other than to sleep an hour or two at the most. He lived in his loft, on the uppermost floor of this tower. That entire floor, and the open deck above, were where Hugh devoted his nights to the passionate study of the universe. Hugh wondered what Morgana thought of this utilitarian chamber, but he wasn't going to ask.

Her fingers clutched at the throat of her gray silk kirtle. Without the vest, it had no more shape than a night rail. Hugh blew out the flame in the nearest lamp and crossed to the other. As he reached for it, he nodded toward one side of the bed, saying, "Do humor me by taking off your boots. I've got an aversion to being kicked in bed. You can take your pick of the pillows."

Morgana's head tilted to one side, her expression puzzled. Did he really think he could just order her to sleep and she would? Suddenly it occurred to her that she could just bide her time and wait for him to go to sleep. Then she could search his clothes for the key. It wasn't necessary that she fight and argue to get downstairs. There were always other ways to get what she wanted.

She tried to remove her shoes the way he had done, by balancing on one foot to pull off the first. That feat wasn't possible with hot Irish whiskey boiling through her veins. Her sweaty hand slipped off the heel of her boot, and she stumbled. Hugh caught her before she tumbled to the floor.

"Be careful," he said. Strong fingers gripped her elbow, steadying her. Morgana still felt like she was teetering. She tried to tell herself that this was the reality, not the vision. The few times she'd had visions in the past had been the same. She had difficulty afterward separating what was real from what was not.

"My head's gone to mush," she informed Hugh petulantly. "And it's too cold in here. There's no fire."

"I've got plenty of quilts." Hugh steered her to the edge of the bed and sat her down. Putting out the lamp could wait a moment longer. "Besides blankets, it helps to have a drink each night before I go to sleep. Whiskey warms the blood."

"I'll say it does." Morgana let go of her neckline with one hand and wiped her fingers across her face. "I've never felt so strange . . . ever."

"Is that so?" Hugh knelt at her feet, took one in hand and began unlacing the boot, keeping his head bent, not wanting her to see his expression.

Fascinated, Morgana stared at the top of his head and the wide, wide ledges of his shoulders, jutting sideways below it. Even doing such a simple task as unlacing a boot made the network of musculature across his upper chest and shoulders ripple and bunch. If there were actually bones underneath all that flesh, she couldn't see a one of them. Tempted, she reached out to touch his hair, fingering one of the smoothly plaited braids at his temple. "Did you wear your hair like this in London?"

"Och, no." He shook his head, lifting her right foot to slide the unlaced boot off. "I kept it clubbed."

"What's clubbed?"

"Tied at the nape of my neck and tucked under, so no one can really tell how long it is. The queen says too much hair is a sign of poor breeding. Most courtiers keep theirs short to suit her. She has a weakness for mustaches, though, and beards. Says those are manly."

Morgana pressed her fingers over her mouth to hold back a giggle. Something turned loose her tongue, and her thoughts spilled out. "I heard she's got a red mustache . . . and shaves it off just like a man."

Hugh glanced up at her face to judge the quality of that silly comment. He didn't approve of malicious gossip, or indulge in that sort of behavior himself. Knowing that he was always subject to recall to London, he didn't intend to develop any bad habits that would come back to haunt him.

Realizing how seriously he was studying her face, Morgana pressed her lips together and looked up at the ceiling. Oddly enough, she found a square hole in that open-raftered ceiling. She hadn't seen that before, and she'd thought she'd done a good job examining the empty room. "What's that?" she asked him. "A priest hole?"

"No, lady. This is a tower, or have you forgotten that? A tower is built for defense. In case of siege, each floor can be cut off from the one below it. That's a trapdoor, only I've removed the door."

"There's another room up there?"

"Aye, my loft." Hugh nodded, setting to work on the left boot. She bounced backward, sinking into the feather mattress as she tried to bend far enough back to see into the room above.

"How do you get up there from here?" she asked, wiggling enough that her dangling feet were hard to capture.

"You don't!" Hugh caught hold of her left boot, stilling it so that he could untie the laces.

"Why not?"

"What good would a tower be as a defensive works, if one could just get up to the next floor without a fight?"

"I don't know. This is the first tower I've ever been in. We live in a manor house." Those words were out and spoken before Morgana realized what she'd said. She blinked again, having shocked herself. "I mean, we used to live in a manor horse...house."

"Which just goes to prove that towers still serve a very useful purpose."

"My father said they are death traps, now that cannons can level even the stoutest walls."

"So, you know a lot about warfare, do you?"

"Oh, no. Nothing." Morgana shook her head. She shut her mouth and bit her cheek. It was too numb to feel anything. She'd never been really drunk before. Her own numb sensations fascinated her nearly as much as watching Hugh's muscles. She poked her fingernail into her cheek, testing the limits of the numbness.

The leather laces noisily whipped out of the eyelets each time Hugh stuck his finger under the crossover and pulled back. His hand felt very firm and determined at her heel, the pressure indicating that he wasn't letting go till the job was finished.

The sides of her boot flopped open, and the tongue fell out. He tightened his grip on her heel and lifted her ankle with his other hand, drawing the shoe off. Morgana let herself giggle again. Her feet were ticklish.

Hugh took both shoes in hand and set them at the foot of the bed. He looked up at her and frowned to see her poking her finger at her jaw. "What are you doing?"

"My face is gone all numb. It's most peculiar. Is it because of the whiskey?"

"Most likely." He stood up, both knees cracking loudly.

"You have very noisy joints." Morgana shook her head. "Is that what you meant by saying no one ever accused you of sneaking up behind them?"

"That's what I meant." Hugh padded barefoot to the lamp, intending to put it out.

"I would like another glass of whiskey." Morgana said, putting forth her first of many planned demands.

He frowned at her. "I don't think you need another."

"But it feels very good," she argued. "I mean, not the feeling all hot and sticky, but the numb part feels very good. My jaw doesn't hurt right now. Nor do my arms or my neck."

She got out of bed and came over to where Hugh stood under the lamp, holding her right hand up for his inspection in the light. The whiskey appeared to have made her oblivious of how loose the neckline of her undergown was. She leaned toward him, displaying the bruises on her wrist and hand, and unknowingly showed him her splendidly un-injured breasts.

Hugh took a deep breath as he took her hand in his. His scowl darkened as he examined that complicated structure of bone and sinew that composed a delectably delicate hand. He threw mental reins on his rising interest in what lay exposed by the gaps in her gown, reminding himself that he was first and foremost a man of caution. Not a man of passion.

"See. It's very bruised. Maybe another whiskey would make me forget how badly it hurts. And you should look at my neck. James Kelly struck me with the handle of his sword, right here." She turned around, lifting hanks of tumbled red hair from her neck, exposing that sensuous curve to Hugh's hungry eyes. "I'm sure there must be some sort of mark. I can't begin to describe how much it aches right here.... Why are some men such bastards?"

Hugh laid both of his palms on her white shoulders. There was a terrible mark to the left of the fragile bones of her spine. Hugh knew better than to touch it. Instead, he carefully turned her around to face him. "I can't explain why some men are cruel and hateful, Morgana. They just are. I'm sorry, but I don't think there is enough whiskey in the world to make your pains go away."

"Then why did you practically insist I drink it?"

"Because its most consistent effect is to put tired people to sleep."

"Oh," Morgana said, making her voice bright and full of energy. She turned around, walked to the bed and sat. "It doesn't seem to work that way on me. I don't feel at all sleepy. Only I never talk this much, and I'm talking a lot. That's peculiar, too, isn't it?"

Hugh blew out the lamp. The bedding rustled, and he assumed Morgana was settling into it. He waited for his night vision to adjust to the dark before moving to his side of the bed. Mostly he had to feel his way. His bedchamber was blessedly dark at night, which was why he slept here. Before he got into bed, he unfastened his trews and slid the garment off.

Even on the coldest winter nights, Hugh slept nude. He stretched his back and his arms, then lay down, lacing his fingers under his neck.

He managed to lie perfectly still, but that wasn't the case with Morgana. She wiggled and squirmed. Turned one way, then another. She pulled up the covers, and minutes later tossed them back to the foot of the bed.

Upstairs, the clock in his study tolled the hour of one. She sat bolt upright, saying, "What was that?"

"The clockwork."

"Is it going to do that every hour?"

"No." Hugh summoned the answer from a deep well of patience.

"It chimes one bell every quarter hour."

"Sweet Saint Brigit." She flopped onto her back. The bed bounced. "I'll never go to sleep. I can hear it ticking."

"You can't hear the clock ticking. It's too far away to hear that, and you haven't been quiet long enough to hear anything but your own movement."

"I hear it ticking," she repeated. "It's too dark in here. I don't like it."

"Morgana," Hugh said dryly, "how old are you?"

"Two-and-twenty."

"And I'm four centuries older than Methuselah," Hugh snapped. "Is lying a practiced art with you?"

"I'm two-and-twenty years old, Hugh O'Neill. How old are you? Seventy?"

"What's that supposed to mean?"

"You sound like a crabby old man."

"You sound like a spoiled seven-year-old. Be still and be quiet. Go to sleep."

"No. You're the one who insists I have to sleep here with you. So you have to put up with the consequences. I'm not sleepy."

She turned over, rocking the bed, dragging covers thither and yon. God only knew what she was doing on her side of the bed. Hugh considered taking her pillow and using it to suffocate her…at least as far as the point where she'd drop into a dead faint. He ground his teeth together. No doubt about it, now she was definitely being perverse—like all the rest of her English sisters. Obviously he'd only had to wait her out to discover her true nature.

"You shouldn't do that."

"Do what?" Hugh asked tersely.

"Grind your teeth. It a very bad habit to acquire. You'll break perfectly healthy teeth. Then you'll lose them, and you'll wind up a toothless old man who has to eat mashed foods and pudding."

Hugh laughed bluntly, unable to imagine himself either old or toothless. He abruptly turned onto his side, facing her, and stretched out his hand till he found her hip. She wasn't under the covers, but then, neither was he. They had enough whiskey coursing in their veins to have no need for covers right now.

Morgana became very still and awfully quiet as his fingers splayed across her hip, gripping her firmly enough to turn her toward him. "What are you doing?"

"My lady, you've told me no twice when given a direct order. Did you parents not instill an understanding of obedience and law in your head?"

"I haven't seen either of my parents in six years."

"Are you using that as an excuse for doing whatever the hell it is you want to do, lady?"

"Sorry. I don't follow you."

"All right. I'll make this even simpler, so your limited, womanly brain can understand. Do you know how to follow an order?"

"Of course I do. I wouldn't be alive today if I didn't know how or when to follow orders."

"Then follow this one. Shut up and go to sleep."

Hugh pushed her hip away and turned to his back. Blessed silence followed, so he laced his fingers behind his neck once more and closed his eyes.

Morgana rolled onto her back once he'd released her hip, and for several minutes listened to the ticking of the clock, which reverberated on the rafters, his breathing, and the constant thrumming of her heart in her ears. She could hear her throat creaking when she swallowed. The drip of water off the roof, and the lap of the lake against the rocks below the castle.

Oh, she could hear and identify all kinds of sounds. Beams creaking. Stone contracting. The rush of a bird's wings as it took flight from the roof. The distant thrumming of a bodhran and the rattle of crystal glassworks tinkling in the wind. And running under all that, there remained the rumble of thunder as the storm continued its relentless drive southward.

Knowing she must get away from him now, Morgana took a very deep breath and turned her face toward Hugh's. "I'm not sleepy."

Hugh sat up. He swung his legs off the bed and stood. Morgana raised up to her elbow, looking for his shape in the darkness. She followed his moment with her eyes, and listened to the sounds his body made as he moved. Though the night hid all the details, she could tell he was naked, because his thighs made a curious whispering sound with each step he took.

The thought of his nudity brought other images to her mind, images she'd prefer not to see again. James Kelly on top of her. The visage of the warrior-god that had ridden across the Blackwater and saved her. Her own terrifying vulnerability when that warrior's eyes had locked on to her, showing her the true meaning of blood lust.

A shiver of fear cooled Morgana's skin. For the most part, Hugh O'Neill had been very kind to her and didn't deserve to be manipulated. Was it going to matter what bed she woke up in when the sun rose?

It was not as if she actually had a reputation to protect in society. No, not at all. Were the truth to be admitted, socially she was ruined. A pariah. In Dublin, old friends alternately called her a whore, a witch or Ireland's richest widow. Her dowry was immense...consisting of all the Ormand and Kildare lands combined, demenses, castles, vast plantations, and the greatest library in the world outside the Vatican.

That left Morgana in more danger than ever. It wasn't just Lord Grey who wanted to force her into an unholy marriage. Each and every greedy upstart who came to Ireland to steal the country blind wanted to get his hands on the Fitzgerald wealth. And not one gave a damn how they accomplished bringing her to the altar.

Ruined reputation or no, it still mattered to Morgana whose bed she woke up in come sunrise every morning. Since Gregory O'Malley's death, Morgana had always managed to wake up alone. She no longer cared how many people called her a whore. What mattered was that she wasn't one.

It was very, very important to her that she not succumb to becoming one simply because the temptation to give in to a man had become impossible to resist.

For those complex reasons, she did at this moment, regret provoking Hugh O'Neill. God help her if he ever figured out how desperately she had to work to manipulate him.

Glass clanked together. A cork popped out of a bottle. Liquid gurgled and splashed. The cork squeaked when it was roughly replaced. The man in the shadows turned and trod softly back to the bed. Morgana sat up. Hair raised at the nape of her neck and down her forearms, as she dreaded the coming explosion.

Her good vision picked out the flat expanse of Hugh's belly just before his leg disrupted the sheeting.

"Round one to you, lady. Sit up and take this drink from my hand. You're going to need every drop of it. Don't tell me on the morrow you weren't given fair opportunity to have a night of peace, or that I didn't behave as a gentleman up until this point. I am claiming round two, and the balance of this night's excesses and pleasures, with no quarter given. Prepare for a prolonged siege, lady."

Chapter Eight

Morgana scooted backward, mashing a pillow at the small of her back. Her shoulder blades contacted the deeply carved headboard. She could just barely make out the rim of the glass in his hand. The smell of liquor swam pungently in her nostrils now, as it had done earlier. She swallowed dryly, asking herself whether she dared throw the glass's contents at him, or onto the floor or the bed.

It wouldn't be the first time she'd opted for the coward's way out.

Almost as if he knew what she was thinking, Hugh threw the corked bottle on the mattress between them. Morgana mentally refused to pick up that gauntlet. She held onto her glass, and didn't spill a drop as the bed shifted, taking his weight.

Hugh O'Neill eased into a relaxed pose beside her, his knee propped and supporting his arm and his glass of whiskey. Morgana had no trouble whatsoever defining his purposeful leisure as the greatest threat she'd faced from a man yet. She racked her brain, seeking some kind of advice from Grace O'Malley to get her past the bubbling tension in her belly.

"Tell me," Hugh said, much too easily, to Morgana's way of thinking, "do you prefer having a candle burning or the dark? Both suit me, though I will admit I enjoying watching a woman take her pleasure."

"I would find candlelight limiting." Morgana answered. *Not to mention humiliating and degrading. This proves he thinks I am a whore.*

Now that the bed was still and there was no danger of spilling the liquid on the sheets, she brought the glass to her mouth. The very last thing she needed was more spirits. Her reaction to the whiskey was no act. Wine she might have some tolerance to, but not this potent brew. Maybe, she thought, it would be better if she was drunk.

At that thought, she drank deeply.

Hugh matched her, keeping the rim of his glass to his lips as long as she did hers. "For the record, I must insist that you keep up with me, lady. Drink for drink. Kiss for kiss. Touch for touch." His hand touched hers, taking the glass away. "You may stand up and take off the kirtle. You'll want something to cover you decently when you leave in the morning. There's a peg on the upper right-hand side of the dresser that you can hang it from. It will have fewer wrinkles if you put it there. You may suit yourself in that regard. It's your dignity that's at risk."

"How generous of you to mention dignity. Since you brought up the subject, isn't this the appropriate moment to request that you unlock your door and let me leave? That way, you will have the silence and sleep you asked for."

"It's too late for that, Morgana. I don't like being manipulated. You've roused the demon. You'll stay till you've satisfied him. And you'll come back and appease him in all our future dealings."

She didn't like the sound of that. As she left the bed, groping her way to the dresser, she considered her chances of finding that key, of scaling the wall to the trap in the ceiling, of throwing herself on his mercy. Her fingers gathered silk into handfuls, bunching it, lifting the gown up and over her shoulders.

She wasn't frightened, not really.

It wasn't as if she were saving herself for some future husband who would love and cherish her above all else in this world, save God. No, no. Sooner or later, her luck was going to run out. Lord Grey had stated his demands in perfectly blunt and clear terms. She could service his entire army, for all he cared. He wanted only her moneys and properties. That was only one of the reasons she was on the run.

At least here, in this room, the man she was going to allow to bed her granted her some choice. She found the peg and hooked the gown over it.

"Is there a hairbrush here?" she asked, tugging at the few pins that remained in her hair.

"You'll have to feel for it." Hugh answered. "Last time I saw it, it was on the second shelf up from the counter, next to my porcelain shaving mug. Does that help?"

"Yes, thank you." Morgana patted her way across the shelf, taking care not to tumble things over onto the cluttered counter. "You ought to have a wardrobe brought in. The one down in the solar is practically empty, and obviously rarely used by anyone. It's not so tall or wide that it couldn't be brought up the stairs."

"That won't make the task any less difficult."

"Agreed." Morgana found the brush. She pulled her braids over her shoulder, feeling for the ends and the threads she tied around each braid to secure it. She used her fingers to comb through the braids and open them, then closed her right hand over the handle of the brush, and, as quickly as her hand allowed, smoothed her hair into one smooth fall. She dropped the brush twice.

"Your hand still hurts. Come here, and I'll brush your hair for you."

"Are you certain you want to do that? I've got an awful lot of hair."

"The more the better," Hugh responded. He tucked their glasses on a ledge in the headboard and turned to the side of the bed. She put the brush in his hand and gave him her back, standing before him. Hugh opened his legs, drawing her hips between the grip of his knees.

He gathered the sheet of sweet-smelling hair into his hands, marveling at the weight and silky texture of it, regretting the lack of light that would have allowed him to fully appreciate with all his senses the pleasure of brushing her hair.

Each crackling stroke of the brush sent a maddening tumble of silk into his lap and onto his thighs. He was hard as a rock. She nestled back against him, the cleft of her bottom so very close to his stiffened manhood that he ached, because he could feel her heat.

Still, he was in no hurry to take her. Years of studying the night sky had taught him that his best times were always those to come in the wee hours of the morning, before dawn. It was not yet gone two o'clock. The night was his to savor.

"Have you ever cut your hair, Morgana?"

"My mother used to trim it a little bit, if she thought the ends were too dry."

"You like it this long, then?"

"I know how to work with it, to make it look pleasing for those who have to look at me."

"My sisters cut theirs quite short, to my way of thinking."

"Inghinn Dubh's hair looked quite long. It's a very nice color, black. Rich-looking. Red isn't very appealing."

"Do you know what Inghinn Dubh means in Gaelic?"

"No."

"Dark daughter. She was Sorely Boy Mac Donnell's second wife's pride and joy."

"That's a curious way to state a fact. How many wives does he have?"

"The usual Celtic three."

"Why do you say the usual three? Are Celtic men all bigamists?"

"Nay." Hugh laughed easily. "There's an old tale that says a man's first wife is chosen by his father for her properties and dowry. His mother chooses the second to guarantee production of a son and heir. The son chooses his third for companionship, while his parents pray that she will outlive them all.''

"There must be a meaning there I'm missing...about the third."

Hugh tossed the brush across the room. It clattered onto the dresser, knocking something else that dropped loudly to the floor. His hands swept around Morgana's waist, turning her to face him, pulling her body onto his as he lay back on the bed.

"Aye, there's a moral lingering in the tale. It means by the time a man gets round to picking the third, he's so old he needs a nurse's care—and the same for his parents."

Her breasts and belly flattened on his. Fingers splayed across his chest, tangling in dark, curling hair.

"And where are you in that astounding process, Hugh O'Neill?"

"I am stuck in limbo. My mother has already died, so there's no one about to choose wife number two."

"You're married?" Morgana said with some shock.

"I was. Though it wasn't my father who chose the bride. Queen Elizabeth did that. Margaret died three years ago, from the usual complication of marriage, childbirth. Both she and the child succumbed to fever shortly after my son's birth."

"How dreadful for you." Morgana murmured sincerely.

"In truth, I regret that I never knew Margaret very well. It was a marriage of state, forced on the both of us. I was ordered to play a certain part, and so I did. Beyond leaving me with a great feeling of emptiness, it's all behind me now."

Morgana could see that they had much in common in that regard, though she was not free to openly sympathize. He'd opened a road into her compassion, making her ask, "How old are you, Hugh O'Neill?"

"Five-and-twenty. Decrepit and ancient. Tottering into my dotage." His hand spread across the back of her head, drawing her mouth down to his.

"That's hardly old at all," she replied.

"Sometimes it feels as though I've existed for ten lifetimes and never lived one."

Morgana shivered as his lips bloomed over hers. His heat invaded and enveloped her. Wonderfully strong arms clasped her to him, with every inch of her torso from throat to belly in contact with him. His shaft prodded her softness, hard, hot and huge. She couldn't comprehend how anything so big would fit inside her, but knew from experience that mystery was one of the most lasting pleasures of good loving.

She wanted to give away neither her ignorance nor her experience. So she concentrated on meeting the demands of his mouth and feeling his smooth lips gliding over hers. They were alternately soft and then hard, rough and gentle. His shaved whiskers teased and burned and scratched her lips, making them all the more sensitive and aware of each nuance of his mouth's touch upon hers.

Marriage had told her that men liked putting their tongues in a woman's mouth during mating. Her sister-in-law, Grace O'Malley, claimed the way they used their tongues separated the lovers from the rutters. Morgana had never known there was a difference until Hugh O'Neill sent a probe spiraling past her parted lips. She clasped her fingers to his shoulders and yielded, thrilled by sensations she hadn't dreamed existed.

All at once she was overwhelmed by his flavors and textures; whiskey and salt, the astringent he splashed on his cheeks after he shaved. She loved the rough feel of his whiskers against her tongue, the hardness of his teeth, the stab of his tongue delving deep into her mouth, the teasing flick as he skittered across her gums and ran circles around her tongue.

She could have spent hours and hours going no further than just kissing, but Morgana wasn't directing this play. Hugh O'Neill was in complete control. His right hand slid down her hip to grasp the back of her knee, drawing that soft inner flesh high over his hair-roughened thigh. His left arm tightened across her back, and he rolled her over, pinning her underneath him.

His rod bucked against the opening of her portal. Nothing else could possibly have made her more acutely aware of the drastic change that had taken place in her body while she was lost completely in the artful joy of kissing. A seeping wetness drenched her nether lips. Deep inside her belly, something pulsed, driving her to madness, urging her to rock her hips hard against his.

His teeth nipped at her throat. His tongue laid a hot trail across her jaw and circled her ear, racking her with delicious shudders of purest pleasure. She thought she was going to die when he drew completely away from her, grasped her body under her arms and lifted her higher across the bed. She didn't understand how he could leave her for even that short moment.

His hands cupped her breasts, forming them as suited him, and then his mouth closed over one, suckling her nipple deep, deeper inside his mouth than seemed possible. His tongue worked against the hard palate at the roof of his mouth, driving her over the edge into utter abandoned ecstasy.

She tried to stifle her moans of pleasure, to keep her cries to some sort of ladylike demeanor, but that was impossible. She caught his head between her hands, trying to draw him off, but only succeeded in accomplishing a transfer to her other breast. He made her throb and ache and writhe beneath him, begging for more, for everything that he could give her.

Hugh caught hold of her hands, restraining them as he moved deliberately down her belly. He tasted her curls and bit the plump mound of Venus, deliberately leaving the marks of his mouth upon each quadrant of her belly. Then he made his tongue into that hard, tormenting probe that had teased and toyed with her mouth. He wedged her thighs wide apart with his broad shoulders and tasted her.

His tongue entered her, tickled her, tormented and teased her, preparing her for the entrance of his shaft inside her. Morgana arched and strained against him, struggling to free her hands from his containment, to somehow reach that impossible place he was so ruthlessly determined to drive her to. Her whole body tensed, every muscle drawing tight as a bowstring pulled to its farthermost limit.

Then his tongue scraped across some infinitesimal pleasure spot that only he seemed to know of, and everything shattered. Morgana's scream went on and on, as unstoppable as the climax rushing through her. Hugh moved up her body, lifting her legs as he brought his mouth back to hers.

His tongue flicked across her lips, bringing the taste of herself to his flavor and imprinting both on her tongue.

His hands plowed into her hair, drawing it back from her face.

"Now, lady—" his voice was fierce, husky, possessive "—you belong to me, and no other. From this moment forward, you are mine, my consort, my queen, my woman."

He drove his shaft downward into her, his mouth covering hers, taking her scream of surprise inside him. Shockingly aching need drew Morgana's body back into that taut, aching, tension she'd felt only moments before.

This lesson in true lovemaking was complete. She knew exactly where he was taking her now. No guilt-ridden shame at enjoying such a union completely was going to hold her back.

The fullness his shaft caused matched the growing ache for more that ran rampant inside her. She would never get enough of him, taste enough, feel enough. Not of this. She wrapped her legs tight around his back, bringing him down to her, asking for all of him, in the only way she knew, letting their bodies become the only necessary instrument of communication between them.

She thought she had learned it all then. But never had she been more wrong. The point of joining was only the beginning. The touches, the tastes, the sounds, the sensations and the raging emotions continued to build and increase and drive both of them to the brink of madness and beyond.

Her climax in the beginning was child's play, compared to the hard, physical work of his. Each and every time she thought Hugh had peaked and spent himself inside her, he hardened again. He pulled back, switching tactics, changing focus, drawing out the pleasures that could be wrung from them, like the last drops of precious honey squeezed and scraped from a comb.

He switched moods like lightning, changing from tender to demanding and finally to pure driven need that sent them both over the edge, into wrung-out exhaustion. He collapsed upon her, buried deep, his member throbbing and pulsing, his seed filling every empty crevice inside her.

Nothing, nothing Morgana had experienced in her lifetime, could compare to this. How she kept from crying, she would never, ever know. Or how she kept from babbling out her ignorance before, as compared to her insight and knowledge now. Somehow she kept her tongue behind her teeth, instead listening to the wonderful sounds of his ragged, exhausted breathing.

A full quarter hour ticked away before Hugh could bring his head up from collapse upon Morgana's shoulder. Before he could summon the strength to take his crushing weight off her body, soft and squashed beneath him.

He rolled off her, pulling her against his chest, one possessive arm refusing to part with her or give her any space. Sweat held their bellies together. The chamber was ripe with the heady scent of raw sex, great sex, the best he'd ever had. He scraped his fingernails across her belly, gathering the tangles of red hair and looping it across her damp shoulder.

He smoothed his hand up her stomach, gently cupping her breast, and bent his head to kiss each orb one more time. He turned his face up, studying hers in the womblike darkness. Her eyes were open, her lips were parted, and from what he could tell, she looked replete. "Are you still awake, Morgan?"

"Yes, wide-awake, Hugh."

He laughed and caught a handful of the top sheet, using it to wipe her down, to dry the dampness from her skin, so that she wouldn't get chilled. "Then I won't tell you that a man's natural inclination immediately after lovemaking is to drop off in a stupor of sleep."

"Oh?" She didn't waste her breath contradicting a known fact.

"Oh, yes. Surely you've noticed that one outstanding male fact over the years."

"Possibly." Morgana sat up and took the sheet from his hand, doing for him what he'd done for her. "I can't say I've paid any particular notice. Men seem to sleep any time of day or night, without any trouble. I suppose that's just one of the ways in which we're different." She paused in her ministrations at his loins, to ask permission before she continued. "May I touch you . . . here?"

"You may do anything you like . . . there."

"Kiss you?"

Hugh's breath caught inside his chest. It wasn't possible that he could return to life after his last strength-sapping climax. "Anything you like, Morgana."

Her fingers slid around the base of his shaft, gently cupping him, holding the flaccid organ erect as she bent her head and kissed him. Her tongue came out and licked him, then circled around and around.

Hugh shuddered from the pure pleasure of her touch, but even when she took all of him into her mouth, suckling much more tentatively than he had suckled her breasts, his rod remained soft.

He let her continue, because it delighted him and there was some pleasure to be gained from the touch of her mouth upon him. It was a pointless exercise, and he knew the reasons why. He just thought better of telling her she was wasting her time.

The clock banged out the hour of five. Hugh drew her off and put her glass in her hand, saying, "Suckle on this. I'm going down to the lake for a wash. There's water in the pitcher at the basin, do you care to use it."

"It's too dark to see what I'm doing."

"Fine. I'll light one of the lamps for you."

Hugh rose from the bed, searched the Welsh dresser for his flint and iron. He found a plaid first, and draped that over his shoulder. Morgana watched him strike sparks against a twist of lint, then touch the flame to the lamp's wick. He adjusted the flame, then closed the lantern's glass door.

Hugh glanced to the bed, where she sat, wrapped in sheet. He caught a small spurt of laughter behind his teeth and smiled wolfishly at her. "I'm tempted, lady." He nodded to indicate her fetching position, long legs exposed, plump breasts pressed up by the clasp of her arm across her chest and that splendid head of red hair spilling all around her in flaming curls.

Tempted, yes. But not hardened enough to act on the temptation. What man could be? He'd just spent three hours in a constant state of erection, spilling his seed inside her five separate times, only to come back moments later as hard as he'd been before. That sort of performance put him in the same category as a randy goat, and hadn't happened since he'd passed the age of nine-and-ten.

He caught up a wedge of soap and slung the tartan around his body, tucking it once at his waist for modesty's sake. As he fastened the plaid, he spied the object that had made so much noise when it hit the floor several hours ago. The gold-handled dagger he'd pried out of her fingers the night before.

Hugh bent and retrieved it with his own hand, marveling at the few hours that had passed since then. It felt like much, much more, felt as though he'd know this woman named Morgana for an eternity. He picked up his belt and his sheathed dirk, taking those with him from the room, too.

Last, he took his key from his doublet's pocket and headed for the door.

"I'll be back," he promised.

"Will you?" Morgana asked, doubt and remorse echoing in her voice.

Hugh looked to see whether there was a pout on her mouth. Damned if there wasn't. That halted his progress. He stood a moment longer, staring at her, thinking of the exact words he wanted to say. A current of underlying tension formed between them during the wait. Finally, he had it all organized.

He moved his eyes in the direction of the glass in her hand. "Finish your drink, Morgana. All of it. I can't stand waste. When you've done that, clean yourself up, make the bed up decently and take a nap. I may be gone a couple of hours—more or less I can't say. When I do come back, I expect you to be as willing and eager as you were a few short hours ago. Don't try to manipulate me with sulks and pouts or tantrums.

"To make your status perfectly clear to you, you're my leman now. You'll do as I say or have cause to regret it."

Morgana didn't blink, or allow a single muscle anywhere in her body to react. As hard as it was to do, she met his penetrating stare without flinching. After a long delay, she lowered her lashes, then looked up at him, saying, "By your command, my lord."

"Exactly," Hugh snapped, angered by the sarcasm implied in her words, although vacant in her tone. "By my command!"

He jammed the key in the lock and twisted it, opened the door and slammed it shut behind him. He'd been going to give her the freedom of his house, let her roam at will. But not now. He thrust the key into the lock again and turned it. Just maybe, he'd leave her locked in till noon. That might cool her heels. He put the key on the nail above the door and went down to the lake for his morning swim.

Hugh O'Neill's daily schedule was as well regulated and predictable as the quarter-hour chime of his imported clockwork. At a quarter past six, he was in chapel, to hear Loghran O'Toole say mass and to receive communion with his sisters and Inghinn Dubh.

By seven-thirty, he had had his breakfast and stood behind his uncle's chair as the boards were cleared and morning hall assembled. The ladies retreated to see Inghinn on her way home. The day's cases consisted of a dispute over payment between a landlord and his tenant in the village and one over licensing of the beggars allowed to work inside the village precincts. A widow had petitioned the laird to dispense rough justice to her unruly son, and a dispute between two unneighborly neighbors took up the majority of the morning's session.

Hall ended at ten, giving Hugh the first chance he'd had to meet with his kerns since they'd returned to Dungannon the night before. Kermit reported that James Kelly was doing his best to antagonize his jailers and pick fights with other detainees bound over for trial at Fort Tullaghoge.

Donald the Fair gave a tally of the weapons collected and coin taken, and displayed jewels and other odd trinkets on a felt cloth for inspection by all participants in the raid.

It was left up to Hugh how to disseminate the wealth, including eight horses. The Arabian, having been judged the property of Morgana of Kildare, was removed, along with her tack, back to Hugh's section of Dungannon's stable. Hugh kept the unopened saddlebags at his feet during the meeting. Before they broke up, he handed Morgana's knife to Art Macmurrough and asked what he made of the blade.

The elder took the finely crafted dagger in hand and examined it, testing its weight and balance and remarking upon the superb skill of the Irish goldsmith who'd made the handle.

A walnut-size bead of amber encased in a circlet of pure gold formed the base of the handle. The gem gleamed the way the fiery sun did at the summer solstice. In the center of the bed was a blooming cinquefoil, perfectly preserved.

Macmurrough turned the jewel so that the sunlight shined through, illuminating the ancient flower. He grunted deeply, then said, "Cinquefoil—the most potent herb. Carried in a pouch, it gives one eloquence when asking favors of officials, and ensures that favor is granted the bearer."

"Aye." Hugh nodded approvingly, adding, "The points of the five leaves of the blossom represent love, money, health, power and wisdom."

What he did not add to the Irishman's summation was that to the queen's alchemist, John Dee, amber stood for the element of fire. To an astrologist like Hugh, it represented the planet Jupiter, the most powerful planet in the heavenly constellations. Truly, the amber gemstone was a rare and potent jewel, as unique as the knife itself.

"Can you tell who it belonged to?" Hugh asked.

Macmurrough made a rumbling noise in the back of his throat, clearing it. "Aye, the ogham inscription on the blade names it as property of Gerait Og Fitzgerald, ninth earl of Kildare. How did you come by it, my lord Hugh?"

"I took it from my guest, Morgana."

"The woman the soldiers were after?" Macmurrough asked.

Hugh took the knife in hand again. "The same."

"That's no mere trinket," Macmurrough said uneasily. "It's a ceremonial knife."

"Oh?" Hugh said, impressed with the scope of Macmurrough's knowledge. "How so? What sort of ceremony?"

Macmurrough's brow pleated deeply, and he cast a sideways glance at Loghran O'Toole, which Hugh took to mean that Macmurrough had misgivings about speaking frankly before the priest. Whatever his reservations were, he overcame them. "I'm only judging by the ogham inscription, my lord. Knives like this come in a set, with various tools, pens, blades, and certain other magical paraphernalia. Wizards use them in conducting their black masses and wickedly evil ceremonies. The ninth earl of Kildare was a warlock, Lord O'Neill. You should destroy the knife before it brings you evil.''

"Don't be ridiculous," Hugh said. He slipped the blade back into his sheath, the discussion over, as far as he was concerned.

"It's no' ridiculous," Art argued heatedly. "If you're of a mind to keep the knife, take it to Sir Almoy at Dunrath Temple. Ask him to exorcise the evil from it before you use it. Blood spilled with that blade will come back to haunt you, unless you are a Fitzgerald and have the right to use it."

Deliberately changing the subject, Hugh asked, "What happened to the man Brian brought down with his musket at the crossroads?"

Macmurrough scratched his head. "Didn't find any trace of his body, just his horse. Brian says he put the bullet in his chest. I looked for a trail of blood, but the rain pretty well washed that from sight."

"So we don't know if the man's alive, or whether he'll show up at some later date with a full battalion, looking for the rest of Kelly's patrol," Hugh concluded.

Kermit Blackbeard scowled. "Odds are he's dead."

"Kelly's got a son in the regiment. Young one, wet behind the ears. Corporal John Kelly. Some say he's another crack shot." Rory offered that bit of gossip to chew. "Does any investigation occur, young Kelly will be behind it."

"Any chance that he was the seventh man taken down at the crossroads?" Hugh asked.

"No chance, O'Neill," Macmurrough insisted.

Their business completed, Hugh adjourned the meeting, after telling the men to be ready to ride north with him the next morning, May the seventh. Knuckles cracked in anticipation of traveling into Antrim, a province in a state of turmoil. Any chance of sighting Francis Drake's warships appealed greatly to Hugh's ready kerns. Hugh shouldered Morgana's heavy saddle packs and headed for his tower.

It was not yet noon, so he went up to his study. Her weighty packs thunked heavily on his worktable when he slung them off his shoulder. Hugh unbuckled one of the paired sacks and dropped out its contents. He had to pull hard on the tightly packed mass of clothing in order to remove it from the pack.

Hugh O'Neill prided himself on being thorough and leaving no stone unturned—in any endeavor. Still, he almost missed the most important find of all by not unrolling the assorted and uninspiring clothing in the second bag.

Seven documents had been carefully concealed inside the rolled skirt of Morgana's only complete change of clothes— a black serge convent habit.

The documents, the deeds, the map and the letter from Bishop Moye of Armagh paled beside the revealing importance of the clothing itself.

Morgana Fitzgerald was a consecrated Arroasian nun.

Her heavy wooden rosary and crucifix dropped from Hugh's hand as if made of molten lava. He sank onto the stool beside his worktable, deeply shaken by the enormity of the great sin he'd committed. All he could think from that point on was, *Dear God, what have I done?*

Book 2

The Earl of Tyrone

Same old slippers,
Same old rice,
Same old glimpse
Of Paradise.

"June Weddings"
William James Lampton

Chapter Nine

Catherine Fitzgerald paced round and round the bed where her kinswoman slept with the ease of an infant. *Why will you no' listen to me?* Catherine exclaimed, exasperated by the restrictions placed upon her in death. Mortals simply wouldn't listen to the dead's voices unless they were hit over the head with something outlandish. Then they might listen to an urgent warning.

Exhausted by wasted pacing, Catherine sat at the foot of the great bed. *Can't you see you've made a mistake, girl? Why didn't ya weep or rail at the awful man when he left you like he did? How could you just shrug your shoulder, as if to say it's nothing to you?*

Catherine heaved a deep sigh. Men, especially those from Ulster, were a race apart from women. Their words, deeds and manners defied explanation. Hugh was as exasperating a master as his bloody-minded grandsire, Conn O'Neill.

What had Morgana Fitzgerald done after the cold bastard stomped out the chamber, issuing his orders right and left like he was God Almighty's right-hand judge? Why, to Catherine's mortification, her grandniece had done each thing Hugh ordered her to do.

Never mind that it took no more than a moment or two! It was the principle behind such orders. Morgana was a Fitzgerald.

Come, girl. Catherine gave the bed a hard shake. *Get up. I want you to come walk with me outside the castle walls. You must see where these barbarians put my grave. I'll no' rest until the ground around me is blessed. Will you not get up, you lazy girl? The O'Neill opened the door an hour ago. You can go free!*

In her exasperation, Catherine shouted her last words. To no avail. Morgana slept. Oblivious of the tracking in and out of a dozen household servants. Oblivious of the aroma of the hot meal laid out for her on a table beside the bed.

When the last servant had gone, Catherine gave the open door her hardest push. It slammed against the frame and sprang open again. But when Catherine turned to look at the bed, a sunbeam entering the westward cross-and-orb cut a brilliant path across the wood floor and shone brightly on the covers at the foot of the bed. Catherine could not pass over a direct beam of daylight. She faded back into the shadows, powerless and silent, condemned to wait endlessly for the night to return.

Morgana woke late in the afternoon, refreshed from hours of needed and undisturbed sleep. She yawned and stretched her arms wide, cognizant of exactly where she was and how she'd come to be in Hugh O'Neill's bed.

The sun had traveled during her long sleep to the opposite wall. A bright cross-and-orb sunbeam warmed the light covers lying over Morgana's feet.

That wasn't the only change in the chamber. The door stood wide open. A table and two short benches graced the previously vacant interior wall. Morgana's saddlebags lay on one of the benches. A candelabrum holding eight candles—only one of them lit—focused her attention on a delectable assortment of food spread out on the linen-covered table.

There was also a crucifix on the stone wall, a prie-dieu set before it, and a trunk of clothing that Morgana recognized from the solar.

Morgana slipped out of bed, reaching for her kirtle. First things first. She hurried to the table and lit the other seven tapers.

Her hunger ran deep at the sight and smell of food. She shoved her saddlebags aside and sat. Eagerly grabbing the loaf of bread, she broke it in two, then stuffed half with tangy cheese and slabs of delicious honey-cured ham.

A painted china pot steamed as she poured its herbal contents into a cup. Morgana concluded that the tray had been delivered only a short while before she woke up. She had absolutely no curiosity about who had brought all these things into the chamber while she slept. What mattered to her was appeasing her hunger.

Until her belly was filled, she couldn't concentrate on other things. Like where Hugh O'Neill had gone and when he would come back.

She took clean stockings from her saddlebags and checked her boots. They were thoroughly dry now on the inside, for which she said a quick prayer of thanks.

The trunk provided Morgana with an adequate assortment of clothing, replacing the baggage lost in her hasty flight from Benburg. It contained everything she needed: combs, kirtles, petticoats, stockings, richly woven surcoats, overskirts, lawn chemises and bodices, and several very finely embroidered stomachers.

Morgana closed the door for privacy as she washed and dressed. She tamed her hair into a neat chignon fastened by a gossamer net. Decently dressed for the first time since she'd arrived at Dungannon Castle, Morgana decided the time had come to explore it.

She tiptoed to the door, opened it and looked out, investigating this newfound freedom.

She saw no one on the landing or the stairwell, though she heard voices coming from below. That decided the course of her inspection. She lifted her hems and carefully made her way up the winding, dark staircase.

There was no doorway to the uppermost room. The stairwell simply opened into a massive round loft some twenty feet in diameter, filled with brilliant sunlight.

Morgana exhaled in surprise. All sorts of curious contraptions, tables, shelves, furnaces and materials crowded the sunny room. The oddest of all was a huge cylinder of polished brass. It was as tall and as big around as a fully grown man. It appeared to be perfectly balanced in a peculiar angle by a metallic construction of wheels and bars and puzzling belts and pulleys.

She thought at first she'd entered a stillroom for making whiskey, but the airy chamber lacked all the telltale scents of liquor preparation.

Drawing closer to the brass contraption, Morgana saw that a smaller cylinder rose from the first and passed clear through the slate roof. Numerous open skylights in the roof proved the cylinder jutted up like a tilted chimney several feet beyond the roofing. Some sort of chair had been suspended off the floor beneath the contraption, in an odd upside-down position.

"How very strange," Morgana murmured. Her fingers touched the ring of fitted brass where the larger tube encased the smaller. She dropped to her knees to examine more closely the upside-down chair. Bending her head to see the bottom, Morgana spied a very small tube protruding like a teat on a cow's udder. A ring of ivory fitted over that.

"I call it a stellar octascope," intoned a voice as bland as a Jesuit's and sober as a judge's. Hugh O'Neill stepped out from between facing rows of tall shelves jam-packed with more oddities and curios.

Startled, Morgana clutched her heart. Her alarm eased the moment she recognized the speaker was Hugh. "My lord, you frightened me. I didn't know anyone was up here. What is a stellar octascope?"

"A fixed tube through which I may examine the same portion of the sky each sunrise." Hugh sauntered into the light carrying a small wooden box with glass circles packed in excelsior.

Morgana frowned at the odd little pieces of glass she saw in the box and shook her head. She hadn't wanted to confront Hugh O'Neill until she found out what condition her horse was in. So that she could tell him exactly how soon she expected to depart from Dungannon Castle. Now she had no point from which to bargain—or dictate.

"Come here." Hugh set the wooden box on his cluttered worktable, motioning to Morgana. "Showing you what a looking glass is is easier than trying to describe it."

Morgana did not care much for the dark expression she perceived on his face. Perhaps he didn't like having intruders enter this chamber. And she felt very much like an intruder.

She gave one last look at the odd mechanism, and made up her mind to be strong. She squared her shoulders, certain that doing so would enable her to withstand any demands he put to her. She came to his table, not knowing what to look at first. So many odd things were spread across it: feathers, glass bottles, metal mechanisms, flasks and tubes, a mortar and pestle, and small piles of chemicals laid out on bindles of brittle white paper.

All at once it came to her that this tower room was very like her grandfather's study at Maynooth, before the whole castle had been razed. Was Hugh O'Neill a warlock? She looked for a pentagram and a crystal ball and found none.

He'd picked up what Morgana thought was a hand mirror. Then she saw that it had no silvered back. It was clear glass, encased in a carved wooden frame. She'd gotten close enough that Hugh O'Neill only had to reach out his hand to draw her closer to him—which he did, apparently without thinking.

Hugh drew her over to the scope. "I am studying the rising of the sun and the planets in the sky. This octascope merely allows me to examine the same section of sky each time I come up here. Much as the seafarer uses scopes to look for land in the distance. Come up on the roof and I'll show you what I mean."

Hugh retained hold of her hand, leading her up the wooden steps to the roof of the tower. He kept numerous scopes set up there, but to begin with he took out his pocket scope and put that in Morgana's hand. "See that oak tree on the side of the hill?"

"Yes." Morgana moved back from the edge of the turret. Below was a lake of shimmering water, and she didn't like looking down at that at all.

"Good. Look through here until you find the tree, then adjust the tubes by turning them gently until you bring the tree into clear focus. When the scope is focused, there should not be any blurred edges. That's right. Make the separate tubes smaller or longer, whichever your eyes need to see it clearly."

"I see it!" Morgana had some idea of how to work that instrument. Grace O'Malley had one very similar to it. In just a moment, Morgana had a solid fix on the distant oak. "This brings it much closer, doesn't it?"

"Aye," Hugh agreed. Again his hand closed over Morgana's, and he led her to a stationary scope at least four times the size of the hand-held device. He sat down on the wooden seat below it and drew Morgana onto his lap. Turning the scope toward the oak tree, he focused it to his eye, then leaned back and invited Morgana to look.

Very conscious of where she was sitting, Morgana tried to keep her bottom as still as possible. But with Hugh's arm circling her waist and his cheek flush against hers as he adjusted the scope, she couldn't help remembering what had transpired between them during the night.

"Here, look now. I've got it focused just right." Hugh drew back his head, yielding the eyepiece to Morgana.

"Oh! That's impressive," Morgana declared. "Why, the leaves are so close, I can see the veins on each leaf, and the bark on the trunk of the tree."

"So you can." Hugh inhaled deeply of the clean scent of soap clinging to her hair. In bright sun, her hair was the color of flames. His fingers twitched to tug the dark netting loose and let those magnificent tresses fall into his hands.

"This is incredible!" Morgana said excitedly. "It almost looks like I could reach right out and pluck the baby acorns off the tree! Amazing." She swung around on Hugh's lap, looking at his face. "And the really big one inside? What will that do? Put things a mile away right in front of my face?"

Hugh smiled, pleased by her reaction, but to answer her he had to shake his head. "No, it won't do that. It's for looking at the stars. Do you know about astronomy?"

Morgana laughed, her back resting easily against Hugh's chest. "What I know about the stars in the sky could be put into a thimble. I can locate the North Star, but I couldn't navigate my way anywhere without the sun rising and setting in the same places every day."

"It doesn't, though." Hugh corrected her, pointing out to her the scope's undercarriage. "By tracking where the sun rises every day, I can prove that the earth is circling the sun just like Copernicus did."

"Why would you want to do that?" Morgana couldn't help asking. To her practical mind, such study seemed frivolous.

"Well, for one reason," Hugh said gravely, "keeping track of the movement of objects in the sky allows me to predict with certainty when celestial events will happen."

"Like what?" Morgana laughed again. "The second coming of Christ?"

"No." Hugh solemnly shook his head. "Solar or lunar eclipses and the rising and setting of certain stars, the passage of comets and arrival of meteor showers."

Morgana was well educated, but he might as well have been speaking Greek, for she understood less than half of what Hugh said. "I think it would be ever so much more useful to be able to predict tomorrow's weather."

"Tomorrow's weather is easy to predict, my lady. The sun will shine all day, and the night will be crisp, cool and clear. The following day will be wet and damp and miserable again."

"And how is it that you know that?"

Hugh raised his arm and pointed to the southern horizon, where the tops of yesterday's slow moving storm could still be seen in the far distance. "That has been the pattern of the weather for the past month. Two to three days fair, then more wind and rain swoops down from the sea. Tomorrow, you will have good sun for your journey to Dunluce. If we ride hard, we'll make good time and be at Mac Donnell's demesne before the next storm breaks."

Morgana's eyes were very solemn and intense, studying his face. "Are you going to escort me?"

"Of course." Hugh kept his expression blank. He knew her purposes now, but she had no reason to confide in him, unless she trusted him. It was quite obvious that she didn't.

"Well." Morgana got to her feet, her hands busily dusting her skirt, though there was nothing on the cloth that needed brushing away. "That is wonderful news. I don't quite know how to thank you."

"You don't need to express any gratitude for common courtesy. We Irish always open our homes to travelers and pilgrims. That is a fundamental Celtic trait."

Morgana nodded, thinking that her home had once been as gracious and as open to travelers as his. Now she had no home at all. She felt bad that she'd never be able to reciprocate in kind.

Hugh adjusted the scope, turning it north, toward Slieve Gallion's purple peak. "Would you like to see the road we'll be traveling? Tullaghoge is in the next glen, but with this scope it is possible to see the high cross at Maghera."

"You can see from here to the high cross at Maghera?" Morgana asked in an astonished voice. Landsdowne Abbey was an hour's ride east of Maghera. "How far away is that?"

"Hmm..." Hugh considered the distance as he adjusted knobs to bring that Celtic cross into clear view. He didn't think it important to mention that only on the clearest days, like this one, was such a sighting possible. Today Hugh's scopes could see fifty miles or better.

Once the scope was adjusted, he relinquished his seat to Morgana. It wasn't right that he continued to treat her as familiarly as he had during the night. Her status as a religious troubled him greatly. It seemed natural to want to hold her and touch her. He refused to think of what had passed between them last night as a sin.

Loghran would tell him otherwise, and Morgana's confessor would surely tell her the same. Hugh did not intend to let his emotions get away from him again. She would be perfectly safe in his care on the journey to Dunluce.

"Goodness, I see it," Morgana whispered.

She was obviously awed by the distant sight of the sacred high cross, Hugh thought. St. Patrick had converted the kings of Ulster there, and together the kings had built the cross in Patrick's honor after his passing, commemorating the day of their baptism.

"It's just the tiniest speck in the distant hills, but I can see the cross, and the stele beneath it." Morgana's whisper rose to outright praise. "I'm impressed, Hugh O'Neill. This is a wonderful tool!"

Morgana stole a glimpse of Hugh's solemn face. He was so distant, so very formal and reserved, completely lacking the passion he'd exhibited the night before.

"Have I done something wrong?" she asked.

"What makes you ask that?"

Morgana took a deep breath. A gentle wind played havoc with Hugh's long black hair, ruffling it over his brow and his cheek. And the day's bright sun gave proof that his beard was red, even though he kept it cleanly shaved. That told her

he was a man of deep contrasts, extremes and possibly op-
posites.

"I'm not certain what makes me ask that." Morgana
made an effort to explain her question. "I seem to sense that
you are distancing yourself from me. Am I keeping you
from something important?"

"Not at all." Hugh stroked the hair out of his eyes and
turned so that the wind was in his face and not behind him.
"My time is my own. When the sun goes down, we are expected to attend supper in the hall. Now that you've had the
chance to recover somewhat from your adventure, I must
present you properly to my uncle and my sisters. You
needn't worry that you'll be the focus of censure. I made
certain no one knows about—" he paused just long enough
for Morgana to wonder why "—about last night."

She made no effort to hide the deep breath she needed to
take before launching into discussing that topic. "I con-
clude you have some regrets, then?"

"I didn't say that," Hugh said very quickly. "And you
shouldn't, either. What happened happened, and can't be
undone. There's no good to be accomplished from flaying
ourselves and wearing hair shirts for a natural sin. Even in
your state—"

"What state is that?" Morgana interrupted him deliberately. "You haven't been thinking you forced me, I hope.
Don't you think I made a conscious choice at the time?"

"Did you?" Hugh's brow lowered.

"Yes, Hugh O'Neill, I did make a choice. After what you
witnessed yesterday, you should realize that I would not let
any man take me unless I wanted him, as well."

Morgana's frankly spoken words put him back two full
paces. He regarded her more soberly than ever. "Forgive
me, I am not used to ladies speaking bluntly about matters
regarding bedding. I certainly didn't expect to hear that
from a . . . a . . ."

Again his words halted, as though he'd just realized what
he was saying and clamped a vise on his tongue.

"A what?" Morgana asked as she rose to her feet. She put a hand out to steady herself. Standing caused her to see the shimmering sunset glazing the lake. That touched off her sense of vertigo.

"A whore?" Morgana asked, putting her own words to what he wouldn't say. "If that's what you think I really am, I shouldn't think plain speaking about intercourse would cause you to color to the roots of your hair."

"I am most certainly not!" Hugh emphatically denied his outright and obvious blush. "No one would dare think of a novitiate as a whore, and I resent that accusation. As I tried to explain earlier, there is no sense trying to put a hair shirt of guilt on either of us for what happened. It just did. I'm certain your confessor will find some means to absolve you of whatever sin you care to call it. Rest assured, in my eyes you are most certainly not a whore. That you even say that is blasphemy to my ears."

"Novitiate? Confessor? Blasphemy?" Morgana's voice rose somewhat, for she was more confused than ever after his very strange dissertation. "You've got that wrong, if you think I am in need of a confessor for anything. Do you realize I killed a man yesterday?"

"It was self-defense," Hugh argued. "That's not the same thing as murder."

"Really?" Morgana countered. "Had I had my way on the riverbank, I'd have murdered five more without so much as a dram of remorse. They deserved to die. My little brother, an angel only six winters old, was poisoned by one of Kelly's bastards. They cut down eight men before my eyes at Benburg, then turned on me. It was my life or theirs."

"That proves it isn't murder," Hugh reasoned. "You needn't worry about losing your state of grace."

"Grace!" Morgana laughed, pressed to say more than she knew she should by the raging emotions calling for revenge that he set loose within her. "Know you this, sir—the very last thing I seek on this earth is a confessor to listen to my sins. I was damned to an eternity in hell long before last night, Hugh O'Neill.''

"This is upsetting you." Hugh took hold of her arm, drawing her toward the stairs leading back into his loft.

Any other time, Morgana would have stood her ground and argued there, but the high tower gave her vertigo and the shimmering water made her nauseous.

"I'm not a whore and I'm not a witch!" she declared ferociously, as if saying that out loud denied the terms completely.

"No one here has said you were," Hugh snapped in retaliation. "I refuse to listen to you disparage yourself with such unseemly terms. Do so again, and I'll be pressed to do something about it. Is that clear?"

Hugh felt her hand trembling where it clamped on his forearm. As they went below, he studied her grimly set profile and worried that he'd caused her more grief. Her face was now as pale as candle wax.

"Have you eaten?" he asked concerned. He led her to his worktable and brought a stool to seat her.

Morgana didn't argue as she sank onto the stool. Her head was doing things again. The circular room around her seemed to spin on a separate axis. "Yes, I ate."

Hugh cast a glance over the cluttered table, looking for the bowl of fruit Mrs. Carrick had brought him that morning. A sampling of last winter's apples was all the fruit available this early in the season. He took up one, and cut the fruit in half with Morgana's golden dagger, examining it for spoilage before offering Morgana a crisp, peeled slice.

As she chewed on that, he brought another stool to the table and sat, clearing his machines out of their way. When he moved the last, an arbalest, he uncovered her wooden rosary and crucifix. Deliberately ignoring those objects, Hugh cut another slice from the apple and handed it to her.

"You know, I did tell you that I have the rolls from all the monasteries and abbeys in Ireland."

The apple was on the edge of being overripe, grainy in texture and bland in taste. Morgana swallowed it, then reached across the table and pulled the rosary to her. "How did you acquire this? It looks just like the one in my saddle-bags."

"That's because it is from your saddlebags, Morgana Fitzgerald."

"You went through my things?"

That accusation stung. Hugh cut the remainder of the apple into quarters, then turned the blade toward her, exposing the ancient ogham writing on it. "This knife is the reason I looked inside your bags. I shouldn't think that would come as such a surprise to you. O'Neills are capable of reading ogham and divining the meaning of crests and symbols. This knife was made for Gerait Og Fitzgerald, the ninth earl of Kildare."

"And it belongs to me!" That response was delivered with considerable heat.

"I have not questioned that, my lady. Be assured that when the time is right, it will be returned to you. I do find my curiosity deeply aroused by an Arroasian nun traveling Ireland armed to the teeth and prepared to die defending herself. The nuns who lived at Saint Mary de Hogges's Abbey were reportedly a penitent order, consecrated to vows of silence and poverty. In my understanding, their mission is committed to unbroken prayer and atonement for the sins of the entire world."

"You've got that right." Morgana snapped. "What's your point?"

Exasperated, Hugh thundered, "Aren't you an Arroasian?"

"No. I am most certainly not. When the deeds to my dower properties failed to arrive, they tossed me to the wolves. Likewise, my brothers were expelled from the good sisters' charitable orphanage, on the grounds that I was available to care for them."

Hugh said nothing for a long while, as he carefully considered her words. It relieved him on one hand, and troubled him deeply on the other. He had to know for certain her exact status with the church. That was most important to him.

"Are you telling me you did not take your final vows?"

"Hugh, surely you know the general rule of the orders. A woman, even one who is a propertied widow, must be twenty-one years of age before she can profess her final vows."

Her words rocked Hugh to the bottom of his soul. He reeled from them, staggering with the import of everything she'd just said.

"Are you telling me you are also a widow?"

The words had already been spoken. Morgana had no chance to retract them. "Can we deal with one question at a time? I asked mine first."

"Yes." Hugh felt like swearing. "I am aware of the general rules of most orders. There are exceptions made, but not without special dispensation from the pope. But you told me last night that you are twenty-two years of age."

"Now, this year I am twenty-two, sir. I was expelled from all hope of sanctuary when I was ten-and-seven."

"Good heavens!" Hugh exclaimed, elated by that word in one way and distressed in another. "Where have you been living for the past four years, then? Surely you have not been wandering the island with two young boys, trying to evade English capture."

Morgana inhaled deeply. Would it help Sean's cause to answer that question honestly? She didn't think so. Hugh O'Neill wouldn't like any answer she gave him. "Suffice it to say I have good friends in both high and low places. I have learned to survive, sir. Nothing else matters in this life."

"Answer me this—did you enter the convent after your husband's death?"

Morgana glared at him, refusing to answer that question by remaining silent. She didn't like to think of the sad and agonizing months of her short-lived marriage. It was too painful.

Hugh lifted his hand in a gesture that as much as said he was brushing her willfulness aside. He reached across the cluttered table for a pack of scrolls. "You don't need to answer that question. If you prefer, I shall look it up for myself."

"His name was Gregory O'Malley."

"The privateer?" Hugh barked, stunned. "Grace O'Malley's legendary twin brother was your husband?"

Morgana swallowed hard. She'd not fall apart or break down now, just because this bastard Ulsterman was pushing too close to her truths. "Aye, he was a good man, and I'll not hear anything bad said about him. Be warned, O'Neill."

Talking ill of a dead man was the last thing on Hugh's mind. Especially not a dead man as renowned and revered as Captain Greg O'Malley. Had O'Malley lived, Drake would have lost his admiral's rank by now. He took a deep breath to calm himself as he cast the scrolls back onto the clutter.

"How did you come to know James Kelly?"

On safer ground, Morgana managed a civil answer. "One cannot live in Ireland and not know James Kelly. He has insinuated himself everywhere, and made himself indispensable to both Lord Grey and Lord Sidney."

"Lord Grey is responsible for closing the last of the Pale's hallowed abbeys," Hugh acknowledged, "Sidney for managing the government."

"Yes," Morgana replied. "But James Kelly is ever eager for advancement. When I first heard how they stripped everything of value from the abbey, it seemed like retribution from a just God to me. I repented that wickedness. The sisters didn't deserve being brutally raped by Grey's army.

Later I learned Lord Grey's true purpose, and why his army behaved so brutally.''

"Are you implying they were after you?" Hugh didn't follow her reasoning. "How do you figure that?"

"Yes. The English also had the convent's roll, and access to the Christian names of all the nuns living within its confines. They specifically wanted James Fitzgerald's eldest daughter. I think that was the only time in my life that luck has actually been on my side. No one on earth knew that I had found a safe haven on Clare Island save Grace O'Malley.''

"Clare Island," Hugh murmured as he reached across the table and secured another apple from the basket. He began to peel it, turning the apple round and round against her grandfather's blade. "That's west, in Connaught, is it not?"

"Yes." Morgana also reached across the table, but what had caught her interest was a miniature brass cannon. She rolled it toward her on the wooden wheels affixed to its cart.

The cannon was as long as her forearm and as thick around as a musket barrel. It was complete right down to a tiny wick sticking up from its flash box. She lifted it to her nose and sniffed, inhaling the scent of smoke, saltpeter and gunpowder. "Does this work?"

"Aye." Hugh severed a portion of the peeled apple, offering it to Morgana. She refused it with a shake of her head, so he ate it. "It's a deadly toy, when packed right."

"How curious." Morgana rolled the cannon aside and brought another machine from the clutter. "This looks positively diabolic. Grace O'Malley has something just like it. How do you use it?"

"It's called a pistol. It works on the same principle as a musket. You pack it with shot pellets, powder and ignite the wick in the flash pan. Trouble is it's likely to blow one's hand or head off before it hurts anything else. I'd feel much better if you would put it down carefully and not touch it again."

Morgana had no problem following that request. Muskets scared the devil out of her.

"So you are intimately acquainted with Grace O'Malley, are you?" Hugh asked.

"We're still friends," Morgana admitted nonchalantly.

"How long were you married to her brother?"

"Why do you ask?"

"Surely you know it's no secret Drake is out to capture her. Warrants are posted in every port for her arrest for piracy."

"Yes, it makes it rather hard for her to carry on the family trade now, I daresay." Morgana folded her hands on the empty table space before her. "But I doubt Francis Drake will ever take her in. She's a better sailor than he is."

"You know that from experience?"

"Aye, to my sorrow I do. I'm no sailor, because water terrifies me deeply, but she can outsail Drake blindfolded."

Hugh laughed deeply, amused by that candid observation. "The great Captain Drake would take exception if he heard you say that to his face."

"I harbor little interest in coming face-to-face with Drake," Morgana said. "So he's safe from my opinions. Do you know Grace? Have you met her?"

"Aye, once, when she accompanied Greg to London to receive his letters of marque from the queen," Hugh replied.

"My, my, you've seen and done everything, haven't you? I wouldn't have imagined you'd ever step foot out of Tyrone. Not after what they did to Shane."

Hugh bit into the apple, savoring the last morsels of the juicy core before casting it away. "I was already in London when Shane was murdered. I'd been living there for eight years, as a page to the queen, then a squire to Sir Raleigh. You should be familiar with fostering. It's a common enough practice here and in England."

His admission made Morgana look at him intensely. "How old were you when you went to England as a page?"

"Not quite ten." Hugh took a cloth from the table and wiped his hands, then carefully cleaned Gerait Og's blade. He set the knife down on his opposite side, well away from the reach of Morgana's hands.

"I'm not going to stab you," she told him.

"Don't think that I would allow you to do such a foolish thing. It doesn't bear speaking about."

"So." Morgana retreated to their earlier topic, the matter of her knife tabled for the moment. "You were a page to the queen, and a squire. Did you complete the standard training in arms and become a full-fledged knight, sworn and dedicated to Her Majesty, Elizabeth?"

"I did," Hugh affirmed with a solemn nod of his head.

"I'll bet that made your uncle Shane happy."

"Actually, Shane would not have cared one way or the other, though I was confirmed as the earl of Tyrone while he was still alive and could make note of it. You see, English titles make little impression on the people of Ulster."

That tidbit stunned Morgana. "You're the earl of Tyrone, too?"

"Unfortunately, yes." Hugh sighed deeply. He glanced toward the open skylights in the roof, then got up from his stool and began closing down each opening by cranking the gears controlling them with a long iron rod.

Morgana followed him to watch the lowering of a second skylight. A set of gears worked by a linkage of iron chain controlled the high in the ceiling devices. She shook her head, marveling at the curiosities. "I've never seen such a plethora of devices. Are you responsible for making all these things?"

"Guilty as charged." Hugh smiled at the rafters over his head, concentrating on working the mechanisms.

"What other conveniences have you got up here?" She wandered off a little distance, examining whatever came to hand. She put a hand out to a pipe with a spigot on it. A steady but slow drip of water came out of it and landed in a large tub set on the wooden floor. "I thought I'd stumbled across your whiskey still when I first looked in here. What's this do?"

"Och," Hugh said, and put the iron crank back on its holder on the wall. "That's water. I've got a cistern on the roof for collecting the rain. Saves having to run buckets up and down the stairs."

That wasn't exactly an original concept, Morgana knew. Most larger houses had some means of collecting rainwater, though she'd never seen any funneled into a device on the roof, because water weighed so much.

"My grandfather had a room like this in Maynooth, but it was in the dungeon. We weren't allowed to go down there when I was small. After he died, I went exploring, and got a terrible whipping for sticking my nose into things that I shouldn't."

"Rightly so," Hugh commented. "There's many things here that would be a danger to a child. I wouldn't want any children mucking about up here, which is why I chose the most inaccessible room to conduct my experiments in. I will admit that my first reaction to your appearance here was to shout at you to go away."

Morgana was only half listening to him, caught up as she was in the fascination of watching the steady drip, drip, drip, of the beads of water out the odd spigot.

As when she'd examined his big octascope, she tilted her head down to look inside the tube, trying to figure out what mechanism kept water from gushing out. Her fingers gave the knob a sound twist, and she was instantly washed with water all over her face. "Oh! Help! How do I stop it?"

Water splashed into the bottom of the tub as Morgana twisted the knob more to shut off the flow. Hugh's hand closed over hers, turning the cock across the pipe. "What's that saying about curiosity and cats?"

"You needn't laugh at me," Morgana said as she wiped her face off with her left hand.

"I'm not." Hugh chuckled. "Look here, Morgana. The cock is open, and the water flows when this bar is straight up and down with the pipe. It's closed, and water doesn't flow when it's horizontal, or across the pipe. Understand?''

"Yes," Morgana said, very aware of his large hand covering hers and his other hand resting on her shoulder as he gave his instructions. "Again I've stuck my nose where I shouldn't."

"A wet face seems punishment enough. You might consider asking me how things work before rushing ahead into who knows what, hmm?"

"Yes, milord," Morgana said, chagrined. "What I wanted to ask was why the water drips when it's shut off. Caskets of wine and ale don't drip. Couldn't cocks like that suit your purposes here?"

"No." Hugh shook his head. "There's too much water in the container on the roof. It blows out a stopcock that isn't screwed into place. However, I am working on perfecting the valve. A few pieces of leather have worked to stop the drip for a while, but it always comes back."

He brushed a drip off her chin, then kissed her wet mouth. "You taste very refreshing, Morgana Fitzgerald. Too bad we must go down to hall now. Otherwise, I'd be tempted to tarry a while in my feather bed with you."

"That's assuming I'm willing, correct?" Morgana asked.

"Are you?" Hugh inquired silkily.

Morgana wiggled her fingers out from under his. She shook her head a little bit. "Not if I must present myself shortly in the hall and deal with your sisters again. I fear they took a bad view of me the first time."

"Actually," Hugh drawled, following her back to the table, "they are very curious to meet you again, and asked me all sorts of questions about why you didn't come down to hall this morning. I kept them at bay with a recitation of your numerous injuries, which, I might add, do not seem to be impairing you any now."

"I've an ache or two that I haven't forgotten," Morgana admitted shyly. A blush ran up her throat and spread into her cheeks.

"Truly?" Now that he knew she wasn't a nun, Hugh felt much, much better inside. He found he had a very hard time keeping his hands off her, as if her body were silently screaming out to him, *Touch me, hold me, love me.* Testing his feelings, he took the napkin he'd laid aside in hand, folded it and lifted her chin to mop up her face. "You look beautiful wet, Morgana. I want to lick each droplet from your lashes, your brow, your cheeks."

Instead, he blotted the moisture away, and at the same time examined her closely for signs of injury that his father or his sisters might remark upon when they went to hall. The swollen and cut lip she'd arrived with had gone down appreciably. So, too, had the large knot on her jaw. In its place was a darkening bruise. Mrs. Carrick's ministering with the leeches had removed most of the discoloration around her right eye.

He tossed the cloth on the table and dropped his hands to her shoulders. "Tell me truthfully, Morgana—do you feel up to managing a hard ride at dawn tomorrow?"

"I'll manage it," Morgana assured him.

"Would you actually tell me if you were in any discomfort or pain?"

"Certes," Morgana lied.

One of Hugh's very dark brows hiked up in a bold arch, as if to question the truth in her words.

"Well, I would," Morgana insisted.

He said nothing to that, but his fingers tightened on her shoulders, turning her around so that he could examine the back of her head, neck and shoulders.

"We shall consider it a good thing in the coming days that I know better than to trust words spoken by all perverse Englishwomen. You are the worst liar I have ever met, Morgana Fitzgerald."

"And what makes you say that?" Morgana demanded in an outright challenge.

Hugh's arms circled her so that his hands could release the small bow tied in her chemise, exposed by the sweep of her boat-necked bodice. When Morgana started to bolt away from him, he caught her and held her still.

"Whist, woman, I'm not going to undress you. I simply want to see how the bruise on the back of your neck is coming along."

Hugh was glad she wasn't facing him when he drew the soft cloth down and exposed the terrible dark bruise marring the triangular rise of flesh from her shoulder into her long, elegant neck.

Mrs. Carrick should have leeched it, and had Hugh spied it in time, he would have ordered that done. It was too late to remedy now. The purplish mark would have to heal naturally. Touching it reminded him of the brute who had left the mark on her. Hugh set her chemise in place again, turned the young woman to face him and deftly retied the bow at her distinct collarbone.

"It must look awful, since your mouth is so grim."

"I am controlling my temper," Hugh replied tersely. "Seeing that mark makes me want to go to the dungeon and give James Kelly another sampling of the power of my fists."

"You can't do that when you told him to his face that you wouldn't lower yourself to strike him again."

Hugh solved that problem easily enough. "Then I shall order Kermit Blackbeard to beat him to a bloody pulp."

"Let's go and do that now," Morgana declared. "I want to watch."

"No, you will not," Hugh answered, without a moment's hesitation. "I may allow you to come to the stone of the O'Neills to give testimony against the cur when the gathering convenes, but I assure you, Morgana, you will not witness his punishment or his death."

That particular statement didn't satisfy Morgana's driving need for revenge. However, she wasn't going to engage in foolish arguments with Hugh O'Neill about what he would or would not allow her to do. She would do what she must do, always.

"I believe it would be appropriate for you to let your hair down from this net," Hugh said as he quickly dispensed with the few pins holding the netting secure. As her hair tumbled free onto his hands and her shoulders, he added a reason for that request. "It is not necessary that you display your wounds to the public eye. There will be ale and whiskey flowing in my hall this night, as well as many people with long-standing grudges against Kelly. It would serve no purpose to incite a mob. I want justice served so there will be no challenge to the clan's authority over its sons by our English overlords. Do you understand that, Morgana?"

"No," she admitted truthfully. "I want Kelly dead. Preferably by my filleting him from throat to groin with my own knife. That's what I want."

"Well, then, we are at cross purposes. I, too, want him dead. Only I want that life forfeit to written and incontestable law. Kelly is my kinsman, my brother under the ages-old law of the clans. The baron has the power of pit and gallows in all matters regarding people born of clan O'Neill. I have that power over all who live in Tir-Owen and Tir-Connail—in short, all of Ulster. That right supersedes English law.

"Kelly must go to trial and be judged by his peers. Nothing less is acceptable. So I ask you, as a favor to me, wear your hair down, so that it covers the marks he left on you. You will have your revenge in the end."

"You ask too much of me, Hugh O'Neill."

"Then you must forgive me, Morgana Fitzgerald of Kildare, for I must ask for nothing less than the best of you."

Morgana replied with firm conviction, "You haven't the right to ask me anything, Hugh O'Neill."

"Oh?" His eyes darkened with deliberate heat, reminding her that she'd already given her consent to anything he desired from her. "Is that the way you think to play this?"

Shouts came from below stairs. "My lord Hugh! My lord Hugh!" The thunderous tramp of boots on the steps accompanied the breathless heralding of trouble to come.

"My lord Hugh!" Rory O'Neill shouted as he burst into the loft. "James Kelly's caused a revolt in the gaol at Fort Tullaghoge! Shamus Fitz has been overpowered. Kelly and four other villains have escaped!"

Chapter Ten

After Hugh O'Neill departed in haste, Morgana thought better of going down to hall alone. She retired to Hugh's feather bed on the lower floor, prepared to content herself with whatever was left over on the table for her supper.

Mrs. Carrick had not forgotten that there were other guests to the house, and came shortly after sundown bearing a heavily laden tray. She didn't bat a single eyelash at finding Morgana resting in Lord Hugh's bed, which made Morgana wonder if that was commonplace.

"Oh, you shouldn't have troubled with me," Morgana protested as she got to her feet.

"Sure and I should be troubled. You're young Hugh's guest, milady. We couldn't let you starve up here in his drafty old tower." Mrs Carrick set the tray down and lighted the candles on the table beside it. "Hugh never meant to leave you stranded."

"I don't feel stranded," Morgana replied. If anything, she felt relieved that she hadn't had to present herself in the vast hall, where the evening's supper and entertainment were about to commence.

"Ah, well, but you are. O'Neill and his men are ever on the march somewhere. Come, sit you down, my lady. You need to build up your strength for tomorrow's journey. Young Hugh told me you are determined to go to Dunluce, come what may."

"I really haven't any choice in that, Mrs. Carrick."

"No, and I canna argue the wiseness of that, either. But at least you will have young Hugh and his kerns accompanying you, so you will make that journey safely." Mrs. Carrick uncovered her trays, and an appetizing aroma lifted to Morgana's nose, making her realize how hungry she'd become. "Though it is my opinion that it is too soon for you to travel at all. You've been through much, milady."

"Thank you," Morgana said graciously. "But again, Mrs. Carrick, I haven't any choice in the matter. I must be at Dunluce before May tenth."

"Humph!" Mrs. Carrick wasn't convinced. "That's the trouble with you young folk, you're always in such a hurry. You do not take the time to enjoy the moment."

That reminded Morgana of the delightful moments she'd spent in this room only the night before. Mrs. Carrick couldn't have been more wrong. For Morgana had enjoyed every minute she spent with Hugh O'Neill.

"Oh, and before I forget it, Brigit will be bringing you up hot water to wash, as well as your mended garments. We repaired and cleaned what we could. Such fine clothes shouldn't go to rags. Not much could be done for the skirts, but Hugh's told me he's provided you well with others."

"Thank you, Mrs. Carrick, that was very kind of you." Morgana said sincerely.

"'Twas the least we could do, milady."

When she'd eaten her fill, Morgana again had the luxury of soaking in a hot tub. She found the day's lack of exercise had allowed most of her muscles to tighten, thereby letting her know that yesterday had been a day filled with excesses of all kinds.

Content, she retired early, to be ready for an early departure the next morning.

Morgana Fitzgerald was sleeping soundly when Hugh O'Neill returned from a fruitless ride across Tyrone. The clockwork's iron hammered the hour of four. Hugh dropped his plaid to the floor and shivered the way a dog shakes water from its coat just before he crawled into bed.

Morgana stirred awake, recognizing the scent of the man drawing her into his encompassing arms. "Hugh, you're back," she said. "Did you catch him?"

"Nay." One gruffly spoken word told Morgana all was not well beyond the confines of Castle O'Neill. The impact of Hugh's body against hers told her more, that he was wet and cold, tired and exhausted, from a hard, futile ride. His damp brow dropped to her shoulder and lay there, as if he were seeking comfort.

Without a second thought, Morgana wrapped her arms around him. Her hands soothed the tired and knotted muscles at the back of his neck. She touched the sodden queue dripping cold water on his back.

"My lord!" Morgana exclaimed. "You're soaking wet!"

"I hadn't noticed, for I am fair burning for you, my lady."

Hugh's unshaven cheek nuzzled against her neck, and she felt the heat of his breath caressing the soft curves of her ear and the press of his nose against her temple. "Ah, Morgana, you smell so sweet and fresh."

"And you are as cold as marble, and wet, too." Morgana shivered where his damp chest glazed her breasts and belly, dampening the sheer lawn of her night rail.

"Blame the moat. I could not come to you smelling of horse and sweat." Hugh caught hold of a blanket at their feet and pulled it over his back. He shuddered deeply, then nestled down against her, seeking her heat as a ward against a cool spring morn. "I have been thinking long and hard, Morgana of Kildare."

"Oh?" Morgana murmured, adjusting her body to accommodate his. "Pray tell me what your thinking long and hard has led you to?"

"Kelly has escaped my justice, your revenge, and the retribution of clan O'Neill. The bastard is as slippery as an eel, though I believe he had help from within to make good this escape. He will make more trouble for you."

Morgana lifted an unconcerned shoulder. "The man has been the bane of my existence for the last year. I have always managed to outwit him. In truth, my lord, he's not as cunning as he would like us to believe."

"Maybe not." Hugh was willing to grant that much. "But he is as tenacious as a hound with the last bone from the feast between his teeth. He'll return with more men, now that he knows you are here."

"All the more reason for us to part company soonest," Morgana said plainly, giving no hint of the deep regret that caused her to feel.

Hugh lifted his head somewhat, so that he could use his sharp eyes to divine her features. The chamber remained trapped in the stygian darkness that precedes dawn. No waxing moon or fading hearth fire cast romantic light on Hugh's private bed. He sighed as he traced his forefinger down her profile, needing no light to confirm her quiet, solitary composure.

Morgana Fitzgerald's mettle had been tempered in the hot forge of the fugitive's life. Nothing on this earth that Hugh did would cause her strong will to break.

"Morgana, this is no game afoot here. You must tell me what it is Kelly truly wants of you. How else can I protect you?"

"You cannot protect me, Hugh O'Neill. No one can."

"Ah, Morgana, in that you are wrong." Hugh let a deep breath fill and expand his chest. His hips nestled against hers, their legs entwined on the rough linen sheeting. "You are perfectly safe here in my tower."

"Do you think I am a bird you can cage? I am not."

"I did not say that. Castle O'Neill is safe. The English cannot touch any of us here. Kelly knows you are traveling to Dunluce. I say we wait awhile, delay the journey, say a week or more. You need the time to recover."

"I don't have so much as a day to waste, Hugh O'Neill."

"Ah, but you are a maddening, iron-mouthed woman, unbroken to the bit. What cannot wait a day or a week? Whose life depends upon this journey of yours?"

Morgana put her hands to his chest and pushed him away. The next earl of Kildare's destiny hung on her journey. "The sun will be rising anon. I must go."

The bed shifted as she climbed out of it. So resolute was her tone and her mood that Hugh thought she would storm out the unlocked door and depart without him. "Morgana, I have just ridden ten leagues through the night and back. Come, stay with me a while longer, till the sun rises. I will not allow you to leave Castle O'Neill without me."

"You cannot stop me by your command. I am a free woman, Hugh O'Neill, and you have no cause to detain me or delay me," she argued.

"I am not commanding you to come to bed and let me sleep an hour or two. I am asking you to let me rest. Is that so unreasonable that you must fly into the night?"

He heard her sigh deeply, troubled and uncertain, as if delaying her journey were more dangerous than running headlong into danger.

"You are a bold, bad man," she whispered.

Taken aback, Hugh said, "Why say you that?"

"You ridicule my urgency."

"Then explain it to me, or else let me sleep, woman. The sun will not rise for another two hours. Come, Morgana. This is a foolish argument. Get you back into bed. A quiet sleep in my arms will not harm you."

He couldn't have been further from the truth. Did she get back into that bed with him, she might never have the strength to leave it.

Morgana put down the flint and iron she'd taken up to light the candles. Her body trembled and quaked, chilled by the cold that had seeped in with the night. She crossed her arms, compressing the dampness he'd transferred to her night rail against her breasts, in a futile effort to warm herself. She recognized a new weakness inside her, a crack in her armor through which she had allowed Hugh O'Neill to wedge a toehold in her soul.

It would be far better for the both of them if she left him now and went on her own. Quietly, so as not to alert him to her intentions, Morgana gathered up her saddle packs, her clothes and her boots. Then she slipped out the open door and tiptoed up to the loft to dress.

Hugh unlaced his fingers from behind his head and sat up. He was tired, yes, but not exhausted. Odds were he'd not sleep a wink even if the woman did come back to bed and be reasonable. He'd want to finish what he'd started, and bed her thoroughly. That would only delay their departure.

So he, too, climbed out of bed. His toes found the plaid he'd dropped, and his fingers fumbled over the stacks on the Welsh dresser until he found a clean sark, hose, trews and a belt. As the morning was crisp and cool, he added a quilted doublet to warm his chest. He bumped into the new table and bench added to his furnishings for her comfort and sat to lace up his cross garters and boots.

Finished, he caught up his sword belt and scabbards and stood in the bartizan stairwell, fastening the clanking metal armaments to his hips, waiting for her to descend the steps from his loft. He did not have to wait long before the sounds of wools and linen swishing from the landing above informed him of her descent.

Morgana had lighted a torch, wisely choosing not to try to manage the stairs without light. She came round the curve and stopped several steps above Hugh when she spied him standing on the landing, blocking her way.

"My lord," she whispered.

"Don't 'my lord' me, you willful wench. I'm up. We'll go now." He turned to a closed door on his left and hammered his fist on the wood, hollering, "O'Toole, *à moi!* We ride to Dunluce!"

Beyond the oak door, a muffled voice returned sleepily, "Christ and him crucified, are ye daft, man? We just went to bed!"

"Rise, you lazy bounder, and fetch the men. Meet me no farther north than Tullaghoge."

That said, Hugh O'Neill reached up and took Morgana's heavy saddle packs from her shoulder. He gestured for her to take the lead on the stairs, since she was carrying the torch. Morgana smiled as she brushed past him, holding up her hems so that her step was sure. "Thank you, my lord."

Hugh grunted out of sorts and followed, unwilling to say anything civil to that.

The pink glow of sunrise was just glazing the hills and the cloudless sky as Hugh and Morgana rode out the north gate of Castle O'Neill's village. Ariel was in fine mettle, restless and ready to run, and skittish of the dun stallion, Boru, that Hugh rode.

Hugh tossed Morgana a half loaf of rye bread as they galloped up the hills toward distant Slieve Gallion. "Best save some of that. I can't say when I'll have more to offer you."

Morgana held back a chuckle over his snappish temper and secured the bread inside a tuck in her Irish mantle. She put her heels to Ariel's sides and let the mare set her own pace following the stallion.

A heavy mist clung to the low spots outside the township's walls and blanketed the moat, obliterating the castle on the crannog from Morgana's sight. Soon it would rise. Morgana felt confident the fog would linger on through the early morning. She couldn't think of a better way to escape her worries for Sean's safety than to be taking action, and to have that action obliterated from common sight by thick and encroaching fog.

Content for the first time in days, she followed Hugh O'Neill north through Tyrone, certain that this time, nothing untoward would impede her path.

They rested the horses at noon at a little wood on a rise just to the north of the high cross of Maghera. True to Hugh's orders, his kerns had caught up with them before they skirted round the village of Tullaghoge. Rory and Brian O'Neill had been the last to catch up, bringing with them a packhorse loaded with provisions for the road.

Morgana dismounted and walked the kinks out of her legs. She let the men take their privacy first, in the small wood, while she walked Ariel a bit to cool her down.

"We've made good time," Hugh said, and fell into step beside her, his large shadow looming over hers as she circled the wood.

"How much farther is Dunluce?" Morgana asked him.

"Another ten leagues, easily, due north." Raising his right hand, he pointed to a nearby mountain peak. "That's Carntogher, the last peak of the Sperrin Mountains. The land levels out somewhat between here and the coast. It's not as hilly or as heavily wooded. The last leg becomes so rockbound, it wears out the seat of your trews and the iron shoes of your horse."

"For someone who's been away for such a long time, you're amazingly familiar with your land," Morgana observed.

"I've spent a lot of time riding, familiarizing myself with old memories. Truth be told, mistress, it feels good to be home."

Hugh grinned so endearingly, it made Morgana's heart throb. He was so open and appealing that it hurt to know she could never stay with him. Not that he'd asked.

No, aside from that one mention of her being his leman, immediately after they made love, he'd not brought up the subject of her remaining at Castle O'Neill again.

Which was fine, since she couldn't stay, for now she cared about what became of Hugh O'Neill. Any soul so unlucky as to be linked to a Fitzgerald soon found himself in the unenviable position of having legions of enemies.

"You're very quiet, lady." Hugh took Ariel's reins from Morgana's hands. "Here's a good place for the mare to graze."

He pointed to a shady spot under a bower of pines, where the grasses and ferns flourished. Morgana picked a moss-covered stone in the shade of the pines as a place to rest and have some privacy from his kerns. She leaned on the rock and calmly folded her gloved hands in her lap.

"Hugh..." She chose her words with care, not wanting to alert him to anything being different, now that they'd come this far. "I think the time has come for you to give me back my knife. One never knows what might be in the woods, ready to take a bite out of a lady's exposed backside."

The grin on his face enlarged appreciably as he turned around from tying up Ariel. "My lady, if you're going to expose your derrière, perhaps I'd best stay close by to enjoy the performance."

"You most certainly will not," Morgana said primly. He came to her with open hands, grasping her shoulders to draw her to his chest.

"Och, Morgana, but you're a temptress of the worst sort. Do you know how much I want to kiss you and bed you, right here in this shady bower?"

She didn't resist the pull of his hands, and she lifted her face to meet his lips. One more kiss of sweet remembrance would be a secret treasure to comfort her in the uncertain future. One more taste of his lips couldn't hurt, if it provided a lifetime of comfort for the rest of her accursed days.

His hands tightened on her back, lifting her against the sun-warmed heat of his quilted doublet. Morgana wound her fingers into his hair and kissed him deeply, taking a last loving taste of the happiness and fulfillment she could never have permanently.

For the duration of his kiss, Hugh's hands roamed over her body, as familiar to her as his face had become in the past days and nights. Then he gripped her shoulders fiercely and set her back from him, at arm's length. He scowled darkly.

"Look at the callow fool I've become! Forgive me, I know no sense of decorum when I'm near you, my lady. From the moment the sun broke through the fog, all I've thought about is spreading your flaming hair on God's green grass and making love to you until you cry out my name again. Don't be long, Morgana. I can't bear to have you out of my sight."

He abruptly pulled her knife from his waist and put it in her hands. Then he turned and strode down the rocky rise to where Loghran O'Toole, Kermit Blackbeard and Shamus Fitz lounged beneath a fragrant, blooming hawthorn.

Morgana stood watching Hugh O'Neill's upright back as he walked away. Another spell of her grandfather's came to mind— *By oak, ash and thorn, the fairy's magic is born.* That chant she had learned in her cradle. Wych elms, rowans, oaks and hawthorns were potent, magical trees.

Gerait Og had told her the Tuatha de Danann, Ireland's mystical people of yore, lived on in such magical places. The ancient forces slumbered in the soil beneath the trees, waiting to be enchanted back to life. One day soon, the old man had told her, they would come back, when all the petty wars between the clans ended and all Ireland united under one high king—the *ri ruirech Eirinn.*

Though jaded by all that had happened to her, Morgana believed in her grandfather's truths. It would happen someday, and lucky would be the men and women of Ireland who lived to see their true king crowned on the hill of Tara. To that end, she must give her all to see that her own line continued into the future. There must always be Fitzgeralds in Ireland. Sean was their future.

As Hugh O'Neill sat down to rest beside his companions, Morgana began picking out the freshly gathered cockleburs caught up in Ariel's tail. She knelt beside her horse's hooves and plucked each precious little herb from Ariel's feathery fetlocks.

It was only a mere handful, but the littlest amount of a powerful herb was more than enough to cast a powerful spell.

Visualizing all the kerns and Hugh sleeping, Morgana ambled to the highest point of the rise. There she knelt and dug a small hollow in the rich, damp earth. As she blew the cockleburs off her hand into the tiny pit, she chanted, "Agrimony, agrimony, keep safe watch over the men on this hill while they sleep."

She covered the cockleburs with the soil she'd loosened and got to her feet, brushing the damp earth from her hands.

Smiling at the ease with which any spell could be cast, Morgana strolled into the woods to take care of her business there. When she emerged from the wood, three of the seven men were nodding against the support of as many trees.

Hugh's eyes were as heavy-lidded as the rest's, but he'd forced himself to stay awake till he spied Morgana returning from her sojourn into the woods. He patted the earth beside him, motioning for her to sit with him.

Morgana knelt just to the side of him and put her hands to his broad shoulders, dusting off the hawthorn blossoms that had fluttered on the easy breeze to his shoulders and snared in his head. "You are dusted with bread-and-cheese blossoms," she said softly, so as not to disturb the dozing kerns.

Hugh plucked one blossom from his thigh, where it had fallen at the stroke of her hand. "'Tis called quick or Mayflowers hereabouts. Hawthorn, that most magical of herbs, symbolic of the planet Mars, guarantor of fertility, chastity and constancy."

He crushed the blossom between his fingers and thumbs and rubbed its tangy, aromatic juice across her brow. "You are mine forever, Morgana Fitzgerald, anointed thus under the spell of the hawthorn tree."

"You know about magical herbs?" Morgana asked, sitting back on her heels, shaken by the blithely spoken spell he'd just cast.

"I haven't become a devotee of the art, but I know a thing or two about what helps one to get along in this troublesome world." He yawned deeply and pointed down the hillside, to the little river winding through the valley. "Take those willows on the bank of the river. An infusion made with the supple bark of a willow can cure a serious fever."

His hand dropped from his upraised knee to pick a violet from a small clump of weeds flourishing under the shade of the hawthorn trees. "And if you pick the first violet of the spring, your dearest wish will be granted."

Morgana looked around them. Clumps of violets rioted out of every loamy crag in the rocky earth. "I don't think you've picked the first violet of this spring, my lord."

"Ah, but how do you know that I haven't done so already, and made my wish, weeks ago, when the blooms first appeared?" Hugh posed his tantalizing question with a smile and twirled the dainty blue flower between his fingers.

Morgana set her hands to massaging the taut muscles of his shoulders through the weight of his doublet. "I don't," she said, responding to his smile with one of her own. "Did you?"

Hugh turned his head so that he could see her face as he tucked the blue flower into her crown of fiery braids. "Perhaps I did. I seem to have everything a man could ever want at hand."

"Save a good night's sleep," Morgana teased gently, diverting his attention with a look around at his sleepy kerns.

"None of us would be so tired if you had half the sense God gave the sparrows." Hugh chided her softly, testing her mettle. To his mind, the highest mark of a man and a woman's breeding showed in how they behaved in a quarrel.

"Oh, so it's my fault you Irish are dropping in the traces, is it?" Morgana laughed ever so softly. "Look at poor Rory.

He's been dead asleep from the moment he dropped out of his saddle and wound up in a heap right where he lays.''

"It's your fault we left Castle O'Neill before the cock crowed, it is,'' Hugh reminded her. "Accept the truth.''

"And so I have done.'' Morgana put her thumbs into the hard work of softening tightly bound muscles, up and down the thick column of his neck.

"That feels *so-o-o* good. Don't ever stop.'' Hugh's head bobbed forward as he relaxed, satisfied deeply by her sparring answers, which raked pleasantly but didn't cut to the bone.

"I won't,'' Morgana promised absently.

Art Macmurrough's snores buzzed like a buck-toothed saw against hardwood. Young Brian was sprawled on a bed of fiddlehead ferns. A damselfly flitted in and out of the folds and tucks of his tartan.

O'Toole was the most alert. His eyes drooped to slits. His head kept nodding, jerking against the trunk of the hawthorn tree.

Rory, Kermit and Shamus whistled in their sleep. Donald the Fair looked like a sleeping angel. Morgana almost felt sorry for them. They had been riding all through the night, chasing after James Kelly, while she had been sound asleep, getting plenty of rest.

"Help yourself to the bread and meat. There's plenty of mead,'' Hugh said around a ferocious yawn. "You get to stay awake and stand guard, my lady. It's the penalty you pay for routing us all from our beds.''

"Very well.'' Morgana watched him stretch out on the cool earth, settling most contentedly against her spreading skirts. "I shall stuff myself like a yearling pig and drink till I pop.''

"You have my permission to do exactly that.'' Hugh pillowed his head against his bent arm and closed his eyes.

A moment later, as Morgana set the skin of mead aside after quenching her thirst, his eyes were closed and he was sleeping as peacefully as all his mighty kerns.

It almost wasn't fair to take such gross advantage of them. Morgana refused to be bound by scruples. Not now, when she was within five miles of the house where her brother, Sean Fitzgerald, lived.

Chapter Eleven

If it was possible for Morgana to make a break for free-dom, so that she could travel the rest of the journey alone and unimpeded by the Irish, now was the time to do it.

Hugh's randy stallion had made it impossible to tie Mor-gana's mare up with the rest of the horses. Ariel was set apart, tied separately on the northern edge of the wood-land.

Morgana headed crosslots to intercept Ariel. In her sad-dlebag was a map constructed by one of the Franciscan monks of the abbey at Landsdowne. Bishop Moye had given Morgana the map when she stayed overnight in Armagh. Its first marking signified the high cross at Maghera. From here on, the way to Landsdowne Abbey was clearly detailed for her. Morgana would have no trouble traveling the road on her own.

She opened a saddlebag and reached inside, searching for the documents under her clothing. She came up empty, but that didn't alarm her. The bags had been moved and re-placed on the saddle. So she slapped Ariel's rump to move her around and searched inside the opposite pack, standing on tiptoe to see inside the deep pocket.

For a moment, she thought she'd lost the document—all the documents—but then she remembered she'd hidden them in the hems of her old black serge habit. Morgana carefully removed that garment from the bottom of the pack, taking care not to disturb any of the other valuable contents of the pack. She unrolled the skirt and tore loose the stitching in the hem, removing all seven of the documents stored there for safekeeping.

Now that the English were as far behind her as the river Blackwater, she no longer had to worry about being captured. Nor did she worry about James Kelly's escape from the dungeon at Fort Tullaghoge. He was too smart not to have immediately fled south to the safety of the Pale.

She unfolded the map and studied it, orienting herself with the high cross, the nearby peak of Carntogher Mountain and the woodlot marked on the map. When she was certain her directions were correct, she led Ariel quietly over the crest of the hill.

She found a rock suitable for mounting. As she gathered the reins in her hands, she looked at the hilltop that separated her from Hugh. She didn't feel right deserting and deceiving Hugh O'Neill, but she didn't see that she had any choice. It was better for Sean Fitzgerald's sake that Morgana go the rest of the way alone. Saying a special prayer to Saint Brigit, Morgana set off along the heavily wooded track to the next village.

Tyrone, Morgana now knew, was one dense forest after another. They all seemed to be separated by little valleys where some clearing had taken place, enough for the planting of grain fields or some other husbandry. But most of the glens and vales were tree-covered. Without Bishop Moye's map, she'd have been lost before she was out of hearing distance of Hugh O'Neill. She managed to find her landmarks and made the correct turn at each crossroads.

In the space of an hour's fairly pleasant ride, Morgana arrived at the triple-arched, stone bridge in the valley crossing the river Bann. At the bridge she was rewarded by being able to see the rising tower of Landsdowne Abbey above the forest line. According to her map, the house of five white gables was nestled two miles north of the abbey, in the cleared hillside behind it.

Morgana had envisioned Carrew Cottage in her mind a hundred times over the past year, but not once had her imagination provided her such rich and fluid details as she spied on the winding road up from the bustling community of the Dominican abbey. The cottage she'd pictured in her mind had a slate roof. In reality, it was thick with aging thatch. Low whitewashed walls gleamed in the afternoon's bright sun, against a splendid backdrop of spring-green beech trees.

Lazy smoke drifted out of a rock chimney. Someone was to home, if hot fires burned in the hearth. Encouraged, Morgana increased Ariel's pace, leaving the little village and the abbey behind her.

A bevy of black-faced sheep clumped beside a pool in the meadow below Carrew Cottage. Behind the beech trees, a forest of tall green pines added plenty of shelter against frequently hard and cold north winds. Hedgerows bordered each field. Low stone walls separated one small plot of grain from the next, in typical Irish order.

As she came within hailing distance of the cottage, Morgana drew back on Ariel's reins. Cautious, and concerned that she not give herself away or bring any undue notice from the village or the abbey in her direction, Morgana did not call out a greeting.

But then, she saw no one in the cottage's yard to give that greeting to.

She let her horse walk at a measured pace that took them up the winding path between hedgerows and low stone walls to the yard outside the cottage.

All the while she held herself back, Morgana's heart thrummed a heavy cadence in the pit of her stomach. Her mouth was dry. She didn't dare think about what she would do if Sean was not here at Carrew Cottage. Or if one of Walsingham's agents had gotten here ahead of her.

It was too quiet, too silent, for a house where an eight-year-old boy was supposed to live in the virtual obscurity of a large, bustling Irish family. Except for the sheep bleating in the lower field and a line of wash fluttering on the breeze, the place was silent and still.

Alarmed, Morgana drew her *sgian dhu* from its hidden sheath and gripped it fiercely in her hand as she dismounted onto the stepping-stone outside the stable.

"Hallo!" she called. "God and Mary keep all who live in this house. Is anybody to home?"

The stillness shattered with the sound of a door slamming. Ariel snorted. The sheep in the field bleated. Morgana turned toward the yawning dark cavern of the barn, locating the direction of the slammed door. Behind her stood the idyllic house, with its five whitewashed gables, one marking each new and taller addition to the long, sprawling length of it. It was as silent as a Protestant church on Tuesday.

Her nostrils widened as she picked her way through the mud to the yawning doors of the barn. The soil at her feet was ripe with the scents of the stable, horse and cattle, though not a single animal was in sight.

A rude lean-to henhouse in back of the barn boasted a molting assortment of fowl, chickens and geese, far enough away from the back of the house as not to become a nuisance.

A handful of wooden toys scattered between the wash line and the back of the house gave mute testimony that children resided in this house. But none was visible now.

Cautiously Morgana stuck her head inside the barn door. "Captain Tanner," she called out. "Are you here?"

A bucket tipped over from the loft and crashed to the dirt floor. Inside the air turned explosive as a man in the loft shouted, "Jesus, Mary and all the saints! Are ya trying ta kill me? Who is that sneaking up on me ta scare the wits out of a man? Jesu!"

"Captain Tanner?" Morgana asked again, hoping to identify the man in the shadowy darkness over her head.

"Captain Tanner, my arse! There's no pirates swinging from any yardarm in this landlocked hell!"

A wooden pitchfork flew out of the loft and landed in a pile of straw two feet shy of Morgana's boots. Morgana held her ground, refusing to jump back several feet. "Are you Luke Tanner, then?" she demanded.

Blinding rays of sunlight slanted holes through the barn's black shadows. Each ray shimmered with dust and swirling chaff. Morgana blinked the dusty rain out of her eyes and glared up into the hayloft as a man straightened out of the massive pile of hay, hitching a saffron shirt into a pair of gray trews.

"Who is it that wants ta know?" he demanded.

A halo of ungoverned hair wreathed his sweaty, gleaming brow. A scowl blacker than winter thunderclouds marred the weathered lines of his face. The too-long, bewhiskered jaw and massive frame below it lent the landlocked pirate an air of comic menace. He matched the description Morgana had been given—beetle-browed, foul-tempered, and bigger than any man alive.

Morgana took a deep breath of relief, cutting to the point. "Where are the children?"

"Who is that wants ta know, I asked?" he demanded with arms akimbo, broad fists parked on his hips. The meat fleshing his upper arms bulged under the strain of his rolled-up sleeves. As intimidating as his stance was, Morgana still noticed the scuttle of someone's legs as that someone burrowed into the hay behind him.

Her own brow darkened measurably. "I'm Morgana O'Malley. I've come to fetch my brother, Sean."

"Well, and ta be sure, ye've come ta the wrong house, ya have, then, Morgana O'Malley. There's none but Tanner's get here. Get ye gone, wench! I've work ta do."

"I can see what philandering work you do." Morgana had no patience for his bluster. She'd been told the old pirate Luke Tanner was no fool, and that his appearance could be most deceiving. She didn't retreat, as he'd commanded, but she did put away her knife.

She came farther into the aromatic barn, removing her kidskin gloves. He growled in a menacing manner as he snatched up another fork and heaved a shower of straw in her direction.

"See here, Tanner," Morgana said briskly as she side-stepped the cascade of hay and chaff. "I haven't any interest in masquerades or games. Time is of the essence. Call Sean out of hiding. I must be off with him to Dunluce with all due haste."

"Sean, Sean," he barked. "I've Toms and Johns and Iains under me roof, but none here called Sean. Go away, gel, I'm busy."

Exasperated, Morgana threw the edges of her Irish cloak off her shoulders. She also fixed her arms akimbo and put her hands on her hips, declaring, "Each of us knows who the other really is."

"Do we, then?" The man's falsetto-voiced question bordered on mockery. "Ya don't look the least familiar ta me."

"I've proof of my identity," Morgana argued. "There's no need for you to be rude."

"I said I've work ta do. Get you gone!"

"Aye, and I said I know what work you're up to, man." Morgana stood fast, directly in the path of his next forkful. "I bring greetings from Timothy Moye. He bids you open a casket of your oldest brew and give me a taste of the devil's drink. If I'm satisfied by it, I'm to take two barrels to the laird of the Glens as payment for your last quarter's rent."

That secured Tanner's intense inspection once more. He jammed his fork into the hay piled in his loft and bent over the rail. Broad-knuckled, stubby fingers gripped the aged wood. For a farmer he had very, very clean hands. But then, Morgana knew, this man was no farmer—nor ever would be. His powerful voice shook the rafters. "There's no papists here, lassie! We're God-fearing Protestant folk one and all!"

"When Queen Dick sits on the throne!" Morgana tossed this last at him with some heat. He was being most stubborn, and she was nearly out of convincing phrases to prove she was from Bishop Moye and not a Protestant spy ferreting out priests in all their various disguises.

He swung his leg over the side and grabbed hold of a smooth pole, sliding down it as nimbly as a first mate managing a ship's rigging. On the ground before her, Lucas stood nearly toe-to-toe with Morgana, peering at her face in the dusty light, as if that would prove who she was, when he'd never laid eyes on her in his life.

"So you're O'Malley's widow, are you?" he demanded, wary and distrustful still. "How'd the poor bastard die?"

"Unshriven and unrepentant, in the arms of two dock-side whores, drunk as a lord!" Morgana snapped, adding, "God forgive and save his immortal soul, for I haven't."

Luke Tanner burst out with a roaring laugh. "Bless my soul, that proves it! You're the sod's true widow! Only a long-suffering wife could sound so thoroughly disgusted."

Morgana failed to find any humor in a single word either of them had said. In her book, a philandering husband was no laughing matter.

"Welcome to Carrew Cottage, Lady Morgana." His manner changed all at once. Captain Tanner swept a gallant arm over his vast waist and bowed deeply to her. "Forgive my distrust. I take no chances. We expected you two days ago. Hence, I feared an impostor had come in your place. Come, step with me out into the light and let me get a good look at you."

"Where is Sean?" Morgana asked. "I haven't much time."

The elder wouldn't answer that question. When they were outdoors, in the afternoon sun, he said, "Och, now, I can see the red hair of the Geralds in you, aye, that I can. What kept you?"

"Foul weather, and a tail of English scouts determined to stop me."

"Humph!" He nodded, motioning with his head toward the house. "We heard there were redcoats patrolling Armagh."

"A number of them. Some five or six are dead now. One particularly bad sort escaped detainment at Fort Tullaghoge, and remains on the loose."

"Would I know him?"

"Since you've been landlocked a few years now, it is possible you've heard of the man. James Kelly is his name. I hear he has a son also in the queen's service, a musketeer by the name of John."

"Never heard of either of them," Captain Tanner replied. He put his hands to his mouth and let loose a whistle, signaling all within hailing distance that all was well. The notes he trilled had a familiar ring to Morgana's ears, matching the clear whistle Grace and her brother, Greg, had used. Chagrined, Morgana realized that if she'd used the same signal when approaching the cottage, she might have had a better reception.

A closed door at the back of the cottage opened and a blowsy woman looked out. "Who is it then, Luke?"

"The guest we were expecting. Set the table, Marie, and tell the young'ns they can run out and play agin."

He stamped dirt off his muddy boots and turned back to the open door of the barn, hollering. "Come out quiet now, lads! 'Tis safe!"

Quiet was not the way Morgana would have described the explosion of lads from the cottage or the barn. They dropped from loft doors, burst running from the barn door and shambled up from the cottage and the privy. A full dozen handsome red-haired lads, and almost as many with dark and sandy heads, too.

Luke Tanner's teeth gleamed in the strong sun. "We saw you comin', the minute you crossed the bridge."

Morgana turned to scan the hillside and look down at the peacefully flowing river in the bottom of the valley. Sure enough, from the vantage point of Carrew Cottage there was a clear view of the bridge and the road leading uphill past the village and the abbey.

And to Morgana's embarrassment, she realized how easily she could have ridden into another deadly trap. She turned to look at Luke Tanner with some respect. He wasn't the fool she'd first thought, when she spied him trysting up in the barn's loft. That, too, had probably been a ruse.

"Now, then, lass." His grin turned wolfish. "Which one of these fine lads do you intend ta claim is your lost brother, Sean?"

Morgana turned around to discover that the boys had lined up with regimental precision, from the oldest down to the youngest. Every young face mirrored Luke Tanner's wolfish grin. The smallest could be no more than six years of age, the biggest were as tall as she, and they might have been any age from fourteen years to twenty.

The bottom of the row had only one redhead in it. So did the top. But in the middle range, where the ten-year-olds surely had to be, every boy sported hair the color of a winter fire, as red as Morgana's own. She blinked, surprised.

Luke Tanner laughed. "Stumped, are ya, then, lass?"

"Yes," Morgana agreed reluctantly. "Finding a specific boy by only the color of his hair would be like looking for a needle in a haystack in this mob."

She crossed the short distance to the line, smiling at the boys' proud postures and grins. The young ones looked healthy and well fed. She had to give Tanner credit for putting on a good show—not that she had time now for theatrics. She nodded to each boy as she walked up the long line, then came to a stop in front of the smallest redhead in the lot.

A pair of solemn pale eyes looked back at her without so much as a blink from underneath a shock of brilliant red elflocks that hadn't seen a trim in months. The small boy's neck was very thin, and he stuck out by the fact that his large head seemed too big for what clearly was a frail body beneath his woolen tunic.

He was much too young and small to be Morgana's ten-year-old brother, Sean. Still, his solemn, freckled face brought her to a dead halt in her progression up the line. Morgana dropped to one knee, grasping the boy's shoulders, her eyes moving over his face and down his body to his toes. Her heart slammed to a stop inside her chest.

Lucas Tanner just barely caught the lady's whisper: "Sweet Saint Brigit, Maurice, is it you?"

The boy cast a fearful look up to Tanner's grave face. All trace of his affable smile was gone. Tanner nodded once, a silent signal that released the boy from his previous orders. Maurice Fitzgerald threw his arms around his sister's neck, crying, "I thought you'd never come, Morgana! Me and Sean gave up!"

The line broke as Sean Fitzgerald bolted out of his place in the ranks and ran to his sister to embrace her as hungrily as Maurice did. Both boys swamped Morgana with their arms, hugging her for all they were worth.

"Well, now, will ya look at that?" Luke Tanner drew a handkerchief up from a pocket and blew his nose, moved by the loving reunion playing out before his eyes. "Come now, come now, get out of the sun, all of ye. What have I told you lot? You never know who watches who in the hills."

Dazed and overwhelmed by emotion, Morgana was led inside the cottage by her brothers. Her head was spinning dizzily. Her heart was pumping hard. She kept Sean and Maurice at her sides. Their arms remained tight around her waist. In the cool darkness of the cottage kitchen, they found a bench and sat. Her head throbbed from the survey of faces she loved so much, but had almost forgotten in their long separation.

"You've grown so much I'd have never recognized you," Morgana told Sean as she ruffled his sun-glazed red curls. "But I'd have known Maurice anywhere."

She hugged the youngest to her heart, rubbing her cheek against the top of his small head. "How? How did you get here? I was told you were dead, and shown your grave."

"I was bad sick," Maurice said solemnly.

"Aye," Sean added. "They gave him the last rites, Morgana. Tanner and me decided it was best to let the word out Maurice had been killed."

Morgana shook her head. "And I believed it. Do you know what a start you have given my heart?"

Maurice put the blame for the lies Morgana had been told on his older brother's head. "'Twas Sean's idea."

"And it makes good sense," Sean declared righteously. "That way, if something happened to me, Maurice would be there to carry on Father's name."

"So it would," Morgana had to admit. She looked up at Luke Tanner, further respect for the grizzled old man shining in her eyes. "I don't know how you did it, Tanner, but I thank you from the bottom of my heart."

"Humph," he grunted. "No thanks necessary, lady. I fulfilled my deathbed oath to O'Malley. A man's to be judged by the bond of his word, that's all. Now, you boys get. You've chores to do before supper, and we grown-ups have need for words. All of you, scat!"

He ordered every lad out of the cottage's huge kitchen with a wave of his hand, including Sean and Maurice. Morgana let her brothers go reluctantly. Luke Tanner was correct. It was time the adults had a talk.

After the bright, sunny day, Morgana's eyes refused to adjust to the kitchen's cavernous shadows. Overhead, a deep loft intensified the strong contrast by allowing a direct ray of brilliant sunlight in through two unshuttered windows.

She couldn't see into the loft, except to pick out bunches of herbs that hung from the rafters to dry. The kitchen smelled of musty, damp thatch, coriander, garlic and thyme. The stone floor was dry underfoot.

A goodly fire blazed on the floor of a wide hearth. Huge, blackened iron pots hung from swinging iron hooks over the fire. It was a simple room. Utensils hung from crowded racks suspended from the joists supporting the loft.

Tanner invited Morgana to his table. They joined a white-bearded old man already seated at a bench there. He held a crust of bread in one of his thin-skinned blue-veined hands. His most curious feature was his clothes. He wore a linen tunic bearing the red cross of a crusader knight. Under that, Morgana saw an ancient coat of chain mail. The blackthorn walking staff of a pilgrim lay across his lap.

His great age not withstanding, he stared at Morgana with intensely alert eyes. Spellbinding eyes that made her feel as though they penetrated her skin, to seek out her soul. The longer he stared at her, the less aware of the busy workers in the kitchen Morgana was.

"Do I know you, sir?" Morgana asked quietly.

"Somewhat." His noble head inclined in acknowledgment of her greeting. "I am Almoy, the preceptor of the temple of Ireland."

"Oh?" Morgana said, surprised. "Then I do know of you. We have corresponded in the past."

Before she fled Dublin, Morgana had carried out the terms of her father's final letter. The vast library of the Fitzgeralds was to be consigned to Sir Almoy of Dunrath Temple. Morgana's last contact with Grace O'Malley had been on board the *Avenger,* where every document and history had been carefully packed away, stowed for the journey around Ireland. "Why are you here, sir?"

He nodded gravely. "I am here at Carrew Cottage to bring you a warning."

"Warning?" Morgana frowned. "What sort of warning?"

"The deed you carry that is signed by your father, bequeathing Gerait Mor and Gerait Og's library to the priory, must be destroyed. There must be no record found of what became of that library, least it fall into the hands of Lord Grey."

"Well, that's easy enough to do," Morgana replied. "It can be burned the moment I hand it to you, if you can prove you are Sir Almoy to me."

"I do not have to prove anything to you, lady," Sir Almoy declared. The young woman's temerity in challenging his identity rankled him. "I cannot touch the document. Were I to do so, I could not destroy it. Tanner will agree to do that, do you give it to him. In the scheme of things, it will be better if you do not know specifically what happens to the document."

"This is very strange. I cannot destroy such an important document on an old man's whim. It goes against my father's instructions to me."

"Cantankerous whelp!" Sir Almoy sputtered. "My instructions supersede your father's."

The Templar raised his right hand in a gesture Morgana recognized—thumb, index finger and little finger raised in a powerful hex. Knowledge of what he was struck her. He was a wizard. As powerful as her grandfather! She ducked reflexively, as though he were about stone her.

"Do not dare me to cast troubles on your head, daughter of Fitzgerald," Almoy told her solemnly. "You have troubles enough facing you."

"Yes, I do." Morgana took a tankard of ale in hand and calmly sipped its contents. She told herself she wasn't rattled by old men gone far beyond their prime. This man across the table from her looked frail enough to be blown away by her breath. But powerless he wasn't!

God help her, she didn't want his hand raised against her. She tilted her chin proudly and challenged him. "Give me sufficient reason to destroy the deed, and I may do as you say."

She was really asking for sufficient proof that he was Almoy of the Knights Templar, and Almoy knew it. He dropped his hand to the trestle. Morgana gasped as that same hand appeared to sink in and out of the wood. He studied her reaction somberly. "You do not frighten easily."

"That depends," Morgana admitted. "What is it you want of me? The library is yours to do with as you like. I am a messenger, naught else. As the deed belongs with the collection, proving your ownership of the whole, what is your point?''

It was instantly obvious that the old man didn't like the question. Prepared to wait him out, Morgana brought the cup to her mouth and drank deeply.

Almoy chose his moment to speak well. "You must bring the O'Neill to Dunrath Temple.''

Morgana choked on the strong ale. She set the tankard down with a snap, sputtering, wiping spilled ale from her bodice.

"What are you talking about?'' she said, unable to hide the shock of his demand from her face. There was something most peculiar about the way Almoy stared at her. He couldn't possibly be reading her thoughts. She looked at Luke Tanner and found his face about as confused as her thoughts. "What's this about? There is no O'Neill, Sir Almoy.''

Almoy interrupted with soothing words that had the effect of settling Morgana back on the bench opposite him. "You have a destiny to fulfill, beyond the security of your family name. A child is involved, and only Hugh O'Neill has the power to bring that child into the orbit of my teachings. Hence, you, Lady Fitzgerald, must bring me the O'Neill.''

Morgana wanted to say that she had enough trouble on her hands worrying about the safety of her brothers. She didn't need the added burden of Hugh O'Neill and some unnamed child.

"None of this makes sense," she argued.

"Neither does the Holy Trinity make sense in your woman's head. Some things you must leave to faith. In good time, you will see and understand the purpose of my request. I speak of things that come to pass in the distant future. Bring me the O'Neill. That is all I have to say. Good day, milady.''

Sir Almoy rose to his feet, passed his blackthorn staff before Luke Tanner's blank face and murmured, "You will forget my visit, sir."

Almoy shuffled slowly to the door of Carrew Cottage. He left unanswered questions in Morgana's head. How did he know that she knew Hugh O'Neill? A shiver flashed up Morgana's spine as she, too, got to her feet.

Luke Tanner put a hand to Morgana's elbow to steady her. "Are you leaving so soon, Lady O'Malley?"

"I fear I must," Morgana replied, turning her thoughts to the business at hand. "I trust you have horses, Captain Tanner. Daylight is wasting."

"Aye. The lads should have the boys' ponies saddled. Mind Maurice's cough. He's not as strong as Sean."

Chapter Twelve

The sense of urgency that had propelled Morgana throughout her journey north returned the moment she crossed the threshold and saw how far the sun had shifted in the balmy afternoon sky. Spring days were not all that long. She did not want to be on the road after dark, traveling alone with two young boys.

She realized she couldn't protect Sean and Maurice's lives all by herself. She must ride back to the woodlot where she'd left Hugh O'Neill and his kerns. They would be rested now. They would also be available to protect her brothers.

She came to that final decision while standing on open ground between the cottage and the barn. She turned a full circle, searching for Sir Almoy. He had vanished from sight, which was very odd, because he'd stepped out the door of Carrew Cottage only a moment before she had. "Where did Sir Almoy go?"

"Beg pardon, milady?" Luke Tanner asked. His face was as blank as a chalk slate.

"The old man." Morgana shaded her eyes with one hand, searching the road winding downhill to the village. She turned to look at the paths that wound into the beech and pine trees topping the rise.

A host of young lads bustled about, attending to their chores. But no ancient knight walked the fields or shambled between the hedgerows.

"Where did he go?"

"Where did who go?" Luke Tanner asked with beetling black brows. "Lady O'Malley, I am the only man in this vicinity. Who are you talking about?"

"I'm talking about the man who was just in your kitchen, that's who I'm talking about." Morgana said exasperated.

"There was no one in my kitchen save old Mab, who cooks for the lot of us," Tanner answered. "She gave you ale and kept her mouth shut while we discussed the boys. Lady, are you certain you are in fettle enough to finish this journey? You may tarry here the night, and ride out in the morning."

Morgana snapped her mouth shut, her brows lowered in concern. She was not given to imagining things. All the same, she pinched her arm, making doubly certain she was awake and not dreaming this strange encounter. As slowly as the old man had walked, proving his great age, she knew he had to be somewhere in plain sight.

He was too gaunt and too old to stoop to hide behind a hedgerow, which was silly anyhow, because there wasn't a hedgerow situated on the downhill slope that couldn't be seen perfectly from where she was standing at this exact moment.

"Tell me I am imagining seeing an old man in a Templar's tunic and chain mail, then," she quipped lightly.

Thoroughly confused, Luke Tanner laughed. "Lady O'Malley, there are no living Templars. The last died seventy years ago, at Stranhurst Temple in Tir-Connail."

A cool wind sent a chill across Morgana's neck. She turned to the barn. A tall lad came forth, leading Ariel and two ponies. Maurice and Sean came running after saying goodbye to their friends.

"Seventy years ago?" Morgana repeated. "Is that so?"

"Aye," Luke Tanner said emphatically. "Don't know why you should ask about that. Here are the boys, ready to go, as I promised ya."

Tanner bent to pick up young Maurice and carry him to the ready horses.

"I'm going to miss ya, sprout," he said affectionately. "Ya won't be forgetting everything I've taught you, will you?"

"Och, no." Maurice threw his arms around the huge man's neck, hugging him in return. "You've been a right nice bear of a man, Captain Tanner. Haps I'll come back and visit you when you're ready to put to sea again."

"Won't be doing that until this crew is trained properly." Luke Tanner pinched Maurice's nose playfully. "That's some time in the future, I vow. Still, you know how to find me, correct?"

"Aye, aye, Cap'n." Maurice saluted as he sat on his saddle. "A whistle over the bounding main."

"And you, too, Sean." Luke turned to make his farewells to Sean. The boy put out his hand and grasped Tanner's meaty palm firmly.

"A thousand and one thanks to you, sir. We stand in your debt forever."

"Och, don't go maudlin on me, boyo. Mind the lady, and keep a good watch on Maurice. He's not as strong as he looks."

"I'll take my most excellent care of both, Captain," Sean said proudly. "And I'll speak to the powers that be regarding your pardon."

Tanner chuckled, clapping Sean on his back fondly. Then he turned to boost Morgana onto Ariel. He found that the lady had opened a saddlebag and removed a dark cloth from it. She unrolled it partway, then paused and looked at Tanner with eyes full of gratitude.

"I can't repay you for your loyal service adequately, Captain Tanner, but I can give you this."

"You owe me nothing, lady." Luke Tanner shunned any reward. "O'Malley gave me payment enough a long time ago. He was a good man for the sea."

"Take this anyway. It was Greg's. He'd want you to have it as a token of his appreciation." Morgana shoved a jeweled brooch into his hand, covered by several folds of crackling parchment, the deed to her father's library. She took a deep breath, as if she might be plunging headlong into deep and unknown waters. "You'll know what to do with it, I believe."

Tanner unfolded the crackling parchment and saw the gold brooch lying inside it. His eyes were glistening with tears when he looked up at Morgana again. "Damn my foolish eyes, but I recognize the crest, lady. 'Twas Greg's favorite brooch. I'll cherish it always. Keep the paper, though. I've no use for it. I send the boys down to the abbey for their lessons with the friars. Me, I can't read a word. Never could and never will. I'm too old to learn at my age."

"Then do what you like with it, as well," Morgana answered confidently.

If Tanner had no conscious recollection of the ancient man's words, he'd likely follow every suggestion the wizard had planted in his head. Just as Morgana was going to do. Powerful magic such as Almoy possessed wouldn't go unheeded. Tanner boosted her up onto Ariel, then stood back to watch them go. A phalanx of lads escorted them to the gates and waved them goodbye.

Outside the gates, Morgana turned back to look at the cottage and the strange crew that inhabited it. Tanner waved an enthusiastic goodbye. Morgana had a momentary vision of him lighting a candle with twists of torn parchment.

That image made her smile.

"So." She turned to her brothers, saying, "Tell me all that has happened to the both of you. I want to know each and every adventure that you have had in the past year and a half."

Hugh O'Neill was not a happy man. Loghran O'Toole knew there was not a thing he could do to improve Hugh's sour mood. So Loghran chose to give Hugh something else to do in the face of a woman's deceit. Loghran galloped uphill to the promontory overlooking both the Maghera and Kilrea glens. Hugh stood there, scouring the countryside with his spyglass. His expression darkened with unreleased temper.

Loghran drew in his reins and dismounted, saying, "She didn't go south, O'Neill."

"Aye, damn your sleepy head, O'Toole." Hugh snapped closed his spyglass and swiveled on his heel to glare at O'Toole. "Some fine gillie you turn out to be, protecting me and mine with your life, you do."

"My lord . . ." Loghran began.

"Don't grovel, damn it. She didn't go west. She didn't go south. She didn't go north. Yonder she comes with Rory and Brian from the east. Now what did I tell you when we woke up? East, I said. East to Landsdowne Abbey! Would you listen to my laudable reasoning? No! So I've stood here wearing this hill to a nub. I've paced, while all my fine kerns travel yonder and back, bringing me empty hands and foolish reports. You're an old worrying ass, O'Toole, admit it."

"My lord," Loghran sputtered. "I was thinking of your safety. It was imperative that you remain here, waiting. There's an English fort, unchallenged, east of Ballymena. You know perfectly well that Kelly must have headed there, since we didn't find him south of the Abhainn Mor."

Hugh raised a silencing hand. "Don't say it!"

Loghran said it anyway. "I couldn't let you go there."

"Augh!" Hugh shouted, pushed beyond his patience by Loghran's misplaced sense of loyalty, which made him treat Hugh as though he were an unweaned boy. "When are you going to get it in your head that you don't *let me* do anything? I've had all of your mothering I can stand, man!"

"Oh? So it's mothering that I do, is it?" O'Toole snapped. A delicious grin lighted his face, because Hugh had taken the bait. He dropped his hands to his sword belt and unfastened it and cast it to the earth. He put up his fists in a defensive stance. "I'll show you what mothering is, then, whelp. You've gone daft over a skirt, you have, you fool.''

Provoked past any point of reason, Hugh threw his own sword to the ground. "Think you can take me down, old man?"

"I do! I'll mop what's left of this worn-down hill with you, lad.''

Hugh didn't bother answering. He acted.

Launching his whole body at his mentor, he wrestled Loghran to the ground. The time had come to prove who was the boss between them once and for all.

They scuffled for a good while. Not even the sound of numerous horses' tramping hooves disturbed the wrestling match on the top of the hill. Shouts began to add spice to their grunting and huffing wrestling match.

Rory O'Neill cleared his throat loudly. "Milord Hugh, there's a lady and children present.''

"Hold yer damned tongue behind yer teeth!" Hugh grunted ferociously. "I'm not stopping till I've pinned this miserable Viking get's ears to the bloody earth!''

Hugh's kerns took up sides, cheering their favorites. Hugh and Loghran rolled over and over in the dirt. Whoever wound up on top tried to pin the other, and failed miserably. Morgana scowled darkly at the two men wrestling like bad boys in a village square.

One minute Hugh was winning. The next it was Loghran O'Toole who'd gained the upper hand. Sean jumped down instantly and got involved in the fracas, calling encouragement to whoever was on top.

Only Art Macmurrough made any remark about Morgana's sudden reappearance in the fold. He cut her a chilly yet fatherly glance and said, "You'll be answering to himself for running off like that.''

That spoken, Macmurrough jumped into the circle around the fighters. He shouted, "Pin his ears back, O'Toole. Teach the whelp to respect his elders!''

"That will be the day!" Donald the Fair called out as he offered a hand to Morgana to help her dismount. "Mind you, you'll be wishing you hadn't started this, come time to mount up and ride again, lady."

Ignoring the handsome kern, Morgana stomped to an opening in the circle around the fighters. On her way, she snatched up a good-size stick from the ground. She watched the fierce struggle for a moment or two before deciding this was a pointless show that certainly wasn't fit exercise for her young brothers to watch.

O'Toole grunted as he flipped Hugh onto his back, pinning his shoulders in the dirt as he roared, "Tell me when you've had enough, boy!"

Morgana lifted her stout stick. Kermit Blackbeard saw her do that, and lunged for her. He wrapped a brawny arm around Morgana's arms, trapping her stick in midair. "Ah, ah, ah... No, ya don't, milady."

"Unhand me, you miserable cur. I intend to stop this nonsense immediately."

"Nonsense it isn't!" Blackbeard roundly argued. His arm tightened, and he wrenched the stick from Morgana's hand and tossed it far down the hill. "Next to me, O'Toole's the strongest man in Ulster. Hugh beats him fair and square, or he doesn't. No interference from you."

"One of them is going to be hurt!" Morgana shouted in the kern's face.

His black beard split wide open in a brilliant grin. "Aye, so one will. But one of them is going to win. My bet is it's going to be O'Toole. You're not changing the outcome, you aren't."

"Let my sister go, you beast!" Maurice shouted, launching an attack Morgana hadn't expected.

Stung by the delivery of a hard shoe to his shin, Kermit looked down and spied a small red-haired boy flailing at him. His laughter roared in Morgana's ear as he caught Maurice up in his other arm and stood holding the two of them helpless prisoners in his fast grip.

As Maurice let the whole world know his opinion of that, the fight ended. Hugh held O'Toole's shoulders pinned to the earth while the kerns counted a loud chant to ten in a unified, triumphant voice.

"I'll be damned," Kermit Blackbeard said in amazement. "He did it, fair and square."

Hugh got up, dusting his clothes off and glared at Kermit. "Of course I did it fair and square, ya senseless lout! Let go of my woman!"

He let his fist fly at Kermit's face, pasting him a good one. Then Hugh caught Morgana as she was dropped to her feet when Kermit toppled into the dirt. Maurice had to fend for himself.

"Are you all right?" Hugh demanded, concerned only for Morgana and what ills she might have suffered while she was out of his sight.

Breathless from having all the air squeezed out of her, Morgana stared up at Hugh's dirty, sweaty face and threw her arms around his head. "You've been hurt! Loghran O'Toole, how dare you strike the man you've sworn fealty to! I'm tempted to murder you with my bare hands!"

Every kern on the hill roared. Even Kermit Blackbeard laughed as Donald the Fair hauled him from the dirt where he'd landed.

"Who's this?" Donald wanted to know, pointing to the small boy trapped under Kermit's leg.

"My brother!" Morgana yelled. "And don't any of you hurt him! He's been sick!"

Hugh grinned wolfishly. He turned back to Loghran O'Toole and taunted him. "Hear that, old man? That's exactly what you sound like, with your womanish plaints assaulting my ears. Have you got it in your head now that I'm capable of defending myself?"

O'Toole ignored that remark as he got to his feet, beaten fair and square. Art Macmurrough shook his head, as though he'd taken the beating instead of O'Toole. Hugh laughed in triumph and returned his attention to Morgana.

Her hands stroked over each lump on his face and fussed with the tears in his doublet and sleeves. Hugh knew he'd never feel more like a king among men than he did at this very moment, with Morgana's hands comforting him.

"You came back," he said, amazed by that truth. "I thought I'd lost you for good."

Morgana pressed his hair away from his face, then shied away from the intensity she found in his eyes. "Aye, I came back."

Hugh cupped her face in the palms of his hands. "I'm so glad that you're here. I couldn't bear losing you."

Art Macmurrough grunted in disgust. "Well, go on then, O'Neill. Be a bloody fool for a woman. Kiss her. While yer at it, tell her how we all enjoyed every minute of your foul temper. Don't forget mentioning the long ride covering every trail from here to eternity looking for her. Go on, you damned lovesick fool, kiss her!"

To Morgana's surprise, Hugh did exactly that—kissed her full on the mouth, in front of God and every-body...including both of her brothers.

"Morgana!" Sean screeched, shocked. "Have you forgotten that you're a lady?"

Hugh lifted his head from his woman's lips and glared at the impudent boy daring to insult his lady. "Who the hell are you, little man?"

Morgana couldn't get out of Hugh's arms quickly enough to clap her hand over Sean's mouth and silence him. The boy drew up to his full height, glaring at what he perceived to be an Irish ruffian, and declared to Hugh, "I happen to be John Gerald Fitzgerald, sir. Who the bloody hell are you?"

Hugh growled darkly in Morgana's ear, disliking being topped by a mere whelp of a boy—even in so base a skill as cursing.

"I happen to be the *O'Neill!*" Hugh's roar was like a lion's, in full and terrifying volume. "Swear at me again,

Kildare, and I'll skin you alive with the first strap I lay my hand on.''

No fool, Sean leaped behind the biggest man present, Loghran O'Toole. "Morgana, do as you bloody damn well please," he replied.

Maurice broke the terse silence following that injudicious gibe with a burst of delighted, childish laughter. "Morgana, Sean's about to piss himself."

"The devil I am, you little monster." Sean struck out from behind Loghran to pound his little brother. Loghran caught Sean by the neck of his tunic, yanking him back.

"One battle at a time, bantling." He turned to Hugh, deferring to his judgement. "Are we skinning wee brats alive or riding to Dunluce?"

Hugh cast a look around the assembly, wanting to know first of all whether they had heard the deference in Loghran's question. The fact that every man present met Hugh's eyes proved that they all recognized what O'Toole now acknowledged. Hugh could beat them all. He grinned broadly with satisfaction.

"We're riding to Dunluce." He reluctantly released Morgana. "You have some explaining to do, lady. You will ride with me on Boru."

Morgana knew when not to argue. She turned to help Maurice to his feet and dusted the backside of his trews free of dirt.

She thought she heard Kermit Blackbeard grumble over the attention she gave Maurice. As she straightened from neatening the small boy's clothes and releasing him to run to his pony and mount up, Morgana met Kermit's harsh and condemning gaze evenly.

"The boy has been ill," she explained quietly. "I am not coddling or spoiling him unnecessarily. Walsingham did his level best to poison him."

"Aye-yah." Kermit cleared his throat, unrepentant. "Did I say a thing, lady?"

"You don't have to, when your Irish eyes condemn so eloquently," Morgana countered.

"And you should let the little man in him stand tall," Kermit replied. "He's a brave laddie, taking me on for your sake. Don't discount the heart in him. Size and age isn't everything."

"I don't," Morgana said. "I'm hoping you don't, either."

"Och, he's a wee small, is all." Kermit shrugged. "He'll grow."

Satisfied, Morgana tucked a button that had come loose from Maurice's shirt into the pocket of her skirt. She drew her cloak over her shoulders and crossed the hillside to where Hugh stood, discussing the road ahead and the rest of the journey with Loghran and Donald the Fair.

When Hugh finished his conversation, he boosted Morgana onto Boru's back, then mounted behind her. The kerns were moving out in single file up the northern track. Sean and Maurice rode side by side between Kermit and Rory. Brian and O'Toole brought up the rear, both hauling brushy limbs cut from the trees to obscure their horses' tracks.

Quiet for the first portion of the ride, Morgana rested against the support of Hugh's chest, feeling very glad to be back in the strong circle of his arms.

There was very little conversation as the band rode north. Everyone seemed to be thinking his own thoughts. Morgana certainly was caught up in her own. She marveled over the fact that she felt so good, now that she was back with Hugh. She put aside the troubling question of what Sir Almoy wanted of him. She would deal with that when the time came, not before.

Some distance past Kilrea, Hugh's chin nudged the top of Morgana's head. "You'll notice I did not ask where you went."

"Aye." Morgana nodded, and scooted farther back into the press of his thighs. "I noticed you did not ask."

His knees tightened. "Don't distract me."

The stallion galloped forward. Hugh's physical signals could be interpreted by both the horse and Morgana. She smiled at the distant black hills on the northern horizon. "How much farther is Dunluce?"

Hugh brushed an annoying mosquito away from Morgana's cheek. "Far enough. We'll make the inn at Colraine by dusk. Dunluce will keep till the morrow."

Morgana scanned the sky, looking for the moon. High tide was her deadline. If she missed the tide, she'd not get Sean and Maurice on board the *Avenger* for the voyage to France.

"Don't want to talk about it, do you?" Hugh said.

"I'll talk." Morgana replied. "I just don't know what exactly you want me to say."

Hugh's chest expanded and contracted against her back. Wisps of red curls lifted from the crown of her head and fell forward to kiss her brow. The breeze made by Boru's forward movement laid them back on her crown. She'd lost the violets Hugh had placed in her coiled braids.

Morgana decided to risk all. "Do you know of a man named Almoy?"

"Aye," Hugh said. His lips nuzzled against her temple. The temptation to kiss her intimately overwhelmed him. He pulled his cheek away, and shook his head to clear it.

Morgana frowned at the sharply descending path of the hillside before them. The troop had spread out quite far. Maurice and Sean were out of hailing distance. She shifted and cast a look around Hugh's shoulder to see how far back those riding behind them were. O'Toole was a small figure in the distance. He raised his hand in a signal, acknowledging her. Morgana waved back.

She sat up straight and said, "Have you ever had any disagreements with him?"

"None that I know of." Hugh slipped his hand inside her cloak. He would rest it on her waist, that was all. He was a soldier, leader of this patrol. He wouldn't get distracted by a woman again. "Have you?"

"Disagreement, no. Though I have dealt with him through the post. Dealings regarding the disposal of some of my father's estate. Possessions, not properties, mind you."

Morgana looked to the west and read the sun. Long hours remained before sunset. Impatient for the ride to end, she shifted again, then laid her hand over Hugh's.

Hugh had made some conclusions from what she'd said. "So, now you've met him face-to-face, you've got questions about Almoy's trustworthiness, do you?"

"How did you know that?" Morgana wondered—and not for the first time—whether Hugh O'Neill had the ability to read her mind. What she didn't want him to read.

"It's logical." Hugh shrugged. "You disappear, then return, and now ask about someone you've never spoken of before."

"What do you know about him?"

"Gossip, rumors. None of it true, I'm certain. I've been gone from Tyrone fifteen years."

"You knew him before you went to England?"

"Aye, I took lessons under him."

"In what? Magic?"

Hugh laughed. "Why do you always ask about magic? Has it some importance to you?"

"Suppose it does?"

"I have found in my years that there is usually a rational explanation for all things considered to be magical, mystical, or unexplainable. You just have to look for the true reasons and meaning behind the things that happen. No, I did not study the magi's art under Almoy at the priory. I studied Greek and mathematics. He is a brilliant man, and a superb teacher."

"So you know him quite well," Morgana concluded, more puzzled than ever. Why should the man appear to her, when he could just as easily have transported himself to Dungannon and appeared there to Hugh in person? "Have you ever seen him appear right before your eyes and speak to you, then disappear right after?"

"You mean as a ghost materializes?" Hugh wondered how they'd gotten off on this tack. "I must give you credit, Morgana. You are very entertaining, exasperating and befuddling."

"What I mean is, have you ever thought you've had a conversation with him? Then, a little while later, realized it was not possible."

Now she was touching on what Hugh viewed as dreams, daydreams, of which he was fond. But that didn't mean he would admit his fanciful thoughts. "No."

"So if he said something important to you in such a visit, or asked you to do a specific thing, would you do it?"

"Suppose I ask you to stay the night with me in my bed at the Bonnie Foyle Inn at Colraine tonight? Would you do it?" Hugh let his breath warm the inner caverns of her ear.

"Probably," Morgana replied without hesitation. "Once I made certain Sean and Maurice were sleeping for the duration of the night."

Hugh's pulse jumped a beat. He slid his hand upward and cupped her breast. She closed her eyes, leaning into his hand, giving him all of her to touch and fondle.

"I'll make it my mission to see that the boys are exhausted and ready for the deepest sleep. My promise, my sweet."

Morgana's eyes opened. She turned her face slightly, looking up into his. "Am I shamefully wicked to give in to you so easily, my lord?"

"There is nothing shameful in your giving in to me. I think you are enchanting, quite the most beautiful woman I have ever laid eyes upon in my life."

"That is very kind of you to say, sir." Morgana's cheeks dimpled. "Enchanting is a reference to things magical, isn't it?"

"Is it?" Hugh drawled. His hand tightened over her breast, coaxing a firm response from the nipple underneath her gown. "Do you find this magical, lady? I find it highly natural. It is a normal response of a healthy, loving woman to her lover's evoking hand. Not magical, but surely mysterious."

As he'd also coaxed a blush onto her cheeks, Morgana took firm control of his hand and lowered it back to her waist. "Control yourself, my lord. I have agreed to meet you late tonight at the Inn at Colraine. *Attendez-moi.* We were speaking of Sir Almoy. What is he, really?"

"An alchemist."

"An alchemist? Is that all?" Morgana couldn't believe that simple explanation. She patted Hugh's hand, detaining it. "I would, sir, have you remember we are in public and you must respect me. Now, about Almoy. Why only an alchemist?"

"Well, he is that. And more." The corners of Hugh's mouth twitched at the skillful way Morgana chided him back to perfect, gentlemanly behavior. He loved her all the more for that.

"And more?" Morgana looked off into the far distance, where a low line of shadowy haze lay over the sunny horizon. She wondered whether it would rain on the morrow, as Hugh had predicted. Time would tell, she concluded.

"Well, somewhat more," Hugh responded, misinterpreting the nature of her wonderings. "When I was a boy, I was told he was a Templar Knight. Now that I have all the facts to mind, I know the Templars were disbanded two hundred years ago. Most were martyred. I expect he is in reality a knight of the order of the Hospitaliers of Saint John of Jerusalem. His age may have affected his mind."

"How old is he?"

"Old," Hugh said emphatically. "No one knows exactly. By my reckoning, he is well over a hundred."

"A hundred!" Morgana repeated. Her great-aunt Eleanor Fitzgerald had lived to a great age—her nineties. Rarely did anyone live past the century mark. If they did, they certainly couldn't walk two leagues as if it were a race to the hill of Tara. Almoy had disappeared from her sight, vanished, the moment he stepped out Luke Tanner's door.

"Aye, well . . ." Hugh shifted on the saddle, a bit uncomfortably. He rubbed his leg to smooth out a wrinkle in his leather trews. Exactly where Morgana's bottom made him acutely aware of his aching loins.

"So what else do you know about him?"

Hugh shrugged. "Why are we talking about an old man? Was he your brother's caretaker?"

"No. Heaven forbid the day. We Fitzgeralds have had enough trouble being branded as warlocks and witches. I wouldn't dream of turning my brothers over into the care of an obvious eccentric."

"You're speaking from ignorance. The rabble in the street do no worse when they call a woman a witch and demand the authorities burn her. If we all fell into that trap, nothing new would ever be discovered. We'd still be burning folk for saying the world is round."

"I'm not accusing him of anything. I'm trying to understand how it was he appeared to me at Landsdowne. It was very strange. Unexplainable. One moment, he was there, and the next he wasn't. He also told me I must bring you to him very soon. There is a child he expects you to bring him as a new pupil."

"What child?"

"Now that's what has me stumped more than anything. He didn't say what the child's name is."

"How odd. Are you certain he wasn't referring to one of your brothers?"

"No. He wasn't. I'm certain of that."

"Speaking of your brothers, the boys look healthy enough to me. You told me one had been poisoned."

"Aye, Maurice. The little one."

Hugh hated to be the one to break the news to her, but both boys were little. No match for Walsingham's spies, thugs and deputies. "I would know the truth, Morgana. Are your brothers the only reason you came back to me?"

Chapter Thirteen

That Morgana delayed her answer too long was answer enough for Hugh. He revolted against being second in Morgana's thoughts.

"Forget I asked that," he snapped. He dropped his hand from her waist and used it to change his hold on Boru's reins. "Don't struggle to come up with some explanation that coddles my vanity."

"Wait!" Morgana raised a silencing hand against his brief tirade. Again, too little action, too late.

Hugh's spurs dug into Boru's sides. The stallion shot forward on the downhill slope. Morgana caught hold of the short pommel to steady her balance.

"'Tis perfectly obvious what is my use to you." Hugh bit out each word, hurting himself as well as her, with the telling. "You have need of a protector. So do those small and innocent boys. Correct?"

"Hugh!" Morgana's shout was torn from her lips as Boru galloped down the dangerous slope. His hooves struck the rocks with jarring ferocity, and Morgana's bones took the impact. Boru stretched out, giving his all to Hugh's demand. Morgana grabbed Hugh's hands in a vain attempt to pull back on the bit.

"Don't!" Hugh warned. He used one hand to keep Morgana's hands at bay, the other to skillfully guide his horse.

"Unlike his master, Boru is a sensitive beast. Desist, Morgan le Fay. Bewitch me not with your schemes."

"Bastard, you'll kill us all!" Morgana hissed through her clenched teeth. Hugh laughed boldly.

Brush ripped at their clothing. Stinging limbs scraped at their arms and faces. Morgana held her breath on the mad race to the very bottom of the steep hill.

There, a swiftly flowing brook cut a cleft in the stones, leaving a shelf of rock overhanging the brook. Hugh's kerns waited there, dismounted to drink and ease their horses. Morgana's brothers splashed in the shallows under Shamus Fitz's careful watch.

Boru thundered toward them all at breakneck speed. Hugh risked what a cautious man never would, listening only to the roar of the rushing wind in his ears, which abolished Loghran O'Toole's whoop of alarm.

Morgana half turned. At least her head turned, or her neck bent. Somehow she managed to get a clear view of Hugh's dangerous, mood-blackened face.

"I came back because I need you!" she shouted.

For a heartbeat, in the stallion's headlong rush to the bottom, Hugh's eyes locked on Morgana's. He judged what he saw there, and it wasn't fear.

No, no, his Morgana did not know the meaning of fear. Even now, when both their lives hung by a precarious thread, she was as bold and hardheaded as he. He almost shouted the triumph of his knowledge of her to the heavens. Her courage matched his own.

A shivering hand pressed against his heart. Hugh turned his attention back to Boru, guiding the horse to a surefooted stride down to the rocky ledge. Then he drew back on the bit. The stallion dropped his haunches on command and skidded to a breathless halt before the startled kerns and the two boys.

"Cor!" Sean Fitzgerald whispered. He didn't know whether to throw up his hands and shout or jump into the shimmering pool of water and get out of the way.

Maurice dropped onto his bottom at Shamus Fitz's feet. He was incapable of saying a word as his sister and the O'Neill came to a standstill a king's yard from his nose.

The great horse snorted in Maurice's face. Then Boru tossed his mighty head, shaking black mane and forelock for all he was worth. Maurice thought the stallion laughed at him. The O'Neill was certainly laughing.

Hugh's laughter cut the kerns' silence in two. He tossed his reins into Brian's hands and dismounted. Exhilarated by the wild ride, he reached up and brought Morgana to the ground. Her hands clamped on to his shoulders. Her lips were white-ringed as she unlocked her teeth. "My brothers are here because I have to keep them with me!"

"For the time being." Hugh set her down with a snap and released her waist. He bowed and turned to the boys. "Lads, your sister needs your attention. Walk her to the woods, then escort her back to me."

He gave the whole company his back, and walked into a bower of blooming hawthorn and strawberry trees.

"Cor," Sean repeated. Maurice put up his hand to stroke the velvet nose of the stallion blowing hot wind in his face.

Morgana grabbed Maurice's fingers. "Don't, Maurice! This is a war-horse. Never risk your fingers round a beast like this."

As she took Sean by the hand and walked them to the woods, Morgana's very words echoed in her head. How much did she risk, dancing with fate around the O'Neill?

She ducked under the hawthorn and straightened in the wood beyond it. Hugh had gone in the same direction. She saw no trace of his passing as she walked the boys into an oak grove.

When she came out from taking her own privacy behind a patch of honeysuckle, she found Maurice collecting wildflowers. He raised a handful to her nose. "I picked them for you, Morgana. What are they?"

"Windflowers, wood anemones." She knelt beside him, inhaling deeply of the sweet woodland flower. Casting a glance around, she found prettier clumps of bitter vetch and yellow pimpernels at the child's feet. Maurice had unerringly picked healing plants. "They smell wonderful, don't they?"

"Oh, aye, they do. Sweet as buttercups." Maurice stuck his nose into his fistful of blossoms and came up with yellow pollen smeared on his freckles. "Could you make me a May crown? I didn't have one this year."

"You didn't? Oh, we must remedy that right away, mustn't we?" Morgana hugged him fondly.

"Make one for everybody." Maurice shoved all his flowers into her hands. "I'll pick more."

"Do," Morgana told him. She sat on her heels to weave the blossoms into crowns. Maurice ran farther afield to find more of the same blossoms. He came back with an armful of white beauties. Morgana had the first crown ready. She settled it on his head with all the solemnity of a bishop crowning a king. "Windflowers, windflowers, listen to me, make this boy as strong and as sturdy as the nearest oak tree."

"Tha's a spell." Maurice wrinkled his pollen-dusted nose. He put a finger to Morgana's mouth to silence her. "Yer not supposed to do that."

"Who's to tell?" Morgana lifted a brow as she asked her question. "Not you, my love."

"Oh, no . . . it sounds like poetry to me. Is this periwinkle here? What do I say when I pluck it?"

Morgana's busy fingers stilled as she looked at the poisonous lavender flowers Maurice was about to pick. "Wait." She had to think of the incantation and count the days since the new moon. As a potion, periwinkle was a singularly powerful herb to invoke against poison. "All right, love, say this. I pray thee, *vinca pervinca,* that thou outfit me so that I be shielded and prosperous and undamaged by poisons and water."

"That's a very good spell for me," Maurice said solemnly. Then he repeated her words exactly, and picked all of the sweet blossoms at hand and gave them to Morgana. "Will you make one for the O'Neill, and his horse, too? They are both strong as oaks already, but I don't want to slight them."

"You have a kind heart, little brother." Morgana tucked three of the brightest periwinkles into the crown on his head. Working as quickly as he found flowers, Morgana made rings of greenery and colors.

"What are you doing?" Sean asked as he emerged from behind an oak, tying up his trews.

"Morgana's making May crowns," Maurice explained.

"Did you make me one, Morgana?"

"Sure and to be certain she did." Maurice went through his collection of flower crowns till he found exactly the right arrangement to fit Sean's head. "This one."

He held up a crown of mixed blooms, and plopped it onto Sean's silky head. "It's got yellow gentian in it, to break hexes and protect you. You need it."

Sean pulled the flower crown off to study it a moment, then nodded his approval. "Were you scared, Morgana?"

"Scared of what?" Morgana asked absently. She knew perfectly well what Sean meant by his question. She finished tying the last wreath and stood.

"Scared of the war-horse." Sean's attention focused on the flower rings looped over Maurice's forearm. "Let me pick the one for Morgana, Maurice. Hers needs to be the prettiest."

"Then it's this one," Maurice held out the ring with the most flowers bunched in it. Morgana dutifully bent to have the crown placed on her head. Both boys had hands in settling the wreath around her coiled braids.

"That's very pretty," Sean said. His small face twisted for a moment, in his deep contemplation of their efforts. "I've come to a decision, sister."

"Oh?" Morgana turned both of them toward the fast-running brook beyond the trees, more their escort than they were hers. "And pray tell me, what would that be?"

"It's my duty as the eldest Fitzgerald to get you another husband. 'Tisn't safe for you to be roaming the isle, a widow woman up for grabs by any scurrilous lout. Father would want me to do what's best."

Morgana managed to hold her tongue and resist the urge to laugh at Sean's audacious assumption. He took himself so seriously. Being the next earl of Kildare was as heavy a burden as being an outlaw, especially for a boy only ten winters old. "Sean, if there was someone Father wanted me to marry, he would have written and given his command."

"Ah, but there you are wrong, Morgana. Father doesn't know of the troubles we've had in his absence. He isn't like me. I know you like to do what you like. But if Father knew about Lord Grey, he'd be grievously upset. Wouldn't he, Maurice?"

"Oh, aye, he would. We get a letter from France every month. Mother is most distressed about you."

Sean dug an elbow in his little brother's side, not wanting Maurice to steal his thunder. "Father might approve a match to the O'Neill. I heard tell he was made an earl in England."

"And who told you that?" Morgana demanded. "Macmurrough?"

"I don't know any Macmurroughs," Sean said soberly.

"Well, it makes no difference," Morgana replied. "Because that is none of your business, Sean Fitzgerald. I don't recall mentioning to you that I want to be saddled with another husband."

"Don't know why you wouldn't." Sean shrugged. "The right husband is good for a woman, especially a sister to an earl."

"You will keep your big mouth shut about such things. Unless you want your ears boxed, little brother. Don't be shaming me with such talk."

Undaunted by her scolding, Sean ducked under the drooping branches of the hawthorn and emerged onto the rock overlooking the brook, announcing, "Hallo, we're back. Look, isn't Morgana pretty?"

Morgana held her peace. Sean, she knew firsthand, was as willful a Fitzgerald as she. Worse, if she added all the catering that had been done in the early years of his life, because he was an earl's heir.

Given the tempering of proper aging—like good wine and whiskey—most Fitzgerald males managed to control the urges to dominate all and sundry within range. If not that, then they grew up to be charming brutes whose easy smiles won more friends than enemies.

Though each kern looked when Sean made his blatant invitation for a compliment, only Hugh O'Neill actually took the bait.

But then, Hugh stood head and shoulders above any fold of ordinary men. His eyes met Morgana's. Banked heat simmered in their brown depths as he plucked a periwinkle from her crown and twirled the single bloom under his nose.

"Sorcerer's violet becomes you, my lady. I vow, I am under your spell. You are fetching. Very fetching, indeed."

"Well, they will become you, as well." A touch of perversity edged her lips. "It's a May crown, and all of us must wear it, to please the boys."

"A May crown, you say." Hugh inclined his head, glancing only once at the boys. "Then, by all means, lady. Crown me in this fertile month of May."

Morgana took a ring from Maurice's hand and raised it to Hugh's dark head. "Say the poem!" Maurice insisted. "The one you said for me."

Hugh watched a small scowl knot Morgana's brow, but she smoothed it out just as quickly as it had appeared. His mouth twitched with the urge to grin. He'd expected her to crown him after their harrowing ride downhill, but *not* with a ring of flowers!

"I don't think this man needs to be urged to become any stronger than he is, Maurice," Morgana said, tight-lipped. "I shall have to alter it."

"Make it so," Maurice commanded magnanimously, "if you please."

Morgana held the crown over Hugh's head as she recited a quick spell. "Windflowers, windflowers, listen to me, make this man's hands as gentle as today's spring breeze."

Hugh caught her right hand, staying her from lowering the crown onto his head, adding his own incantation to her verse. "And make this man unforgettable to this dear lady."

Maurice clapped with delight as Morgana lowered the May crown onto Hugh O'Neill's head. Hugh's thumb and forefinger encased Morgana's wrist, his touch as light as the wind she'd invoked. "Is it gentle you want now, my lady?"

Morgana's lips twitched at the corners as she looked to where his fingers lightly circled her flesh. Hugh followed the direction of her gaze. The bruises had yet to fade from her skin. As it was her right hand he held, Hugh couldn't have said whether he'd put the marks there or Kelly had. His intense eyes met Morgana's. Both of them were thinking of her desperate leap out the window of Dungannon's solar.

"Had I held you this lightly, you'd not be here to please your brothers' whims, lady. Fear not my hold, Morgana. It will never harm you, no matter how fierce."

The moment of sublime communication was broken by the restlessness of the others in their party.

"Where's my crown?" Rory demanded of Sean and Maurice. "It had better smell nicer and look more handsome than the one you give Brian."

His brother laughed. "On you? Not a chance."

The crowns were dispensed, and Hugh lifted Maurice up to put the last one on Loghran's white locks.

"Can't say that we see the windflowers against that cotton crop, but the greenery stands out well." Hugh laughed.

O'Toole growled like a wild beast, trying to scare the boy in O'Neill's arms. Maurice only laughed, knowing the men were teasing him.

Loghran took the boy from O'Neill's grip. "You're supposed to be frightened out of your wits when I growl at you, boy. Can't you see that I come from Viking stock?"

"Am I supposed to know that because of your hair?" Maurice asked as Loghran set him on his pony.

"No, because of his size!" Sean corrected. "Don't be a goose, Maurice. Use your eyes."

"Well spoken." Loghran gave Sean a boost onto his pony, too. "Come, lads, we'll take the lead this time. Laird O'Neill can spell himself guarding our rear. My old heart's not up for another trampling."

Hugh's men all mounted and rode out after Loghran. Boru and Ariel were left behind. So were he and Morgana. She hurried across the stone to her horse. Hugh followed.

"Are you intending to mount unaided?" he asked silkily, letting Boru stick his nose ahead of him and butt the mare. Hugh thought that a very direct way of securing a sulky female's attention.

Morgana definitely ignored him. She put her back to Hugh as she untied Ariel's reins. Then she deliberately turned the mare between them so that her horse bumped Hugh back a pace or two.

"Your tactics are obvious, milady." Hugh grinned, admiring the fetching flowers crowning her head.

"Are they?" Morgana paused at a break in the stones, climbing onto the taller as she drew Ariel before her. She was in her saddle when she spoke again, fitting feet firmly in the stirrups. "We must go, milord. I wouldn't want to get separated from the troop."

"Liar," Hugh called as he swung up onto Boru's back. Ariel shied away from the randy stallion. Morgana took the lead, so Hugh offset his stallion two paces behind Morgana's mount. The Arabian sidestepped away from the stallion, as tetchy as her mistress.

The climb up the next hill was just as steep as the ride down it had been. Crowded on the path, Morgana had to give her concentration to Ariel's footing.

"Careful," Hugh cautioned, when the mare slipped on moss adhering to the rocks. He put out a hand to quiet the mare, then let Morgana take the lead on the steep ascent to the top, for safety's sake.

"I am always careful, my lord—" Morgana tossed the taunt over her shoulder "—when the danger is as apparent as the nose on *your* face. Keep that wild horse away from my mare."

"If that was supposed to sting me, it went far wide of the mark." Hugh laughed again at her high dudgeon, which she went to such lengths to keep hidden from others.

Her sparring words pleased him, and so did the tempers that simmered just under her control. She kept their battles between the two of them, leaving others out of the fracas. Hugh liked that trait of hers very, very much. It made her all the more desirable in his eyes.

He waved a magnanimous hand at the riders in the distance. "Go then, catch up with the pack. I'm content to bring up the rear. Remember, Morgana, what you promised a little while ago. You will share my bed tonight."

As tempting as it was to spite him, Morgana held her peace again, not saying a word. She scanned the bluff for the rest of their party and put her heels to Ariel's sides. She knew when to pick her battles and when to save her breath. Hugh O'Neill didn't.

They dismounted at Colraine's largest inn, a tired troop of Irishmen at dusk. Maurice had long since given up the ghost. He slept in Shamus Fitz's lap, his small head bobbing over the big kern's arm.

Kermit Blackbeard dismounted first and reached up to quietly take the sleeping boy from Shamus's arms, so that he could also dismount with ease. The kern flexed his left arm, restoring its circulation. He'd carried the sleeping boy for the past hour, since the sun had begun dropping into the hazy sky over Lough Foyle.

Morgana was glad to have Hugh's help when she dismounted. They had ridden almost nonstop since their short rest at the brook. For some unspoken reason, Hugh O'Neill had insisted they make it to Colraine before full dark set in.

Torches flickered in iron stands, well away from the inn's doors and thatched roof. Loghran O'Toole went inside to arrange for accommodations. Sean sidled up to Morgana to tell her he was hungry.

A groom came out of the stable and collected their horses. Hugh slung Morgana's saddlebags and his own on his shoulder, then took her arm and walked her up the steps into the low-roofed common room. Young Sean proceeded them, his curiosity about this new place dampened by well-schooled caution and road-weariness.

The day's haunch of venison was roasting on the inn's hearth fire, crackling and spitting grease at a boy not much older than Sean who was turning the spit. The smell of whiskey and ale flavored the inn's common room. Barrels of ale were stacked against one wall, whiskey the other.

Few patrons showed any interest in their arrival. Always cautious, Morgana searched the room for redcoats and found none. She got no more than a first look before Hugh resolutely hustled her through a narrow door leading to the second floor. The innkeeper opened a door on a small room and stood aside to let them enter.

To Morgana's eye, the bed looked woefully inadequate. She insisted on inspecting the sheets before she allowed Maurice to be laid down in the center of the bed. She sat beside him, unlacing his shoes, removing stockings and rumpled tunic and shirt.

He needed a bath, but she wasn't going to wake him for one now. A wash in the morning might do. Sean sat himself on a stool and did the same, took off boots and stockings, cast off his cloak and tunic. He stood, hitching his trews to his waist, and turned to Hugh O'Neill as the innkeeper's girl brought a supper tray into the chamber.

"Will you be joining us, sir?" Sean asked.

Hugh noticed that the boy's earlier camaraderie was gone from his demeanor. Now Sean Fitzgerald appeared as formal as one who had been trained at the queen's court. The lad looked years older than his actual age.

That reminded Hugh of his own past, and those first years he'd spent in England, learning the hardest lesson of life—never to trust anyone.

"Nay." Hugh waved the serving girl, Loghran and Kermit out of the room. When he was alone with the Fitzgeralds, he said, "I'll sup below, with my men. The privy is behind the kitchen, if you need it, lad, but take a man of mine with you, should you go out. Lady Morgana, content yourself here with the chamber pot. Colraine is known for river rats and thugs that linger about its alleyways, waiting to rob the unsuspecting."

He set Morgana's saddlebags on the floor beside the bed. Then, with a meaningful look to Morgana, Hugh departed, closing the door behind him.

Sean didn't know whether he'd been slighted or not, and told Morgana so. "Nonsense," she told him. "He's a man grown, and would prefer to sup with his soldiers rather than a boy, Sean. Rank has nothing to do with that."

"Are you certain?" Sean asked. "I am an earl."

"Father is the earl," Morgana reminded him. Their father was still alive, though in exile.

Morgana shed her cloak and went to the basin to wash her face and hands. Sean stuck a pose and repeated Hugh's orders several times, mimicking Hugh's delivery. "The O'Neill commands well, wouldn't you say, Morgana?"

"Aye, he's mastered that art." Morgana soaped her throat and the back of her neck. Sean's voice lacked the depth and power of Hugh's. It wouldn't when he came of age. Morgana's father was a terror in his own right.

"I could learn a lot from a man like O'Neill. Haps I'll ask him to squire me." Sean pulled off his undershirt and dragged a stool to the table and sat.

"You're not sitting to the table to eat like a barbarian," Morgana gasped as she folded the towel she'd used and hung it on the washstand. "Put on your shirt!"

"Aw, Morgana," Sean complained round a mouthful of bread and venison. "I'm fair starved, and tired, too."

Morgana took the bread and meat out of his hand. "Put your shirt on, you little heathen. Don't insult me. I don't care how far we Fitzgeralds sink in the world, you've been taught manners, and you'll use them."

"What makes you think my stomach knows the difference between eating while wearing a shirt or going naked?" Sean grumbled. He got up and grabbed his shirt, jerking it onto his skinny arms. He didn't go so far as to tuck it in before he sat once more. "Let me eat in peace."

Morgana handed him the biscuit she'd taken from his hand. She saw no point in telling him she'd let him skip some polite rules. He hadn't washed before he ate, but he would wash before he went to bed, or the two of them would be going head-to-head. If it came to that, Morgana vowed, she'd come out the winner.

Morgana took the damp towel to the bed to mop up Maurice's face and hands, then washed his feet before settling him under the covers. She kissed his brow, marveling anew at the miracle of his existence. His quiet breathing was a gift from God. Thinking that, Morgana sat to the table, but did not eat.

"Now what's wrong?"

Morgana looked at Sean for a moment before her troubled gaze went back to Maurice. "I don't think I can put my thoughts into words, Sean. I haven't had time to reflect upon what it means to me to have Maurice alive and well. I mean . . . the last I heard, he was dead."

Sean cast a glance over his shoulder to the boy in the bed, speaking between hungrily wolfed bites of food. "He pulled through the worst of it, but he's still sick. Can't eat sometimes. He's just a little boy, Morgana, but he's very brave."

"I know." Morgana nodded. "You are too, Sean. I'm sorry for my curt words a few moments ago. I forget what's most important sometimes."

"Aye." Sean mopped his plate with a wedge of bread. "God's truth, Morgana, sometimes I'm scared out of my wits. Suppose one of those kerns comes to kill us when we sleep?"

"You don't mean Hugh's men, do you?" Morgana asked softly. Her trust of the O'Neill extended to his band of men, with one exception. She didn't trust Loghran O'Toole, who would just as well have been done with her several nights ago. She hadn't forgotten his order to cut off her hand. She wanted to know whether Sean felt the same unease regarding Hugh's gillie.

"I don't know who I mean," he replied. "We can't trust anyone who knows we're Fitzgeralds. I wish I was anyone but John Gerald Fitzgerald, the outlawed heir of Kildare."

Morgana could think of no platitudes to offer her brother. Hollow words of comfort did neither of them good. Sean would know them for the lies they were, anyway. "You'd best wash and sleep awhile, then. I'll watch over you."

Sean cast the remains of the loaf on the platter and stood. He stretched, then ambled to the washstand and completed his ablutions with a ten-year-old's lack of enthusiasm for the task. As for going out to the privy, he declined, making use of the chamber pot.

"Say your prayers," Morgana said, from old habit.

"To who?" Sean asked. "There is no God."

Morgana stared at him, momentarily stunned. That he should feel the same way she did astounded her. He dared to voice his blasphemous doubts out loud, proving he had more courage than she. "They say we must keep our faith and hold on to our beliefs even in the darkest moments, Sean."

"That's another lie they've fed us," Sean responded. He climbed into bed and sat there, staring at Morgana with old, old eyes in his too-young face. "Gods and saints, fairy tales and legends—this whole land is full of them. Everywhere we go there are shrines and crosses and monuments to leprechauns and Little People and the Tuatha de Danann. It's all a bunch of nonsense. You don't believe any of it, do you, Morgana?''

The test was to say she did when she didn't. That would prove she still had some faith left within her. But at this moment, with the most uncertain of all tomorrows facing them, Morgana wouldn't compound her errors by lying to her brother. "Sleep on your thoughts, Sean. We'll talk about it in the morning."

She thought perhaps Hugh O'Neill, who could explain why and how the sun rose each morning, could prove to Sean that a kind and benevolent God ruled the cosmos. She couldn't. Not any more than she could swear to the boy that, come tomorrow morning, they would wake to see the new day.

Hugh found Morgana seated at the small table with one candle lighting the remains of her meal when he came up to bed. The boys sprawled like littermates on top of each other, fast asleep.

Morgana, on the other hand, looked as miserable as could be. She lifted her face up to Hugh's as he took hold of her hand. "Come with me," he urged.

Her head dropped in a tired nod of acquiescence, and she rose, accompanying him to the adjoining chamber. Loghran O'Toole got to his feet, his face a mask of grim, tight-lipped shadows. Morgana felt the disapproval of his glare before he gave her his back and slipped into her brothers' room and firmly shut the door.

Morgana stared at the closed door, even as Hugh's hands unlaced her short bodice and freed the ties of her skirt to let both garments fall to her feet.

"Hey." Hugh caught her chin, turning her face to his. "I'm here, lady."

"He disapproves of me."

"Who? Loghran? He disapproves of everyone who gets close to me. Don't let it bother you."

"No, it's more than that." Morgana shook her head. Hugh's deft fingers released her braids, and they fell down across her shift. "He makes me feel guilty."

"He makes everyone feel guilty. That's what priests do best."

"He is a priest?" Morgana stepped back. "A Catholic priest?"

"As Catholic as they come—an Augustinian." Hugh's wolfish grin nowhere near appeased her shock.

"That Viking—" Morgana sputtered "—warmonger is a priest?"

"Would I lie about something like that?" Hugh caught her shoulders and pulled her to him. "Forget Loghran."

"But he rides into battle with you. He paints himself blue from head to toe and wields a sword and a battle-ax. He can't be a priest. They aren't supposed to kill people."

"So he takes the term *soldier of Christ* literally."

"Don't joke about this."

"All right, then." Hugh held her at arm's length. His fingers were tight on her upper arms, and his gaze was direct and solid. "You tell me where it is written that a priest cannot be a warrior? Pope Julius was a better general than a pope. Jesuits manage to blend the two, else the church would have no inquisitors to put heretics to death."

Morgana choked down a cold laugh behind her hand, thinking of how her grandfather had died after being accused of witchcraft. "This is wrong. I can't stay with you tonight, Hugh."

Hugh pulled her to his chest and wrapped his arms around her. He held her as gently as he'd held her wrist earlier, implying no restraint, intending only comfort.

"What is wrong about it, Morgana? You are safe with me. No harm will come to the boys while Loghran guards them."

"You don't understand," Morgana argued. "And I can't explain it well."

Hugh tightened his hands on her shoulders. "I do understand. I've been where you're standing, afraid of everyone, not knowing who I can trust. Let it go, Morgana."

"I can't." She shook her head and refused to meet his eyes. "It's no use."

"What is this really about?" Hugh asked. "Tell me. Don't blame it on a wash of conscience because Loghran gave you the cold shoulder when he went into your room. Tell me the truth for once, Morgana."

"You think I know the truth? You fool yourself."

"No, lady. I do not. What is it you want from me? Why did you come back to me? Tell me the truth about that. We'll work the rest out from that point forward."

He was asking too much of her. Asking that she go inside herself and look at the motives for her own actions. Morgana refused to do that.

Hugh dragged her up to his mouth, kissing her deeply, passionately, with all the hunger he felt growling for release inside him. He wanted to devour her, taste her, fill her. He denied himself anything more than the taste of her lips yielding to his demand for so much more. Then he set her back from him and dropped his hands to his sides.

"What is it that you fear the most, Morgana?"

"Tomorrow," she whispered, and tried to get back to him. Hugh put out his hand, stopping her. He shook his head.

"What about tomorrow frightens you? Tell me!"

"You won't be here."

"I will," he responded with assurance.

"No, you won't." Morgana shook her head. "We are both cast adrift. The bonds holding the rest of the world together by convention are severed by our status as widow and widower. I am fair game. You are a free agent. Nothing binds us."

"You forgot to mention desire. I want you, Morgana.
You fair burn for me." His hands slid down her arms till he
found her hands and brought them up to his lips to kiss each
palm.

"It's a pointless liaison that I should not have allowed to
begin. I knew better, Hugh." Her eyes remained fixed on
Hugh's as she told him her one truth. "You have no future
with me. I am an unacceptable choice, even for a leman.
Your gillie-priest, or whatever O'Toole is, knows that."

"You should have the grace to let me be the judge of
that."

"It is the truth. Do you think I can be happy for even a
moment, knowing the time will come when you are forced
to cast me out? I know what troubles tomorrow brings. I've
seen it too many times."

"I've already told you, I will be here for you come morning. Come every morning."

"I would like to believe such a sweet lie, my lord." Morgana stroked her hand across his smooth cheek, then
dropped it to her side.

"It is no sweet lie, my lady."

"No, my lord, I know better. To love and kiss me brings
the curse of the Fitzgeralds to your door. I will not seal your
death warrant. I can't do that to you." Morgana caught up
her clothes from the floor and fled. "I'm sorry, Hugh, I
can't."

Hugh recaptured Morgana before she reached the adjoining door. He turned her back to the oak, holding on to
her struggling hands. "Isn't it a question of *won't*, not
can't?"

Morgana wrenched one hand free of his control. "I refuse to bandy words with you. It's pointless and impossible. Let me go, Hugh."

"No. I will not. Did you hear that, lady? I said, I *will*
not."

Hugh caught hold of Morgana's chin, lifting it till she
looked him squarely in the eye. "My lady, that means I am

making a conscious choice to stay with you. It is not whim nor fancy. No queen, with all her power and authority, has ordered me to your bed to service you and bring more loyal subjects into her kingdom. No priest or father of a virgin has caught me in flagrante delicto and driven me to make a guilty vow to love, honor and cherish you all the days of my life. I am here because I want to be here with you.

"You, Morgana Fitzgerald, widow of the late pirate Greg O'Malley, sister to two outlawed lads fleeing Erin for their lives, outcast, whatever you call yourself. I am here, standing beside you, wanting to love you and hold you against me."

"You're a fool to risk everything you have for me. I tell you, I am not worth the sacrifice."

"Pray tell me, Lady Morgana, whose life are we speaking of risking? Whose property? Mine? I own nothing. Yours? I see no properties and deeds attached to your hand. In all truth, my lady, what have I to give you? My body, my mind, my wits. Naught else. I have lived by my wits since I was your brother Sean's age. I have survived, alone all the years since but for the counsel of a bloody-minded Irish priest. And for the first time in years, I feel alive, truly alive, and part of this world, because being with you makes it so. Stay with me, Morgana. I need you so much, and in my cold, unfeeling heart I believe you also need me."

His hand cupped her cheek and his mouth touched her trembling lips. As he kissed her, Hugh could taste how strongly her urge to run away from him was. He could no more let her go than he could stop the eternal beating of his heart. She surrounded him, infused him, filled each of his senses, until he was drowning in the need to feel her body throbbing close to his.

Hugh swept her up in his arms and carried her to the bed. He laid her down upon the pristine sheeting and removed her shift, then sat back upon his heels, marveling at the splendid generosity of a God who made a woman's body so beautiful to a man's eyes.

His only thought was to worship and adore her with his lips, his tongue, his body, soul and mind. Then he realized that what he wanted most of all was just to love her, hold her and satisfy her. If doing that would bind her to him, the rest of his days on this earth would be happy days, halcyon days of splendor and joy.

For Morgana it was the most tender loving she'd ever experienced in her life. Sweet and fulfilling, abolishing for the duration of the night all the demons and shadowy threats that plagued her days.

She didn't think about her duties, her brothers, her father, or any of their multitude of enemies. She thought only about Hugh and how to please him, satisfy him with hungry kisses and soft, sweetly shared touches.

This loving was all that truly mattered in life—being bound to a good man. Hugh had made his choice to stay through her darkest night. And if they loved hard enough and long enough, perhaps tomorrow morning would never come.

Chapter Fourteen

The chamber was very, very dark. Maurice woke up hungry. He didn't know where he was. Momentary panic sat him bolt upright. A fearful scream crept up the back of his throat. Then Sean stirred beside him. His warm hand soothingly patted Maurice's back. Sean mumbled, "Go back to sleep, Maury. 'Tis early yet."

Reassured, Maurice knuckled the sleep from his eyes. He yawned so deeply his jaws cracked. When he took his knuckle out of his eye, he saw that the window above the bed was open. Maurice got up, standing on the mattress to peer out into the predawn night. Nothing looked familiar about the broad river coursing beside the building where he was sleeping.

Not so much as the faintest glow of sunrise lightened the inky night sky. Maury scratched his belly and got up, tiptoeing about, seeking the chamber pot. He almost stumbled over a big man sleeping on the floor.

Maurice hunkered down so that he could bring his face close enough to the snoring man to identify him. It was the very tall Loghran O'Toole.

Satisfied by that conclusion, Maurice stepped over Loghran to reach the chamber door. There would be a privy outside. He had only to find it then come back to bed. Sean would get him something to eat. Maury knew how to be patient.

He closed the door ever so softly, so that he wouldn't wake Loghran or Sean. Maurice strained his eyes, making out several other doors along the narrow hall that dropped by a stairwell into the common room of the inn. All was quiet below, save for the snoring of the men sleeping there.

Maury's bare feet made no noise as he padded through the common room. Outside, the air was damp and cool. Fog rose from the river. Its tendrils feathered out like a wet blanket across the yard, clinging to the ground and the bases of each building.

Overhead, the starry night was crystal-clear, and a quarter moon cast dim light on the earth, showing Maurice the way to the privy. Maury hated going inside a privy—they were dark and rank, unpleasant things. He took a deep breath, determined to hold it for as long as it took to relieve himself, then ducked behind the door.

James Kelly jerked when Corporal Williams jabbed his fist between his ribs. "Sir!" the young soldier hissed in an excited whisper. "Wake up. A boy just left the inn!"

"Wha'?" Kelly shot upright, looking blindly around him, numb with fatigue. He'd been trailing Hugh O'Neill with only one untrained corporal backing him up. He had yet to find another complement of English soldiers to draft more men from, and wouldn't until he reached Derry, or backtracked all the way through Ulster to Carrickfergus.

Williams poked him in the ribs again and pointed across the foggy yard. "Sir, a boy just went inside the privy. I'd stake my soul on his being a redhead, sir."

"Is that so?" Groggily Kelly hauled himself out of the haystack. He straightened his jacket and drew his sword, then crept to the door of the stable, shouldered Williams aside and looked out.

Not that there was anything to see, save more Irish mud, broken harness trees and garbage.

"How'd you know his hair was red?"

"The moon, sir." Williams pointed to the pale orb rising in the east. "Late-rising quarter moon tonight, sir. I saw him plain as day."

Kelly slumped against the door frame and scowled into the stable's depths as he scratched vigorously at his hair. Of thirty horses boarded here, he recognized only one, that prime Arabian mare that belonged to Morgana Fitzgerald. He hadn't laid an eye on the woman.

His teeth set on edge. He had racked his brain for a suitable means of taking the woman captive without risking his own recapture by the O'Neill. Kelly had gone to sleep trying to work out some solution to that dilemma. Now this fool corporal had woken him up to tell him a redheaded boy had to take a piss.

Kelly dragged his hand over his face. "How old is the boy?"

"Five, six maybe. A little fellow."

Kelly held back the urge to brain Corporal Williams. Good soldiers were made, not born. "Listen to me, young man, the woman I'm looking for might be accompanied by a boy, but he'd be nine or ten years old by now. I'd take it as a personal favor to me if you'd just stand your watch and let me get a few hours' sleep. I'm after bigger quarry than pissing six-year-olds, understand? Wake me when you see people stirring about the common room. We'll need time to saddle up and get into position to follow O'Neill. Is that understood?"

"Yes, sir, Captain Kelly. I've got it right now. I'll keep a sharp eye out for an older boy."

"You do that," Kelly grumbled as he retreated to the haystack. He sheathed his sword before he laid down and closed his eyes. Walsingham always saddled him with imbeciles. Just once in his career, he'd like the chance to work with someone competent and capable.

Maurice didn't return upstairs directly. He knew he should have done so, but he hadn't seen anything when they arrived the night before. He wanted to explore and discover things, sample the ale in the common room, find out how many horses were inside the stable and discover whether there were any whores in this particular establishment.

The sun was definitely on the rise when he scurried back up the stairs. He was worried, too, because he reckoned he'd been gone too long. Sean might notice. Maury knew better than to do anything that would make Sean mad. He'd smack the eternal daylights out of Maurice.

Sure enough, the moment Maury's bare feet touched the cold planks of the upper floor, Sean let loose a bloodcurdling scream that would have woken the dead two counties away.

"Uh-oh!" Maury whispered. He froze on the landing, staring down the long, dark hall, wondering where he was going to hide. Anyplace in the world would do. Maurice opened the first door he came to and jumped behind it, shutting the door hard.

He was so intent on listening to Sean's screams, trying to make out what he was saying, that he didn't notice the commotion he'd started behind him.

Morgana shoved Hugh off her and sat bolt upright. "What is it?" Hugh asked sleepily.

"Someone's come in the room."

"What?" Hugh rolled over, cocking his ear to the sound of bashing and footsteps and somebody shouting ... next door. Some of the words were low and deep—a man's voice. The other was a shriek, like a woman's, but not exactly.

Hugh sat up and reached for his trews. He hadn't quite got hold of them before the connecting door between the rooms burst open. Morgana yelped and grabbed the covers up to her throat.

Loghran O'Toole ducked through the doorway, carting someone rolled up inside a quilt. He stomped across the small room and dumped his burden onto Hugh's bed. "Damn my soul to hell and back again, O'Neill. You started this. You'll damn well make it right. Deal with this brat. He thinks I've killed his brother.''

Morgana drew back against the bedstead. Sean fought his way out of the quilting, heaping the worst sort of curses on Loghran's eternal soul.

Maurice whispered, ''Uh-oh,'' and slithered into a heap against the hallway door.

Hugh lighted a candle just as Sean's head emerged from the swaddling. The boy sputtered all sorts of words, but then went silent as a stone when he spied Hugh's sleep-tousled hair and angry visage, and Morgana's face, pale against the headboard.

''What's this about?'' Hugh demanded tersely.

''That monster devoured my bro...'' Sean's voice petered out as he realized what exactly he was seeing. ''Morgana, where are your clothes?''

Hugh restated his demand. ''I asked what all the shouting is about, boy. You'd better give me a straight answer now.''

Sean gulped. His head swiveled about, and he found Maury cowering behind his hands and knees.

''Jesu!'' Sean gasped. ''Maurice James Fitzgerald, what in the name of creation are you doing there?''

Morgana tilted her head to the side, blinking, staring past Sean's shoulder. Maurice peeked through his fingers and whispered, ''I didn't see nothin'! Honest to God!''

Sean climbed off the bed, trailing the quilt around his legs, screaming, ''Damn you, Maury, ya scared me half to death! I thought that Viking murdert you! Where'd you go?'' Sean dropped down to the floor beside Maurice and dragged the little boy to his chest. He shook him hard, and then, wrapping his arms around Maurice's head, he crooned to him, a litany of ''It's all right, it's all right. I'm not mad, I'm scared.''

Hugh got his trews pulled up his legs and stood to fasten them. Morgana found her shift and dragged it over her head. As Hugh shoved his arms inside his shirt, Sean looked him square in the eye and did the impossible; he apologized. "I'm sorry, sir. I woke up and Maury was gone. It scared me. I didn't know he was in here with you."

Hugh threw the curtains back and opened the window, letting rosy daylight spill inside the chamber and the brisk morning breeze off the sea. The fresh air also removed some of the ripe scent of sex from the closed room. To Hugh's chagrin, it didn't go far enough.

He stood back a moment, blinking, as he stared at the stable yard. What he'd thought he'd seen wasn't there. He turned around to deal with Morgana's brothers. They were the reality, the human reality. A flash of red darting round the edge of the stable back to the river could be anything.

Hugh stamped into his boots and said, "Right, lads. Which one of you wants to explain first?"

Morgana tucked the sheet into a toga and stood up.

"On second thought..." Hugh stepped before her, accurately deducing that she would go to any length to protect those boys. This situation, Hugh decided, needed to be handled man-to-man. "Boys, both of you come with me. Lady Morgana needs time to dress."

Hugh secured both boys and hauled them out the doorway into the hall. The last glimpse Hugh had of Morgana was of her jaw sagging another inch in shocked surprise.

They sat on the stairs, Maurice and Sean on the top step, Hugh on the third one down. "What happened, Sean?"

"Like I s-s-said," Sean stuttered, "I woke up and Maury was gone. O'Toole was sleeping across the door, so I asked him where Maury'd gone. He just grunted and didn't answer, so I clobbered him."

"Sounded to me like I heard more than one clobber," Hugh said.

"Ya might have." Sean wasn't going to condemn himself with his own mouth. He'd done some kicking and cussing, too. "The thing is, he threw his quilt over me, and I thought he was going to murder me, too."

"I see." Hugh stroked his jaw. His day-old beard rasped against his fingertips.

"Then he dumped me on top of you." At that point, Sean shied away from looking at Hugh as he added, "And Morgana."

Keeping this conversation on the business at hand, Hugh turned his gaze to Maurice. "And where were you, little man?"

"I had ta go to the privy." Maurice would not raise his head from his folded arms.

"Get off, Maury, me and O'Toole were fighting for nearly a half hour." Sean hit him in the shoulder. "You were gone too long just for a trip to the privy."

"I was." Maury defended himself verbally as he rubbed his shoulder. "I got sort of distracted. Lord O'Neill, there's two redcoats sleeping in the stable."

Sean drew in a hissing breath and hit Maury hard. "You little liar, don't go making things up just so you don't get a skelping."

Hugh put out a stilling hand, intercepting Sean's fist. "I don't believe I asked you to pound your brother to a pulp, Sean. So, you were distracted by soldiers, Maurice. How many were there?"

"For the love of God," Sean swore. "Don't get him started, sir. Maury sees redcoats everywhere. He's a bloody chickenheart, he is."

"Two." Maurice looked up at Hugh with watery blue eyes, so identical to Morgana's that whatever animosity Hugh retained at the intrusion in his bedchamber evaporated.

"Can you describe them?" Hugh kept his voice soft.

"Umm..." Maury nodded. "Old."

"How old? As old as I?"

"Umm," Maury frowned. "More like Macmurrough."

"Who's Macmurrough?" Sean asked, exasperated.

Hugh waved a silencing hand. "Right, then, what about the other one. Is is big or tall? Fat or skinny?"

"His name is Williams, and he's like Rory, only he's got a red coat on, and a long sword and black boots."

"Did you hear the other man's name?"

"Oh, um, Captain, maybe. I dunno."

"Captain." Hugh repeated that word out loud. He got to his feet, towering over both boys, even though he stood on the steps below them. "Sean, take Maurice back inside your room and tell Loghran I want to talk to him out here in the hall. And, boys, both of you are to stay inside the room until I come for you and Morgana. I'll have some food sent up. Understand?"

Sean understood that the interview was now over. He stood up and discovered that, on the landing, he was nearly eye-to-eye with the O'Neill. That restored his determination to speak his mind.

"Sir, we need to speak man-to-man about my sister. I see that you have something else on your mind, so I will table the discussion for a more opportune moment, but I will not, under any circumstances, allow my family honor to be tabled indefinitely."

"Is that a challenge to a duel I'm hearing?" Hugh asked incredulously.

"I believe so, sir." Sean put his arm around Maurice and walked away, leaving Hugh O'Neill to make whatever he would of Sean's most serious words.

Loghran found Hugh still grinning when he caught up with him in the common room. "What's going on?"

"We're being spied upon." Hugh shook Kermit awake and roused Brian and Rory. "I believe Kelly is trailing us. Go out and have a look, lads. Loghran go down to the church and find out if there have been any English troops moving through the area in recent days. Luck may be with us. I don't believe Kelly's found any reinforcements, else he'd have attacked us in force on the road. And while you're at chapel, O'Toole, see if you can hire three or four red-haired altar boys to ride with us to Dunluce. Report back to me in one hour, saddled and ready to ride."

* * *

The bells signaling the end of morning mass were ringing when Morgana and her brothers came out of the inn to mount up for the last day's ride to Dunluce. Hugh, carrying her saddlebags, slung the heavy pack onto Ariel's saddle and fastened the straps.

A stiff wind from the north had dissipated the morning fog. Morgana had fastened her hair under a netting to keep it out of her eyes. She took the extra precaution of binding it now underneath a kerchief. Last, she drew on her kidskin gloves. The palms and fingertips were showing their age and the use she'd put them through in the past year. Still, they were the last pair of gloves she owned. Use them she would, until they fell apart completely.

Maury and Sean were not in the least surprised to find that three red-haired boys had joined their troop. Names were exchanged and caps admired.

As Hugh boosted Morgana onto her saddle, she scanned the group. "We are missing O'Toole and Shamus."

"That's right." Hugh answered cryptically. He didn't want Morgana to worry. He hadn't mentioned the soldiers tailing them.

"How far is Dunluce?"

"A league and a half, north by northeast. We'll ride straight through, and be there well before noon."

"When's high tide?" It was Morgana's last question, for the time being.

Hugh turned round to look at the moon. He finished buckling the last strap on her saddlebag and patted her hip reassuringly. "After midnight, by my judgment. You won't miss it, I promise you."

Taking him at his word, Morgana turned her attention to her brothers. It had been decided, for safety's sake, that Sean and Maurice would each ride double with a kern and the new boys would ride their ponies.

Hugh boosted Sean onto Boru, then sprang up into the saddle behind him. Maurice was almost completely hidden by the drape of Art Macmurrough's ample plaid. They rode across the wide bridge over the Bann into Antrim. At the crossroads before Portrush, took the lesser road east, between Aghren and Ballyreagh.

Tyrone's forests were far behind them on this leg of the journey. The hills leading to Ballyreagh were less steep, and the closer they came to the coast, the rockier the landscape became. What trees there were began to show the marks of the relentless north Atlantic wind.

A tall bank of clouds loomed on the northeast horizon, flat-topped and billowing underneath, and the sunrise bore a distinct and lingering aura of red—a portent of a stormy afternoon.

Castle Dunluce could be seen from miles away, high on a promontory overlooking the sea. Even from a distance, the castle looked formidable and impregnable. The closer they came to it, the less appeal it had for Morgana's eye. She urged Ariel to catch up with Boru, specifically to ask Hugh questions about the inhabitants of the austere structure. But when she did catch him, she had something even more important to ask about.

The north wind now howled in their ears. It swept over the top of the black granite cliffs, tearing the words from Morgana's mouth as she shouted her questions to Hugh.

"Who built Dunluce?"

"Originally?" he shouted back. "Normans, I think. A de Burgh, possibly. The Scots wrested control of it some time ago. Why do you ask?"

"It looks a dreadful place."

"Wait till you step inside it. It's worse than you can imagine. Haunted, they say."

"By whom?" Morgana asked.

"By every race known to Ireland. Look, there's the road, or what passes for one here. We'll cross via the drawbridge, provided I've got credentials enough to get us inside."

"Isn't the Mac Donnell your vassal?"

Hugh grinned, and the wind whipped his hair across his brow. Sean looked up from the drape of Hugh's plaid to squint into the wind and see where they were going. He'd been very quiet since coming face-to-face with Morgana in the bedchamber where she'd spent the night.

"Sorely Boy's my vassal as much as he's any man's vassal."

"What does that mean?" Sean asked.

"That means never turn your back on him, lad," Hugh answered with blunt authority. He waved Morgana ahead of him on the narrow track winding up the rocks to the castle gate. When she was well surrounded by the five kerns who remained with him on this leg of the journey, Hugh dropped back to use his spyglass and search the plateau for O'Toole and Shamus Fitz. They had remained behind in Colraine to investigate any redcoats lingering in the vicinity.

As he closed the glass to put it away, he noticed that Sean's fingers fairly twitched on Boru's pommel. Except for the one question asked in the presence of his sister, Sean Fitzgerald had been a silent companion from the start of the ride till now.

Hugh opened the glass full out and asked, "Do you want to have a look, Sean?"

"Aye, sir, I do."

Hugh put the spyglass in his hand and instructed briefly, "Twist it to bring things into focus. There, that's right. What do you see?"

"Rocks, a bent tree and the sky, sir." Sean swiveled in front of Hugh, scanning to the south and west. "Who is it you are looking for?"

"O'Toole."

"Oh." The boy took the spyglass from his eye and twisted it closed. Curious, he opened it and closed it twice before handing it back to Hugh to put safely away. Hugh clucked to Boru and turned back to the road. Boru trotted briskly up the hillside.

"I hope nothing I said or did caused any friction between you and your gillie, sir," Sean said stiffly. Hugh was well aware of what it cost a proud boy to apologize. He'd been in Sean's shoes most of his life—at the mercy of powerful barons and lords who had the queen's ear.

"It would take more than an insult or two to put something serious between Loghran and I, lad. He treats me like I'm his errant son."

"I see," Sean answered, but Hugh knew that he didn't.

"Perhaps the easiest way to explain what I mean is that Loghran has been a father to me when I've needed fathering."

"Is your father dead, sir?"

"Yes," Hugh answered concisely. "I never knew him, though my uncle, Matthew, tried to take his place."

"Like me and my father?"

"Possibly. How long has it been since you've seen your father?"

"Years, sir. Once or twice he came to Clare Island and visited, but he has always gone back to France to raise his army."

"You and Maurice lived on Clare Island with Morgana and her husband?"

"No, not then. Only after she was widowed and she came out of the convent." Sean's shoulders went up and down. "She sent us away. Said it wasn't safe to be staying in a pirate's compound. I always thought it was because she's afraid of ships sinking."

Hugh mulled over that insight as he came abreast of the others waiting outside the castle gate for the portcullis to be raised. Some fool as old as Sorely Mac Donnell manned the gatehouse.

"Open the gate, Donovan," Hugh raised his voice to be heard above the howl and whip of the increasing wind.

"Who is it that wants in?" asked a small girl who poked her head out the wicket portal.

Hugh glared at the impish face regarding him with the curiosity of a sun-warmed cat. "The earl of Tyrone," he barked at her.

"Och, Donovan," she said, loud and clear, as she withdrew from the wicket. "Ya best let the man in. He's full of himself, he is."

Morgana ducked her head and hid a smile behind her glove before managing to straighten her face and look back at Hugh. "Clearly we're all going to hell in a handbasket together, my lord, if this is the state of things with the next generation. No respect for their elders."

"Don't goad me," Hugh warned. "I've got troubles enough getting what little respect I do get, milady."

Only one of the huge barred doors swung open, both the old man and the girl powering it. The girl ran ahead of the retainer, and was first to take hold of Ariel's bridle when Morgana drew to a halt.

"Who are you, milady?" she asked curiously as Morgana dismounted.

"I'm Morgan O'Malley," Morgana replied, with a smile for the dark-haired child. She was all eyes for the band of red-haired boys dismounting and stretching their legs.

"Are ye Irish or Scots?" she asked next.

"Irish," Morgana replied. The statement was out before Morgana realized what she'd said and how proudly her voice sounded to her own ears. Her smile broadened on her face, but it wasn't reflected back at her in the eyes of the somber child.

"Oh," the child said, crestfallen. She stood very still, watching Hugh dismount. He stood back from Boru, allowing Sean to spring to the cobblestones.

"Who are you?" Morgana asked her.

"Me? Oh, I'm the Mulvaine." There was a light lisp in her voice, the result of her missing several prominent milk teeth while permanent ones descended into place. "I've been watching out the wicket for ever so long, waiting for someone special to come." Her eyes left Hugh, and she looked at each adult member of their party with an intensity that seemed uncommon for so young a child. "He's not here."

"Who is it you are looking for?" Morgana asked.

"Why, the O'Neill," the child replied solemnly. "I'm going to be a sorcerer's apprentice. The O'Neill is to take me to the master."

Morgana blinked in surprise at the child's guileless statement. The doors of the hall burst open then, spewing hounds and servants and a blustering old man in plaid trews and a tartan slung across his shoulder. The girl ducked under Ariel's belly and ran away before Morgana could tell her another word.

Sorely Mac Donnell bellowed out a greeting, and Hugh went up the steps to meet the elderly leader. In the bustle of being presented and welcomed, Morgana did not think of the strange little girl with the clear gray eyes again till much later in the day.

Chapter Fifteen

Inghinn Dubh rushed to the hall the moment she was informed that the earl of Tyrone had come to call upon her father, Sorely Mac Donnell. Her eagerness for company was chilled when she saw who Hugh O'Neill escorted into Sorely's hall. That bedraggled, wretched woman he'd pulled out of the Abhainn Mor.

Still, it was Inghinn's duty to act the gracious hostess to all her father's guests. The name the lady gave had some meaning to Inghinn. Grace O'Malley frequently visited Dunluce. As she escorted Morgana to the solar, Inghinn did her best to draw in her claws and make polite conversation.

"So, you're an O'Malley. Do you know the Lady Grace?"

Morgana knew a test when she heard one. She smiled politely back at Inghinn. "I am related by marriage to a woman named Grace O'Malley. She is my late husband's sister. Is she the Grace of whom you speak?"

"You're Gregory's widow?" Inghinn choked, and she colored to the roots of her lampblack hair. She stopped walking and dropped into a deep and graceful curtsy to Morgana. "Countess, I beg you, forgive me. I did not realize to whom I was speaking."

"Nonsense." Morgana caught Inghinn's wrist to stop her from making an unnecessary show of obeisance. "You do not have to curtsy to me, Inghinn. That old title passed to

Gregory's heir several years ago. I am no longer a countess, and to tell the truth, I never felt I was from the start."

"Oh, I am so embarrassed." Inghinn laid her hand on her breast, still apologetic. "Why, I snubbed you abominably at Dungannon. Please, I beg you, forgive me."

"There is nothing to forgive. We barely met in passing, and I will be the first to admit that I was woefully lacking in any and all graces at the time. Come, we will be friends from here out, correct?"

"Certes, my lady." Inghinn ushered Morgana into the cheery solar that overlooked the sea. "Welcome to Dunluce."

A bank of beautiful mullioned windows gave a dramatic view over the distant stony formation called the Giant's Causeway. Now that her eyes were shielded from the sting of the wind, Morgana could appreciate the wild and natural beauty of the northern coastline. She really hadn't been able to do so on the ride across the bluff.

"What is that curious rock formation?" Morgana asked Inghinn, pointing to an upright tor nearly as tall as the basalt cliffs themselves. "Hugh has already described the wonder of Finn mac Cool's bridge, but we couldn't see those tors from the road."

"It's called Chimney Tops," Inghinn explained, then joined Morgana at the mullioned windows to point out other curiosities. "Antrim has not much else to boast about, save our wild weather and the stark beauty of the coast. Those beautiful gray mountains rising from the sea are in Scotland. It's a lovely view, isn't it?"

"Oh, yes." Morgana considered the whole scope of the dramatic formation of sea, earth and sky. To the northwest, both sky and sea were a threatening, ominous bluegray of a new storm bearing down on Ireland. Directly over the castle, white, fleecy clouds ran fast across the brilliant azure sky. "Why, were I to live here, I'd be driven to paint such beauty."

Inghinn chuckled softly. "Many of us are. I try with my watercolors and conte, but I fear my efforts are never as splendid as the real thing. My sister Leah was very gifted with paint and brush. She did many of the oils you will find scattered about the manse. Father keeps them as a reminder of her."

Morgana shook her head, marveling at the dramatic splendors framed by the window. Looking at the dark, ominous clouds in the northwest made her shiver.

"It's going to storm," Inghinn said, reading Morgana's thoughts.

"It most certainly is," Morgana agreed. "How safe and protected is your harbor?"

"Very." Inghinn pointed to the jutting black stones at the base of Dunluce. "You can just see the entrance to the cove. It's well sheltered from the north wind. Father's ships ride out most storms there. I'm told, by those who know, that the trick is to put into port before a storm."

A genuine smile creased dimples in Inghinn's creamy Celtic complexion. She was just as beautiful as Morgana had suggested to Hugh. She and Inghinn were of the same age, both in their early twenties, but two women could not have been more different. Inghinn was delicately formed, graceful, as feminine as damask linen. Standing next to her, Morgana felt toweringly tall and overdeveloped. For a moment, she saw Inghinn as a formidable rival for Hugh's affection.

Morgana put that negative thought aside as petty and selfish. Hugh was entitled to any woman he wanted. Theirs was not a permanent liaison. Come tomorrow morning, Morgana would be gone. It would behoove her not to dwell on Hugh, longing for what she could never have.

They made small talk into the late morning, then went down to the hall for the midday meal. Sean cajoled Hugh into loaning him his spyglass. He wanted permission to stay the whole afternoon on the parapets, watching for the *Avenger* to come. The Mac Donnell said that was impossi-

ble when a storm was brewing. He did send one of his retainers out with the boys to let them look for a little while,
but when the storm hit, everyone was back indoors.

The fires in the great hall's hearths were kept well stoked
all afternoon because the storm brought a bone-chilling cold
north wind howling over Antrim. Great, booming claps of
thunder rattled the rafters in the castle's roof. Frequently
lightning struck hard enough to shake the stone walls.

A constant bustle of servants and the commotion of boys
dominated the midday meal in Sorely Mac Donnell's hall.
Hugh O'Neill had brought with him a handful of extra ex-
citable boys. Like Sean and Maurice, each wanted to be
where the next crack of lightning was going to strike, to see
if Dunluce's thick walls would shake.

Morgana and Inghinn visited pleasantly amid the ebb and
flow of the menfolk's more heated conversations. Morgana occasionally heard snatches of politics and religion,
punctuated by outlandish oaths regarding the sport of kings,
horse racing.

An hour into the storm, Maurice gave up trying to keep
up with Sean and contented himself with playing chess
against the Mac Donnell's confessor, lame Father Eddie.

The little girl with the gray eyes put in an appearance
shortly after Maurice settled in at the chessboard. Morgana
saw her peeking out from behind a pillar, studying Maurice
and the chess pieces with a covetous eye. Morgana hoped the
boys would have the good manners to invite the child to join
the game. Neither Maurice nor the old Cleric took any note
of her.

"Who is the shy little girl?" Morgana asked Inghinn.

Totally unaware of the child, Inghinn turned to look and
then returned to Morgana, shrugging a negligent shoulder.
"That's Cara, my half sister Leah's child." Inghinn added
a deep sigh to her answer. "She's as wild as the weather. Ignore her. She's only looking for attention."

Morgana wanted to say that the little girl had claimed she
was seeking the O'Neill, but something made Morgana keep

that remark to herself. For some reason, Hugh did not want to be called by that title. His kerns did so with impunity, but no others did.

A short while later, Hugh separated himself from conversation with Sorely Mac Donnell and his sons and crossed the vast hall to where Morgana stood in conversation with Inghinn and her sisters-in-law.

His arm slipped easily around Morgana's waist, and he kissed her cheek. "Did you miss me, my dearest? Inghinn, you're looking beautiful as ever. Your father tells me Red Hugh O'Donnell called upon him yesterday, asking for your hand in marriage. May I be the first to congratulate you?"

Morgana blinked in surprise. Inghinn shyly blushed over Hugh's compliment and accepted his congratulations with grace.

"You know full well I have always had a special place in my heart for the O'Donnell," Inghinn admitted. "Thanks to your sisters' gracious hospitality, and the fact that you had returned at last from England, O'Donnell became jealous enough to rise out of his complacency and ask Father for my hand. I feared I would wither away here in Dunluce forever." Dimples flashed in Inghinn's cheeks as she added, "I'm not getting any younger, you know."

"We couldn't have that, now, could we?" Hugh laughed as he gave a brotherly kiss to Inghinn. He winked over the top of her dark head at Morgana. "You can't go wrong with old Hugh. He's a bookish man, but fair. Likely he'll worship the ground you walk on, as well he should."

"Please, don't go on," Inghinn insisted softly. "If you will both excuse me, I must see what progress Brenna is making toward supper. My lord." Inghinn curtsied deeply to Hugh. Gracefully lifting her skirts just clear of her dainty feet, Inghinn withdrew from the hall.

Her ladies took that as a signal to withdraw, also, leaving Hugh and Morgana alone with each other.

"I thought she'd never leave you to me," Hugh whispered in Morgana's ear. "Let's stroll on the parapet and watch the storm. I want to have a look to the south, to see if Loghran and Shamus Fitz are coming to the Castle gates. They should have been here by now.''

"Why did you leave them behind?" Morgana asked.

"To check out the rumor that James Kelly was sighted in Colraine,'' Hugh explained bluntly. "Come, the parapet is this way."

Morgana declined, with good reason. "We'll get struck by lightning."

"Nonsense,'' Hugh insisted. He steered her toward an open door into the gallery. "The parapet I'm talking about has a covered walk. I promise, you won't even get wet."

"You certainly appear to know your way about Dunluce," Morgana remarked.

"I suppose I do. I've spent some time here. Sorely has the uncanny ability to involve the O'Neills in his devious and sometimes nefarious schemes. For the sake of peace with England, I'd rather he didn't, though."

The castle was huge, full of unending corridors and shutoff rooms. Hugh's denial notwithstanding, Morgana was convinced he rather liked being a frequent guest here.

Some of Dunluce was in dreadful repair, and crumbling, Morgana discovered as they went up to the parapet that ran the full width of the castle's northernmost seawall. Hugh had to put his shoulder hard into an oak door to force it to open. There was evidence that the outer wall had collapsed and been repaired. The cliff face on which that edge stood gave Morgana vertigo at the sheerness of the drop into the crashing sea.

No sooner had they left the solid confines of stout stone walls than the cold banshee wind howled and tore at Morgana's skirts, batting them against her legs. Hugh laughed as the wild wind struck his face. He leaned over the balustrade and looked down at the foamy surf beating at the solid rock on which Dunluce stood, dominating the sea.

Hugh turned to Morgana, hand out and fingers beckoning to her to come close. "You must see this. It's magnificent. The sea boils against the cliff."

Teeth chattering, Morgana said, "I'd rather not."

"What?" His brow twisted above his so endearing brown eyes. "Are you frightened, Morgana?"

She took a deep breath of salty, spume-tasting air, whipped to frenzy. Rain slanted in under the roof of the parapet and beat at Hugh's tunic, flattening his hair against his brow. He was in his element, delighted by nature's tempest. She swallowed and made her feet bring her forward to him, but when she reached the edge, where she could look down and see the crashing waves, she turned her face into Hugh's chest, refusing to look.

Hugh's laugh sounded so gentle as he drew her close. His breath warmed her ear. "So, at last, I've found your specific weakness. Tell me, my love, it isn't the heights that bothers you, is it? It's the water."

Morgana rubbed her hand across her face. Her skin felt clammy. Her stomach rolled. She gripped his tunic and lifted her face to look over the edge of the stones. Far, far below them, white water pounded against the rocky cliff, foaming and gurgling as it curled up the wall, then sank out to sea again.

"Aye, it's the water." She pressed her fingers against her mouth and shut her eyes. Hugh's arms tightened around her. A soft kiss soothed her brow.

"Ah, Morgana, my love, why is it you never tell me what to expect from you? Do you want to go back in?"

"No." She shook her head, taking control of her stomach and her head, determined to face her deepest fears. "It's wonderful out here with you, the wind and the wet, the chill and your heat."

"My heat, eh? Do you know how you tempt me with words like that?" His fingers lifted her chin, tilting her face so that his mouth could join with hers. His tongue slid past her lips in that dueling dance of mating that only he could do so well. His kiss was hot and full of his spice and over too soon. "Shall we go indoors and find some quiet alcove where we can tuck ourselves away and out of sight?"

"There is no such thing as a quiet alcove in a storm like this, my lord," Morgana told him.

"My bedchamber at Dungannon, my lady. It's the perfect refuge in a storm. The walls are so thick, it's like some deep cocoon buried in the earth. Safe, warm, and womblike. I'd give my all to be there with you right this moment."

Morgana knew exactly what he meant. She rubbed her brow against his shoulder, content to stand in the circle of his arms while the elements did their worst around them. No force on earth would move Hugh O'Neill's arms from her body. That made her feel more secure than she'd ever felt in her life. Not even the roiling sea could bother her, so long as Hugh had his strong arms around her.

Hugh spread his fingers in the coils of her hair, gently massaging the silken tresses encasing the back of her head. "The storm will pass soon, Morgana."

"Aye." She looked to the gray belly of the storm, where lightning gilded the dark. The clouds ran fast overhead. Those still coming from the north were less intense now, and the slanting rain was no longer so fierce. "It will pass before dusk."

"And then what, Morgana?" Hugh asked somberly. "Is this the end for us? Are you leaving me?"

"What do you mean?" she asked, startled by so direct a question.

"You know what I mean." Hugh slid his thumb under her jaw to tilt her face to his. "Are you going back to the sea? Will you climb aboard Grace O'Malley's ship and sail away without ever looking back at me? Is that what this is about?"

Morgana took a deep breath. "Hugh, there's things about me you don't know."

"What? That you can fight as well as a man? That you are the softest woman that ever scuttled a ship or slit a throat? That you are terrified of drowning, and fear the wind will rip you down from the heights? Which truth don't I know about you, Morgana of Kildare?"

"I don't have a choice about the life I must live, Hugh O'Neill."

"You do," he solemnly said. "You could choose to live with me."

"No, that is not one of my options, Tyrone." She called him by his title purposely, to remind him of who and what he was. Laying her hand upon his cheek, Morgana drew one finger across his mouth. "I can't stay. Neither, my lord, can you."

"So it is goodbye when we go down to the ship." It wasn't a question, so Morgana didn't attempt to answer it. Instead, she lifted her mouth to his and kissed him, giving what she could give him for this moment.

Knowing exactly what her kiss meant, Hugh lifted his mouth from hers. After a minute of solemn study, he smoothed a damp, fiery curl from her cheek. "I won't let you go without a fight, Morgana."

"And I wouldn't stay without the biggest fight you'd ever think to join in, my lord."

"Are you challenging me? You don't know how I fight. No holds are barred. No tactic is too underhanded. Have you given any thought to the fact that you may at this very moment be carrying my child?"

"That argument doesn't bear talking about, Hugh. I'm barren."

His brow lowered. "You don't know that."

"I was married for three years, Hugh. It's true. Don't try to tell me Greg may have been the barren one. He fathered three bastard sons. The fault lies in me."

"No." Hugh refused to accept that, and shook his head vehemently in denial of it. "Pray tell me, how old were you when Fitzgerald gave you over to a privateer twenty years your senior?''

''That doesn't matter.''

''Just answer my question.'' he demanded impatiently.

Morgana sighed, reluctant to give him the answer he wanted to hear. ''Four-and-ten.''

Hugh closed his eyes briefly, seeing red beneath the shut lids. Would that the earl of Kildare stood before him. Hugh's hands would be around the man's throat. How could he have sacrificed so young a daughter, simply to further his ends? He did not ask his questions aloud, because he knew that Morgana would refuse to put any blame on her father's head. She did not see herself as the rebellious old earl's pawn, and would deny it to Hugh most vehemently.

Around them, the gale battering Dunluce's stout walls seemed insignificant in comparison to the temper Hugh felt brooding inside him. The injustices done to Morgana blinded him to all else. As he gazed down upon Morgana's set expression, his own jaw set, stubborn and intractable.

''Then you weren't married three years, lady. It was a little over two. You forget, I have those convent rolls to study and consider. I never forget a date. Two years is no test, when a man is gone away to sea more than he is to home and hearth.''

''Oh?'' Morgana answered. ''Have you thought that perhaps I did not sit at home sewing when my husband went to sea, sir? Haps I went with him on his many voyages.''

''Why do you argue with me, when you know as well as I that the truth is something else? You did not go to sea with Greg O'Malley. You lived at his estate in the Pale, and when and if he visited you, it was not for the purpose of getting you with child. I know, Morgana. I know, because I have made love to you and your body tells me a different story than this one you make up to convince yourself. Your marriage was for political reasons alone, the same as mine. The security of O'Malley's name was all you got out of the union. I want you to stay in Ireland with me, Morgana, as my wife.''

"What you suggest is impossible, Hugh. You know it can never be. Desist, I beg you.''

"I'm a cautious man, Morgana. I don't scatter bastards wherever I go. I don't leave their mothers scratching for sustenance wherever they can find it. Stay with me.''

"Hugh, you know I can't. It is only a matter of time before some false charge laid against me in Dublin reaches London and a writ is issued for my arrest.''

"Then stop the madness. Do not continue it,'' he reasoned. "Don't go back to sea with Grace O'Malley. For God's sake, Morgana, what can be in that for you?''

"How can I not? Do you understand what it is like to be exiled, an outcast, banished? I am here in Ireland for one purpose only. To bring Sean out.''

"What if I tell you the true reason you came to Ireland was to meet me?''

"You live in a fool's paradise. Hugh, I was born a Fitzgerald. I will always be a Fitzgerald.''

He brought two fingers to her brow and tapped her temple. "Here, inside here, you will be a Fitzgerald, until the day your submit your will to mine. Then, my love, you become an O'Neill, my wife, the O'Neill's lady. Whatever you were before will be lost to history and the past. You have a future, Morgana. I can give that to you.''

For a long, long moment, Morgana stared at him in dumbfounded silence. He was talking about marriage... as if her agreement were the sole ingredient necessary. Morgana found her thoughts flying instantly to embrace such a fantasy. To be Hugh of the O'Neills' wife and woman, mother of his sons... Then she shook her head, denying the possibility.

"You can't think of such a thing,'' she told him.

"I cannot think of anything less.'' Hugh drew her against him and kissed her deeply. "We belong to one another, Morgana. Why else have the Fates brought us together?''

She laid her fingers on his lips when he raised his head from hers. She would not allow the noblest man she'd ever known to become an outlaw. "No, Hugh. I will not let you sacrifice your future. I'm not worthy of you."

"Morgana." His tone changed, becoming stern and autocratic. The air about them became heavier, laden with thunder rumbling across the water and reverberating against the cliff. "Do not play games with my words. I have planted my seed inside you. I have marked you for all time as my woman. I won't let you go."

"Then we are truly at an impasse, Lord Hugh. Like it or not, when Captain O'Malley embarks from Mac Donnell's dock, I will be on her ship. The *Avenger* is the only place on this earth where I truly belong."

"This is utter madness! Why I am standing here in the rain, discussing something so ridiculous with a woman?" Hugh's exasperation got the better of him. "Is it that you think that I am a weak man? That I don't know my own mind, or cannot act to prevent a mere woman from defying me?"

"Tyrone, don't ask more than I am at liberty to give."

"I can. I will. I do," he asserted with grim determination. "I ask no less from myself—the best each of us has to give. I'll find a way, Morgana. Resolve yourself to that. I'm intractable, driven, and harder than any man you'll ever know. I won't be thwarted. So fight with me all you like. Say no at every turn. But know you this, I will have my way in the end. If not today, then tomorrow."

The storm passed quickly. So did Hugh's somber mood. Still there was no sign of Loghran or Shamus Fitz riding across the barren hills toward Dunluce. The moment the sun escaped its prison of heavy clouds, Hugh insisted they go out and explore the beach down below Chimney Tops to see what the storm had washed ashore.

That activity promised to fill the last hours of daylight, when the wait for Grace O'Malley's *Avenger* would become agonizingly tiresome. Morgana needed the distraction of a walk, needed to expend her energies on something positive. So, too, did her younger brothers. And if it did nothing else, the walk might distract Hugh O'Neill from his determined effort to convince her to stay in Ireland with him.

The sea remained choppy and rough, even as the tide ebbed. A hard wind came out of the north and roared through Dunluce's sea gate in the hours preceding sunset.

A fair collection of merchantmen had taken safe harbor from the storm at Sorely's sheltered dock. Morgana seemed to be the only one surprised to find ten seaworthy ships moored in the lee between the rocks. Every ship belonged to the Mac Donnell. The old man of Dunluce proudly invited his guests to take a closer look at his well-built caravels. Morgana declined that invitation. She wouldn't board any ship one minute sooner than she absolutely had to.

Sean and Maurice weren't so easily put off. They thought the Mac Donnell's suggestion a grand idea, and said so. Nothing could be done to satisfy the two of them except to give them permission to go with Sorely when he boarded his longboat to go out and inspect each ship for storm damage.

Little Cara Mulvaine tried to get on the long boat, but she was turned away. Sorely told her to "get," and she scuttled out of sight before the old man wagged his cane at her.

Morgana scowled as the longboat's crew put their backs to the oars. The more she was around the Mac Donnell, the less she liked him. She didn't care for the idea of her brothers being on board a ship of any sort when she wasn't there to watch over them and protect them. Accidents happened on ships—too frequently, to her mind.

Consequently, Morgana's mood took a dark turn. This time, she couldn't attribute it only to her proximity to water. She stood on the rocky shore, glaring at the longboat, watching the oars stroke through rough water. Hugh took hold of her arm. "Come, Morgana, let's take that walk down to Chimney Tops."

"I'd best remain here till the boys return."

"And worry yourself into a high dudgeon? No," Hugh insisted, with a firmness that brooked no argument. "We're walking, just you and I."

So Hugh thought, until they reached a lower level on the winding steps carved out of the cliff. Cara Mulvaine popped out from behind a tumble of fallen rocks.

"I kin show ye the short way to Chimney Tops." Cara cast a brilliant, almost adoring smile at Hugh.

"I think I know the way, girl," Hugh answered. The curious stone was visible, a mile or so down the curving beach.

"My lord, don't be rude." Morgana immediately latched on to the child's offer. She didn't want to be alone with Hugh now. She was tired of defending her decision. He wanted to wear down her resolve, and continue to raise arguments for which she had no answers. "Why, that's just where we were going, Hugh and I. Lead the way and we'll follow you, Cara."

The child skipped ahead, taking a quicker path down to the black sand beach. Hugh grumbled under his breath. Cara's path narrowed so much he had to fall behind Morgana and let her squeeze through the rocks on her own.

The shorter path proved to be worth it when they stood on the beach, at eye level with the sinking sun. It blazed like a red fireball, reflected a thousand times off the glistening, choppy water. The black basalt cliffs all along the shore from Dunluce to Ballintoy glowed crimson.

"Isn't this magnificent?" Morgana said with candid admiration. The surf roared. The wind ruffled her ears. She could taste salt on her lips and feel the steady drum of the sea in her chest.

"Splendid," Hugh said tersely. A string of redheaded boys from Colraine and four O'Neill kerns had claimed the beach before them.

The three boys convinced Cara Mulvaine to show them the best places to catch crabs and squid. Hugh and Morgana walked hand in hand on the black sand shelf exposed by the receding tide. The children scattered ahead of them, whooping and shouting over each crab they scared up out of hiding.

On the farthermost outcropping of sand below Chimney Tops, Morgana found a beautiful conch shell as large as both of Hugh's hands.

"Look, Cara," she called to the little girl, trying to entice her into conversation. "Isn't this the most beautiful shell you've ever seen?"

Cara Mulvaine came close enough to look at the large seashell as Morgana rinsed the sand from inside it in the water pools about the basalt tower of rock. Cara stuck out a dirty finger to touch one of the spines. She said, "It's dead."

"Well, yes, the animal that made the shell is gone now, I hope." Morgana tilted the shell, exposing its glossy pink interior. "I mean, I wouldn't want something awful to pop out when I put it to my ear to listen to sea."

"It's no good ta anyone dead. I ken where the best mussels are. They're good eating. Jus' crack the shells and swallow 'em."

"Well, I think the shell is pretty. My mother collects pretty things, like seashells and—"

"My mother's dead," Cara said, interrupting her.

"Oh, I know, dear," Morgana said gently. "Your aunt Inghinn told me that. I'm very sorry you lost your mother."

Cara lifted her hand to her face, touching one finger to her nose. Her eyes glazed over. She turned a full circle and wound up facing west, staring hard at the castle at the top of the cliff. "There's a fire coming."

"What did you say?" Morgana asked as she got up from her knees.

Cara pointed at Dunluce. "Fire storm," she prophesied. Her plain English bore no hint of her Celtic roots. "This night, Dunluce will burn."

"What?" Morgana said, disturbed by the child's words and the trancelike quality of her stance. Morgana grasped Cara's shoulder, to give the girl a little shake. Cara jerked out of the trance like a dreamer being woken.

That startled Morgana more than girl's odd behavior did. A forbidding voice echoed inside Morgana's head, repeatedly whispering, *Wake not the dreamer*. Shaken, Morgana felt a shiver whip down her spine as she realized dusk was upon them. The sun was completely gone from sight.

Cara blinked twice, then regarded Morgana with a normal, childish expression indicative of nothing. "Say that again, Cara. What do you mean?"

"Dunno." Morgana's request for clarification went unanswered.

Cara Mulvaine spied a ship on the water west of Sorely's cove. She ran that way, climbing over rocks and jumping into shallow pools of seawater, oblivious to her clothes.

She climbed onto the last stone, pointed at the ship and yelled in Irish.

One of the Colraine boys had to translate Cara's words for Morgana. "She says a whole fleet of fire ships are coming and the *Revenge* is leading them to Dunluce, mum." He scratched at his head, confused, then slapped his cap back in place over red curls and a sunburned nose. "Cara's got the sight, you know. Sure hope she's not right. Drake captains the *Revenge*."

"Hugh!" Morgana panicked. She gathered up her skirts and ran to Cara, caught hold of the girl's arm and dragged her to Hugh. "Hugh! Hugh! Dear God, those boys just told me this child has the sight! There's a fleet of warships coming. Cara says it's the *Revenge*. Did you bring your spyglass?"

"Och! Lemme go!" Cara Mulvaine twisted her arm to escape Morgana's detaining hand. "Ya ain't supposed ta touch me."

"Be quiet, child," Morgana told her. "Hurry, Hugh. Look. Tell me it isn't Drake. Tell me those ships aren't English."

Hugh was one step ahead of her, positioned high on the rocks, taking a good long look through his spyglass. While he did that, Morgana waved everyone in from the outer rocks.

Dunluce stood three full miles back, across the open, unprotected beach. Morgana searched the cliff face, seeking any kind of trail that would get them quickly to the top. She couldn't think what they'd do if the guns on a warship started firing at the beach. Where would they hide? How could they survive a barrage of cannon?

"Put your caps on, all of you! Hide your red hair!" Morgana shouted. Fear edged her voice. "It isn't the *Avenger*. I'd know Grace's black sails anywhere. None of those sails are black. Tell me, Hugh. I've got to know."

"Calm down, Morgana," Hugh snapped the glass closed and returned it to his pocket. His jaw was set, his mouth grim. "They're just carracks and caravels."

"Just carracks!" She choked. "A carrack carries thirty guns. They're not supposed to be here. Not today! Heaven help us! Come, Cara honey, hurry! We'd better run."

Hugh took hold of Morgana's arm. "Don't alarm the children, Morgana. We walked down here. We'll walk back. Donald, get the boys moving ahead of you. Ho, Thomas, we're going back to Dunluce."

"Lemme go! I don't wanna burn!" Cara Mulvaine sank what teeth she had into the back of Morgana's hand.

Morgana let go of the little girl's arm and yelped. Cara took off running. Morgana looked for dripping blood. Hugh collared Thomas from Colraine. The procrastinating boy needed an impetus to follow orders. A swat to his butt got him listening.

"I can't believe that child bit me!" Morgana exclaimed as she tied a handkerchief over the wound Cara had left in her hand.

"I can't believe you brought all these brats down here with us, when you know I wanted to be alone with you."

Incensed, Morgana shouted back, *"Vous êtes impossible!"*

Then she refused to leave her beautiful shells behind. She ripped the scarf off her head and made a satchel for the shells. Hugh couldn't get her to leave until she'd collected every one and threaded her arm through the cloth bundle.

"Let's go, Morgana, now!" he shouted. His spyglass had confirmed the prey the English fleet was after. Far out in the deep water, the black sails of Grace O'Malley's *Avenger* tacking hard to port, making a desperate run for the open seas. "Lady, I said now!"

Those words had no more than left Hugh's mouth then all hell broke loose. Seven guns on the *Revenge* fired, one right after the other.

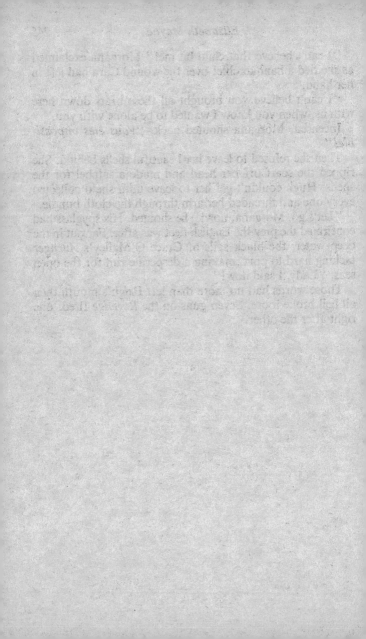

Book 3

The O'Neill

"Play the man, Master Ridley; we shall this day light such a candle, by God's grace, in England, as I trust shall never be put out."

Addressed to Nicholas Ridley (1500–1555) as they were being burned alive at Oxford, for heresy, October 16, 1555.

Hugh Latimer

Chapter Sixteen

The boom of cannon fire put purpose in Morgana's movements. Hugh no longer had to urge her to get moving, he had to run hard to keep up with her. She bolted in a desperate attempt to get off the promontory of stone that jutted so far out into the open sea. She fled back to Dunluce, with one thought in mind. To get her brothers off Sorely Mac Donnell's ships!

Her first burst of fear-driven speed took her as far as the opening of the cove. Dunluce was still a difficult mile west, through wet sand and descending dark.

A sharp pain throbbed in Morgana's side, telling her to stop. She couldn't rest for one heartbeat. Her brothers were on Sorely Mac Donnell's ships. Sir Francis Drake was bearing down upon the Mac Donnell's harbor. The danger pushed her past her usual endurance.

Gasping for breath, she came to the stone wharf cut into the hideaway harbor. She caught herself from collapsing by grasping hold of a wooden upright on the short pier. She dashed her sleeve across her eyes, clearing them, panting hard, trying to restore her breath.

The barrage of cannon drummed erratically. It wasn't her imagination. The crescendo of booming noise was closer, more distinct, and louder than thunder.

The boys from Colraine came running behind her. Hugh, Donald the Fair and Rory and Brian O'Neill were only steps behind them. Morgana cupped her hands to her mouth and tried to shout, to hail the nearest of the ten ships moored in Sorely Boy Mac Donnell's bay.

She had no wind. Her voice rasped out of her expended lungs, a breathless croak. Mac Donnell's vassals and retainers had heard the cannonade and come pouring out through Dunluce's sea gate. Morgana felt a measure of relief on discovering Loghran O'Toole and Shamus Fitz were with them.

Darkness slid over the water fast, complete and total, all at once. While men shouted and boys yelled, Morgana jumped from the stony wharf onto a currach. She didn't have the breath to yell a warning, but she had the strength to row a currach out to the ships. God willing, she'd get her voice back quickly.

"Just what do you thing you are doing, lady?" Hugh got his hands on the currach's mooring rope before Morgana did.

Morgana picked up the tiny round craft's paddle instead. She explained, "Got . . . to . . . warn . . . the . . . ships. . . ."

"It's being done as we speak." Hugh's voice took on a dreadful authority. "Give me your hand, Morgana. You're retiring . . . inside the castle, where it's safe."

"I'm not . . . going anywhere . . ." she gasped, "without . . . my brothers!"

"Morgana, don't make me use force." Hugh took hold of the paddle and removed it from her hands. The currach tipped. Water swirled inside it, wetting Morgana's hems and boots. Hugh caught her wrist when she reached for the paddle. She was so upset she didn't realize the twig-and-goatskin craft was filling with water at her feet.

Hugh's gentle but firm grip on her forearm was all the hold he needed to haul her tiny boat back to the wharf.

Loghran O'Toole cupped his hands to his mouth. His voice boomed over the water, alerting the nearest ship to the coming danger. One of Mac Donnell's retainers held up a lamp, opening and closing the door of it, signaling the far-thermost caravels.

Hugh lifted Morgana clear of the tipping currach and set her on the steps beside him. "Hush now, my love. The boys will be back in plenty of time. Don't be frightened. Dunluce is impregnable."

"You're dreaming if you think that." Morgana shuddered, but she clung to him even as she spoke. She wanted to believe the castle could withstand anything. She knew better. Maynooth had been reduced to rubble by English cannons in a matter of hours.

"I am positive of it." Hugh cupped her face between both of his hands and kissed her. He let his lips give her confidence and soothe her terror. She calmed somewhat, and her breathing slowed. Hugh hugged her and smoothed loosened tendrils of her fiery hair away from her face. "You'll be all right. The boys will be fine. I promise you."

"Oh, Hugh!" Morgana cried out, close to tears. "You're so calm, so solid. You're my rock."

"Here now, love, look—Inghinn Dubh is here. See how calm she is. Inghinn knows there is nothing to panic over. Dunluce has been put to siege a hundred times. We all know exactly what to do. Inghinn, sweet, take Morgana to the solar. I'll send the boys up as soon as they are back on land. I promise."

"Oh, Hugh, what will you do?" Morgana let Inghinn put her arm around her waist.

"Whist," Inghinn said as she led Morgana away from the commotion and up to the sea gate. "You know how men are, dear. They don't like explaining themselves until after they've acted."

If that wasn't a truism, then Morgana didn't know what was. The people of Dunluce weren't alarmed that English warships were bringing battle into their domain. They'd been through this same drill too many times of late.

Once they reached the solar, Morgana found all of Dunluce's womenfolk standing at the mullioned window, looking out over the sea.

Dunluce's harbor was difficult to see, because the cliff hid it partially from view. The battle wasn't happening in the cove. It was happening out in plain sight on the open water. Except it was dark as pitch out there. The moon wouldn't rise until nearly morning. Starlight offered no help visually. But each time a gun fired, the flash of gunpowder allowed the women to pinpoint the constantly moving combatants.

"What's going to happen?" Morgana wanted to know. "What brought this on? How did the English know we were here?"

Inghinn pulled Morgana away from the window. She sat her down on a chaise and handed her a hot cup of milk, well laced with Dunluce whiskey.

"Drink this, Morgana. It will calm you and stop your shivering." Morgana gulped the drink. It burned and made her cough. Inghinn sat beside Morgana and held her own cup between her white hands. "You mustn't think the English are after you."

"Oh, but they are!" Morgana insisted. "My brothers are outlawed by an act of proscription."

"Tell me what son of Ireland isn't?" Inghinn replied. "You shouldn't take warships personally. They can't know from such a distance who's ashore."

"They could. There are spies and traitors everywhere."

"Well, I wish I could say that's not gospel, but I know better. We've been through a dozen nights like this since Ash Wednesday. It's my father's fault, you see. He's at war with Queen Elizabeth, and Drake in particular. They can't agree on who has the right to the sea. Father's too stubborn for his own good."

"That has nothing to do with me or the boys. Grace O'Malley was coming here to Dunluce to pick up the boys and take them to France. She's supposed to be here to-night."

"I'm certain she will be." Inghinn said with purpose. "Grace is always prompt."

"She won't come with an English fleet out there."

"The fleet is supposed to be at Glenarm, my eldest brother's castle, on the east coast of Antrim. It's been under siege the past twenty days. Don't ask me why they've come back to Dunluce. Someone must have told Drake that Father pulled all his ships home to refit them."

"That's exactly what I'm talking about. There are English spies everywhere in Ireland."

"And that's a fact of life, Morgana. But you shouldn't be worried about their presence here. It just means we are in for a noisy night. Not even the infamous Captain Drake has the firepower to actually strike the manse. The cliff is too high, and the rocks will keep all of his ships at a good distance."

"Not if he gets into your father's harbor."

"He won't," Inghinn Dubh said with authority. "We'll be fine."

Whether it was the toddy or Inghinn Dubh's calm assurance that pacified Morgana, she couldn't have said. But after reflecting on the probability of cannonballs rising the full height of the cliff to bring down the roof, Morgana relaxed.

Antrim wasn't the flat meadowland of county Kildare. Antrim sat high above the sea, on cliffs, cut deeper and deeper each year by the waves of the sea.

Feeling a little chagrined, Morgana allowed Inghinn to take her to a bedchamber to change her skirts and stockings for dry garments.

When they returned to the solar, Morgana joined the watchers at the window, determined to content herself with observation, not despair.

Rory O'Neill escorted all five boys up to the solar and turned them over to the women. He requested that they keep all of them out from under the men's feet. None of the boys would be any use in defending Dunluce, Roy explained, though he assured each boy he'd make a fine soldier when he grew taller and stronger.

"You should have come with us to the ships, Morgana!" Sean chirped excitedly. "They're better than Grace's old trap. Twice as big, too! The caravels' holds are enormous! You wouldn't believe how many tons of cargo can be stored inside them. Sorley said I could be a cabin boy now. He's got ships that sail to the Windwards. Two have been round the Cape of Good Hope, to someplace called Madagascar. Grace never sails farther than the Canaries."

"The Mac Donnell's got cannons on his drum towers!" Maurice added. His eyes were huge with wonder. "He says if Drake comes close enough, he'll blow the *Revenge* to kingdom come."

"I'm hungry," Sean said, interrupting him. His candid statement brought a storm of agreement from the other boys.

Feeding them gave the women something to do. Supper had gotten sidetracked by cannon fire.

The Mac Donnell's daughters hustled the servants away from doorways and windows and back to work. The hall was lighted with torches and the food brought to the table. Morgana took charge of making certain the boys washed before they all went downstairs together.

Cara Mulvaine was already to table. Seated in her grandfather's high-backed chair, she had helped herself to a platter full of crisply roasted drumsticks and scones topped with cheese. Three stripped bones were piled beside her pewter plate, leaving grease stains on the table linen.

"Cara!" one of her aunts scolded. "You've come to the table filthy! Go and wash your dirty face and hands!"

"Wha' for?" she mumbled around a mouthful of chicken.

James Mac Donnell's wife had no intention of taking back talk from a child. She marched onto the dais, headed straight for Cara.

Maurice halted behind a pillar in the hall, tugging on Morgana's hand, stopping her. "She's gonna get a skelping for sure, isn't she?"

"And well she should," Morgana said briskly. "It's bad manners to eat before company, and worse manners to talk back to your elders."

The eight-year-old girl was no fool. She saw her aunt coming and ducked out of reach under the table. She popped up from under the long drape of linen several feet away from the Mac Donnell's chair. She had a chicken leg in each fist. Her head turned from side to side, and then she chose her route of retreat and ran as fast as a rabbit from the hall.

A door to the kitchen slammed in her wake. Arliss Mac Donnell muttered under her breath as she took the dirty plate and the pile of chicken bones from the table.

"That child is going to be the death of me," she said to Morgana, by way of apologizing for the girl's behavior.

"Of all of us," Inghinn lamented. "Haps now you can see why I said she's wild as the wind. No one can control her, and God knows, Father tries. Come, Lady Morgana, sit you down. Boys, there's plenty of room here on the benches. We won't stand on ceremony tonight, but we will say our prayers as soon as we are all to the table."

Morgana sat to the long bench and was immediately flanked by her brothers. The Colraine boys filled the left end of the bench. The Dunluce ladies lined up opposite.

The meal began as soon as the oldest of Sorely's daughters-in-law finished saying the blessing, with a spontaneous addendum extolling the virtues of the warriors battling outside the great hall.

"God and O'Neill rout the English," Maurice added.

"Amen!" Sean concurred in a strong, sure voice.

Morgana tipped her head to the side, looking at Sean as Inghinn handed him a large plate of steaming breaded fish. "So, you're on speaking terms with God again, are you, Sean?"

He set the plate down on top of his and crossed himself quickly.

"Aye, sister," he answered solemnly, hands busy with the concentrated work of selecting his choice and moving the fish to his plate. He passed the fish to Morgana and continued speaking. "I've had the opportunity to reconsider my words."

"And what have you concluded?" Morgana inquired. She put a fillet on her plate and offered the dish to Maurice.

"I've concluded that I was speaking when I shouldn't have. Maurice reminded me how many times I've called on the Lord and he's answered my prayers. I shouldn't doubt his existence. It was wrong of me not to have faith, just because I was tired and wanted to eat. Please pass the peas, Lady Inghinn."

"He's not telling the whole truth," Maurice chirped from Morgana's opposite side.

"And how do you know that, squirt?" Sean cast a dark look in Maurice's direction, which Maurice didn't see, because he was occupied with picking the biggest piece of chicken from the platter before him.

"The O'Neill said he'd skelp you if you said there wasn't a God again."

"You didn't say that to him, did you?" Morgana asked, aghast at the thought of her brother publicly denying the existence of the Almighty.

"Not exactly." Sean ducked his head and started eating. "It just came up in our man-to-man discussion."

Intrigued and horrified, Morgana had to know more details about this. "And just what was this man-to-man discussion about?"

"Marriage, honor, duty, and lots of other important man things." Sean crammed a chicken leg in his mouth, stopping the flow of further words with food.

"Where babies come from, mostly." Maurice supplied the missing topic in a blithe soprano voice that carried to the rafters like the high notes of a hymn during mass.

Young Thomas set down the last bowl to make the rounds and asked in an incredulous voice, "Did the O'Neill tell ya where ya get 'em?"

"No," Maurice answered solemnly. "He didn't hafta. Me and Sean already seen how it's done."

Morgana choked. "Boys!"

"Well, we did," Maury insisted, turning his wide, innocent blue eyes on Morgana. "Last night, when you and the O'Neill were doing—"

Morgana put her hand over Maurice's mouth, but not quickly enough to stop the giggles from both ends of the table. "That's enough, Maurice James Fitzgerald."

"If we all listen very hard, we can hear the brass cannons on the east tower." Inghinn tried to divert the boys' attention. "I'm certain I heard it firing."

That put paid to the boys' interest in relationships. Cannons fascinated every one of them. They delved into the food before them with a vengeance, wanting to finish and be excused to go find the east tower, the west tower, and any other part of the castle that had cannons on it.

As soon as the meal was finished, Inghinn's sisters-in-law retired.

Inghinn summoned Donovan to take the boys on a short tour of the battlements. After the silver-haired retainer led the boys out of the hall, she explained to Morgana her reasons for sending them on a tour.

"I hope I haven't offended you by doing that. It's going to be a long night, and I know how curious little boys can be. If we let them see the battery, they might bed down a little easier when the time comes."

"I suppose you are right," Morgana replied. "Sean and Maurice have watched cannon fire before, but perhaps the other boys haven't."

"Donovan won't let them get close to the battleworks. But it won't hurt for them to look about a little bit."

Morgana ran her fork over her plate, pushing the food she hadn't eaten aside. She couldn't have explained why she felt like talking to Inghinn; she just felt the need to confide in someone. Women, she knew, understood each other.

"I don't suppose this is going to end before the tide rises, will it?"

Inghinn lifted the bottle of wine and filled Morgana's goblet to the rim. "No. I don't think so."

Morgana picked up the gold goblet and drank from it. "I can't think what to do now. Grace won't dock here, with all this barrage going on. I may have wasted all my efforts bringing my brothers out of hiding."

"Don't look at it that way. When Father comes to hall, he'll surely know Grace's alternate plans. She'll go to another cove. Antrim is full of safe harbors for those who know the seas. We'll wait awhile and see."

"Hugh took me out on a parapet during the storm this afternoon. Would you mind going there now? I want to see what's happening."

"That's probably where the boys are. I should have thought of asking you if you wanted to go look, too. Bring your wine. I'll show you the way."

The galleries were spookier in the dark of night than they had been that afternoon, when Hugh walked Morgana through Dunluce's twisting and turning corridors. Even with oil sconces burning every twenty feet, the castle felt frighteningly dark and ominous.

"Everyone tells me this place is haunted," Morgana said matter-of-factly. "I can believe it now."

"You should. It is." Inghinn laughed. She held her lantern higher, lighting the steps that wickedly curved through the old tower to the parapet. Several torches also lit the way, but the dark spots were treacherous and the worn stones easy to trip upon. "I've lived here all my life, and it doesn't bother me. Sometimes our guests have a bad night, when it storms and the wind howls. But to tell you the truth, I've never met any of the infamous ghosts that are supposed to live here. Cara sees them all the time.''

"Funny you should mention that." Morgana took care lifting her hems so she wouldn't stumble. Talk of ghosts didn't frighten her, not when the living had such power to scare the wits out of her. "The boys tell me she has the sight. I would expect that means she can communicate with ghosts and spirits, too.''

"More like imaginary playmates, I would say. There aren't any other children in the house, and I suppose she is lonely for company her own age.''

"Cara is the only child here in this castle?" Morgana asked, astounded.

"Aye, she is." Inghinn nodded. "Father put a lock on the dungeon to keep her out of there, but she still finds ways to get down to the caves without notice. Sometimes she disappears for days, and I have to turn the whole place upside down looking for her. I'll be glad when the banns are read and I leave Dunluce for good. I won't be looking back brokenhearted or homesick. No, I'm looking forward to having my own family. And with O'Donnell, I won't be squandering my life on sons to sacrifice on petty wars. He's a scholar, you know.''

"I've never met him.''

"Well, you will." Inghinn insisted. "You will come to the wedding with Hugh O'Neill.''

Morgana didn't say that was unlikely, since she was leaving Ireland for good tomorrow morning if all went as planned. She wouldn't be going anywhere if Grace O'Malley's *Avenger* didn't dock at Dunluce. The appalling thought followed that neither Sean nor Maurice would be leaving, either.

They stepped out onto the parapet through a door that was already open. A great glow of light filled the doorway, more light than torches and lanterns were able to provide.

The boys and old Donovan were running straight at them, yelling and screaming.

Cara Mulvaine sat on the stone balustrade, rigid with horror. Her hands were pressed to her small head. Her mouth was wide open in a scream of terror. Red and yellow flashes of light outlined her body and her dirty, torn dress.

Sean skidded to a halt and grabbed hold of the girl, yanking her off the edge of the parapet. They crashed to the floor as a deafening explosion erupted in the harbor. Blistering fireballs flew skyward. Tongues of flame licked out of the cove into the air. Burning wood landed on the roof of the parapet.

Maurice threw himself against Morgana's knees, tumbling her backward into the stairwell. The next flash blinded Morgana as she landed hard on the steps. Both she and Maurice were trampled by boys running for their lives. Everybody's screams echoed in the bartizan.

Gunpowder was exploding on the ships in the harbor. A rain of fiery wood splattered against the castle walls, hailed down on the lead-and-slate roofs. Donovan and Inghinn shoved the screaming Cara out of the way and slammed the heavy oak door shut.

Sean threw himself down on Morgana, burying his face in her neck. "God save us, we're gonna die!"

Stunned, Morgana clutched his head, her first instinct to see to her brothers' safety. She found no blood on either of them, no cuts, no injuries. She got them up, pulling both onto their feet. "Stop screaming."

"Fire storm, fire storm!" Cara Mulvaine chanted, catatonic with fear. *"Play the man, Master Ridley..."*

"Shut up!" Sean screamed at her.

"Quiet!" Morgana commanded. "Where's Hugh? Cara, shut up! Where's the O'Neill?"

"At—at—at—the—the—wharf," Maurice stuttered. "I s-s-saw him."

"Donovan, take the children to the hall," Morgana and Inghinn Dubh said at the same time.

"Don't leave us!" Sean screamed.

Morgana yanked his hands away from her waist and shoved Maurice into his arms. "Get Cara and bring her down to the hall. Take care of Maurice. Do it, Sean Fitzgerald!"

"Play the man, Master Ridley..." Cara Mulvaine's singsong chant echoed eerily in the roar of the fire.

Inghinn caught hold of Morgana's arm and pulled, transmitting terrified urgency through her touch. Both of them ran down the twisting steps. The children's cries chased after them. The Colraine boys huddled in a knot at the base of the stairway, heads covered by young arms.

"To the sea gate," Inghinn gasped as they dashed into the gallery above the great hall. James's and Albert's wives, and all the castle servants, streamed across the hall below.

"Get blankets and wet them. Bring buckets and water!" Inghinn shouted orders as they ran. "Form a bucket brigade. Arliss, fetch your medicines."

There wasn't time for more. Inghinn yanked on Morgana's arm, turning her into the stairwell that dropped to the sea gate. The door had been barred. It took both of them to lift the beam of wood off its rack.

Inghinn fumbled in her pockets for her chatelaine's keys. Her hands shook as she thrust a key into the lock and turned it.

Morgana grabbed the door handle and yanked on it with all her might. Smoke rolled through it into the castle proper.

Blinding light filled the end of the black tunnel. "Hugh! Hugh!" Morgana screamed. She ran straight to the fire and tripped.

She fell onto a soft pile of bodies. Men gasped for air in the fierce cloud of blackening smoke. "Hugh!"

Morgana grabbed the first limb she found, yanking on it. The mound shifted. Inghinn grabbed a hand and pulled. Someone threw a bucket of water on their backs. The pile on the ground shifted. Another slosh of icy water roused the fallen. Men crawled on their hands and knees to the open

door. Others got their feet under them and staggered to the
open door. Servants, all water bearers now, set down buckets and grabbed burning people, yanking them inside the
castle.

"Hugh!" Morgana screamed again, choking on the
smoke, feeling each inert body she crawled over. "Here!
Inghinn, here's your father!"

A huge flame licked across the roof of the cave, blackening the stone. The heat singed Morgana's ears and nose as
she ducked underneath it. She covered her mouth with her
hands, eyes open and stinging, searching for more bodies
amid the splash of the tide surging up the seagate.

The last two were pulled by their feet back to the steps.
Morgana heard Inghinn choke. She felt Inghinn's hands
pounding on her back, dragging her away from the wall of
flame engulfing the seagate at the mouth of the cave.

"Hugh, Hugh . . . Hugh's not there," Morgana croaked.

"Your hair's on fire!" Inghinn screamed. Her words
failed to register on Morgana.

"Hugh's not there," she repeated hoarsely.

Buckets of water were thrown at her and Inghinn as they
staggered through the oak door, and then it was slammed
shut. Morgana stood rigid, drenched in the wash of liquid,
choking, barely able to breath for the searing heat that filled
her lungs.

Someone pulled her out of the smoke-filled stairway and
up into the castle's great hall. Unrecognizable, fire-
blackened bodies were laid out on the cold stone floor.
Sorely Boy Mac Donnell coughed as if to expel a lung.

Morgana wiped her hands across her eyes, searching for
Loghran, for Hugh, for Rory O'Neill, for anyone she could
recognize. Inghinn collapsed beside her, sinking to the floor,
coughing puffs of black smoke out of her mouth.

"Oh, God, no, not this, not this." Morgana turned away,
burying her face in her hands. The sound of hammering on
the huge doors of the hall made her stop crying and look up

at the massive carved planks of wood, barred to keep the enemies of Dunluce out.

She seemed to be the only person in the hall aware of the racket. Morgana stumbled to the door, but for the life of her, with the size of the beam of wood that ran across it twelve full feet, she saw no way to open it by herself.

A small wicket door to the right had a steel grate fixed into it. Morgana twisted the iron hasp and dragged the porthole open. She stood on tiptoe, putting her face to the iron grate, blinking owlishly out. Fresh air washed her nose and mouth. As of yet, there were no fires in the castle's ward. "Who is there?"

"Jesus be praised, it's about time someone answered this door!" Loghran O'Toole stuck his face to the grate, nearly nose to nose with Morgana. "Would it be asking too much for the door to be opened for the earl of Tyrone or must we stand out here while a rain of cinders burn the clothes off our backs?"

"Loghran?" Morgana said, dazed.

Loghran didn't recognize the black face looking back at him. He didn't recognize the voice either. He did recognize the language spoken.

"Lady O'Malley, would you be so kind as to..." He started out speaking with the soft accents of a man using persuasion to get what he wanted then wound up roaring with a vengeance the command, *"Unbar the door!"*

Stupidly, Morgana lurched away from the violent shout that was literally yelled in her face. She pressed her hands to the sides of her head, and stared at the workings of the door, baffled by a command that she couldn't possibly obey with any sort of alacrity.

When she didn't respond with the speed that Loghran thought she should, he began pounding on the door again with the handle of his sword.

Morgana found the iron hasps on the wicket and shoved at the first bolt. It had been oiled. The other two hadn't. They stuck fast to their iron casings. She got the lower one unstuck, the topmost wouldn't budge. She needed something harder than her fingers to release it. There weren't any hammers or tools nearby. She clawed at the iron bolt, scratched and pulled. It wouldn't come apart. A glance at the chaos in the hall proved she had to deal with the door alone.

Desperate for a tool, she remembered her knife and lifted her skirt, taking Gerait Og's golden blade from its sheath at her knee.

Hugh was outside that wicket.

Loghran had said he was. Morgana believed Loghran. She believed God wouldn't take Hugh O'Neill from her. Not now. Not now that she'd found him. She laid the handle against the iron bolt and pushed, putting all of her weight into the work of moving the frozen bolt. It gave very little to her pitiful bit of force.

Morgana pressed her forehead against the wooden door. She smelled rust and iron, tasted it mingling with her own sweat when she licked her parched lips. She closed her eyes, desperate to summon the strength necessary to open the door.

Loghran's sword beat the tattoo of a bodhran summoning the Irish to war. Morgana opened her eyes to the sight of her grandfather's amber jewel, pressed to the wood between her face and the great doors of the hall. They focused on the seven-petaled blossom of cinquefoil embedded in the amber. The herbs' powers came to her like a revelation.

Morgana stepped back, amazed at the power she held in her hands. "Sweet Saint Brigit," she whispered. She held the answer to her desperate prayers in her hands!

This time, when she closed her eyes, it wasn't in defeat, it was in prayer. "Jesus, Mary and all the saints, give the hardness of gold, the weight of amber and the power of cinquefoil to my hands. Let me open this door so that love can fill my heart and my soul. Bring my love to me, whole and unscarred, so that I may prove my love for him all my days. Do this in Jesus' name and I will serve him faithfully, atoning for all my sins, making reparations for my wickedness, amen.''

Morgana opened her eyes and studied the last bolt with care. Suddenly she knew where the best place to put pressure was, and how to wield a knife to do the job necessary. She bit down on her lip as she pushed. Rust drizzled out of the frozen bolt and the iron guard. She pushed harder, putting her shoulders to the task, bracing her legs apart to have the most leverage.

The iron gave way all at once, with her fingers curled around the handle and the blade, shoving the bolt free of its home. It snapped into the iron guard so hard, Gerait Og's blade flew from Morgana's hands. The knife spun through the air, twisting and spiraling end over end. It struck hard on a corner of the stone steps at the entrance of the great hall.

The knife shattered, breaking in two. The golden handle skidded to a stop against the bottommost step. The blade kept flying until it was embedded in the wooden base of a standing suit of armor.

Awed, Morgana made a mental leap, recognizing the broken knife as a symbol of her life. That it was broken in two meant the spells were all broken. That knife meant more to her than any possession she owned. It had protected her for the past six years, when she had no one but herself to rely upon. She didn't need that knife any longer. *She had Hugh O'Neill to protect her.*

She turned to the wicket door, and pulled on the handle. It creaked open on rusty hinges. The song of the bodhran ended. It wasn't Loghran O'Toole hammering on the door for admission. It was Hugh O'Neill.

Hugh stepped back and opened his arms. "I knew you wouldn't let me down, love.''

Morgana fairly leapt out the wicket into his embrace. "Oh, Hugh," she said as her arms closed around his shoulders. "I love you.''

Hugh caught her against him, spinning her around, and kissed her. He took two revolutions before he tore his lips from hers to say, "I thought I'd never hear you say that, love of my heart. Now answer me this, while I have witnesses listening. Will you marry me, Morgana of Kildare, or am I going to have to send for the pope himself to coerce you to the altar?"

"I will marry you, Hugh O'Neill." She threaded her fingers into his hair and bent her head to kiss him again.

"Done!" Hugh shouted in triumph as he hitched her higher in his embrace and twirled her around to the cheers of his kerns.

Loghran O'Toole grunted disgustedly as he sheathed his long sword. He waited impatiently for the cheers to die out and the smooching to end. Hugh clapped him on the back once he'd set Morgana to her feet again.

"Congratulate me, old man," Hugh commanded.

"Not before the both of you have confessed your sins and said your vows before God. I've told you plain and simple, I'll no' countenance wickedness and sin, not in you, not in anyone else."

"What kind of talk is that before my bride?" Hugh bristled up, temper edging his manner.

"Straight talk. I won't mince my words to you today, any more than I ever minced them in fifteen years in England. Banish me if you dare, O'Neill. I'll go back to the monastery at Dungannon and live out the rest of my days in peace and tranquillity."

"The devil you will," Hugh responded. "You're sworn to me by a deathbed vow, O'Toole. I won't release you from it until I lie on my deathbed, hearing you recite the last sacraments over me. I'll never get into heaven without your help."

"Without my help, you won't see the cool side of purgatory. Lady Morgana, welcome to clan O'Neill. Now, can we go inside? I'm fair starved, and ready to drop in the traces for a cool drink of ale."

"There's going to be trouble now. Who opened the wicket?" Cara Mulvaine asked from the wicket door. She blinked her unusual pale gray eyes when Loghran O'Toole turned to face her. Then she gasped a small scream, turned and ran from sight.

"Who the devil is that?" Loghran asked, dumbfounded by the small, dirty girl with the bold mouth.

Hugh exhaled a deep, deep sigh and rubbed his hand over his face. His arm tightened around Morgana's waist, keeping her body close to his. "Don't be mad, either of you."

"About what?" Morgana asked.

"Why?" O'Toole growled with a shift of mood as dangerous and dark as Hugh's could be. "Don't tell me that brat is the heiress Queen Elizabeth ordered you to marry when you got home to Ireland."

Chapter Seventeen

Hugh's hand made a rather frantic pass across his face and plunged through his hair. "I would not have stated Queen Elizabeth's orders exactly like that."

Morgana's jaw sagged. "Queen Elizabeth commanded you to marry that child?"

"Now, Morgana," he began lamely, "The queen doesn't exactly realize the Mulvaine is just eight years old. Really, Elizabeth thinks Cara much older...uh, that is...old enough to be married."

"But you're under orders to marry her. You're not denying that?" Morgana gasped.

"No, well, I can't. Exactly." Hugh shot a killing look at Loghran for bringing up this subject at the most inopportune time. He put his hand to Loghran's shoulder and pushed him to the wicket. "Go on! Go in, damn your black Irish heart!"

He turned his scowl on his hooting kerns. They were doubled over with laughter, slapping their knees and howling at the fix Hugh found himself unable to explain.

"Shut yer faces," Hugh growled. He followed that order with a promise to do bodily damage if the lot of them didn't show him the respect he was due.

Morgana was decidedly tight-lipped when she ducked back into Sorely Mac Donnell's hall via the too-short wicket door. Her step was brisk and determined, guaranteed to take her away from Hugh O'Neill. She paused only long enough to snatch the handle of her grandfather's broken knife from the floor.

"I can explain, Morgana." Hugh caught her elbow and yanked her back when she tried to stalk away. "Give me the chance to wet my throat, then I'll explain the whole situation to you, away from these laughing louts."

"I'll just bet you can explain," she answered through tight lips. She jammed the broken knife into the pocket of her skirt, wishing it was whole and she could sink the blade into Hugh O'Neill's heart.

"And I'll just bet he can't," O'Toole interjected unnecessarily.

"That did it." Hugh swelled like a bull inhaling the dust it scored underfoot before a maddened charge. His hand dropped from Morgana's elbow, and the sound of steel scraping out of a scabbard cut through the smoke-tainted air inside the hall.

Loghran spun around on his heel, facing Hugh. "Don't do it, lad, unless you mean to finish it."

"What is the matter with you two?" Morgana demanded.

She put herself between the two of them. If she'd only had the power to do so, she'd have knocked both their hard heads together. She wanted some sort of explanation. Loghran O'Toole was doing his best to incense Hugh to the point of blind anger.

"Stop it! Stop this right now! I don't know why either of you is trying to make the other so bloody furious you could kill each other!"

She put her back to Hugh, confronting Loghran. "You! You're supposed to be a priest. When, dear God, are you going to act like one? Quit goading Hugh. We've been to hell and back inside this castle tonight. Look around you. There are men that need sacraments, and words to ease their pain. Go and do something to help."

Loghran swelled up worse than Hugh had. Morgana saw his fingers twitch at the grip of his sword. She didn't know what saved her from having her head lopped off on the spot for daring to yell at that barbarian. If he was truly a priest, then she was eligible for canonization!

"Lady, step aside," Hugh said from behind her, his voice darker and more dangerous than she'd ever heard it. "No woman fights my battles. Be warned, Morgana. I won't repeat an order—not even to you."

Morgana turned, very slowly, to face him. Her blackened face showed the shock his words registered deep inside her. "So that's the way of it, is it, my lord Tyrone? And if I don't stand aside to let you kill a man that loves you like a son, will you strike me? Cut me down with your sword to get to him?"

She took a deep breath to try and calm the erratic beating of her heart inside her chest. Her lungs hurt. The pounding of her heart dislodged a deep cough. Releasing that didn't calm her.

"Let me make one thing perfectly clear before I give the ground you demand, my lord O'Neill. You owe me no explanation of your queen's command. I, too, am subject to her will, an obedient, albeit reluctant, subject of the crown of England. Marry the child you've been ordered to wed. Do so with all haste, or put it off, as you see fit. Make no allowances for the inconvenience I may have caused you. I will not swear any vow to you, or place myself under your dominion to become your obedient servant."

With all the grace and nobility inborn within her, Morgana gripped the edges of her skirt and spread the scorched and filthy fabric as she bowed deeply to the earl of Tyrone. "Good night, O'Neill. I beg your leave to withdraw."

She didn't wait for him to give that leave. She turned and ran from the hall.

Hugh slammed his half-drawn sword back into its sheath. "Morgana! Come back here! Let me explain!"

Donald the Fair caught him and pushed him back. "Let her go, friend. She won't listen to a word you say now. Give her time to shed her first tears, then try to talk to her. If she's truly important to you, don't rush in spewing half truths and words she'll never believe. Courting a worthy woman is as difficult as taking a castle. Wait. Know your heart and your mind when you speak to her."

Hugh knew sound counsel when he heard it. He didn't want any misunderstandings to exist between Morgana and him. He didn't want there ever to be times of discord, strife or separation. He even realized how unreasonable that need to always be with her was.

The reality of life decreed that there would be times of strife and separation. Their marriage would not be without opposition. The selfsame forces that pulled them apart now would exist as far into the future as he could see. They must learn to handle the disappointments and hurts others caused them, and learn how to overcome them together.

Hugh nodded his head, signaling to Donald that he'd heard his advice and would live with it. Donald's one restraining arm tightened in an almost hidden show of acceptance and brotherly concern. Hugh turned to Loghran. For once, all his words failed him.

What could he possibly say to this man who had raised him? Taught him? Trained him in the ways and manners of an honorable man? Hugh's throat seemed to choke and tighten on itself, making speech impossible, even if he had known what to say.

Hugh shook his head and exhaled, letting all the tension out of his chest. Doing so, he found his voice. "We keep going over the same ground, old man. And I keep thinking things are settled once and for all between us. Then I find they are not. Am I the one in the wrong? Have I not learned all the lessons of life you wanted to teach me? Or is it you who won't let the boy stand on the feet of the man?"

"It's all of that and more, my lord," Loghran said with total honesty. "It hurts me to see you make mistakes that you shouldn't."

"The Lady Morgana is not a mistake."

"She will betray you." Loghran stated what he believed.

"Respectfully, sir, I will tell you that is not a subject for any man to discuss with me. I know my heart. I believe I know what lies in hers."

Loghran took a deep breath, expanding his chest with the tainted air inside the hall. He didn't want to believe the conclusions and sureties logic led him to see. But he knew his duty to Hugh. So he made himself speak the truth, as he saw it.

"I am not saying she will do it apurpose. It will happen because her loyalties will always be divided. She is a Fitzgerald, born to her kin, pledged to them. Her father will come with his French allies and an army of Scottish foot soldiers. Ireland will be plunged into war. I know your heart, Hugh O'Neill. You will never pledge your sword to the earl of Kildare to make a Norman king of this land. That's the truth. Marry her, and you will betray yourself and the people of Tir-Owen, who believe in your leadership."

"Of all the men I know, old friend, I expect you to rise above the issue of race, because you are a priest and you minister to all of God's people. I know no one more Irish in his thoughts, his moods, his eloquence and demeanor, than you. Yet any who looks at you sees you for the stalwart Viking your ancestry made you, just as those who look at me know I am a Celt and in Morgana see the Norman conquerors of this land. When are we going to get past this? When will all of us born on this island become one people, the *Irish?*"

"Well, this is just perfect!" James Kelly sneered.

He stood on a promontory midway between Portrush and Dunluce, glaring at the smoking remains of Sorely Mac Donnell's wharf. The sun had yet to rise, but fires in the harbor and the barn burning within the castle's ward gave him ample light to view Drake's destruction.

"Wouldn't you know that bastard Drake would get in my way."

Kelly's new adjutant, Corporal Williamson, knew when to keep his mouth shut. So did the rest of the patrol. They were all raw recruits just arrived from England to join the regiment bivouacked at Portstewart. Captain Kelly had conscripted six men to fill the vacancies in his patrol.

None understood the hatred Captain Kelly bore his prey, an Irishman named Hugh O'Neill. Yet every soldier among them understood the fierce nature of the competition between the army and the navy. Captain Drake had gotten to Dunluce first and scored the crippling blow.

That stuck in Captain Kelly's craw so badly he refused to press England's advantage and assault the rebel compound from the ground. Kelly claimed he had not enough troops to overwhelm the rebels left in the enclave. Yet everyone of them knew that five miles west in Portstewart, an entire regiment idled.

Kelly swung around from the view overlooking Antrim's raw shoreline. "There's no point in our lingering here. We'll return to Colraine. If O'Neill has lived through that fire storm, he'll be making tracks for Dungannon soon enough. I want to know who each of those redheaded boys were they picked up in Colraine. We'll bide our time and lay a trap there. Remember, all of you, it's the woman I want taken alive. So don't any one of you blunder into killing her. I'll cut your bloody heart out if you do."

It took Maurice a long, long time to find his sister. She was hiding and didn't want to be found. Maury knew that when he slipped under the drape of the curtains that kept the high bed warm. She was weeping. Maury knew Morgana didn't like for anyone to know that she could cry.

He thought that very strange. Girls were supposed to cry when they hurt, when words spoken made them sad, and when people died.

It was easier for women to show their emotions than for men. Men had to be strong, brave and fearless. Men weren't supposed to be hurt by death or the loss of a friend. The way Maury understood it, men had to fight on in battles even when their best friends went down before them. So men couldn't ever cry like women did.

He hoped when he grew up he could be strong and brave, and not cry just because something made him feel sad.

Hearing Morgana cry made him feel the saddest of all.

So when he saw her sitting on the middle of the bed, her knees drawn up and her head bent to them, sobbing so deeply, he couldn't stop himself from climbing into the bed to be with her.

"What's wrong, Morgana?" Maury asked as he laid his hand on her shoulder.

She looked up and wiped her hands over her face, rubbing her fingers under her nose and across her mouth.

"Don't cry anymore, please."

Morgana brought a cloth to her face to wipe away the tears. "What are you doing here?" she said sternly. "Inghinn told me she wouldn't tell anyone where I was, so that I could have a bath in peace. How did you find me?"

Maury shrugged both shoulders and made a face and pushed her damp hair away from her shoulders. It was still wet and it smelled very nice. "I went looking behind every door. Don't be mad at me. I was lonely for you."

"It's late. You should be asleep." She dabbed the cloth at her eyes one more time, and then the tears stopped.

Maurice sat down beside her, certain she wouldn't be sending him away. "The fires are all out."

"Good." Morgana nodded.

"The Mac Donnell burned his foot. The Mulvaine says he's going to be crippled and will need to walk with a blackthorn staff even after the burns heal. And she says they are all going to be very poor for a long, long time. All of the caravels are gone. The fire storm consumed them. Are we poor, Morgana?''

Morgana wondered how to answer that. She took a deep breath and blew it out her lips, then made a Maury face. "I don't know, Maurice. What do you think poor is?"

"I don't know." He fingered the golden medallion of Saint Colm Cille on the gold chain at his throat. Morgana ran her fingers through his damp curls, settling them back from his brow.

"You had a bath?"

"Oh, aye. Inghinn said we all smelled like the fire storm and she wouldn't have us in her beds. We had to troop out to the bathhouse and scrub with the soldiers. The maids took all of our clothes to wash them first thing in the morning and gave us these sarks to wear in the meantime. Sean says Fitzgeralds look stupid in saffron. He looks like a flame in his, but my hair is darker, like yours. Is Papa coming for us?"

"Ah." Morgana sighed, realizing he'd come to the important question. "I thought I explained that Grace was coming for us. She'll take all of us to France, where Papa is."

"You can't go to France, Morgana. You have to stay here. Sean says you have to marry the O'Neill. Our father will be very unhappy if you go to France instead of doing what you should do, 'cause the church has to be obeyed."

"Sean has a self-important opinion of the things he says, Maury."

"You better not tell him that. He'll smack you and remind you that he's the next earl."

"Speaking of which, I did not tell you Father would be on Grace's ship. You shouldn't be expecting to see him if Grace does come. It's too dangerous for him to travel here."

Maury sighed sadly. "I wouldn't mind going back to Captain Tanner's farm. It's fun to live on a farm. I had my own sheep, two goats and a pony. Sean and I liked living there.''

Morgana clicked her tongue. They'd come to the hard part. ''I'm afraid I couldn't take you back there. You would never be safe with Captain Lucas, now that others know you were there.''

''So what do we do?'' Maury asked, very confused.

''I don't know exactly, Maury. I'll have to think about that for a while. I promise you, I'll think of something.''

Maurice seemed satisfied by that. He raised up on his knees to put a kiss on Morgana's cheek. His skinny arms embraced her shoulders. ''You'll think of something good,'' he said confidently. ''You always do. Good night.''

''Good night, love.'' Morgana pulled the drapes back to watch him pad barefoot across the chamber. Her love for the brave little boy brought a smile to her lips. The first she'd felt in what seemed like aeons.

Once Maurice closed the door behind him, Morgana climbed out of the bed. She'd shed enough silly tears over Hugh O'Neill. She wouldn't allow herself to expend any more on a hopeless cause. She crossed to the window overlooking the sea.

This wing of Dunluce, like the solar below it, was much newer than the old Norman drum towers and keep. Here the roof was gabled and steep. Huge windows graced each of the bedchambers that overlooked the sea.

She pushed the shutters wide open on a rose-hued dawn. The night was gone. Mhórning lay upon the land and spread across the mild sea.

The night rail Inghinn had provided Morgana fluttered around her body. A strong wind lifted the damp length of her hair and set it waving like pennants at her sides. She turned her head to the wind, lifting the heavier hanks at the base of her neck, spreading it to dry on the breeze.

As he came out of the bathhouse, Hugh's focus traveled magnetically up the walls of Dunluce. Morgana stood at a window on the third floor, staring morosely at the sea and the rising sun. Her hair billowed like a cloud around her. Hugh rubbed his plaid over his wet head and let the drape fall to his shoulder, unfastened and free.

A trellis of old ivy crept up the gabled wall to her window.

He knew himself for a damned fool then. For his hands itched to dig into that ivy and test its ability to support his weight. He searched his mind for a magical property to give to the vines.

Only an old maxim came to mind: *Where ivy grows, it guards against disaster.* That was enough protection to suit Hugh O'Neill. He put himself to the arduous labor of climbing the ivy trails up to Morgana's window.

She jumped back, startled, when his hands slapped on the windowsill and he lifted his head and shoulders above it.

"Good morning, my lady." Hugh grinned. "May I come in?"

"Hugh!" Morgana gasped. She looked down the sheer wall that dropped to the cobblestoned castle ward. "Are you trying to kill yourself? What are you doing?"

The wind blew his damp hair across his eyes. It ruffled his tartan as if it were a battle flag advancing before the troops.

"What on earth are you doing?" she repeated.

"Coming to my lady the most direct way possible. Say that I may come in, Morgana. I pray the vines will hold my weight for a descent if you refuse."

Her fingers scratched at his shoulders, seeking a grip upon him. "Come in, come in! For the love of Saint Brigit, come in, before you fall to your death!"

"Ah, sweeter words I never expected to hear, my love. Move back a step, my lady. I shall join you shortly."

Hugh put his body to the hardest work of the climb, lifting his own weight over the window ledge, hoping he did so with grace and charm.

Morgana's eyes grew huge as she watched the big man bound over the ledge and come to stand, a towering hulk of bare-armed, bare-chested male, before her.

Hugh caught his borrowed *philabeg* to his waist. He tucked the loosened end under his belt, lest the cloth fall to his feet, leaving him embarrassingly randy and naked before her. He ducked his head slightly and smiled as he explained, "I've just come out of the bath. So I'm a little damp, but when I saw you at the window, I couldn't resist coming to you. May I explain to you Elizabeth's demands upon me?"

"Yes." Morgana nodded. She wanted to hear his explanation, and she told herself she would believe anything.

"It's all because of old Sorely's war with England. I told you he's been fighting Tudors since Henry commanded a navy be formed to make England a strong rival of Portugal. Mac Donnell thought to be Henry's admiral. But he had enemies at court, and was denied the post he sought."

Hugh took a deep breath before he continued. He opened his arms as a gesture of invitation to Morgana, wanting very badly to hold her against him.

She lifted her chin and said, "Go on."

"Here I digress, for I don't know the truth of all of it. I was not witness to those years, because I was not yet born. Some at court say the Mac Donnell sank the *Maiden Anne*, though I have never heard Sorely claim responsibility for that. I do know that when Henry declared himself head of the church in England, the schism between he and the Mac Donnell deepened to bitter hatred. It was blasphemy of the highest order to the Mac Donnell. He set himself against Henry, and has been at war ever since.

"Which brings us to Elizabeth, Henry's daughter and queen of England. When she released me to return to Ireland, an earl sworn and pledged to her, it was with the charge that I put an end to Sorely's rebellion in Antrim."

Hugh dropped his open hands to his sides. "You won't come willingly to me, Morgana?"

"Not before you finish it," she refused.

"I ache to feel your breasts against my chest, Morgana. No other woman I have ever know has moved me as deeply."

She parted her lips to moisten them with the tip of her tongue. That was agony to Hugh, to stand and watch and not taste. He compressed his lips, nodding, forcing himself to go on talking, to explain it all.

"As you are aware, peace is often obtained by marriage. Were you not forced to marry your father's strongest ally when you were but a girl?"

"Aye, I was," Morgana admitted. "I was as formless as Cara Mulvaine on the day of my marriage. Greg O'Malley treated me like a daughter, until one day when he came home from the sea and found I had grown into womanhood in his absence."

"And so I would treat the Mulvaine—were I forced to wed her at this age in her life. No banns were written, no contracts, no betrothals made between the child and I, Morgana. It was the queen's suggestion to me, to secure the peace between us. Forgive me for not telling you this before. It had no importance to me.

"After I first visited Dunluce, I wrote to Elizabeth immediately upon my return to Dungannon. I asked leave of the queen to forgo the match. The girl did not appeal to me. Sorely has poisoned her mind. She thinks England and Elizabeth are her enemies. Her grandfather fosters that hatred, hoping she will become a new pawn in his drive to destroy all who pledge allegiance to England.

"I walk a thin line, Morgana, over chasms more vast than one can imagine. To one hand are the desires of my people to be free of the yoke of English rule, to the other is the awesome power of the crown. Do I topple from the line in either direction, my life is forfeit.

"I will not take to wife a woman who will push me over the brink. I want a helpmate, a woman who understands the thin balance between the power of the state and my right to rule my own lands in peace and tranquillity. All I have I offer you, but I tell you with all my heart, I have nothing more permanent than these two hands, this body and this heart. Do you understand what I am saying, Morgana of Kildare?''

''Yes.'' She nodded solemnly.

''Then what holds you back from coming to me, lady?''

Morgana swallowed. Her stomach quivered as if twenty butterflies were trying to escape it. She wasn't certain she should tell him why she held back.

''You...''

''I what?'' Hugh stepped forward to her, but he checked himself immediately. ''No, I won't coerce you, Morgana. Tell me, in your own way, what I must do.''

''You haven't said that you love me,'' Morgana whispered. She ducked her head, unable to look in his eyes. She feared that he couldn't possibly love someone so unworthy as she.

''Ah, I see.'' Hugh lifted his hands and laid them on her shoulders. His hands were calloused and hard, roughened from the arduous work of training with battle weapons and the interests of man. Beneath his fingers, her flesh was as soft and warm and as smooth as the cloth covering her.

He let one hand slide across her back to draw her softness into his strength. The other touched her chin so that he could gently tilt her face up to his. ''I love you, Morgana, with all my heart and soul. Will you marry this man who has nothing but these hands to offer as service to you all of his days?''

Morgana's chin nudged against his fingers. ''Provided the queen will not summon you to London to be beheaded because of me, I will marry you, Hugh. But she must agree to the match. Else we are both doomed.''

''She will agree, I promise you. I know the secret of gaining Elizabeth's favor.''

Morgana tucked her brow under his chin. Her fingers rested against his breastbone. ''I have one other request.''

"If you are going to ask me to allow your brothers to remain with us, it is entirely unnecessary for you to petition me for so small a duty. They are welcome at Dungannon, at Castle O'Neill, at any holdings of Tir-Owen."

"Oh, Hugh, thank you for that gracious gift, but that wasn't my request."

"It wasn't?" His hand, at the small of her back, tightened, bringing her closer. "What would you ask of me if not that, then?"

Morgana moistened her lips. She met his gaze directly. "You must take the Mulvaine to Sir Almoy."

"What?" Hugh jerked, astounded by such an outlandish request. "Are you out of your mind? I can't take that child from Sorely's house. Didn't you listen to what I said? He sent five of his ships to Scotland and laid siege to Graham Castle to take the girl into his control. Three years ago, Sorely killed the Englishman, Carlisle, that she was betrothed to. Now you want me to incite that madman by taking the girl from him and turning her over to the Templars? Morgana, that doesn't make sense."

"You didn't tell me that," Morgana said in her own defense. "You talked about King Henry."

"All right, so I skipped some of the story. Good God, it's an epic. It would take weeks to recount all of the tribulations of the laird of the Glens. No, Morgana, I can't do that. Don't make Cara Mulvaine's fate a condition of our marriage. She has no place in our life."

"I've made a promise regarding her. If you won't accept that, then you must give me leave to act in my own best interest. I'll speak to the Mac Donnell, reason with him."

"Sorely Mac Donnell does not reason with women. He commands them, and they obey his orders. You would be wasting your breath and provoking his ire. No, Morgana. The matter is closed. Don't bring it up again."

"Do you know how self-important and autocratic you sound?"

"Aye, I do. Will you challenge my authority? Resist it? Do as you please, and provoke me when we disagree? Tell me true, for I would know if I am bringing an obedient woman to my heart."

"There's the rub, isn't it? Haps I have been on my own too long, making all the decisions necessary for my brothers and my survival. Haps I won't make you the good wife you are seeking, even though I love you. Maybe love is not enough in a wife. Or a husband, either."

"No, there must be more. A willingness to compromise."

Morgana trailed her fingers down his chest, to his belly. "Perhaps a willingness to search for solutions, or to find alternate means to solve problems between us, my lord?"

"Tempting my baser inclinations is certainly a creative approach, my lady, but not if you intend to manipulate me."

"I wouldn't dream of doing such a thing, sir. I'm far too direct for that."

"And much too alluring a female. You tempt me now, Morgana of Kildare."

Morgana's fingers dropped to his belt buckle. "I have every intention of tempting you to your very limits, my lord, with your permission . . . of course."

Hugh spread his fingers into her hair, tilting her lips to his. "Granted, my lady. I am your servant always."

Morgana stilled as his lips met hers in a devouring kiss. It gave proof of the banked passions surging between them. She caught the tongue of his belt and yanked it free of the buckle's hasp. Both belt and kilt dropped to their feet. His manhood surged against the soft flesh of her belly. She leaned into him, welcoming the hardness.

Hugh tore his lips from hers, crying out, "Unfair! You are clothed, my lady."

"There is a remedy to that." Deep dimples flashed in Morgana's cheeks as she stepped back, out of his arms. She brought her hands to her throat, releasing the ribbon bow holding her night rail secure. She dropped her arms. The soft linen fell to her feet.

"Splendor of the gods," Hugh whispered. "Diana the huntress could not be more beautiful than you."

His eyes did what his mouth wanted to do, devoured her inch by sweet and lovely inch. His hands accomplished that desire, fanning out to touch her rosy, tilted breasts. They swept down the long curve of her belly, skimmed around her hips to grasp the firm round globes of her bottom and pulled her body flush against his.

Her height made her the perfect fit to his body. Only the slightest boost would be necessary to bring her up that they might couple where they stood. Hugh cataloged that thought for another time, when he wasn't so driven to have her beneath him. He swung one arm under her legs and lifted her, stepping over their discarded clothes as he carried her to the bed.

Morgana wrapped one arm around his shoulders, and the other she stretched out to pull back the bed curtains. "The sun rises, my lord. There will be work to be done this whole entire day."

"We won't tarry overlong in bed, lady." Hugh promised as he set her down upon the feather bed. It cocooned her, swallowing her. The ropes creaked noisily as Hugh added his weight to the mattress. Her legs and arms parted in open and generous invitation to him. Despite his words, he had no intention of rushing through this joining.

Her body was so familiar to the touch of his hands and the taste of his mouth. It was a completely new experience to see that lovely body revealed to him by the clear light of day. He kissed each freckle glazing her throat, and marveled over the coral orbs of her nipples that darkened to ruby after he suckled them.

The most splendid of all was the glistening patch of red curls crowning her womanhood. He lowered his head to kiss them and taste her, and was driven to seek out the delicate nubbin of her sex. It firmed and played hide-and-seek with his tongue, driving Morgana wild and wanton.

She cried out, trying to stop him from sending her over the edge, to the next plateau of pleasure, without him. When her whole body began to throb and pulse with the rising undulations of deepest need, he lifted his head, releasing the hardened bud from his tongue and teeth.

He kissed his pathway up her body, tonguing the depression of her navel, laving each of her swollen breasts. Her sweat was pungent musk to his senses, drowning him in the throbbing desire to be seated deeply inside her.

Her mouth bloomed under his, lips parted, sweet and open. Her knees gripped his hips and her ankles crossed behind his back, drawing him down to her. "Do you love me, Morgana of Kildare?"

"Yes, Hugh of Tyrone. With all my heart and soul, I love you."

"Prove it," Hugh commanded. Morgana threaded her fingers into the dark waves behind his head and pulled his mouth down to hers. Her tongue played the mating game with his.

She gasped with shocking delight when his shaft intruded into her, then shivered as he sought her depths, thrusting deep, till he was seated to the hilt.

"My lord—" she blinked both eyes wide as though his invasion had come a complete surprise "—I fail to see where there is anything left for me to prove. You have conquered me completely. I surrender."

Hugh kissed her brow, and the soft shell of her ear. The kissing and the touching were for her pleasure. What came next was for him. Her surrender wasn't the issue. It was only a signal on the journey to complete union, and the sublime emotion of peace that was sure to come after.

Chapter Eighteen

"Morgana! Morgana!" Sean stuck his head inside another door and shouted his sister's name again. When no answer came from within the empty rooms of Dunluce, he scurried to the next door, opened it and repeated her name.

He was out of breath and exhausted when he came back to the gallery stairs overlooking the great hall. He sank onto a riser, panting, wiping the freely running sweat from his brow. "I can't find her," he confessed. "She's not anywhere on this floor. If you'll wait here, I'll run and fetch some of the servants to help us look."

"No, son, we won't do that," James Fitzgerald said. "They're all working. Tsk, so many dead to be buried. We'll find Morgana, you and I. Let's go up to the third floor."

Sean wiped his sleeve across his face and stood up. He thought that wasn't such a good idea, that they look together, he and his father. God only knew where Morgana was or what she was up to. Sean had given up trying to figure his sister out.

He trudged up Dunluce's main stairwell to the third floor of the confusing castle. One wing took a dogleg to the left of the stairs. Another went straight ahead through a hallway of chambers, each private and closed off from the other.

"Which way first, sir?" Sean jerked at his doublet and tried to pull down the cuff of his left sleeve at the same time.

The earl of Kildare observed his heir and thought the boy looked like a ruffian. His feet were bare and dirty as a kern's. His hair hadn't been cut in months. Otherwise, the boy appeared as healthy as a stoat, sturdy of limb and apple-cheeked.

In contrast, the earl's ermine-lined cape, satin doublet and immaculate hose felt completely out of place in this environment, and they were. Dunluce was nothing more than a decrepit, crumbling fortress on the verge of sinking into the sea where it belonged.

James Fitzgerald looked to the straightaway hall. "This way. You take the doors on the left. I'll look in those on my right."

"Yes, sir." Sean stiffly nodded his assent. He squared his shoulders and started walking forward. The first room was as empty as all the ones on the lower floors. That was to be expected.

Everyone, simply everyone at Dunluce, except for the earl and Sean, was outside attending the mass for the dead.

Grace O'Malley's black-sailed ship had arrived in the harbor after the very last body was recovered. Twenty sailors wrapped in shrouds had been laid on the ground beside the chapel, to be buried at the completion of the mass. Sean had almost fainted dead away when he saw his father and Grace O'Malley walk up from the sea gate and into the chapel yard.

Grace had immediately taken Maurice to the ship. Sean had offered to find Morgana. He hadn't expected his father to insist on coming with him. The earl had said there wasn't any time to waste. Drake could come back. O'Malley had no intention of becoming a sitting duck in Sorely's harbor.

The third door came up empty. Sean turned around to tell his father that news and found him standing in the wide-open door opposite, his ruddy fists on his hips and murder roaring out of his throat.

"Get off my daughter, you rutting Irish pig! Morgana!"

"Uh-oh..." Sean ducked underneath the earl's arm as he reached for his sword and withdrew it. He ran into the room and put himself between the bed and the earl. "Father! I beg you. Listen to me. It isn't what it seems. I hadn't had time to tell you. Morgana got married."

Blood lust, rage and fury were hard emotions to get under control. Somehow, as Morgana and Hugh grabbed the sheets off the bed, Sean's father came to a stop. The blade of the earl of Kildare's steel sword wagged dangerously close to Sean's head, but Sean didn't flinch.

Sean stood his ground, praying his father's bulging eyes would focus on him, not on the naked people in the bed.

They didn't. At least not for a while. They dropped to scan the garments strewn across the floor at Sean's bare feet. A length of Irish plaid, a leather belt, and a bleached muslin night rail.

Sean took another deep breath. The bed ropes creaked. Morgana squeaked. Hugh O'Neill's knees popped as his bare feet hit the floor. "Father, please. I beg you, let me explain," the boy said.

"Married, you say, do you, boy?" The full thunder of his father's voice nearly knocked Sean to his knees. "Explain!" James Fitzgerald shouted. "So what's the bounder's name, what church posted the banns, and when did this blessed event take place? This morning, before the funerals?"

"He's the O'Neill, sir. Hugh, the earl of Tyrone."

"Thank you, lad, but I can introduce myself." Hugh stepped forward with a sheet wrapped around his middle. Sean ducked under his father's blade again and grabbed Hugh's plaid and belt from the floor and boldly handed both to him. "I take it, sir, that you are James Fitzgerald, the earl of Kildare."

"I am."

Hugh snapped the tartan around his waist and fitted it to his hips with his belt. The tail crossed his left shoulder when he strode forward, relieved of the sheet, and extended his hand to the earl. "I am Hugh O'Neill. Your future son-in-law, sir. Sean is stretching the truth to protect his sister."

Fitzgerald's droopy eyelids narrowed. The young man extended his hand as though this were a casual meeting on the streets of London. Kildare had heard Hugh O'Neill's named bandied about in Paris. Rumor had it he was Bess's latest favorite.

There had been a point in Fitzgerald's life when he stood in the same high regard and the queen of England looked upon him as more than just a favorite. Today, older and wiser, he understood what Elizabeth's fleeting regard was actually worth—nothing.

Fickle Elizabeth Tudor, her father's daughter in all things, was infatuated with the chase. Criminally vicious to those she cast aside in her rush to gain the affections of her newest love. Worst, Elizabeth feared aging, hence she perpetually surrounded herself with young, attentive and virile males. The "Virgin Queen" was the laughingstock of the courts of Europe.

Her policies in Ireland were diabolical. James Fitzgerald saw her as the most evil woman alive. His one goal in life was to wrest Ireland from English control. The rebellion he lead in 1569 had caused his banishment, and the proscription of his race. But the battles were not over. Armageddon for Elizabeth Tudor would commence soon.

To that end, James Fitzgerald stood and evaluated this brazen hulk of O'Neill manhood, ripe from the audacious act of swiving Fitzgerald's own daughter. Were he any less than the very man every wagging tongue at Henry's court in Paris claimed was the current paramour of Queen Elizabeth, Fitzgerald would have cut off the man's balls and thrown both him and his cods out the bloody window. Then he would have horsewhipped his daughter and cast her onto the same rocks where her lover lay and waited for the carrion crows to pick their bones clean.

Instead, Fitzgerald had the presence of mind to see a man he could use to get to Elizabeth. Morgana meant nothing to him.

Calmly Fitzgerald lowered the blade of his sword and re-sheathed it. Tempered steel clicked into its guard as the earl of Kildare slowly put out his hand. As he grasped the earl of Tyrone's hand, Fitzgerald said, "I accept your hand in peace."

"I'm glad to hear you say that," Hugh replied. He saw the dead space behind Kildare's blue gaze. "May I suggest we step out and give Morgana an opportunity to dress?"

"An excellent idea. Morgana, bring your packs with you when you come out. Grace is anxious to sail immediately. Sean, go and wash your feet and put on stockings and shoes. You will not insult me further by being dressed like a savage."

The door shut behind the two men's backs. An urge to vomit caused Sean to nearly double in half.

"Sean!" Morgana gasped. "Why didn't you come and tell me he was here?" Morgana sank onto the far edge of the bed. "How could you have brought him up here?"

Sean's jaw sagged. He stared at Morgana in all her terrible *dishabille* and gulped down the lump in his throat. "There wasn't time," he explained. "We were at mass when the ship came. Just he and Grace came up from the *Avenger.* She took Maury to the ship. I had to come with Father. Get dressed, Morgana."

It took Morgana long moments to recover her dignity, but she did. She rose to her feet, wound in a trailing sheet and said coldly, "Do you leave, my lord Offaly, I will."

"Aw, Morgana, it wasn't my fault. I swear. I tried to warn you by shouting your name in every room on the floor below. Father told me to stop shouting and just look for you. He knew what he was looking for, Morgana. I just know he knew. Somehow. Maybe they saw Hugh climb the ivy to your window. Everyone else did."

Morgana didn't need more mortification. She forced a breath to compose herself and let her emotions go, casting all of them out with the expiration of her next breath. *Accept it,* she told herself. *This is the morning you saw coming. Accept it.*

"You're right, Sean. None of this is any fault of yours. Go now. Get cleaned up. I'll be down to the sea gate directly."

Sean stood for a long time staring back at her, a little lordling who didn't know which way to turn at this moment in his life. Then he made up his mind abruptly and ran to Morgana, embracing her, kissing her cheek. "I love you, Morgana. No matter what happens, know that I love you with all my heart. I wasn't trying to compromise you or force the O'Neill's hand. Forgive me."

He turned and ran before Morgana gathered her wits and remembered that neither Sean or Maury knew about her agreement with Hugh. They had just come to the conclusion that they could marry, in this very room.

That put her father's intrusion into her and Hugh's privacy onto a completely different level. He'd known what he was going to find when he threw open the door. What he might not have known was the political value of the man Morgana was bedding. But Sean had given all that away, and Morgana had clearly seen the light of calculation glinting in her father's eyes. He thought he'd found another tool, another ally in his war against the crown.

Morgana caught up her clothes and hurried behind the folding screen to complete her ablutions and dress. She prayed she could get to Hugh and explain before her father ruined everything.

High tide churned up the smoke-blackened cliffs around Sorely Mac Donnell's wharf. It lapped at the lowest door of Dunluce Castle, the sea gate. If it would surge another four feet, the stench of smoke and charcoal might be washed from the rocks. The acrid stink stung Morgana's nose and throat anew.

She emerged from the dark tunnel into harsh daylight. The *Avenger* was moored directly to the wharf. A wooden gangplank stretched across the chasm between ship and cliff.

Morgana walked to the edge, where the mooring ropes stretched from the ship to iron rings hammered into stone.

The pier and its pylons were gone. She didn't look down into the water to see the carcasses of the sunken ships. A sheen of oil, garbage and flotsam floated like a crust on the waves.

Her father and Hugh stood on the bow, engaged in conversation. They both saw her at the same time. Hugh began walking toward her. Her father hollered, "Come on aboard, Morgana. Grace, she's here. Let's get under way."

Grace O'Malley ran up the gangway from her galley. A huge smile lighted her face the moment she spied Morgana standing at the end of the gangplank. "You look wonderful! Come on! Don't tell me you still don't trust your sea legs."

"You should know better." Morgana folded her hands together and stayed where she was, on solid ground.

Grace's black hair streamed into her face as she nimbly crossed the wobbling board. Not one to stand on ceremony, she threw her arms around Morgana and embraced her in a hearty, soul-felt hug. "Look at you, Lady Morgana. Do you know, I've never seen you with your hair hanging loose down your back...."

"Well—" Morgana kissed her friend and hugged her in return "—there's a story to that. You might notice there was one hell of a fire here last night."

"Notice? Dear heavens, Morgana, I fear I started it. I sank two of Drake's caravels just outside the harbor there. Then we doused the ship's lights and ran for cover between Skirres Portrush and Band Haven. We saw the holocaust blazing from there. God's truth, we thought everyone at Dunluce blown to kingdom come."

"Ten caravels were. My only casualty was half my hair. It was singed so badly, I had to cut it just now, when I was dressing."

Hugh joined them, and as Morgana spoke, his hand reached out to touch the curly, silken mass of red that the wind played havoc with. "When did you do this?"

"Just now," Morgana turned to him. "When I realized I had great clumps of it missing. It's symbolic. I've cut all bonds from the past. I hope you understand."

Hugh tilted his head, and a quizzical frown touched his brow. He thought he understood what she was telling him. He spread a handful of the red curls in the sun, before her eyes. "It's lovely. I won't complain." Then he tipped his head and kissed the curls in his fingers.

"Oh, my," Grace scolded. "What's this about, then? A new love, Morgana?"

"Yes. Mhóre than that, Grace. Hugh and I are to be married soon."

"You are!" Grace squealed and grabbed her again, hugging her tight. "Congratulations! He's such a fine figure of a man. Why, I was hoping to steal the man for myself. Your father said nothing when he and Sean came aboard. Does he know?"

"He knows." Morgana and Hugh said in unison.

"Well, this is splendid. Come on, then, come aboard, Morgana. Hugh, you may have to give her a hand. Morgana doesn't like the water much."

"I know." Hugh slipped his arm around Morgana's waist and stood beside her, ready and willing to assist.

"I'm not coming aboard, Grace," Morgana said.

"Och, now!" Grace laughed, waving that comment aside with a flip of her hand. "Don't be absurd. Your father's waiting."

"I'm not coming aboard, Grace," Morgana said, more firmly. "Not today. Not tomorrow. I don't think I'll ever set foot on a ship again. Hugh's going to take me home to Dungannon with him. We'll be married soon. I'm staying in Ireland with him."

"You can't mean that!" Grace blinked. She looked around to her ship and saw James Fitzgerald standing at the near railing, watching and listening. "My lord, Morgana says she's not coming with us. Morgana, what will I tell your mother?"

Morgana looked at her father, then back to her cousin and closest, dearest friend. "You'll think of something, I'm sure, Grace. Tell her I haven't the courage of the O'Malley women. Or tell her that I'm Irish and I'm not leaving my home again. She has the boys. They are what she wanted most of all. I'm old and grown. She'll understand, and she has Father to contend with."

"Grace, it's time." James Fitzgerald unfastened a line and cast it to the shore.

"Morgana, are you certain?"

"Never more certain of anything in my life." Morgana looked up at Hugh and smiled when his hands tightened on her shoulder and waist.

"My lord Father, I've brought the deeds you requested, and the letter from Bishop Moye. If you have need of me, you can reach me at Dungannon. Give Mother my love and tell Sean and Maurice that I will pray for them every day."

Morgana lifted the saddlebag that she'd set at her feet and handed the heavy pack to Grace. "What's in it, gold?" Grace grumbled. "It weighs a ton."

"Gold and jewels and the deeds to all of Father's estates released by the church. It's all there. I included a quitclaim to my dowry estates. I won't be needing any of them, and Father will be needing properties for collateral to pay for his army."

Stunned, Grace O'Malley looked up at Hugh and asked, "Sir, do you realize what she is giving away? The value of her properties. Morgana, your father will mortgage everything to the hilt. It costs a bloody fortune to live in Paris, raising an army."

"I don't think that will matter to Hugh and me. We will have everything we need in Dungannon. He's going to take care of me, and I'm going to take care of him."

"That's right," Hugh affirmed. "Wait here, Morgana. I'll go aboard and tell your brothers we're not sailing with them. Perhaps I can convince your father to come and say goodbye to you."

Hugh took the heavy pack from Grace's hands and carried it onto the ship. He did his last duty where that pack of valuables was concerned by handing it over to James Fitzgerald. "I believe everything inside here is yours, sir."

Judging by the heft of the pack, James had to agree. He looked to Morgana with new respect rising in his eyes. "She's made her decision to stay with you. I don't know how you did it, young man, but I will tell you to remember all your days that she's a Fitzgerald daughter. Mistreat her or dishonor her and you will answer to me."

"I'll take good care of Morgana," Hugh responded. James Fitzgerald didn't intimidate him. He saw the man's worth for himself, and understood how he used each of his children as pawns furthering his political games.

Morgana had made the right decision. Hugh hadn't had a thing to do with it. He knew it—and Fitzgerald knew it, too.

The boys were very sad to learn their sister wasn't going with them to Paris. Fitzgerald declined to step ashore and embrace the daughter he was leaving behind.

Hugh had found the parent he needed in Loghran O'Toole. Morgana, too, must have found someone else more caring than her father.

Hugh unfastened the last mooring rope as Grace gave the order to trim the *Avenger*'s sails.

"Hold! Captain O'Malley, we've got a stowaway!" A crewman hollered from below deck. All heads turned at the howling and screaming coming from the forward hold.

"Damn my eyes, now why am I not surprised?" Hugh pulled hard on the last rope, to keep the ship from slipping away from the wharf.

A sailor brought out a screaming, kicking and howling Cara Mulvaine. Grace grabbed the girl by her ear and marched her over the gangplank.

"For the last time, Mulvaine, you're not sailing with me! Stow away on my ship one more time and I'll tie you to the mizzen and give you forty lashes with my cat-o'-nine-tails. Hold on to her, Sir Hugh."

Hugh had enough to do holding the rope. Morgana caught Cara. "Don't you dare bite me again!"

Grace ran back across the plank. Her crew hauled it in and caught the rope Hugh tossed to them. Cara howled a curse that nearly smothered all the goodbyes being shouted as the ship pulled away and heeled into the wind.

"I hope your ship springs a leak!" Cara screamed. She spat into the sea, then wiped her mouth with a filthy hand.

"You know what, you little heathen?" Morgana said as she firmly jerked the girl around and marched her back up to the sea gate. "I'm going to give you a bath and make you put on a clean dress."

"No, yer not!" Cara argued. "You can't touch me. It's the law!"

"We'll just see about that," Morgana declared, not bothering to point out to the child that she was most definitely touching her. Morgana had a death grip on the girl's wrist, and she wasn't going to let go.

Hugh sucked in a lung full of sea air before he said, "Don't bite off more than you can chew, little mother."

"What's that supposed to mean?" Morgana asked him. "I said I'm giving her a bath. She needs it."

"Some soap in her mouth and a taste of respect for her elders might be in order, as well. But she's Sorely's granddaughter, and his ward. Don't you forget that."

"As if I could," Morgana replied, miffed.

"Ah, Morgana, Morgana, I can read you like the stars already," Hugh said with deep pleasure as he draped his arm across her shoulders and escorted the two ladies back into Dunluce.

When Morgana made up her mind to give Cara Mulvaine a bath, she hadn't imagined the girl would fight with everything she had against such a common procedure. They hadn't any more than gotten inside the hall when the battle began. Cara had the aim of a Dublin brawler and the will to strike back at anyone she perceived as weaker than her.

Thank God Hugh hadn't deserted her and left her on her own to deal with the child. Cara Mulvaine understood one thing—brute force. Hugh had plenty of that. He made one threat to take a stick to her, and Cara shut up. She went quietly to the bathhouse with Morgana and, with grim lips, stood silently by as Morgana filled a tub with steaming water.

"We'll wash your hair first, Cara. Come and bend over the basin for me. I promise not to pull on the tangles when I comb your hair out."

"You're not supposed to touch me!" Cara insisted. Huge tears glistened in her eyes.

Morgana sent a meaningful glance to Hugh's long shadow, outside the door of the bathhouse. He had declined to participate, but had agreed to remain close by as a necessary authority figure.

"We're not going to start on that tack again, young lady." Morgana was certain the girl understood Morgana's meaningful glance to Hugh's shadow. "If you are a good girl and stay still while I scrub your hair, I'll tell you about my adventures sailing the oceans with Grace O'Malley."

"She's a wicked harlot pirate," Cara said as she came to the bench and knelt, then bent forward over the basin.

Morgana picked up a pitcher and dipped it in the tub of steamy water and wet the girl's long, tangled black hair. "So you admire her then, do you? She's my kinswoman, you know. My mother and her mother were cousins. They grew up as princesses on Clare Island."

"Where's that?"

"In Clew Bay, off the coast of county Mayo."

"Is it pretty?"

"Hmm..." Morgana thought the question over as she scrubbed soap into the tresses. Cara's hair was in terrible shape, filthy beyond belief, tangled and knotted. Combing it was going to be an ordeal. "It's a different part of Ireland. Wild gales strip the island bare in the autumn, twisting the trees. There's plenty of rocks and grass and meadows. But it doesn't have the cliffs that Dunluce has. You might like to go there sometime and see it for yourself."

"I only want to go home to Scotland."

"Oh, I see. Is that where you thought Grace was going? If you had asked, she would have told you she is going to

Paris. That's in another country entirely, where they speak a whole different language, French."

"I know that. I'm not stupid."

"Did I say that you were? I think you are a very clever child."

"I'm not. I'm accursed. The Mac Donnell says so."

"Close your eyes tight, Cara. I'm going to rinse the soap out, and it might sting your eyes."

"Then jus' leave the soap in. I do all the time."

"Ah, well, no wonder." Morgana said, finding the reason for the clammy feel of the girl's hair when it was wet. "Wouldn't you like to have soft, shiny hair like mine?"

"Can't be shiny. Mine's black."

"Your aunt Inghinn's hair is very shiny and beautiful, and it is black. She rinses the soap out well, and so do I. It makes it so much easier to comb and brush."

"I don't have no combs. I jus' use my fingers."

That explained something else—the tangles. "Well, that simply won't do, Cara. You're growing up. You can't be a wild sprite running about the moors forever. Close your eyes."

"It burns!"

"Keep them closed. I'm rinsing it as quick as I can."

Morgana gave her a small cloth to press over her eyes and continued with the work at hand. A second soaping and a good healthy scrubbing saw the black curls squeaky-clean to her touch. Rinsing them clean was an ordeal to be borne. The soapsuds did sting. Cara howled about it, but put up with it rather bravely all in all.

Morgana wrapped Cara's head in a towel and set about seeing to the bath. She untied the laces on Cara's wool dress and drew it off her. Morgana had thought the dress in bad shape. Cara's undergarments were worse, torn, ragged, and filthy with caked-on dirt and grime. Her aunts should be doing this for her on a regular basis. Morgana's heart went out to the poor, motherless child.

As she tipped another kettle of hot water into the tub to warm it to a comfortable temperature, Morgana asked, "How long have you lived at Dunluce?"

"A long time." Cara shrugged both shoulders. She stuck her fingers in the tub of water, her eyes downcast. "You're going to have three sons, Hugh, Shane and Brian."

"I am? Those are very nice names for three sons." Morgana reacted to the prediction as if it were commonplace to talk to a seer. "Am I going to have any daughters?"

"No. Your aunt Catherine tries to talk to you, but you don't listen to her. She says she's buried in the wrong place and she can't rest in peace until she's moved to hallowed ground."

Startled, Morgana blinked twice before asking, "What makes you say that? How do you know I had an aunt named Catherine?"

"She married Conn O'Neill and somebody murdert her, but the priest thought she killed herself jumping out the window of the same room you jumped out. She died."

Cara lifted her gaze. She had that same oddly glassy look Morgana had seen before. "I don't want to take a bath. Thank you for washing my hair."

The child turned and walked away from the tub, heading out the door in her shift and old-fashioned kirtle. Morgana caught her in the doorway. "We're not finished, Cara. You'll get in the tub now. Come. I insist."

"You're not supposed to touch me." Cara said in a flat, toneless voice. "Your fingers will fall off if you touch me."

"No, they won't. Come, child. Soap won't make your fingers fall off, either."

They came, then, to the worst of it. Getting Cara shed of that filthy outgrown kirtle and into the tub bare naked. The towel holding her hair up was lost in the struggle, and naturally all that clean black hair tumbled down her back and into the water.

That wasn't a bad thing. Only Morgana had to lift the heavy hair up, wring the water from it and wrap it up in a towel. Cara had sunk down to her chin in the water. But at some point Morgana had to ask her to stand so that she could wash all the underwater parts as clean as her neck, face and ears. That was when Morgana saw all the marks on the girl's body.

The bruises were every color of the bruise rainbow. Yellow and nearly gone. Purple freshly laid on her skin. Blues and grays that were days or weeks old. Horrified, Morgana gave up trying to count the number on just her back.

At first, Morgana was too appalled to say anything. Children were punished for disobedience. Morgana knew from her own observations that Cara Mulvaine was not the most obedient or meek child on earth. The Ten Commandments told every Christian how to live and what to expect of life. Sins were punishable offenses.

This very morning, Morgana had stood behind the bed where her own father had caught her in the act of fornication. She had expected the wrath of his hand to fall upon her. She hadn't managed to work out why he'd spared her a beating. In her heart, she believed any punishment was deserved for being caught in such a flagrant sin by both her brother and her father.

Hugh had something to do with that. On the same vein, had the tables been turned and it had been Hugh who caught her in that same omission, Morgana knew, his wrath would have been ten times greater than her father's.

So it wasn't that she was shocked to see the marks of beatings on an unruly child's body. There were just so many marks, and they were everywhere, except on Cara's face. She had bruises on her small fingers, in the palms of her dirty little hands. A dozen angry red welts crisscrossed her fleshless back, where the sharp bones protruded from the backs of her shoulders. They were fresh, put there this very morning.

"Cara, who is it that beats you?"

Cara looked down on her own shoulder. "Och, tha's the Mac Donnell's blackthorn staff. It doesna hurt anymore."

"He hit you with his walking staff?"

"When I took it to him, aye. I found it and thought he could use it to walk to chapel."

"You brought him a staff and he beat you with it?"

Cara took the sea sponge from Morgana's still hand and lifted a foot from the water and scrubbed the sole. "It wasn't so bad as a whipping with his strap. I sat in his chair and soiled the linen at the table. Am I clean enough to suit you? Kin I have my kirtle and dress back? I don't have another."

Morgana said nothing to that. Too many times in the past three years, she hadn't had another gown to put on, either. "Cara, I want to have both of them washed so that you'll be clean from inside out. I'm going to ask the O'Neill to carry you up to my chamber for me. I'll get you something else to wear from what I have. Will you let him carry you into the manse?"

Cara's face took on a different expression, half calculation, half wonder. "Do you think he would? The Mac Donnell fears him."

"I think he will if I ask him to. But you mustn't fight him or struggle, like you do when I take hold of your arm. I won't have anything but clean toweling to wrap you in, and it embarrasses big men to carry half-naked, squalling children."

"Oh," Cara said to that, as if she had had some revelation. Morgana wanted Hugh to see the marks on the girl. Maybe he would change his mind if he did.

"Would you like for me to help you out of the tub? You can dry off while I speak to him." Morgana offered Cara her hand. The wood of the old tub was furred and slick on the bottom, and the stone floor of the bathhouse had the texture of glass when wet feet touched it. Cara gave the offer a moment's thought, then accepted the help. Morgana shook out a sheet of toweling and wrapped the girl in it. "Dry all your parts, Cara, ears to nose, all the way to fingers and toes."

Cara Mulvaine giggled. Amazed that she could, Morgana went out into the sunlight and looked for Hugh. He sat on a nearby bench. His boots stretched far out ahead of him. His shoulders tilted back against the whitewashed wall. His fingers were neatly laced over his flat belly. His head was cocked to one shoulder, his eyes were closed, and a soft snore whistled out his parted lips.

Morgana woke him, stated her request and gave him the reason she needed Cara carried upstairs to Morgana's guest chamber. It was reasonable, succinctly stated. Hugh's expression indicated refusal, though he delayed answering outright as he thought her request over. He sat up straight, stretched his arms above his head, then stood and looked out over the blue sea.

"Morgana, we discussed this at length just a few hours ago, did we not?"

"Yes."

"You're trying to draw me into a problem that is none of my affair. Cara Mulvaine is a ward of Dunluce. The Mac Donnell is the authority here. If you feel she must be carried somewhere, why don't you go speak to Sorely? Why are you bringing the problem to me?"

"Because you are here, and it is a waste of time to seek the Mac Donnell when you could do the task for me."

"She's eight years old, well into navigating about on her own two feet."

"They'll get dirty."

"Morgana, her feet will be dirty as soon as she walks out of your bedchamber, in whatever shirt of mine it is you intend to put on her."

"Hugh, do you dislike children?"

"You are changing the subject, lady."

"Very well, you've made your point, my lord. Don't feel you need to linger about. Cara and I are dealing with each other just fine. Thank you for your assistance."

"You are welcome." Hugh responded with the same politeness that she gave him. He nodded a dismissal and strolled off to whatever man's pursuits he was about this day.

Cara came out of the bath holding her kirtle and dress in one hand, the toweling to her skinny chest with the other. The castle ward was empty, save for Hugh as he retreated to the postern gate.

"I could wash my dress and my kirtle and hang them in my tower to dry, Lady Morgana. You can go with him, if you want."

"No." Morgana shook her head. "I want to teach you how to comb and brush your hair. If we spend the afternoon together, I think I can teach you to braid it, too."

Cara looked down at the crowd that still grouped about the chapel. "Then we'd better do it anon. I have lessons with the Mac Donnell at vespers."

"What does he teach you, Cara?"

"How to write and script numbers."

"Do you enjoy that?" Morgana slipped her arm across the girl's shoulders as they walked to the manse.

"Aye," Cara nodded. "I read the Bible to him. Some of the names, like Leviticus, are hard to say, but he says I read as well as Uncle James. I like numbers, too."

"So some things you do please your grandfather?"

"Grandfather? Oh, you mean the Mac Donnell. I suppose he is my grandfather. Everyone calls him the Mac Donnell, though. It isn't respectful to address him by any other name."

Chapter Nineteen

The balance of the day passed quickly. There was plenty of work to do at Dunluce. Hugh had little advice to offer the Mac Donnell regarding any means of salvaging sunken cargoes from the ships sent to the bottom of Sorely's bay. Hence Hugh gravitated to other work, where his skills could be of use.

The greatest damage done to the castle itself was in the stable. Its thatch-and-wood roof had gone up in flames. Most of Hugh's kerns were occupied repairing the damage done to that building.

Since the turmoil of the night before, no one had given much thought to the horses. The animals had gotten short shrift this morning. The loss of manpower to Dunluce was staggering, in Hugh's opinion. Sorely was old, and much of his staff had been with him all his life. The casualties among Dunluce's grooms had been substantial.

Hugh took on the task of checking the stable animals for injuries and treating the cuts and burns he found. Boru had a serious blister on his rear left flank. Ariel's worst wound was a cinder flash between her beautiful brown eyes. Both were infested with flies. Hugh cleaned them up and put a generous coating of salve on both burns.

After treating the rest, then mucking out stalls and hauling water and grain to them, Hugh did the unthinkable. He turned Boru and Ariel into the same paddock. Ariel was

definitely in season. Boru intimated he was up to the duty
of siring a foal.

Hugh stayed at the paddock afterward, just to make certain his war-horse didn't inflict any serious damage on the
Arabian. Both were incredible horses, exemplary of their
breeds. He ought to be finding something better to do with
the time he had on his hands, but he couldn't. He was troubled.

He kept thinking back to his last discussion with Morgana. Trying to put a finger on exactly why that talk bothered him so deeply wasn't easy. He gave the lady much
credit. She knew exactly how to couch a request. She hadn't
argued his decision. In fact, her acceptance of his outright
refusal bothered him more than if she'd kept on, asking
again and again, nagging at him.

Not that he wanted a scold or a nag for a wife. No, far
from that, he wanted Morgana to bring him her problems
and openly discuss everything that troubled her. He knew
that she would be a most capable chatelaine and that Dungannon's household would thrive under her management.
She would also be a devoted, loving and caring mother, and
for that he was most grateful.

Ariel chased Boru to a corner of the paddock, then, with
a flirty toss of mane and tail, ran circles around the paddock, teasing him. Hugh grinned as he realized neither horse
needed his assistance, not as a supervisor or observer.
Mother Nature had everything in her capable hands.

As he walked away, he wondered what Morgana would
have to say about his putting the two horses together. With
most of the day now behind him, Hugh wanted to be with
Morgana.

The majority of Dunluce's inhabitants were still occupied with work outdoors. The castle seemed eerily vacant
when Hugh walked through the great hall and up the gallery stairs. A turf boy replenishing peat for the few fire-
places in the main rooms was the only servant he
encountered.

Windows, shutters and all the doors on the third floor of the manor stood wide open. A fresh breeze straight off the sea swept from room to room, lessening the acrid stench of smoke, saltpeter and burned gunpowder.

Hugh heard Morgana's soft murmur as he approached her chamber. Inside the open door, he saw Morgana seated on a stool at the windows. The Mulvaine sat cross-legged before her, having her silky black hair neatly braided. They saw him at the doorway at the same time, and both fell silent.

"After all this time, I should have thought you would be done with the grooming," Hugh said, by way of inviting himself in.

"It took a little longer than we anticipated to get all the tangles combed out," Morgana replied evenly. She turned her eyes back to the braid she was making with her hands. "How have you spent your day, my lord?"

"With the horses." Hugh came to a stop at the only chair in the chamber. It was a high-backed affair, carved with ornamental acanthus leaves. He seated himself and contentedly regarded the vignette before him—lovely woman and child, engrossed in their toilette. "Your mare has taken an avid interest in my charger, my lady."

"Oh?" Morgana's eyes slanted toward him. Hugh clearly saw one dimple flash briefly, though she didn't smile. "Are you telling me that spring is in the air?"

"Aye." Hugh grinned, liking the way she put things in their proper place. "I feel the urge to plow a fertile field or two myself."

His innuendo caused Morgana's eyes to dart over him— from casually leaned-back head to thoroughly relaxed feet crossed at the ankles. She missed nothing in her precise inspection.

"We'll be done here shortly, my lord." Morgana returned her attention to the girl's braids. Cara very intently studied a knotted string at the bottom of one finished braid. She was oblivious of Hugh.

"I see how it's done, lady," she said brightly, turning to look at Morgana. "How often do I hafta do it?"

"Every morning and every night," Morgana insisted.

"There's nothing wrong with doing it in the middle of the day, too," Hugh said with a smirk, although he hid the chuckles that followed behind his hand. Morgana nearly crossed her eyes, glaring at him. The blush that ran up her complexion to the roots of her hair informed him that she'd caught his meaning.

"That's too often!" Cara got to her feet, the second braid secured. She had on a pair of Sean's left-behind trews and a saffron sark of Hugh's. Her bare feet stuck out of the bottom of the britches, nowhere near as dirty as they had been before the bath. "Thank you, Lady O'Malley. I'll remember how to do the braids."

"You look very pretty." Morgana put her brush and comb into the child's hands. "You may keep these, Cara. It's my gift to you."

"Oh, you mustn't. Why, they're silver, both of them."

"I know, but they are mine to give, and I want you to have them and use them."

"Oh. Nobody ever gave me a gift before." Cara blinked in surprise. Her eyes suddenly took on a strange, unfocused look.

Fearing the child was about to cry, Morgana said briskly, "Well. I am pleased to be the first, then. Use them just like I've showed you. I don't ever want to see you as untidy as you were today."

Cara's gaze remained unfocused. Morgana realized Cara was seeing something else, not her surroundings or Morgana's face. It was eerie. Shivers cascaded over Morgana's neck and shoulder.

Cara's fingers skittered across the silver back of the brush. "I shall put it in the east tower as a gift for my guest. He comes anon, to give you blessings and speak with the O'Neill."

"Who comes?" Morgana reached out to touch Cara's cheek. Her touch broke the spell, and the child recoiled, as she had done so often before they became friends.

"You mustn't touch me, lady. It is forbidden."

"Who comes on the morrow, Cara?" Morgana repeated her question, intrigued by the child's visions.

"I do not know his name, only that he told me now, 'If Mohammed will not go the mountain, the mountain shall come to Mohammed.' Lady, will you come back to Dunluce?"

"As the Mac Donnell is Lord Hugh's vassal, I imagine I will. Hugh and I are your neighbors at Dungannon, and you are welcome to come and visit us there."

"I'm glad." Cara smiled, obviously pleased. She made a comical curtsy. Hands that gripped a brush and a comb extended a nonexistent skirt as she bobbed up and down. Then she ran out the door, her two treasures clutched to her chest.

Hugh got to his feet the moment the girl left. He took Morgana's hands in his and drew her up from the stool, then continued to hold both her hands in his. "You have a heart softer than potted soap. Will you be saddling me with every stray waif that crosses the glen? That child is the strangest girl I have ever had the misfortune to meet."

"You can't classify Cara as a stray waif, Hugh. She has a family. They just don't seem to care much for her. I don't see why. She's a sweet child, malleable and painfully eager to please, if one takes the time to get to know her. I intend to ask her to come to Dungannon after we're married."

"You may invite anyone you please," Hugh agreed. "Dungannon will always be open to guests, travelers and pilgrims."

"Then you won't object to my telling the Mac Donnell that we will foster her. I am more than willing to sponsor her, teach her how to manage a household, and equip her with skills that a husband will expect her to have."

"I am afraid to ask what brings on this generosity."

"It's just that I've thought about Cara since we spoke to the issue earlier. I believe when you write to the queen you should have an alternative plan regarding the Mulvaine. It won't wash just to say she's lacking suitable attributes, without giving a reasonable solution to the future."

"You forget the fact that I am not the girl's guardian, or so appointed. She is a propertied Scots heiress."

"All the more reason for you to assert your authority over the Mac Donnell. The queen would make Cara your ward."

"Morgana, you don't understand the facts here. If there is any dispute over Sorely's wardship, it must come from the crown of Scotland. The Mulvaine is a Scot. Elizabeth's interest in her is vengeance against her enemy, the Mac Donnell. The child's a political pawn.

"What happened here last night is a direct result of Sorely's demolishing Graham Keep and the murder of the marquess of Carlisle. Raids go back and forth, from the lowlands to the Irish coast, from Northumberland to Antrim. Drake was commissioned specifically to put an end to it. I'm not going to put Tyrone in the middle of this. My people have enough troubles, without adding Antrim's."

"You are in the thick of it, no matter how you look at it. Listen to me, Hugh, just carry it through. Suppose Elizabeth orders you to marry her, regardless of your wishes in the matter. Cara's properties become yours. The Mac Donnell's problems *are* yours. He is your vassal. You owe him support, protection, the weight and prestige of your office in addressing his petitions to the crown."

"By the same token, in marrying you I take on all the burdens of repeated rebellions of the house of Fitzgerald against the crown, don't I? In the eyes of England, your father is a traitor. You supplied him gold and properties for collateral to build an army to take Ireland from the crown. How far do you think Elizabeth's indulgence to me will carry in favor of our marriage if I lay those facts on the table to her?"

"You're changing the subject. I'm speaking to the issue of the Mulvaine, and the obstacle she is to our marriage."

"So why not tie a rock and a rope around her skinny neck and toss her into the Irish Sea? Let's be done with her once and for all. What is it that you really want me to do, Morgana? Can I have the truth straight out, without all of this extraneous wrapping?''

"I told you the truth when the subject first came up. You brushed my words aside like lint off your sleeve.''

"Tell me again. Plain and simple, Morgana.''

"I promised Sir Almoy to bring both you and Cara Mulvaine to him at the Temple of Dunrath. He wishes to school her. It's that simple.''

"You see fosterage as the means to reach that end?''

"Plain and simple, sir,'' Morgana testily answered him in the very same tone. "You're not leaving me many other choices. I gave my word to do what Almoy asked. I am honor-bound to stand by my word.''

Hugh's fingers tightened upon her hands. "I would have the choices remain open to you.''

Morgana met the intensity of his eyes without flinching. She raised her chin, her jaw setting with unequivocal strength. "People vanish. Children disappear. Fairies steal babies and leave changelings in their places. Make up any explanation you want, Hugh. It boils down to one fact. I will arrange, by fair means or foul, for Cara to escape this beastly captivity of hers. I would rather she was granted permission to leave. If not that, I will kidnap her.

"I would have no qualms about doing so. She is greatly abused by your vassal, the Mac Donnell. Everything I have learned about the life Cara leads here at Dunluce tells me I would be morally right in removing her from the Mac Donnell's domination.''

"You divined all this in little more than one day?''

"I have.'' Outwardly Morgana didn't waver, but it rattled her internally to realize that so much had happened in the passage of so little time. Righteously she declared, "I fell in love with you in less time than that.''

"Now who is changing the subject?''

"Play fair, and so will I. Sow deceit, reap deception. Argue irrefutable male logic, succumb to feminine wiles.

Whatever is necessary. I know how to survive and win, my lord."

"That is pure braggadocio. You are smarting from your failure to move me. The girl will remain here when you and I leave on the morrow. By the time we get to Dungannon, you will have forgotten her and taken up some other righteous cause."

"We'll see."

"You forget, love, that I know what moves you. You have an overwhelming need to champion those you deem victims. You went to great lengths to hide, protect and defend your brothers. It's rather a touching virtue, Morgana, highly admirable. But ..." He released her hands and tapped one finger against her nose. "Don't push it so far that you alienate me."

"Morgana ..." Inghinn Dubh rapped on the open door. "Oh, hello, Hugh. I thought if I found Morgana, I would find you, as well. Are you busy? Could you come down to the hall? My father has found something important that he thinks you must see, Hugh."

Sorely Mac Donnell should have been in bed with his burned foot elevated. Morgana didn't think he'd even gone to sleep since the fire storm. She hadn't, and she knew Hugh hadn't slept. So they should have all been winding down, the way the sunny afternoon was dwindling into evening's shadowy stillness.

But the air inside the great hall crackled with high excitement and unexplained tensions. All of which emanated from the old man agitatedly stamping back and forth on the cold flags of the hearth. His blackthorn staff chattered an impatient tattoo until Morgana and Hugh reached the alcove before him.

"O'Neill, it's about time you showed up. I've been searching all over for you. Look what we found when the tide ran out on the west side of my bay. Donovan, give the scroll to the O'Neill!"

Sorely jabbed the end of his staff at the retainer shoving a round-topped sea chest across the floor on a sled. The chest bore a stamped inscription conveying its contents to the marquis of Winchester, Basing House. Above the inscription was the device of the English crown, two lions rampant, and the initials E.R. Chalked below that was a number, 21.

"Damn me," Hugh whispered, dumbfounded. "William Paulet!"

"Who's he?" Morgana asked.

"Paulet's the royal treasurer. That trunk belongs to him."

"Be damned twice!" Sorely barked. "'Tis the property of the churches of Ireland. Read that parchment."

Hugh took the scroll in hand. It was wet, the seal on it broken. The sodden sheepskin was so soft, opening it made it flop over on itself. The ink had begun to smear badly.

"Sorry, I can't make it out." Hugh squinted to compensate for the lack of good reading light in the hall. He strode to the high board and spread the document on it, then reached for a branch of candles.

The parsimonious Mac Donnell winced when Hugh took the one lighted taper out of its socket and lit every wick. Morgana had already bent over the table and begun to read out loud the only legible column. "Saints Anne and Agnes, Clane, county Kildare, nine crosses, gold, four silver, four chalices—gold—three books—Catholic, gold and jewel jackets—eighteen candlesticks—gold. Hugh, what does this mean?"

"Just one moment." Hugh took a magnifying glass from a pocket in his doublet. He began reading at the top of the parchment, going over each line of blurring script.

"This says it's the consignment of Lord Grey, justiciar of Ireland, transported on the ship, *Margaret Rose,* May ninth, this year, via the largess of Captain Francis Drake, admiral, Her Majesty's navy. Chests numbering seventy in all, shipped from Donegal Abbey to the Tower of London. There to be handed over to the royal treasurer. Sorely, have you opened the trunk? Where are the others? This says there were seventy trunks in all. Good heavens, can the rest be at the bottom of the sea?''

"There are no others that we found. We scoured the shoreline from here to Portrush and the causeway before bringing this trunk to the hall. If there are others, they are at the bottom of the sea with the *Margaret Rose*. Only this one trunk washed up on my shore.''

"Let's open it,'' Hugh said excitedly.

"Nay!'' Sorely shouted, shaking his staff in a threat to strike Hugh if he did. "I've forbidden my men to touch the lock. God strike me dead, there'll be no blasphemy conducted in the hall of the Mac Donnells. It's church gold, stolen by thieving Tudors in the dissolution of the monasteries!''

"We can't know that unless we open the trunk,'' Hugh reasoned. "Morgana, fetch a hammer and chisel.''

"O'Neill, you'll no' open that casket in my house!'' Sorely roared. "If ye must see what I know by faith is true, fetch a priest. No unconsecrated hands will touch chalices of the holy church while I live and breathe. Send for Father Eddie.''

"He's administering the last rites in the village,'' Inghinn said.

Hugh looked about the hall for Loghran. "Inghinn, send to the stable for Loghran O'Toole.''

Inghinn didn't have to go farther than the hall doors to find Loghran. Word of found treasure had spread quickly through Dunluce. Every living soul on the premise streamed into Sorely's hall. Men came in doffing their caps and the women covering their heads, as if they were entering a church.

Hugh moved his magnifying glass over the narrative at the top, rereading what could be deciphered. "This scroll must have come from trunk seventeen when it broke apart. Morgana, didn't Grace say she sank two of Drake's ships before she sped away to Band Haven?''

"Yes, that's exactly what she said.''

"What have you found?" Loghran called over Hugh's shoulder.

"Not me. Mac Donnell's found it, Come look at this cargo manifest. Our good friend Drake had more on his mind than just lessoning our Mac Donnell. Sorely believes he was transporting treasure stolen from the abbeys. This trunk washed up from the tide, intact."

"You jest," Loghran said, stunned. No one looked to be joking. Shamus Fitz produced a pry bar he'd been using in the carpentry work at the stable. He pulled it from his belt and handed it solemnly to Loghran when he'd finished looking over the document.

"I must wash my hands, first," Loghran said reverently, unwilling to touch even the locks without cleansing himself first.

A basin and soap was brought to him. After he washed his hands and folded away a clean linen, he knelt before the trunk, put the bar to the lock and broke the hasp. A hush swept the hall as the onlookers held their breath, waiting to see what the trunk would contain when Loghran raised the lid.

It had been sealed watertight. The memorable scent of frankincense, myrrh and beeswax filled the air the moment Loghran laid back the heavy, lead-lined lid.

Gold gleamed against silk. Each precious icon crammed into the chest had been wrapped in a cope, the outermost garment priests wore during mass. Each embroidered cloth held chalice, paten, crucifix and altar candlestick—all made of pure gold.

With hands that trembled, Loghran lifted out a golden monstrance so beautiful and magnificent in its sunray design that it hurt the eyes to look upon it. He stood it on the high table and bent his knee and his head before it, then crossed himself and backed away.

Slowly he emptied the trunk till he came to the stacks of books lining its bottom. Three illuminated manuscripts as precious as the Book of Kells were wrapped in waddings of damp cloth. Loghran brought the last gold-bound volume to his lips and kissed the jeweled cross worked into its ornate cover.

"I know this book," he said in a shaken voice. "It is the life of Saint Brendan of Clonfert, and belongs to the abbot of Munster. It is priceless, beyond human value."

"I told you so," the Mac Donnell said to Hugh.

Morgana made the sign of the cross and pressed her fingers to her lips, blinking back emotional tears from her eyes. "What do we do with all of this?" she asked.

Hugh looked at Loghran, then to the Mac Donnell. "We return it all where it belongs. To the Dominicans, Cistercians and Franciscans who have been robbed of their holy relics."

Morgana shook her head. "The abbeys and churches have been destroyed. I have just come from the Pale. I tell you there is not a church, no matter how minor, that remains intact. Sidney hunts down priests with a devil's vengeance. They die horrible deaths, martyrs of the true church. All church lands have been confiscated. I know of none that are not occupied by soldiers or taken over by English landlords greedy for more wealth. Most, if not all, of the holy men have been driven into exile."

"And underground," Loghran said solemnly. "The priests and monks are still with Ireland, lady. I stand before you as proof of that."

"Then you tell us, Loghran O'Toole," Morgana said, "where can we send these treasures and relics that belong to the people of Ireland for safe keeping from our governors' greed?"

"Dunluce's east tower is a good place," said the Mulvaine. She squeezed around her grandfather and put her hand out to touch the gold monstrance, a look of awe on her face.

Sorely struck her across her shoulder with his blackthorn staff. "Keep your filthy hands to yourself! No one gave you leave to speak. Get you out of my hall."

Inghinn took up her father's cause, pulling the girl back from the precious ornament. "You mustn't touch these relics, Cara. They are sacred and blessed. Only priests may touch them."

"And those who have been to confession and completed their penance." Loghran injected the instruction to clarify any ignorance in the onlookers.

"The Franciscan abbey in Donegal is secure," Inghinn said. "Hugh O'Donnell mustered all of Donegal to the protection of their abbeys."

"Inghinn," Hugh said, and turned to her, "the manifest states the fleet originated in Donegal."

"Then we must take all of this to the preceptory of the Templars," Loghran concluded. "Sir Almoy's vault is dry and secure. I am told the gospels of Maynooth and all the books of Solomon brought out of the Holy Land by the Templars are in Sir Almoy's possession. He would safeguard these sacred books until we can make contact with the proper church authorities. They will tell us how the items should be dispensed."

"You are absolutely right," Hugh agreed. "As preceptor of Ireland, Almoy is the perfect choice."

"My dungeons are also secure," Sorely offered.

"And wet," Cara said. "Everything rots there. But the east tower is very dry. Anything that you put there would be safe."

Sorely glared at her. Morgana saw him twitch with the urge to strike the girl again. His hatred was palpable, a living thing between the girl and he. Morgana clenched her hands at her sides and thought, *If he strikes her again, I shall kill him.*

Loghran opened the book in his hands. His head wagged sadly. "The child is right. These books must be where it is dry. Your dungeon may be secure, but it will not do. My lord Hugh told me we would be leaving in the morrow. We can transport all of this to the Templars' priory in Tyrone on our way back to Dungannon. It will be safe there for the time being. I'm sure your confessor will agree."

"I do most heartily," Father Eddie said, coming into the hall at last.

"Then I suggest we get everything thoroughly packed for travel. As I remember, Dunrath is a good hard ride from Dungannon," Hugh said wearily.

"You'll need a guide to find the preceptory. It's well hidden," Father Eddie said.

"I can find it," Loghran O'Toole asserted. "Some things one doesn't forget, no matter how long one is away from his homeland."

"Aye," the Mac Donnell agreed. He leaned heavily on his staff as he limped around the high board to his chair on the dais. "I'll sit here and watch the packing. Inghinn, bring fresh linen for the table so that Loghran and Father Eddie can spread the crosses and crucifixes. Arliss, go fetch the seamstress. Tell her to bring a bolt of my finest velvet cloth. I want protective bags made for each object. Donovan, search the manse for a trunk suitable to contain the whole of it, a dry one, with no smell of must inside it."

Cara glared at the Mac Donnell, her small mouth twisted grimly. Morgana watched the girl shake her head as though she were disgusted by the others who scattered to fulfill the Mac Donnell's orders.

Then the child turned and stalked out of the great hall. Morgana sighed, more convinced than ever that the best thing she could do for Cara Mulvaine was to get her out of Dunluce. If Hugh O'Neill wouldn't help Morgana do that, why then, she'd just do it alone.

Silently, Morgana sent a message to the retreating child, *Pack your bags, Cara. You are going to Dungannon with me.*

Hugh O'Neill tapped Morgana on her shoulder. She spun around, startled, scowling at him as darkly as she'd glared at the Mac Donnell.

"Lady," Hugh said in a stern, though soft, voice, "I know what you are thinking."

Chapter Twenty

Morgana had already made up her mind to ride at the back of the procession when they left Dunluce. Today she'd be toasted and roasted over the fires of hell before she spoke to Hugh O'Neill.

They weren't even married yet, and they'd had their first argument . . . over a child that wasn't even theirs!

She took her time getting ready, dressing, fixing her hair so it wouldn't come loose on the day's roundabout ride back to Dungannon. Before he left their bed this morning, Hugh had said he expected to ride hard to Dunrath, leave the treasure at the preceptory, then ride without stopping till they reached Dungannon. That was a fine way for a bunch of Irish kerns to travel, but it was no way for a lady to get about Ireland.

What was the almighty rush? Morgana had wanted to know. Hugh had merely said he wanted to get the treasure off his hands, period. He didn't want to be caught by anyone with that trunk or any of its contents in his possession.

As Morgana came through the hall, she heard the commotion of the horses and the excited chatter of men getting ready to ride. Today there was the addition of a two-wheeled cart and a Mac Donnell driver to bear the heavy trunk to the preceptory. Morgana would have found some way to hide Cara Mulvaine on that cart, had she had her way about things.

But no! Hugh O'Neill had to act the absolute tyrant. He'd threatened to beat Morgana if that child showed up on their journey south, saying that Morgana would rightly deserve punishment for couching a rebellion. Morgana wasn't about to put Hugh to that test. Not that his empty threat had put an end to the dispute. It had only stopped the words. Morgana would find another way, as soon as she could think of one.

When she came outside to the ward, where the horses were tied and the cart was ready to be loaded, she was distracted, wound up in her own deep thoughts. She wasn't paying attention to the Mac Donnell's loud cursing inside the hall.

Hugh's kerns looked up, murmuring among themselves, and turned to the open wicket in the Mac Donnell's great doors.

"It's gone!" Sorely emerged from his hall, shouting, his face the color of chalk. "The treasure's been stolen! The whole trunk is empty. Donovan, who manned the portcullis last night?"

Another murmur went through the people assembled in the castle ward. Heads turned and wagged. The old retainer, Donovan, stepped forward. "I, milord. The gates were closed all through the night. No one went in or out."

"Hold on, Sorely." Hugh ducked out from beneath the too-short wicket door. His face was dark with anger. He flashed a look at Morgana, and she responded with an ignorant shake of her head that said plainly, *I didn't do it.* "If the gates were never opened, then the treasure must be here in Dunluce. Where is the Mulvaine?"

"Aye, where's the deceitful brat? Does she think I forgot her words of yesterday? Nay, I did not!" Sorely came down the steps in a rage. "Donovan, go you and look in the north tower."

"Someone rings the bell at the gate, m'lord," Donovan responded, torn between his normal duty and the order of his laird.

Morgana turned at the compelling sound of the bell at the portcullis pealing. It was too early for visitors. Daylight had just begun to wash away the shadows of the night.

They all heard the chains on the gate squeak as it was being raised.

"What in the name of God is going on here?" roared Sorely Mac Donnell. He caught his tartan to his chest and began limping angrily across the ward to the portcullis gate. Everyone followed him. The kerns and Hugh all drew their swords.

The gate was open by the time the crowd reached it. Outside, on the road up from Bushmills, stood a wagon train drawn by mules. At the lead, stood an ancient man whose white hair and beard trailed down across a snowy tunic bearing the red cross of the Knights Templar.

"Mac Donnell of the Isles," the old man said, and raised his walking staff in greeting. "I am Almoy of the Temple of Dunrath. I have come to Dunluce seeking entrance within your secure walls. A vision, which came to me of late, tells me your east tower is vacant and will hold the remains of the Templars' property secure for a decade to come. May we enter in peace?"

"Of course you can," Cara Mulvaine chirped as she popped out from the gatehouse works. Her hands were filthy from the grease that kept the chains from rusting. "My grandfather has more treasures to add to your cache for safekeeping. Do come in, sir."

Sir Almoy looked down upon the child, smiled an almost beatific greeting and put out his hand to accept her. "Ah, so my apprentice waits for me. Good, good. All is as God showed me it should be. The O'Neill is here, and I see the red hair of the Fitzgeralds among you. Ireland becomes a haven for all of us, from end to end. Lady Morgan, I am grateful to you for doing my bidding. Alas, events changed from when I spoke with you last, though I thank you greatly for hearing my plaint."

"Well, don't just stand there blocking the gate, old man," Sorely cackled. "Come in, come in."

Morgana stood aside with the Mac Donnell as the kerns rushed forward. Each took hold of one of the mules, pulling Almoy's carts and drew it inside the castle's ward. It was an odd-looking procession. No men had accompanied old Almoy and his train of mules. His carts were piled high with every sort of crate, casket and trunk imaginable.

Cara seemed beyond herself, skipping ahead to take Sir Almoy's papery hand and lead him to the old east tower.

"I live in the north tower," she told him excitedly. "But you will like the east tower best, for its mullions open to the rising sun. You are going to teach me, aren't you?"

"Aye," he said gravely. "It is the reason I have come to Dunluce, child. I am glad I arrived in time to stop your journey."

"Oh, I wasn't going anywhere," Cara said, solemn-faced. "I saw you coming. Welcome to Dunluce, my lord. Did you bring my dog with you?"

"Nay, you are not ready for a familiar," Sir Almoy whispered to her. "You have much to learn first. But you will know when the time has come for you to bring the dog up from the sea gate. Now, be quiet and let me speak with your elders. They are confused by what they do not understand."

Confused didn't begin to explain Morgana's feelings. She was knocked off her pins, stunned to abject silence, by this strange and unnatural twist of events. Sorely Mac Donnell's ugly mood had changed to one of kind beneficence. He couldn't do enough to make the ancient Templar comfortable and welcome.

Hugh handed over the mule he'd led to the entrance of the east tower to Kermit Blackbeard and wound his way through the crowd to Morgana. He, too, looked confused.

"Did you also have some indication of this happening, lady?" he asked suspiciously.

"No, I didn't," Morgana said emphatically. "I told you all that I knew. I am as surprised as you."

"Then we have nothing to continue arguing about, do we?"

Rather sheepishly, Morgana agreed. Her ire with him evaporated like smoke. "Just don't say, 'I told you so' or we will."

Grinning, Hugh caught her chin with his forefinger and lifted it. "And nothing to stop us from returning our borrowed boys to Colraine and riding to Dungannon posthaste. Say your farewells. We may as well go while the gates are open."

That was sound advice. The Mulvaine hardly noticed their leave-taking. She was too busy climbing onto the first of Almoy's carts and untying its contents. She called to all the servants to help carry Almoy's many possessions inside the east tower, proud that she had spent the night getting the tower ready.

A curious black-and-white cat popped out from beneath the first tarp Cara lifted. It stretched and yawned, then padded over to the tower's doorway and sniffed its new home. Then it wound affectionately around Almoy's legs as he bade Hugh and Morgana goodbye.

"When you write to the queen dissolving the betrothal," he called after Hugh, "ask to be made the Mulvaine's guardian. She will have need of your counsel when the time comes for her to marry. Ask and you shall receive, my boy."

He beckoned to Morgana to come to him as he took a small pouch from the depths of his clothing. "Here, Lady Morgana. You will have need of this on your journey home and my blessing. Your spells lack potency."

"What is it?" Morgana felt the heft of the small bag. When she drew back the string, she thought she saw gray ashes inside it.

"Pepper and salt, my lady, several pinches of gunpowder, saltpeter and sulfur. All ground as fine as the dust that blows on the wind. Use it only once, and use all of it, then cast the bag to the waters before you. You know its strength and properties. Godspeed, my lady." Sir Almoy made the sign of the cross above Morgana's head.

Then he abruptly laid his papery hand on her brow, to trace another cross on her brow with his thumb. Morgana started, seeing herself surrounded by redcoats. "Hush," Sir Almoy whispered a consolation. "Do not be afraid of the trials to come. You will know the way when you see it. Till we meet again, I give you my thanks for caring for the child. I will protect her as well as I am able."

Hugh rumbled clearing his throat. Morgana tucked the bag in her pocket and took Hugh's arm, allowing him to lead her to Ariel and lift her onto her saddle. She stared back at Sir Almoy, troubled by the vision he'd given her.

No one seemed to take anything Sir Almoy said or did as unusual, though Morgana thought of a hundred questions to ask him. There wasn't time for that. Hugh wanted to be on his way.

The ride to Colraine was unremarkable. The countryside was absolutely pastoral, clean and washed by the storms that had passed in the days before. It was vibrant and alive with the full bloom of spring. The sun warmed the earth. A soft breeze off the sea cooled the skin in the most pleasant of ways.

The small band of Irish kerns and boys began singing their favorite songs with such sweet harmony that it was almost impossible for Morgana to retain that sense of wary alertness Sir Almoy had instilled within her by his touch.

As they approached the bridges that spanned the Bonn at Salmon's Leap, Morgana looked ahead to the village square across the wide river. It was market day and the town was crowded. Drovers had brought their sheep and cattle to town to trade for goods and services. A small traveling troupe had set up a stage for a play to be given later in the day. Two of their members, wearing gay costumes, acted out a small scene from the play to convince the villagers to pay a penny to see the production in full.

"Want to see the play?" Hugh asked Morgana as they rode into the center of the town.

Morgana drew Ariel to stop and look around. She saw nothing to be wary of, found no reason for her growing sense of dread. "I think we'd best return these boys to their parents and thank them adequately for allowing them to come along. They each risked much, if the truth were to be known."

"Aye," Hugh agreed. He looked to Rory and Brian, who'd been drawn off by the actors' boasts. "The boys have had an adventure to talk of long into their old age. I'll wager the coin I give their parents will more than compensate them for any trouble they might have gotten into."

Morgana said nothing to that, her thinking being more attuned to motherly concerns than Hugh's. At least she could say the boys were coming home safe and sound.

Hugh whistled to his lagging kerns, letting Rory know they were riding and not staying in Colraine.

Two of the boys lived in the village and were easily delivered back into their parents' care. Their parents hailed them welcome and gladly accepted the gold coin Hugh gave them for their sons' assistance.

The younger lad, Thomas, lived slightly south of Colraine in a perfect nook in the pine wood forest. They all dismounted when Thomas's parents invited them to stay for lunch.

Morgana marvelled at the welcome and hospitality of the peasants' house. Although the mother shooed Thomas and his siblings out the doors to make room for guests at her table, Thomas's oldest brother stayed. He was nimble with the harp and played the whole while they ate.

Then it was time to go, to face the longer ride to Dungannon. Hugh and Morgana and their loyal kerns stepped out of the cottage to find it surrounded. Six red-coated musketeers stood with their guns primed and ready, awaiting James Kelly's command to slay them all.

"I'm on to your game now. So I'll make a bargain with you, O'Neill." Kelly laughed viciously. "Hand over Morgana Fitzgerald and her brother, and I won't order my men to shoot yours down like so many cattle in a pen. At this range, our muskets will blow everyone of you to kingdom come."

Chapter Twenty-One

Kelly drove his men and their horses hard on the ride south through Tyrone. He wanted to put as much distance as possible between himself and Hugh O'Neill. Not that he was worried about being overwhelmed in a battle. O'Neill knew when he was outgunned. Muskets against broadswords was no contest.

If Kelly would just shut up about his brilliant victory, Morgana wouldn't mind so much. He just kept bragging on and on about how easily he'd done another O'Neill in.

They stopped to rest at, of all places, the Benburg bridge. Ariel was flat-out spent, winded and exhausted. Morgana was thoroughly dismayed.

There at the bridge over the Abhainn Mor, sunset's fading light rubied and faceted the deep, dark water. Morgana dismounted and led Ariel to the bank. As she drank thirstily, Morgana couldn't help thinking how much calmer the Blackwater was now. It ran swiftly under the bridge, swirling into the turn, then crashed over the rocky rapids.

That was the trouble with the Blackwater—the minute you thought you could trust it, it turned dangerously sinister. An owl hooted, and a shiver crept over Morgana's neck. She looked up to the silent sentinel of Owen Maugh, the rock of clan O'Neill. The black castle seated on the top of it had never looked more sinister.

"Stay close to me when it comes time to cross the Abhainn Mor," Morgana warned Tommy's harp-playing brother, Robert, whose only resemblance to Sean was the color of his hair.

"I wish they'd have believed you when you told them I'm not your brother," Robert grumbled under his breath.

"Ah, well, I do, too." Morgana knelt down at the water's edge, cupped her hands and drank to quench her thirst.

"You wouldn't be plotting another rebellion, now, would you, Morgana?" James Kelly said in a silken voice as he put his knee to the rocks beside Morgana. "Just because we're in sight of that old castle of Shane O'Neill's? No one lives there now, you know. And if they did, they wouldn't lift a hand to help a Fitzgerald."

"Hardly." Morgana looked at him, not caring whether her hatred showed in her eyes. He was a disgusting man. No more so now for having stripped Hugh of his dignity and left him and his kerns and all the people at Robert's croft trussed up like pigs for slaughter.

Only one thing reconciled Morgana to this final defeat— Hugh was alive.

She could go to her fate in Dublin knowing that Hugh O'Neill was spared from all further entanglements with her. He knew better than to come to Dublin. So that much was over.

Come tomorrow, she would probably find herself married to Lord Grey. As disgusting as that thought was, its likelihood was evident. She would do Ireland a favor and kill him. She wouldn't fight or struggle against the only future available to her. Her brief fling with Hugh O'Neill was over. All hope was lost.

She resigned herself to her destiny, or would do so as soon as she got Robert released. To that end, she turned to Kelly, needing to torment him before surrendering all.

"Now that you mention it, I'm thinking of all the ways a witch has to kill you." Morgana flicked her wet fingers at Kelly, sprinkling his face with river water. "You won't cross the Abhainn Mor alive. Shane O'Neill won't let you."

He sprang back, stumbling clumsily over his scabbard belt. "Damn you!" he howled.

When he raised his hand to strike her, a black arrow shot through the air between them.

It pinned the cuff of his red coat to the earth.

"To arms!" Kelly shouted as he wrenched his arm free of the earth at their feet. "Mount up, all of you! Get across the bridge! Load your muskets!"

He got his balance and sprang to his feet, grabbing Morgana, pulling her in front of him as he looked desperately around for his attackers. "Where are they?"

"Run, now!" Morgana told Robert. The boy's eyes were huge with fear. He didn't need a second warning.

Kelly's men were all grabbing for their guns. Not one was nimble enough to catch a boy running like a scared rabbit for the forest above the riverbank shrouding Shane's castle.

Kelly wrenched Morgana's shoulder hard as he dragged her between the horses for protection. "They're in the trees! Fire at the damned trees!"

A volley of English gunshots exploded into the wych elms. The great trees guarding the bridge shuddered. A rain of leaves cascaded onto the path to the bridge and into the Abhainn Mor.

They swirled past Morgana as she dug in her pocket for Sir Almoy's bag. She knew exactly what to do with the dust now, bless Almoy.

Kelly was shouting more orders. "Fire again!"

He shoved his horse and Ariel toward the bridge, determined to cross into Armagh. His soldiers put their knees to the ground, forming a flank on the open ground. Heads turned right and left, but they could find no exposed target to fire upon.

Hugh O'Neill carefully assessed the open ground between his promontory overlooking the river and the bridge. He had Kelly outnumbered, though not outclassed in weaponry. He had only two thoughts in mind—keep Morgana alive and stop the English soldiers' retreat.

He turned to Loghran and Macmurrough. "Can you keep them pinned down at the bridge with just arrows?"

"I don't see why not. None of them are wearing armor," Macmurrough said. He sighted his bow again, and sent a missile flying off the cliff into the pack of redcoats below.

"I don't see why we are bothering. Let the woman go. She's not fit to be your wife," Loghran announced.

That did it for Hugh. He threw down his sword, his shield, and his helmet, too, screaming, "For the love of God, Loghran O'Toole, if you say one more thing about the woman I love, I'm going to strangle you with my bare hands!"

Loghran, who never got excited about any of Hugh's dire announcements or threats, blinked his eyes and stepped back two paces from the young man's fists. "You never said you were in love with Morgana of Kildare, Hugh O'Neill."

"Of course I love her, ya damned miserable cold fish-eyed Viking sod! I love her with all my heart and soul! Why do you think I drove us all to the breaking point to get here to this stupid bridge? Just so I could butt my head with James Kelly again? No! I love her, you hear? I love her. I love her. I love her!"

Hugh's voice rose in volume with each declaration.

"Well, that changes everything." Loghran bent down and picked up Hugh's sword. As he put it back in Hugh's hand, he said to Macmurrough, "Go on then, fire at will, lads, what are you waiting for? Pick the bastards off. Hugh's going down the cliff to rescue his lady, aren't you, lad?"

Now it was Hugh's time to lose his wits. He snatched his sword from Loghran's hand and stomped to the edge of the parapet, where Kermit and Shamus Fitz had thrown a rope over the edge of the cliff.

"Milord." Shamus chuckled to clear his throat. "Wouldn't it be easier with two hands?"

"Auagh!" Hugh shouted his frustration to the universe. "Every Irishman's a bloody comic! Just hold the rope!"

He jabbed his sword back in his scabbard and took the rope in hand. Letting himself over the edge of the cliff, he made his way down to the base.

Kelly saw two of his men go down, arrows protruding from their chests, and panicked. He shoved Morgana ahead of him onto the bridge, drew his pistol and pointed the muzzle at her throat.

"O'Neill!" he screamed. "I'll blow her head off if you fire one more arrow. Fall back, men!"

The rain of arrows ceased. Terrified, Morgana looked everywhere, trying to find Hugh. She spied him at the same time the musketeers did. Hugh was exposed on the side of the cliff, speeding down a rope to the running river that cut into the base of the bluff.

"Kill him!" Kelly screamed. "Fire now, ya bastards!"

His command must have been heard at the top of the bluff. Two arrows shot through the chests of two redcoats. They fell forward in the mud, their guns discharging into the earth. The remaining two fired point-blank at Hugh. The reports of the muskets deafened Morgana to her own scream as Hugh tumbled head over heels into the river, out of Morgana's sight forever.

Kelly jabbed his pistol into her throat, grunting, "Move. He's done for. I won't let my reward go now. Move!"

"Just how much am I worth to you, Kelly?" Morgana asked in a cold, calm voice. All her fear was gone now. None of it remained, if Hugh O'Neill was lost for good. "How much is Grey paying you to bring me to Dublin?"

"Never you mind about that! It's enough! Enough to keep me comfortable all my days."

"As much as Sussex paid you six years ago for Shane? That was going to make you a wealthy man. How much was it? A hundred pounds?"

"More, damn it! And it was seven years ago. You're worth five times what Shane O'Neill was. Shut up and move!"

"I'll pay you ten times the amount." Morgana lifted the sack of powders from her pocket. "I'll give you the Kildare diamond now, and tell you where the rest of my family's jewels can be found."

She dangled the small sack before his piggish, greedy eyes. She braced herself on the warped boards of the bridge, knowing she would have one chance. Only one.

Kelly's eyes narrowed. He went so far as to extend his hand. "Let me see the jewel."

Morgana held the sack away from his reach. "First, take your gun away from my face. You can't fire it at this range and not blow your own head off. It's no good to you."

"Let me see the diamond!" he yelled, beyond reason entirely.

"Hold out your hand," Morgana instructed silkily. She moved the sack between them, inverting its contents into Kelly's grasping palm. The instant the powder began to pour, she blew it into his eyes.

He screamed, blinded, and swung his gun around. Morgana ducked under the weapon's barrel. He pulled the trigger, and the flash exploded in his face. His remaining men turned around to find their captain's red coat and hair on fire.

Kelly staggered backward, beating at the flames eating up his wool and linen, scorching his mustache and his vainly pomaded silver hair. He collapsed on his back, writhing in agony, screaming and belching flames of fire out his mouth.

The two redcoats left rushed at Kelly to put the fire out. Morgana ran across the bridge. She tripped on warped boards and went crashing face down on the wooden planks.

"She's killed Captain Kelly!" The soldiers backed away from the burning body of their commander. Both looked at Morgana with hatred in their eyes as she stumbled back to her feet.

She could never outrun them. She staggered upright gripping the stone wall of the bridge. Her only way to avoid being recaptured was the river. Morgana scrambled onto the railing, gathering her skirts and cloak about her.

This time, when she looked into the depths of the Abhainn Mor, she didn't fear drowning. The river had taken her Hugh. She wanted to spend eternity with him. She opened her eyes and her arms wide, embracing death, as she leaped off the bridge into the swirling depths. She called out one word as she fell: "Hugh!"

"Sweet Jesus, what's that noise?" the youngest soldier cried as he came to a crashing stop at the bridge wall, too late to catch the woman before she jumped. His head jerked from side to side, and he dropped his gun to the bridge floor. Both his hands were needed to cover his ears against the deafening, swelling scream rising out the river's gorge.

On the top of the bluff, seven kerns heard the same scream. To a man, they knew what that sound was—the cry of the banshee Maoveen, whose wail for untold centuries had heralded the death of the O'Neill.

"*No!*" Loghran O'Toole grabbed the rope dangling over the cliff. He was gone from sight before anyone could stop him.

Maoveen's scream whipped through the gorge of the Abhainn Mor, gathered force and power from the earth, wind and water, and roared over Tyrone, up to the deserted heights of Owen Maugh, the ancient stone of the O'Neills. She was heard from Armagh to Omagh, from Tullaghoge to Trigall.

At Dungannon, every burning candle was snuffed all at once, blown out by the terrifying force of Maoveen's all-consuming breath.

Chapter Twenty-Two

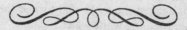

The Abhainn Mor was not unkind. Morgana went into it with her eyes open, expecting a cold, numbing shock. There was no time to feel the cold as she sank into the depths of the wild flow and was caught by swiftly running undercurrents. Water weeds caressed her cheeks and tugged upon her hands.

Air billowed in her gown and cloak, trapping thousands of bubbles that gently floated past her eyes in a mysterious dance to the choppy, glassy surface. Before she lost her breath, her face broke through. The cool touch of the night wind stroked her face and brought the sad lament of Maoveen to her ears.

Morgana spun around, lifting her head and shoulders above the water, in a frantic attempt to locate the source of the song. To one side of the ravine, cliff walls rushed past her. To the other, the virgin forest waved its boughs in a silent salute of farewell.

She was propelled downstream on a billowing cushion of air trapped by cloth in a warm current. When she leaned her head back into the water and looked up, the black wall of the ravine was topped by a canopy of twinkling stars.

Morgana waited for that choking sensation of panic that had always terrified her when she neared water. It wasn't there. She wasn't going to die. The water refused to take her, refused the sacrifice of her life to go with Hugh.

"No!" Morgana screamed, flaying out both arms and legs in a desperate attempt to rid herself of whatever buoyancy it was that kept her on the surface and cheated her of an honorable death.

A swifter current turned her round the bend. Morgana lifted her head, hearing the rush and tumble of the rapids as she tumbled toward them. Now, she saw what was coming, the devastation that would end her life, the battering of her helpless limbs against the rocks that turned the Blackwater into fearsome, foaming white water.

Funny, but she wasn't afraid.

No. Not afraid. She spread her arms across the waves in a welcoming embrace. This would end all of the uncertainties of her life, send her plummeting into a far, far better place. How she wanted to tell Hugh this last truth. She no longer feared drowning or feared the havoc water could wreak because she no longer feared death.

This great river had taken Hugh from her. By its same dark nature it would bring them together for eternity. Morgana lifted her hand in a salute to the wailing spirit of Maoveen, hoping the banshee would add a small prayer for her soul to her funeral hymn.

"I'm not afraid of the water, Hugh."

"I can see that."

Morgana jerked in the weightless embrace of the current, turning to the sound of her lover's voice, seeking his spirit, his soul, knowing he would be there at the final moment to help her into the vail.

But she was surrounded by the dark, by the blanketing fall of night over the turbulent, pulsing river.

"Hugh! Hugh!" Morgana called out his name. "Where are you?"

"Here." He cupped his hands to his mouth and called to her from the topmost ledge of the rapids. "Don't be afraid, Morgana, my love. I'll catch you."

Hugh! She saw him! Standing braced against a rock in the middle of the rapids. "Hugh!"

Morgana began to flail at the water, in a panic to reach him and not be swept past him by the tugging stream.

"Don't fight it! Float. Stretch out your arms." His words came to her when her head went under. She screamed, and a mouthful of water choked her. His name bubbled to the surface as she screamed for him underwater.

The panic and the fear burbled up, strangling her, closing its tight fist across her throat. She made the connection that he was alive. The English hadn't killed him. James Kelly hadn't won. The Abhainn Mor hadn't swallowed Hugh.

"Hugh!" Morgana screamed his name when her face broke water again. "Hugh!"

He dived off the rock, swimming to her. His strong, powerful arms cut through the quickening current. The Abhainn Mor pushed harder on Morgana's clothes, turning her. She spun round and round in the eddying flood as it gathered speed and tumbled toward the rocks. She coughed twice, expelling water from her lungs.

"Hugh!"

"I'm here, my darling." Hugh lifted his face and called to her. That cost him his advantage against the current. Morgana sped past, driven by skirts that had trapped air and acted like a sail. She neared the rapids and screamed. "Hugh!"

"Morgana, reach for me!" Desperately, he lunged after her, driving his arms in powerful strokes going with the current. She spun faster, caught in the tow, turning before his eyes, closer and closer to the rockbound waterfall. He refused to let her go. He could not lose her, now that he knew how much he loved her.

"Hugh!"

"Morgana, I love you! Reach for me!"

Her arms lifted from the surface in a farewell. "I love you, Hugh."

His fingers caught a bubble of cloth and clamped down. Immediately Hugh dropped his body, using his trunk and legs like a rudder against the current. He hauled her to him by the cloth, yard by yard, inch by inch.

Then his hands were at her waist, lifting her above the water. Her back was to him. "Hugh! Don't! We'll both drown."

"Not tonight, my love," he promised. "I've got you. Don't strangle me or choke me. I have no intention of meeting my death in such an ignoble manner. Are you calm?"

Morgana stared at the oncoming rocks. Her hair slid across her back. "The rapids!"

"I know. Brace your body against mine. Lie back on me. I did this a thousand times as a boy, ran the rapids like a trout. Come on, Morgana. Are you ready?"

He yanked her back against him at the last moment, and thrust out his feet ahead of him. They both went under. Hugh clamped his arms around her chest, holding on to her with all his might.

They went into the white water, crashing over rocks, plunging into pools, twisting, turning, swept by the savage, untamed flow of the Abhainn Mor as it coursed down through the rapids that dropped a hundred feet from beginning to end.

Hugh never let go. Not even when stones bashed his head and body and water choked and strangled him. Not even when he knew it was his life for hers. He couldn't let her go. Not now that he'd found her.

Then, all at once, they were airborne, turning head over heels into the pool at the bottom of the waterfall. Hugh expelled the water in his lungs and took a quick breath, knowing what was coming.

They plunged into the pool feet first, welded together by the force of his arms and sank like stones to the bottom. He bent his legs and kicked hard as he could.

He still had hold of her when the current cast them onto the sandy verge, spitting them out of all danger. His heart thrummed a wildly exhilarated cadence. Morgana shivered in his embrace, her arms and legs quaking. Her fingers padded at his forearms like cat feet, claws seeking purchase. She choked on the water in her lungs.

Hugh coughed and raised his head, spat out a mouthful of water, then said, "Want to do it again, my love?"

She choked and coughed then, bent double to expel the water filling her lungs. Hugh managed to sit up and ignore the pains in his back. He cleared his chest, and winced at the pain that caused.

"I don't know," he said, shaking his hair from his eyes. "Maybe it was easier to do when I was a boy and fitted on Loghran's shield."

"What?" Morgana gasped. She turned around in his arms, all blustering woman's fury. Small fists formed against his chest but had little strength left to inflict any damage.

Hugh managed a laugh and covered her hands with his own, holding her against his chest. "No? Bad idea, right?"

"Oh, Hugh . . ." Morgana straddled his legs to throw her arms around his shoulders and kiss him. He beat her to it, tightening his hands on her back, bringing her head down to his for a powerful kiss at the joy of being alive. "I thought I'd lost you for good."

"And I you, my sweet. But as you can see the old gods have no use for our sacrifice, and have cast us back on the shores of life. We'll have a long walk home to Dungannon."

"I'm too exhausted to walk anywhere." Morgana slid her arms around his neck, hugging him, putting a hundred thankful kisses on his face, from brow to chin.

"I'm too sore," Hugh replied. "We'll have to wait here for Loghran to find us. He'll be along shortly, I vow."

Morgana laid her cheek against his and looked to the glen edging the river. It was filled with blooming hawthorn trees. The grass beneath them was so thick with fallen blossoms, it looked like a bed. "Look at all the mayflowers," she said.

Hugh waggled his brows at her in invitation. "A ripe place for soon-to-be-weds to sleep, my lady. A potent and fertile bower. Come."

He got to his feet, lifting her from the river. She was still trembling and weak, but Hugh's strength was coming back. The bumps and scrapes from the rocks no longer mattered. He slipped his arm around her waist and led her onto the grassy verge.

"First," he said briskly, "I will dispose of these wet clothes of yours, and hang them to dry. Then, my love, I will warm you in the best way possible."

"It's a warm night." Morgana stood still for the removal of her cloak. Hugh unhooked his belt and tossed it and his scabbard to the side. Morgana's fingers were at his chest then, no longer passive, for she was as anxious to relieve him of his clothes as he was to remove hers.

"Shall I make you a fire?" he asked when he pulled her body flush against his. The air had pebbled her skin. Hugh gathered her hair off her shoulders, twisting it into a single coil.

"Later." Morgana pressed flush against him, running her hands across his naked torso, warming him the same way he warmed her.

"Ah, Morgan le Fay, you are truly the greatest gift God has ever given me."

Morgana knew exactly when to give in, and how. So she did and was thoroughly rewarded in the giving.

Hugh woke himself up sneezing. Morgana laughed at the shower of hawthorn blooms he sent flying airborne from his face.

"What?" Hugh sat bolt upright, startled out of his hazy, pleasant dreams of making love in the spring grass. A chestful of flowers cascaded to his legs.

"You look like Puck." Morgana giggled.

Hugh looked down at himself and laughed. They were both covered by blossoms. They continued to shower out of the trees like a white rain as the morning breeze stirred and shifted limbs that were heavy with green leaves.

"It's going to be summer soon." Morgana sat up on her knees. She was already dressed in her fitted kirtle. Hugh saw that it was still damp enough to expose her rosy breasts through the cloth.

"Let it turn summer, let it turn fall. Let's stay here in this perfect spot, just as we are."

"Oh, I wish we could, my lord," Morgana handed him his sark which was as damp as her kirtle. "But I don't think we're going to be alone much longer. I hear beaters combing the rushes. They're looking for us."

Hugh hammered his hand against his head, as if to dislodge water from his ears. "I don't hear anything."

"Well, you should," Morgana scolded him. She pointed up the river. Now that the moon had risen, much could be seen. The sharp curve of the Abhainn Mor where it turned away from Benburg. A thin gray mist rose halfway up Owen Maugh and formed a ring around Shane's castle, on the crest. The mist caught the light of the torches and reflected it back down to the water. Searchers had reached the rocks of the rapids and the twenty-foot drop of the waterfall into the huge pool opposite their bower.

Sure as Morgana had said, Hugh's kerns made their way down opposite sides of the river. They were on horseback, to cover more ground, but the purpose of the long staves in their hands, beating at the rushes, was evident. They were searching for bodies.

It wouldn't be long before they came within hailing range. Hugh jerked his sark over his head, twisted it down his torso, then stood to don his trews, and sat to pull up still-wet stockings and boots.

"How long have you been awake?" he asked.

"Long enough to cover you in mayflowers." Morgana laughed.

"Get dressed." Hugh tossed her surcoat to her. The heavier cloth was much wetter than her kirtle. Morgana frowned as she stood and pulled the cold garment onto her shoulders.

"Euch…" She grimaced. She ran her fingers through her hair, then tossed it behind her shoulders. "I suppose now is the time to tell you the worst. James Kelly is most likely dead.''

"What?'' Hugh blinked. He looked up at her from fastening his cross garters. His brow lowered.

"His pistol exploded in his face.'' Morgana explained. "It happened on the bridge, just before I jumped into the water. I'm sorry you won't be able to bring him to justice before your clan, but I'm not sorry he's dead.''

Hugh stood. He crossed to her and pulled her into his arms. They stood looking at each other for a long, long time. "I don't think he matters to me anymore. I don't need to prove myself to anyone, or to avenge Shane's murder, to become the O'Neill. I thought I did, but none of that matters anymore. You are all that's important. We're going to get married as soon as we return to Dungannon. Agreed?''

"Agreed.'' Morgana reached up on tiptoe to kiss him.

Hugh's lips lingered on hers for a long time. Each savored the newness of love in full bloom, and the complete trust and peace that came with it. Morgana had no doubts that the queen would grant Hugh's requests, each and every one of them, down through the years.

And he had no doubts that she would stand by him through thick and thin, through battles and peace, and even the return of the earl of Kildare to Ireland. Hugh laughed.

"What are you thinking?'' Morgana pushed him back a pace, scowling prettily at his grin.

Hugh chuckled some more before saying what was on his mind. "I was just thinking to myself, let Fitzgerald declare himself king of Erin. Then you and I can retire in the quiet obscurity of the hills of Tyrone and live out our lives making babies and living in peace forever.''

"That has a very nice sound to it,'' Morgana agreed. "Father may have an absolute fit, but I second the thought.''

"Excellent.'' Hugh set her back and bent down to gather the rest of their belongings, his belt and empty scabbard, Morgana's dripping cloak and his tartan. He gallantly offered Morgana his arm. "Shall we go and give Loghran

O'Toole the scare of his life? You know they think we are dead. I've got a better idea. Let's head to the road and circumvent them.''

"If they think we're dead, wouldn't that be an unnecessarily cruel joke?"

"I don't know." Hugh gave the matter further thought. "It might make the old sod appreciate me from now on. I came close to killing him at the start of this watery adventure."

"What stopped you?"

Hugh remembered his declaration of love that had stopped Loghran in his tracks. "Oh," he said, not wanting to go into that right now, "as always, it was matter of his not believing how serious I am. We're working on a solution."

The solution would be the blessing of marriage vows spoken over him and Morgana by Father Loghran O'Toole.

"Come on, my love. Let's put them out of their misery. I can see their faces now. They look as forlorn as can be. I can't be so cruel as to make them suffer any longer."

"That sounds like my Hugh talking." Morgana grinned as she threaded her arm through his.

"*My Hugh.* I think I like the sound of that, my Morgana."

They had climbed to the top of the waterfall and were walking outside the rushes on the bank when they were spotted by all seven riders. Four came galloping through the rapids to join the other three bearing down on Hugh and Morgana.

Seven voices shouted at once.

"God and Mary be praised! You're alive!"

Donald the Fair was the first to clap Hugh on the back and embrace him. He shook him hard, laughing wildly. "I know how you did it. Just like when we were boys, feet-first, right?"

"Stand aside, Donald," Loghran said. "Let me put my arms around my beloved son."

The older man grasped Hugh and held him so tight Hugh
thought his back would be broken afresh. Shamus Fitz gave
a shout of triumph and literally picked Hugh up off the
ground in a crushing bear hug. Kermit slapped him on the
back so hard that any water that remained inside Hugh was
driven out by the pounding.

Then they all turned on Morgana, their greeting to her
more reserved and proper. Donald the Fair kissed both her
cheeks and welcomed her to clan O'Neill. Loghran hugged
her and thanked her for bringing Hugh back to them, alive.
Shamus Fitz gave her a bear hug just a tad less ferocious
than that he had given Hugh. Morgana squealed to have her
ribs compressed so tight. Art Macmurrough put his knee to
the ground and kissed Morgana's hand.

Then they boosted the two of them onto a horse, and they
all rode for Dungannon, chattering away like the true, well-
tested friends they all were. Hugh heard confirmation of
what Morgana had told him about Kelly.

"We found out Kelly's soldiers were deserters he'd conscripted in Colraine. The two Lady Morgana let live on the
bridge were both scared puppies."

"You let two redcoats live?" Hugh asked Morgana,
astounded.

"An oversight, my lord. They were young enough to pee
their pants when Maoveen started wailing."

"What's this about Maoveen?" Hugh asked testily.
"That's superstitious nonsense."

Neither Morgana nor any of the kerns contradicted Hugh
on that score. Rory and Brian ducked their heads, then
looked at the lady. "You heard her?" Rory asked.

"I did." Morgana nodded. She knew better than to laugh
at the old ways. Hugh O'Neill did not.

They came to Dungannon anon, and found the gates
draped in black crepe. With a rising sense of alarm, they
rode through silent streets. The bell at the Dominican abbey tolled a death knell.

At the fortress, the gates stood unmanned and wide open.
That in itself was a tradition, when the one who'd died was

within the castle itself. No one spoke as they passed over the bridge to the castle on the crannog.

It wasn't until Hugh dismounted and took Morgana's hand firmly in his that the truth sunk into him. Death *had* come to the O'Neills.

In the great hall of Dungannon, the last son of Conn the Lame was laid out on his bier. Matthew's shriveled, twisted form was dressed in his finest raiment. Death had waxed his skin and ended the pain that had tormented Matthew O'Neill for over twenty years.

Hugh walked into the hall to the soft sound of his people keening, "O'Neill, O'Neill, O'Neill . . ."

Every man, woman and child in the hall turned to Hugh, looking at him for leadership.

His heart sank with sorrow for the uncle he'd never truly known. There'd be no wedding in Dungannon today. He and Morgana would have to wait a little longer to begin their life together as man and wife.

As he felt her hand compress against his, consoling him, assuring him, he knew that their day was at hand. Come tomorrow, their vows would be spoken and a new life would begin.

Epilogue

June 24, 1575
Dungannon Castle
County Tyrone, Ireland

Rory O'Neill went through three horses on the relay from Carrickfergus to Dungannon. He'd waited three weeks for the packet to return with an answer from London to the O'Neill's letters to the queen. If he'd known how to read English, Rory wouldn't have ridden in such haste to have the news everyone in Tyrone waited with bated breath to hear. He'd have read the news himself, then ridden hell-bent for leather to Dungannon.

Word of his arrival at the gates passed swiftly from mouth to mouth and head to head, preceding his arrival at the castle.

The moment Mrs. Carrick heard the news, she hitched up her skirts and huffed and puffed up the hill to the chapel's tiny graveyard. Few at Dungannon had joined the procession from the township's common graveyard to the blessed and hallowed sanctuary behind the chapel.

Loghran wore a cope over his brown robe. He was reciting the last "Glory be to the Father" over Catherine Fitzgerald's new grave, beside Conn O'Neill and his other two wives. Mrs. Carrick respectfully bowed her head and said the proper response, fairly bursting from the effort it took to hold back her news.

Morgana said, "Amen," and laid a bouquet of flowers on the new stone. "Rest in peace, Aunt Catherine," she said out loud.

Oh, I will child. Bless you! Bless you! Catherine said joyously as she hovered over the new grave. *How you did it, child, I'll never know, but I thank you from the bottom of my heart. God bless both of you.*

"Oh, Hugh, it's so sad." Morgana stood above the freshly covered grave looking at the spray of roses she'd laid upon the earth. "Catherine's murder caused so much bitterness and misunderstanding between our families."

Hugh's arm tightened around her waist, holding Morgana against him. "We have to think it's been righted now. I don't suppose we'll ever know who pushed the lady out that tower window. But Catherine is where she belongs now. I hope my grandfather is there to greet her in heaven."

"Do you really believe there is a heaven, Hugh?" Morgana asked. Hugh's arm firmed at her waist and he looked down into her eyes, nodding his head.

"Aye, Morgana. Death isn't the end of life. It's a new beginning. Why, in the isle of the blessed everyone loves one another."

Morgana rested her head on his shoulder. Her faith wavered and she had doubts, but Hugh never did.

"With all my heart, I believe it is so." He solemnly wiped two more tears from her cheeks. "You've a kind heart, my lady. You feel too much, give too much and keep nothing inside for yourself. Trust me, I wouldn't lie to you about something so important as heaven. It exists. Else there would not be angels like you here on this earth."

"Ahem..." Mrs. Carrick cleared her throat. "Begging your pardon, my lord O'Neill. Rory's come."

Hugh lifted his head, scowling at being interrupted in a private moment with Morgana. He had few enough of those in his too-busy days. "What did you say?"

"Ah?" Morgana drew in a sharp breath. "Rory's come!"

"Sweet Saint Patrick, Loghran! Put away the missal and the stole. Run! Rory's come!"

Hugh took hold of Morgana's hand, and they ran down the hill and into the castle ward. Word had spread inside the house, and the great doors burst open. People spilled onto the cobblestones filling the ward as Rory galloped into the bailey. The young man bounded out of his saddle as if he had blisters on his arse, which he did.

He dragged his packet off his shoulder and fell to his knee before Hugh, saluting at the same time he extended the leather packet. "From the queen, O'Neill. The answer to all of our prayers."

Hugh's hands shook as he unfastened the buckle and ripped the packet open. Two scrolls fell out into his hands. He turned them, reading the seals. Only one was from Elizabeth. His heart jolted inside his chest as he broke the seal.

Then his fingers turned to butter trying to unroll the foolscap. He gripped it fiercely at each end and spread it open, scanning Queen Elizabeth's fluid scrawl.

Morgana refused to look at the words. She had her eyes closed, praying for all she was worth, as she had prayed each and every night since the day of their marriage.

Her fingers trembled. She turned the gold band on her ring finger around for good luck. She even said a spell to change bad news to good.

"What's it say?" Loghran came to a breathless stop in the only open space left before Hugh.

Hugh looked up and crushed the paper together between his hands. His face hardened into a solid piece of stone.

"Oh, no." Morgana pressed her fingers to her mouth.

"Her Majesty, the queen of England, says..." Hugh held the moment out just a little bit longer before allowing his face to erupt in a brilliant smile. "...that we are well met and married, Morgana and I! She sends her blessings and prays now for peace in Ireland."

He caught Morgana up in his arms and spun her around in a full circle, then kissed her before one and all.

Loghran slapped his hand over his heart as a deafening cheer rocked the ward of Dungannon Castle. "God bless the queen!" he said jubilantly, then threw his arms around both Hugh and Morgana. "Thank you, God, Mary, and Saint Brendan, too!"

Hugh couldn't resist teasing all these doubting Thomases that he was faced with every day of his life. When were they ever going to have faith in him?

"You might put a little of your thanks to my glib tongue for a change. I told you she would give her blessing. All it ever takes to move Bess is to know how to ask the question. You could do with learning a little diplomacy, O'Toole."

"Congratulations!" Loghran clapped him on his back, ignoring Hugh's provoking gibe. "Both of you!"

"Who is the other letter from?" Morgana asked, having to know it all, here and now. Hugh brought the second scroll up from behind her back, where he'd crushed it when he grabbed her to celebrate. He took time to kiss her again, then tapped her nose with the stiff parchment.

"Ah, ah, ah... You know what they say about curious kittens."

"Well?" Morgana demanded.

"This—" Hugh wagged the document teasingly before her, "—is the wardship of one brat known as the Mulvaine. It authorizes me to arrange her marriage, when the time comes. I'll put it away, my lady, for another day, long, long into the future. At his age, Sorely can't live forever. I've enough headaches for now, dealing with Dungannon and you."

"Oh!" Morgana pinched his ribs.

"Now, answer me true, Morgana of Kildare, am I or am I not the answer to all your prayers?"

"Yes." Morgana's dimples deepened beautifully. She threw her arms around his neck and declared her love for him before one and all. "I love you, Hugh O'Neill."

"And I love you, Morgana O'Neill, now and forever-more."

And at that, the people of Dungannon shouted, "O'Neill, O'Neill, O'Neill!"

* * * * *

Bestselling

author

Ruth Langan

presents

Book III of her exciting Jewels of Texas series

JADE

When the town preacher meets the town madam,
the little town of Hanging Tree, Texas, will
never be the same

The Jewels of Texas—four sisters as wild and vibrant as
the untamed land they're fighting to protect.

DIAMOND	February 1996	PEARL	August 1996
JADE	February 1997	RUBY	October 1997

FREE VALENTINE'S BROOCH!
$9.95 U.S. retail value

This Valentine's Day Harlequin brings you all the essentials—romance, chocolate and jewelry—in:

VALENTINE *Delights*

Matchmaking chocolate-shop owner Papa Valentine dispenses sinful desserts, mouth-watering chocolates...and advice to the lovelorn, in this collection of three delightfully romantic stories by Meryl Sawyer, Kate Hoffmann and Gina Wilkins.

As our special Valentine's Day gift to you, each copy of *Valentine Delights* will have a beautiful, filigreed, heart-shaped brooch attached to the cover.

Make this your most delicious Valentine's Day ever with *Valentine Delights!*

Available in February wherever Harlequin books are sold.

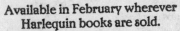

HARLEQUIN ®

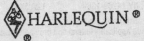

Look us up on-line at: http://www.romance.net

VAL97